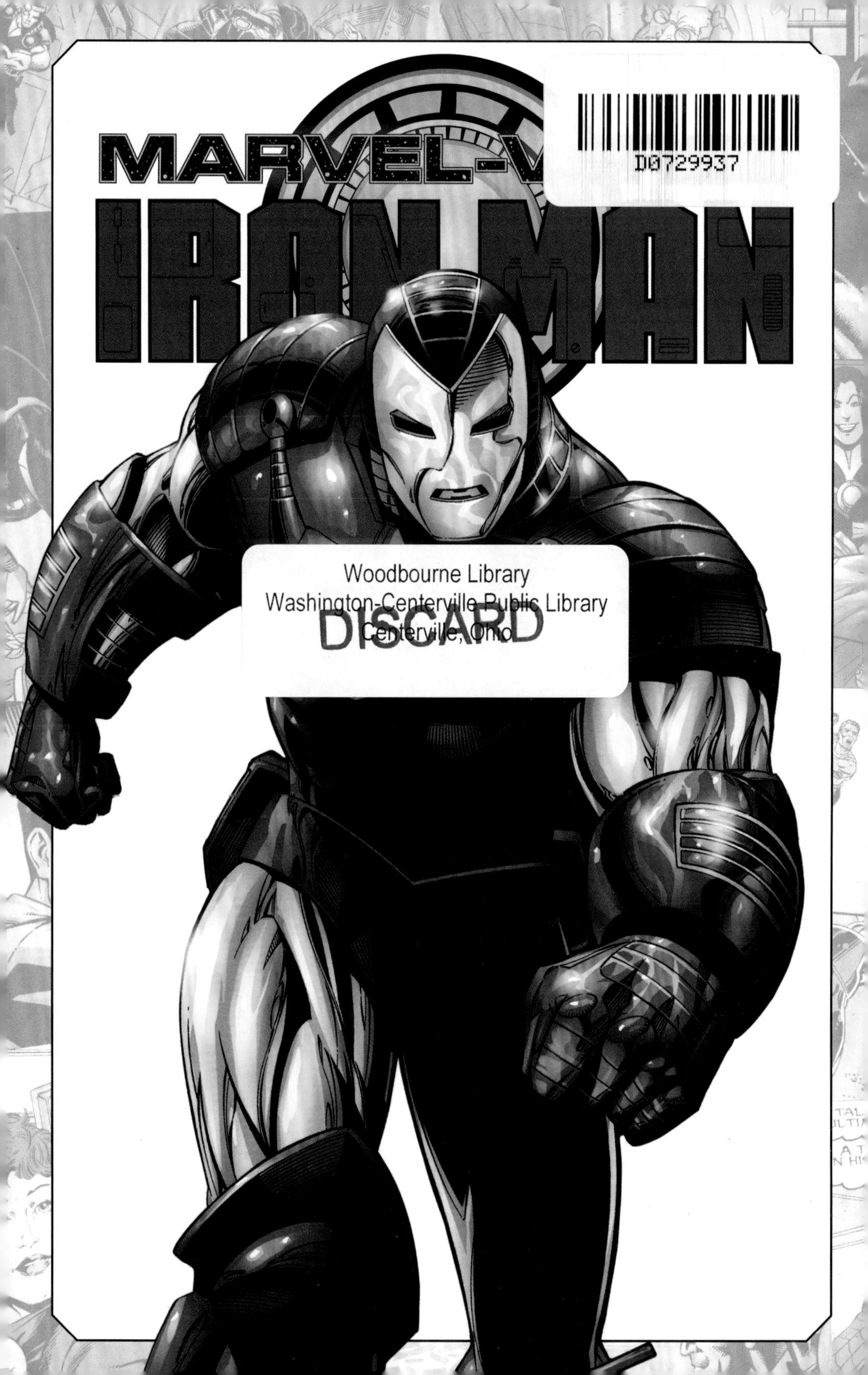
MARVEL-V
IRON MAN

MARVEL-VERSE
IRON MAN

MARVEL ADVENTURES IRON MAN #1

WRITER: **FRED VAN LENTE**
PENCILER: **JAMES CORDEIRO**
INKER: **SCOTT KOBLISH**
COLORIST: **STUDIO F's MARTE GRACIA**
LETTERER: **BLAMBOT's NATE PIEKOS**
COVER ART: **MICHAEL GOLDEN**
ASSISTANT EDITOR: **NATE COSBY**
EDITOR: **MARK PANICCIA**

IRON MAN #234

WRITERS: **DAVID MICHELINIE**
BREAKDOWNS: **BUTCH GUICE**
FINISHES: **BOB LAYTON**
COLORIST: **BOB SHAREN**
LETTERER: **JANICE CHAN**
EDITOR: **HOWARD MACKIE**

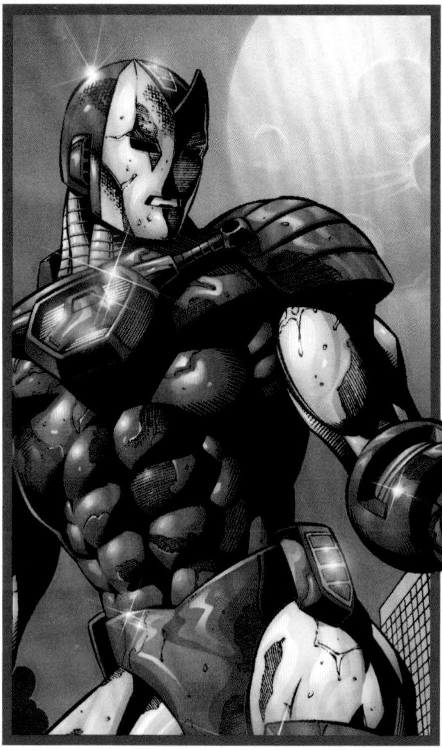

MARVEL ADVENTURES IRON MAN #7

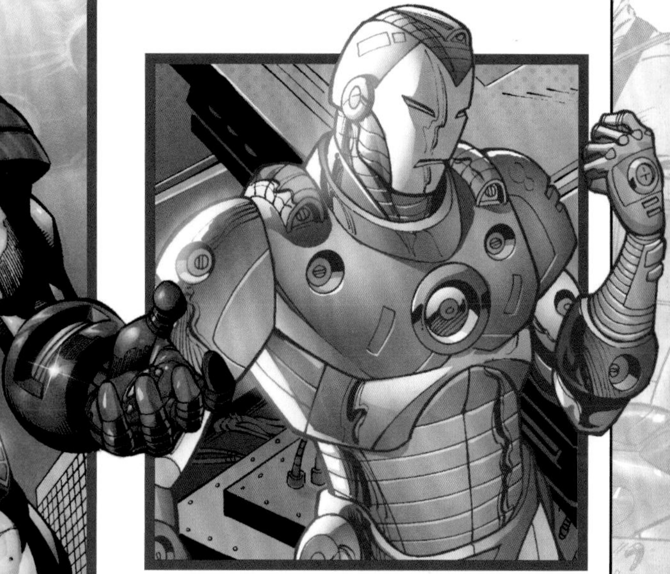

WRITER: **FRED VAN LENTE**
PENCILER: **GRAHAM NOLAN**
INKER: **VICTOR OLAZABA**
COLORIST: **MARTE GRACIA**
LETTERER: **DAVE SHARPE**
COVER ART: **SKOTTIE YOUNG**
ASSISTANT EDITOR: **NATE COSBY**
EDITOR: **MARK PANICCIA**

IRON MAN #1

WRITER: **KURT BUSIEK**
PENCILER: **SEAN CHEN**
INKER: **ERIC CANNON**
COLORIST: **LIQUID!**
LETTERER: **RS & COMICRAFT's DL**
EDITOR: **BOBBIE CHASE**

IRON MAN CREATED BY
STAN LEE, LARRY LIEBER, DON HECK & JACK KIRBY

COLLECTION EDITOR: **JENNIFER GRÜNWALD** ASSISTANT EDITOR: **CAITLIN O'CONNELL**
ASSOCIATE MANAGING EDITOR: **KATERI WOODY** EDITOR, SPECIAL PROJECTS: **MARK D. BEAZLEY**
VP PRODUCTION & SPECIAL PROJECTS: **JEFF YOUNGQUIST** BOOK DESIGNERS: **SALENA MAHINA** WITH **JAY BOWEN**

SVP PRINT, SALES & MARKETING: **DAVID GABRIEL** DIRECTOR, LICENSED PUBLISHING: **SVEN LARSEN**
EDITOR IN CHIEF: **C.B. CEBULSKI** CHIEF CREATIVE OFFICER: **JOE QUESADA**
PRESIDENT: **DAN BUCKLEY** EXECUTIVE PRODUCER: **ALAN FINE**

MARVEL-VERSE: IRON MAN. Contains material originally published in magazine form as MARVEL ADVENTURES IRON MAN #1 and #7, IRON MAN (1968) #234, and IRON MAN (1998) #1. First printing 2019. ISBN 978-1-302-92117-0. Published by MARVEL WORLDWIDE, INC., a subsidiary of MARVEL ENTERTAINMENT, LLC. OFFICE OF PUBLICATION: 135 West 50th Street, New York, NY 10020. © 2019 MARVEL No similarity between any of the names, characters, persons, and/or institutions in this magazine with those of any living or dead person or institution is intended, and any such similarity which may exist is purely coincidental. **Printed in Canada.** DAN BUCKLEY, President, Marvel Entertainment; JOHN NEE, Publisher; JOE QUESADA, Chief Creative Officer; TOM BREVOORT, SVP of Publishing; DAVID BOGART, Associate Publisher & SVP of Talent Affairs; DAVID GABRIEL, SVP of Sales & Marketing, Publishing; JEFF YOUNGQUIST, VP of Production & Special Projects; DAN CARR, Executive Director of Publishing Technology; ALEX MORALES, Director of Publishing Operations; DAN EDINGTON, Managing Editor; SUSAN CRESPI, Production Manager; STAN LEE, Chairman Emeritus. For information regarding advertising in Marvel Comics or on Marvel.com, please contact Vit DeBellis, Custom Solutions & Integrated Advertising Manager, at vdebellis@marvel.com. For Marvel subscription inquiries, please call 888-511-5480. **Manufactured between 8/23/2019 and 9/24/2019 by SOLISCO PRINTERS, SCOTT, QC, CANADA.**

10 9 8 7 6 5 4 3 2 1

MARVEL ADVENTURES IRON MAN #1

BILLIONAIRE INVENTOR TONY STARK DONS THE FIRST IRON MAN ARMOR TO ESCAPE THE CLUTCHES OF THE TERRORIST ORGANIZATION A.I.M. AND THE SUPREME SCIENTIST!

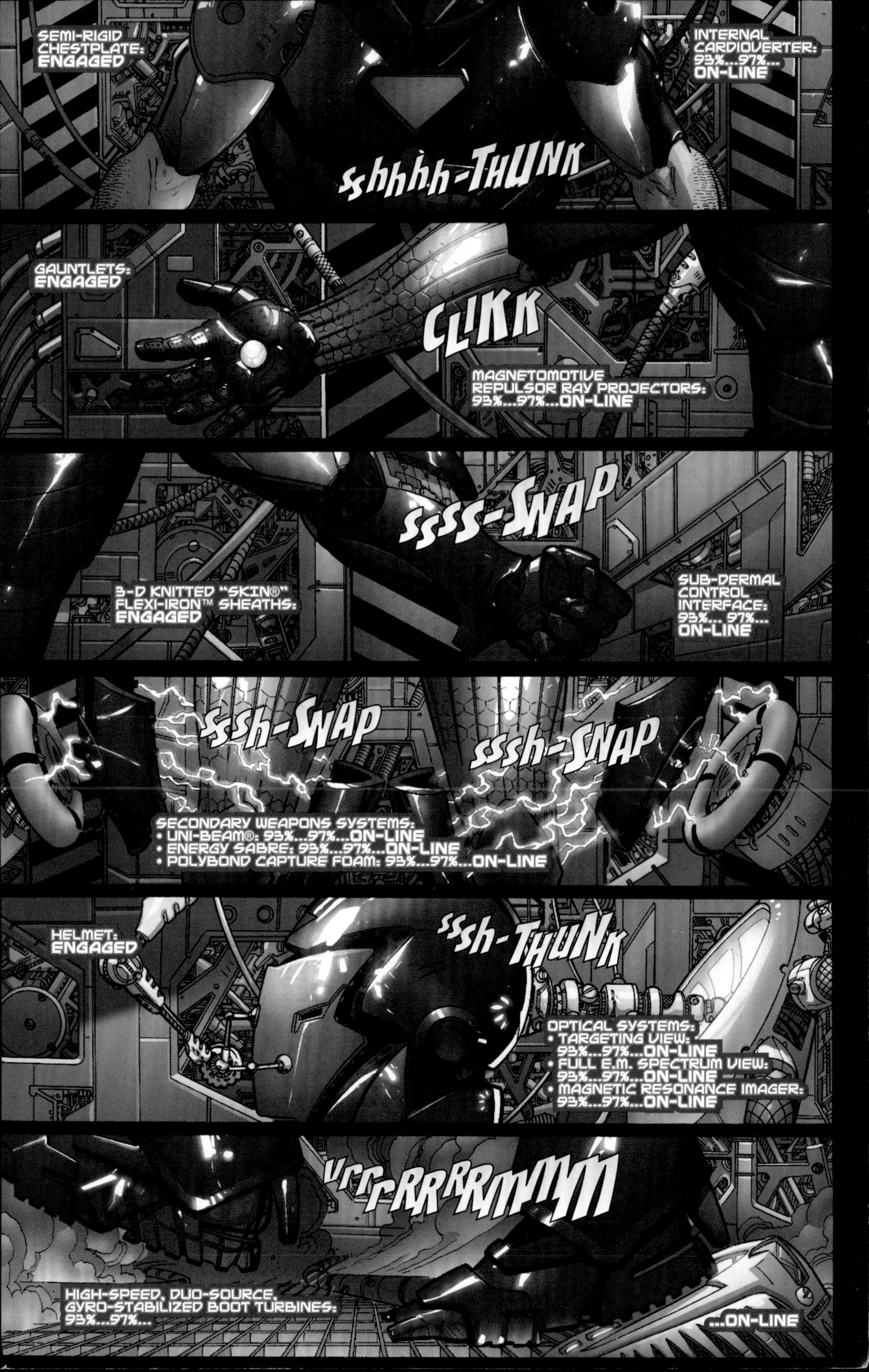
SEMI-RIGID CHESTPLATE: ENGAGED
INTERNAL CARDIOVERTER: 93%...97%... ON-LINE
SSHHHH-THUNK
GAUNTLETS: ENGAGED
CLIKK
MAGNETOMOTIVE REPULSOR RAY PROJECTORS: 93%...97%...ON-LINE
SSSS-SNAP
3-D KNITTED "SKIN®" FLEXI-IRON™ SHEATHS: ENGAGED
SUB-DERMAL CONTROL INTERFACE: 93%... 97%... ON-LINE
SSSH-SNAP
SSSH-SNAP
SECONDARY WEAPONS SYSTEMS:
• UNI-BEAM®: 93%...97%...ON-LINE
• ENERGY SABRE: 93%...97%...ON-LINE
• POLYBOND CAPTURE FOAM: 93%...97%...ON-LINE
HELMET: ENGAGED
SSSH-THUNK
OPTICAL SYSTEMS:
• TARGETING VIEW: 93%...97%...ON-LINE
• FULL E.M. SPECTRUM VIEW: 93%...97%...ON-LINE
• MAGNETIC RESONANCE IMAGER: 93%...97%...ON-LINE
VRRRRRRRMMMM
HIGH-SPEED, DUO-SOURCE, GYRO-STABILIZED BOOT TURBINES: 93%...97%...
...ON-LINE

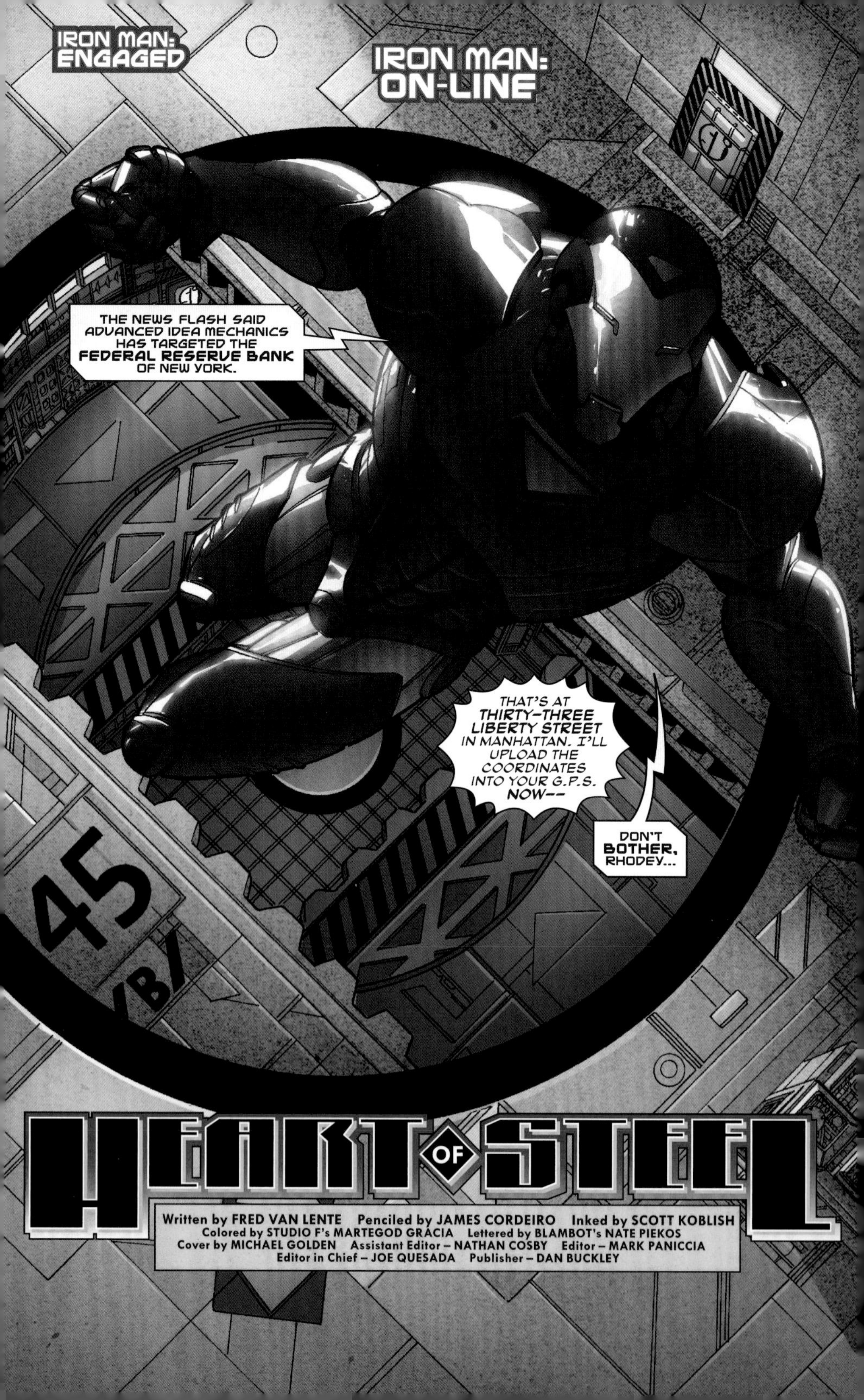
IRON MAN: ENGAGED
IRON MAN: ON-LINE
THE NEWS FLASH SAID ADVANCED IDEA MECHANICS HAS TARGETED THE FEDERAL RESERVE BANK OF NEW YORK.
THAT'S AT THIRTY-THREE LIBERTY STREET IN MANHATTAN. I'LL UPLOAD THE COORDINATES INTO YOUR G.P.S. NOW--
DON'T BOTHER, RHODEY...
45
B
HEART OF STEEL
Written by FRED VAN LENTE Penciled by JAMES CORDEIRO Inked by SCOTT KOBLISH
Colored by STUDIO F's MARTEGOD GRACIA Lettered by BLAMBOT's NATE PIEKOS
Cover by MICHAEL GOLDEN Assistant Editor – NATHAN COSBY Editor – MARK PANICCIA
Editor in Chief – JOE QUESADA Publisher – DAN BUCKLEY

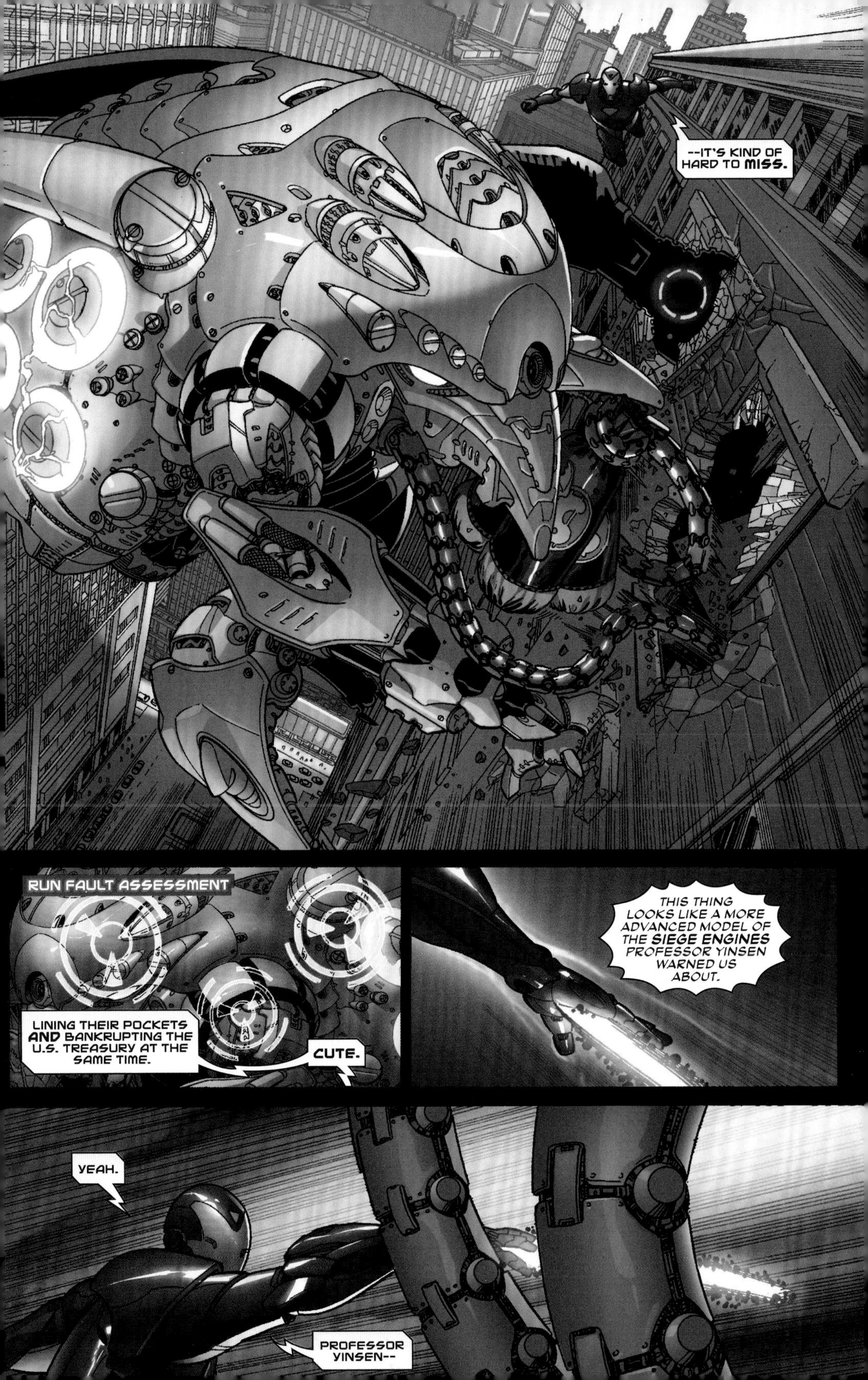
--IT'S KIND OF HARD TO MISS.
RUN FAULT ASSESSMENT
LINING THEIR POCKETS AND BANKRUPTING THE U.S. TREASURY AT THE SAME TIME.
CUTE.
THIS THING LOOKS LIKE A MORE ADVANCED MODEL OF THE SIEGE ENGINES PROFESSOR YINSEN WARNED US ABOUT.
YEAH.
PROFESSOR YINSEN--

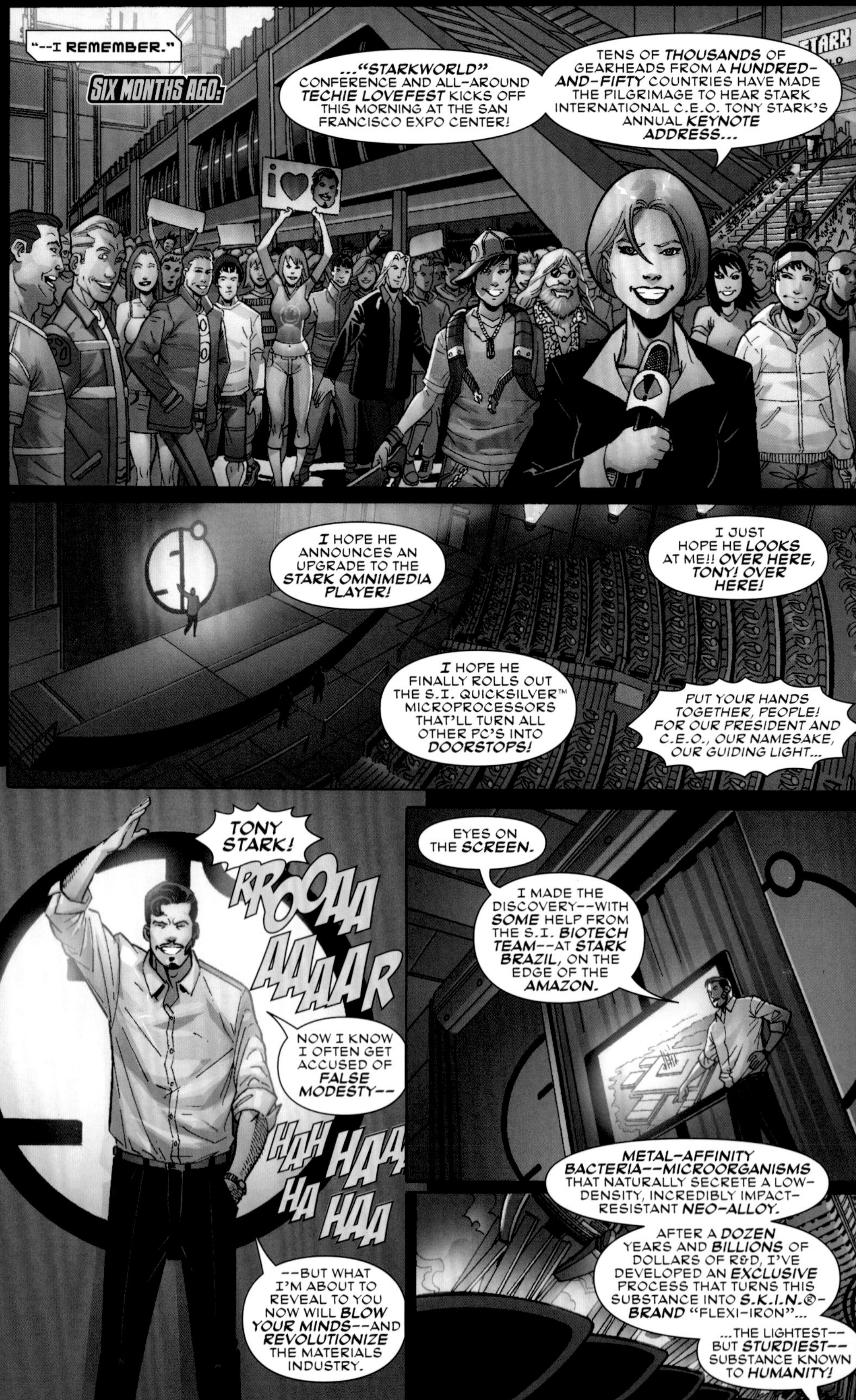

"--I REMEMBER."
SIX MONTHS AGO:
..."STARKWORLD" CONFERENCE AND ALL-AROUND TECHIE LOVEFEST KICKS OFF THIS MORNING AT THE SAN FRANCISCO EXPO CENTER!
TENS OF THOUSANDS OF GEARHEADS FROM A HUNDRED-AND-FIFTY COUNTRIES HAVE MADE THE PILGRIMAGE TO HEAR STARK INTERNATIONAL C.E.O. TONY STARK'S ANNUAL KEYNOTE ADDRESS...
I HOPE HE ANNOUNCES AN UPGRADE TO THE STARK OMNIMEDIA PLAYER!
I JUST HOPE HE LOOKS AT ME!! OVER HERE, TONY! OVER HERE!
I HOPE HE FINALLY ROLLS OUT THE S.I. QUICKSILVER™ MICROPROCESSORS THAT'LL TURN ALL OTHER PC'S INTO DOORSTOPS!
PUT YOUR HANDS TOGETHER, PEOPLE! FOR OUR PRESIDENT AND C.E.O., OUR NAMESAKE, OUR GUIDING LIGHT...
TONY STARK!
RROOAAAAAAR
NOW I KNOW I OFTEN GET ACCUSED OF FALSE MODESTY--
HAH HAA HA HAA
--BUT WHAT I'M ABOUT TO REVEAL TO YOU NOW WILL BLOW YOUR MINDS--AND REVOLUTIONIZE THE MATERIALS INDUSTRY.
EYES ON THE SCREEN.
I MADE THE DISCOVERY--WITH SOME HELP FROM THE S.I. BIOTECH TEAM--AT STARK BRAZIL, ON THE EDGE OF THE AMAZON.
METAL-AFFINITY BACTERIA--MICROORGANISMS THAT NATURALLY SECRETE A LOW-DENSITY, INCREDIBLY IMPACT-RESISTANT NEO-ALLOY.
AFTER A DOZEN YEARS AND BILLIONS OF DOLLARS OF R&D, I'VE DEVELOPED AN EXCLUSIVE PROCESS THAT TURNS THIS SUBSTANCE INTO S.K.I.N.®-BRAND "FLEXI-IRON"...
...THE LIGHTEST--BUT STURDIEST--SUBSTANCE KNOWN TO HUMANITY!

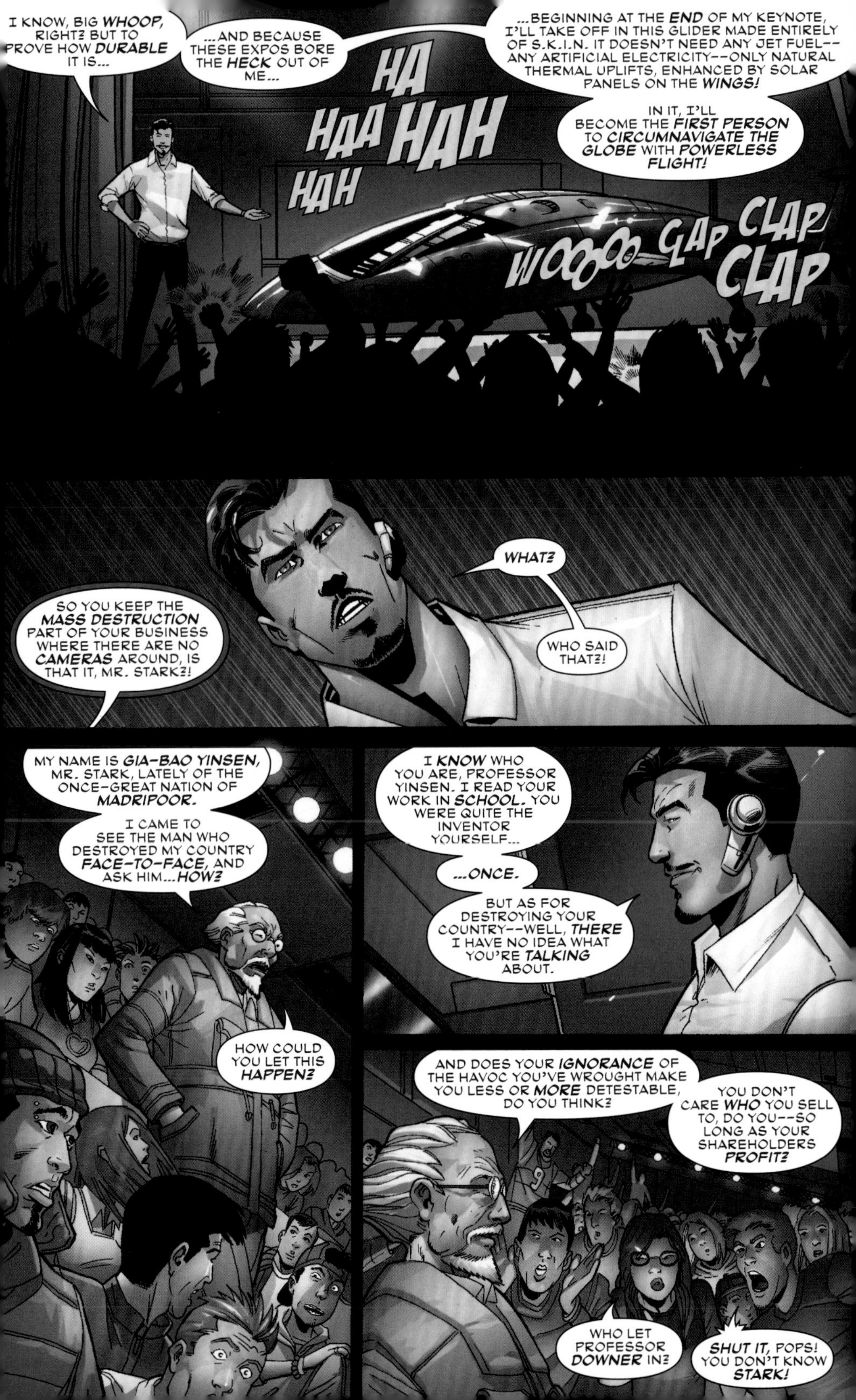
I KNOW, BIG WHOOP, RIGHT? BUT TO PROVE HOW DURABLE IT IS...
...AND BECAUSE THESE EXPOS BORE THE HECK OUT OF ME...
HA HAA HAH HAH
...BEGINNING AT THE END OF MY KEYNOTE, I'LL TAKE OFF IN THIS GLIDER MADE ENTIRELY OF S.K.I.N. IT DOESN'T NEED ANY JET FUEL--ANY ARTIFICIAL ELECTRICITY--ONLY NATURAL THERMAL UPLIFTS, ENHANCED BY SOLAR PANELS ON THE WINGS!
IN IT, I'LL BECOME THE FIRST PERSON TO CIRCUMNAVIGATE THE GLOBE WITH POWERLESS FLIGHT!
WOOOOO CLAP CLAP CLAP
WHAT?
SO YOU KEEP THE MASS DESTRUCTION PART OF YOUR BUSINESS WHERE THERE ARE NO CAMERAS AROUND, IS THAT IT, MR. STARK?!
WHO SAID THAT?!
MY NAME IS GIA-BAO YINSEN, MR. STARK, LATELY OF THE ONCE-GREAT NATION OF MADRIPOOR.
I CAME TO SEE THE MAN WHO DESTROYED MY COUNTRY FACE-TO-FACE, AND ASK HIM...HOW?
HOW COULD YOU LET THIS HAPPEN?
I KNOW WHO YOU ARE, PROFESSOR YINSEN. I READ YOUR WORK IN SCHOOL. YOU WERE QUITE THE INVENTOR YOURSELF...
...ONCE.
BUT AS FOR DESTROYING YOUR COUNTRY--WELL, THERE I HAVE NO IDEA WHAT YOU'RE TALKING ABOUT.
AND DOES YOUR IGNORANCE OF THE HAVOC YOU'VE WROUGHT MAKE YOU LESS OR MORE DETESTABLE, DO YOU THINK?
YOU DON'T CARE WHO YOU SELL TO, DO YOU--SO LONG AS YOUR SHAREHOLDERS PROFIT?
WHO LET PROFESSOR DOWNER IN?
SHUT IT, POPS! YOU DON'T KNOW STARK!

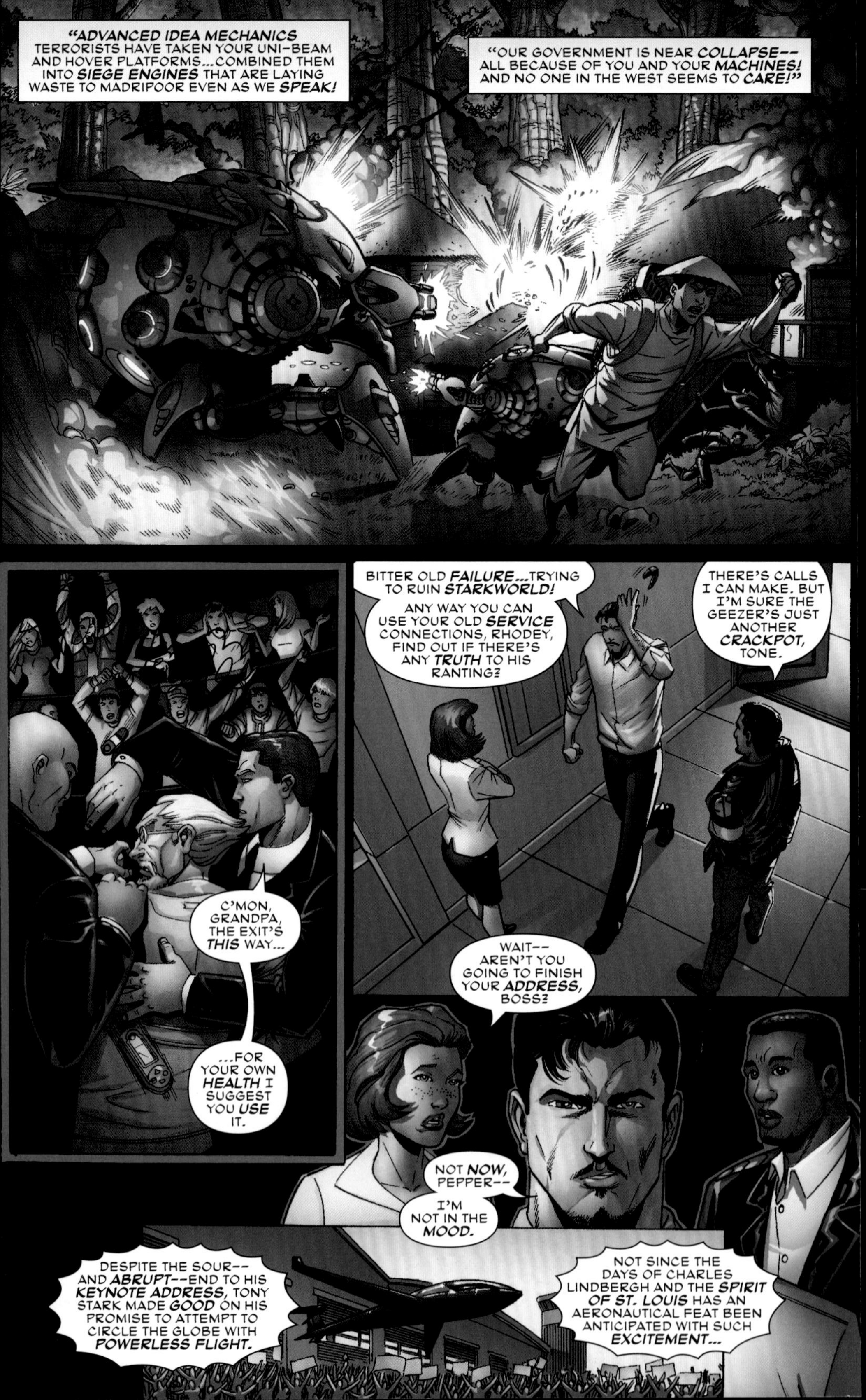
"ADVANCED IDEA MECHANICS TERRORISTS HAVE TAKEN YOUR UNI-BEAM AND HOVER PLATFORMS...COMBINED THEM INTO SIEGE ENGINES THAT ARE LAYING WASTE TO MADRIPOOR EVEN AS WE SPEAK!
"OUR GOVERNMENT IS NEAR COLLAPSE-- ALL BECAUSE OF YOU AND YOUR MACHINES! AND NO ONE IN THE WEST SEEMS TO CARE!"
C'MON, GRANDPA, THE EXIT'S THIS WAY...
...FOR YOUR OWN HEALTH I SUGGEST YOU USE IT.
BITTER OLD FAILURE...TRYING TO RUIN STARKWORLD!
ANY WAY YOU CAN USE YOUR OLD SERVICE CONNECTIONS, RHODEY, FIND OUT IF THERE'S ANY TRUTH TO HIS RANTING?
THERE'S CALLS I CAN MAKE. BUT I'M SURE THE GEEZER'S JUST ANOTHER CRACKPOT, TONE.
WAIT-- AREN'T YOU GOING TO FINISH YOUR ADDRESS, BOSS?
NOT NOW, PEPPER--
I'M NOT IN THE MOOD.
DESPITE THE SOUR-- AND ABRUPT--END TO HIS KEYNOTE ADDRESS, TONY STARK MADE GOOD ON HIS PROMISE TO ATTEMPT TO CIRCLE THE GLOBE WITH POWERLESS FLIGHT.
NOT SINCE THE DAYS OF CHARLES LINDBERGH AND THE SPIRIT OF ST. LOUIS HAS AN AERONAUTICAL FEAT BEEN ANTICIPATED WITH SUCH EXCITEMENT...

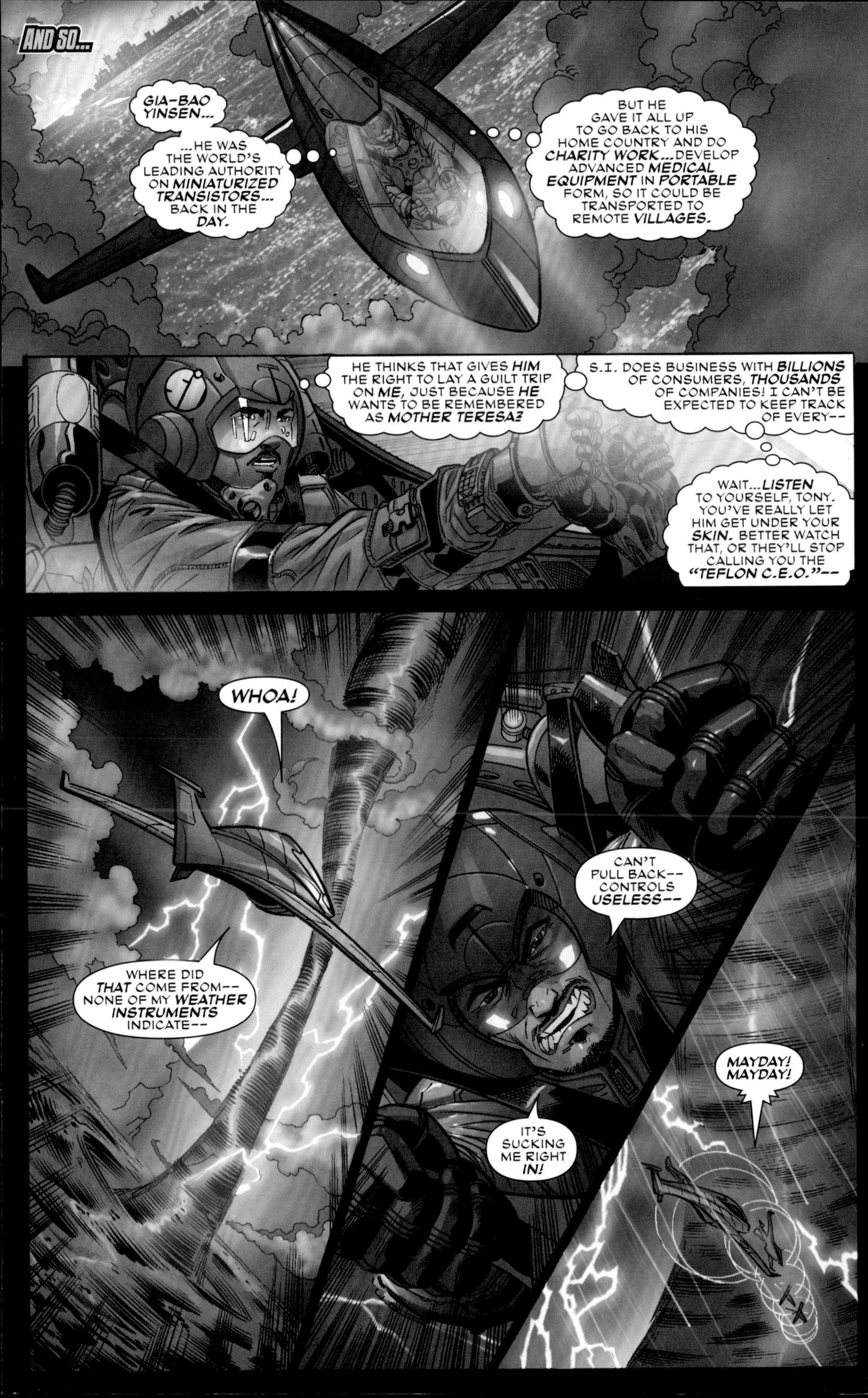
AND SO...
GIA-BAO YINSEN...
...HE WAS THE WORLD'S LEADING AUTHORITY ON MINIATURIZED TRANSISTORS... BACK IN THE DAY.
BUT HE GAVE IT ALL UP TO GO BACK TO HIS HOME COUNTRY AND DO CHARITY WORK... DEVELOP ADVANCED MEDICAL EQUIPMENT IN PORTABLE FORM, SO IT COULD BE TRANSPORTED TO REMOTE VILLAGES.
HE THINKS THAT GIVES HIM THE RIGHT TO LAY A GUILT TRIP ON ME, JUST BECAUSE HE WANTS TO BE REMEMBERED AS MOTHER TERESA?
S.I. DOES BUSINESS WITH BILLIONS OF CONSUMERS, THOUSANDS OF COMPANIES! I CAN'T BE EXPECTED TO KEEP TRACK OF EVERY--
WAIT... LISTEN TO YOURSELF, TONY. YOU'VE REALLY LET HIM GET UNDER YOUR SKIN. BETTER WATCH THAT, OR THEY'LL STOP CALLING YOU THE "TEFLON C.E.O."--
WHOA!
WHERE DID THAT COME FROM-- NONE OF MY WEATHER INSTRUMENTS INDICATE--
CAN'T PULL BACK-- CONTROLS USELESS--
IT'S SUCKING ME RIGHT IN!
MAYDAY! MAYDAY!

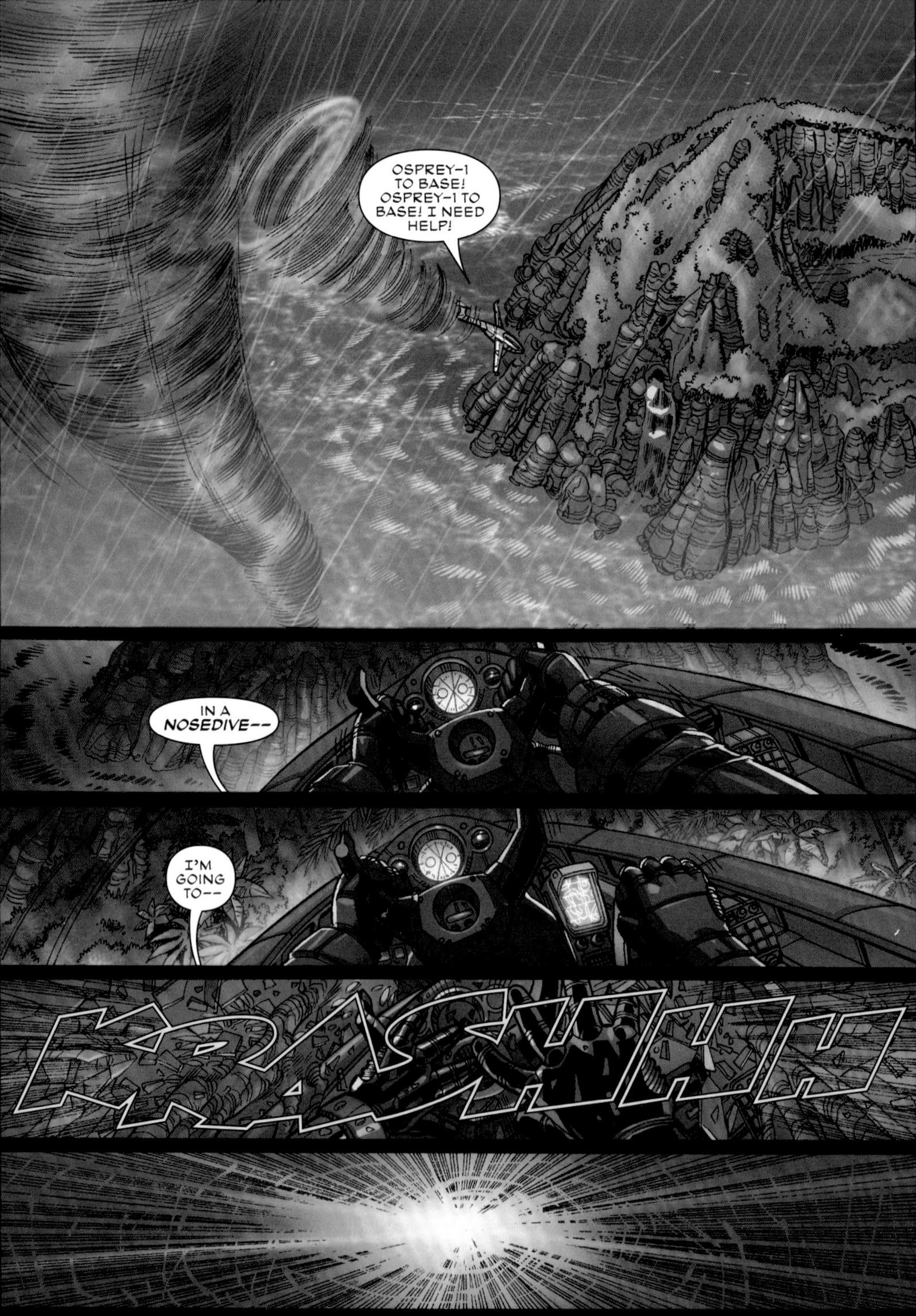
OSPREY-1 TO BASE! OSPREY-1 TO BASE! I NEED HELP!
IN A *NOSEDIVE*--
I'M GOING TO--
KRASHHH

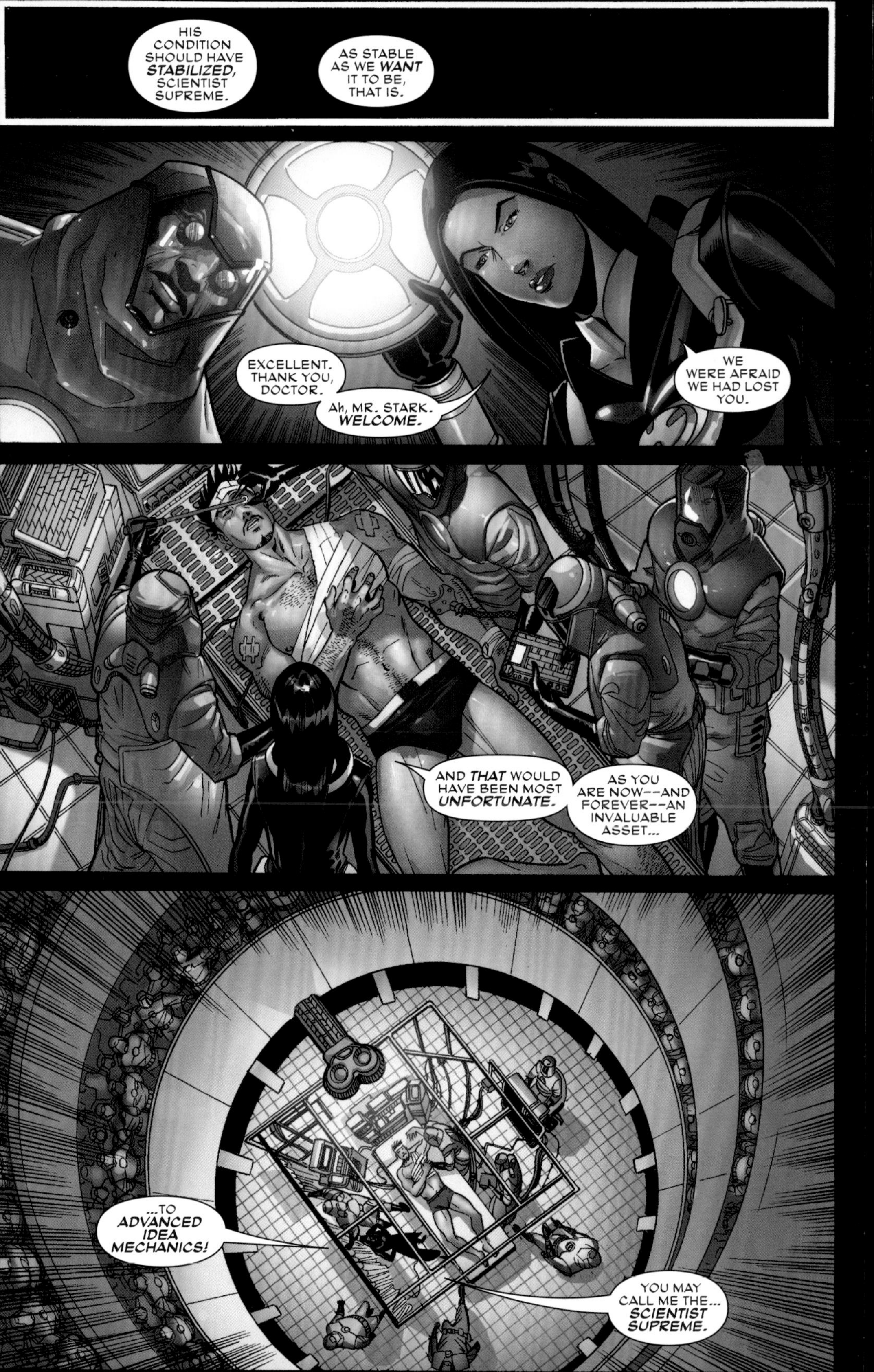
HIS CONDITION SHOULD HAVE STABILIZED, SCIENTIST SUPREME.
AS STABLE AS WE WANT IT TO BE, THAT IS.
EXCELLENT. THANK YOU, DOCTOR.
Ah, MR. STARK. WELCOME.
WE WERE AFRAID WE HAD LOST YOU.
AND THAT WOULD HAVE BEEN MOST UNFORTUNATE.
AS YOU ARE NOW--AND FOREVER--AN INVALUABLE ASSET...
...TO ADVANCED IDEA MECHANICS!
YOU MAY CALL ME THE... SCIENTIST SUPREME.

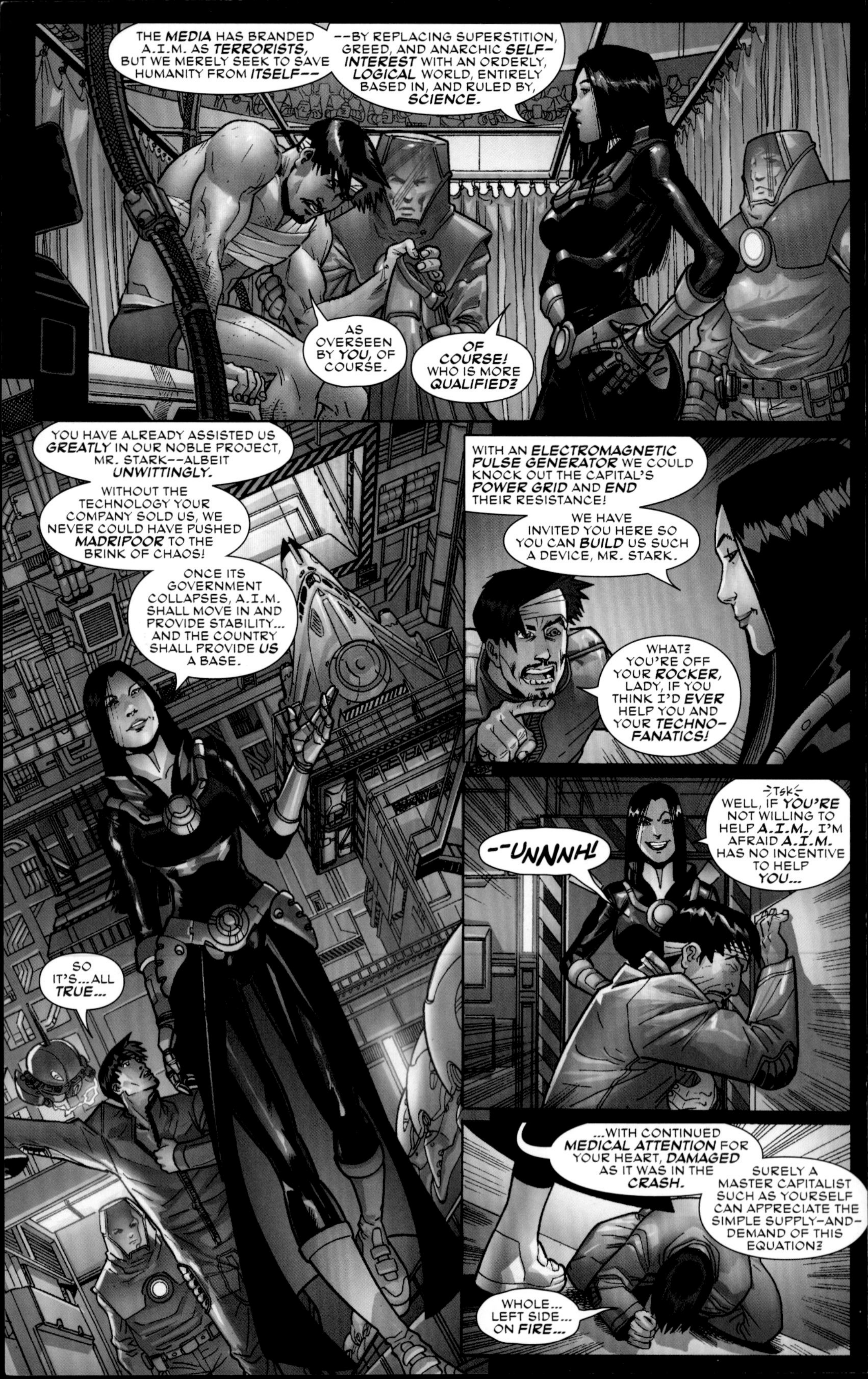
THE MEDIA HAS BRANDED A.I.M. AS TERRORISTS, BUT WE MERELY SEEK TO SAVE HUMANITY FROM ITSELF--
--BY REPLACING SUPERSTITION, GREED, AND ANARCHIC SELF-INTEREST WITH AN ORDERLY, LOGICAL WORLD, ENTIRELY BASED IN, AND RULED BY, SCIENCE.
AS OVERSEEN BY YOU, OF COURSE.
OF COURSE! WHO IS MORE QUALIFIED?
YOU HAVE ALREADY ASSISTED US GREATLY IN OUR NOBLE PROJECT, MR. STARK--ALBEIT UNWITTINGLY.
WITHOUT THE TECHNOLOGY YOUR COMPANY SOLD US, WE NEVER COULD HAVE PUSHED MADRIPOOR TO THE BRINK OF CHAOS!
ONCE ITS GOVERNMENT COLLAPSES, A.I.M. SHALL MOVE IN AND PROVIDE STABILITY... AND THE COUNTRY SHALL PROVIDE US A BASE.
SO IT'S...ALL TRUE...
WITH AN ELECTROMAGNETIC PULSE GENERATOR WE COULD KNOCK OUT THE CAPITAL'S POWER GRID AND END THEIR RESISTANCE!
WE HAVE INVITED YOU HERE SO YOU CAN BUILD US SUCH A DEVICE, MR. STARK.
WHAT? YOU'RE OFF YOUR ROCKER, LADY, IF YOU THINK I'D EVER HELP YOU AND YOUR TECHNO-FANATICS!
-TSK-
WELL, IF YOU'RE NOT WILLING TO HELP A.I.M., I'M AFRAID A.I.M. HAS NO INCENTIVE TO HELP YOU...
--UNNNH!
...WITH CONTINUED MEDICAL ATTENTION FOR YOUR HEART, DAMAGED AS IT WAS IN THE CRASH.
SURELY A MASTER CAPITALIST SUCH AS YOURSELF CAN APPRECIATE THE SIMPLE SUPPLY-AND-DEMAND OF THIS EQUATION?
WHOLE... LEFT SIDE... ON FIRE...

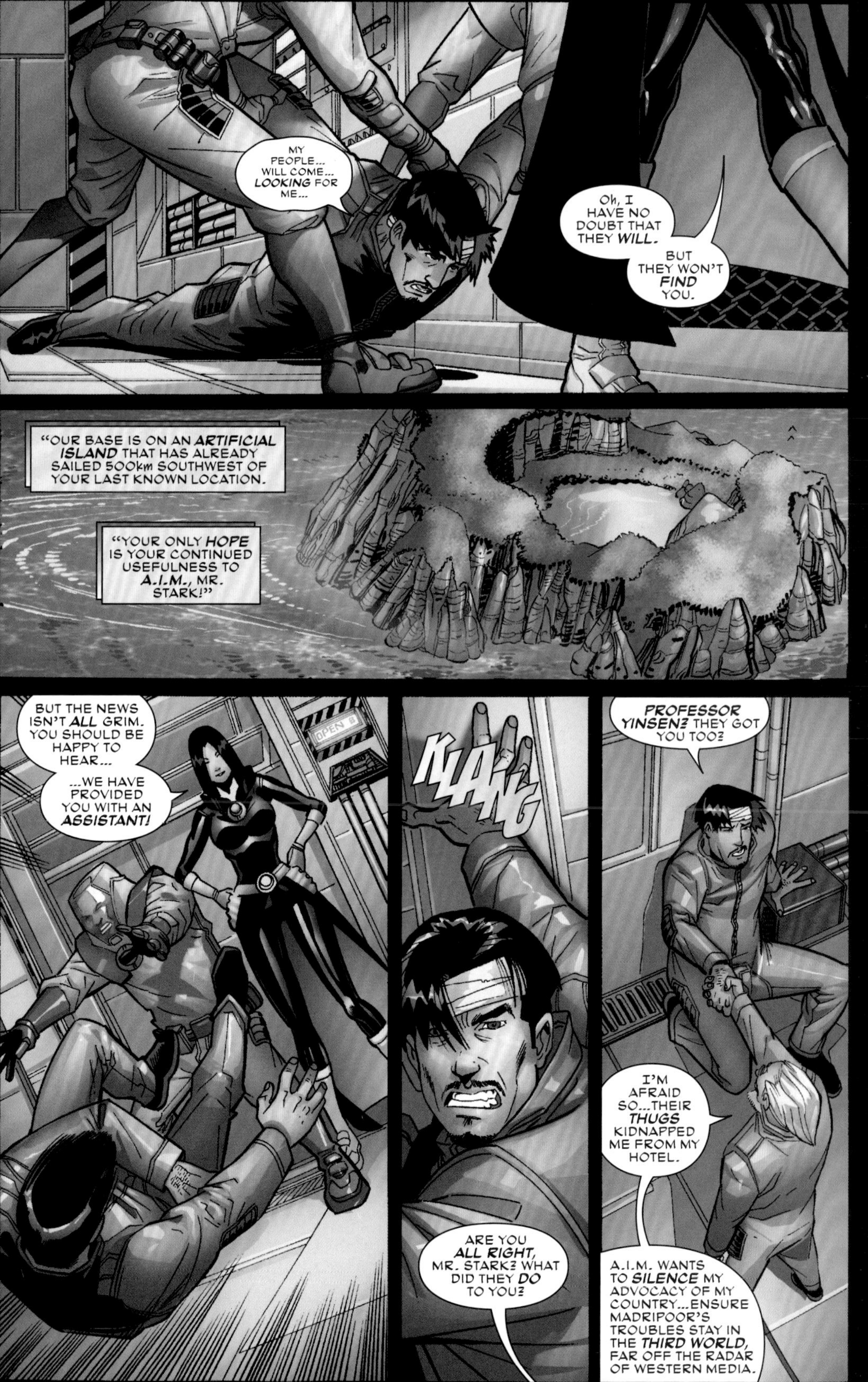
MY PEOPLE... WILL COME... LOOKING FOR ME...
Oh, I HAVE NO DOUBT THAT THEY WILL.
BUT THEY WON'T FIND YOU.
"OUR BASE IS ON AN ARTIFICIAL ISLAND THAT HAS ALREADY SAILED 500km SOUTHWEST OF YOUR LAST KNOWN LOCATION.
"YOUR ONLY HOPE IS YOUR CONTINUED USEFULNESS TO A.I.M., MR. STARK!"
BUT THE NEWS ISN'T ALL GRIM. YOU SHOULD BE HAPPY TO HEAR...
...WE HAVE PROVIDED YOU WITH AN ASSISTANT!
OPEN
KLANG
ARE YOU ALL RIGHT, MR. STARK? WHAT DID THEY DO TO YOU?
PROFESSOR YINSEN? THEY GOT YOU TOO?
I'M AFRAID SO...THEIR THUGS KIDNAPPED ME FROM MY HOTEL.
A.I.M. WANTS TO SILENCE MY ADVOCACY OF MY COUNTRY...ENSURE MADRIPOOR'S TROUBLES STAY IN THE THIRD WORLD, FAR OFF THE RADAR OF WESTERN MEDIA.

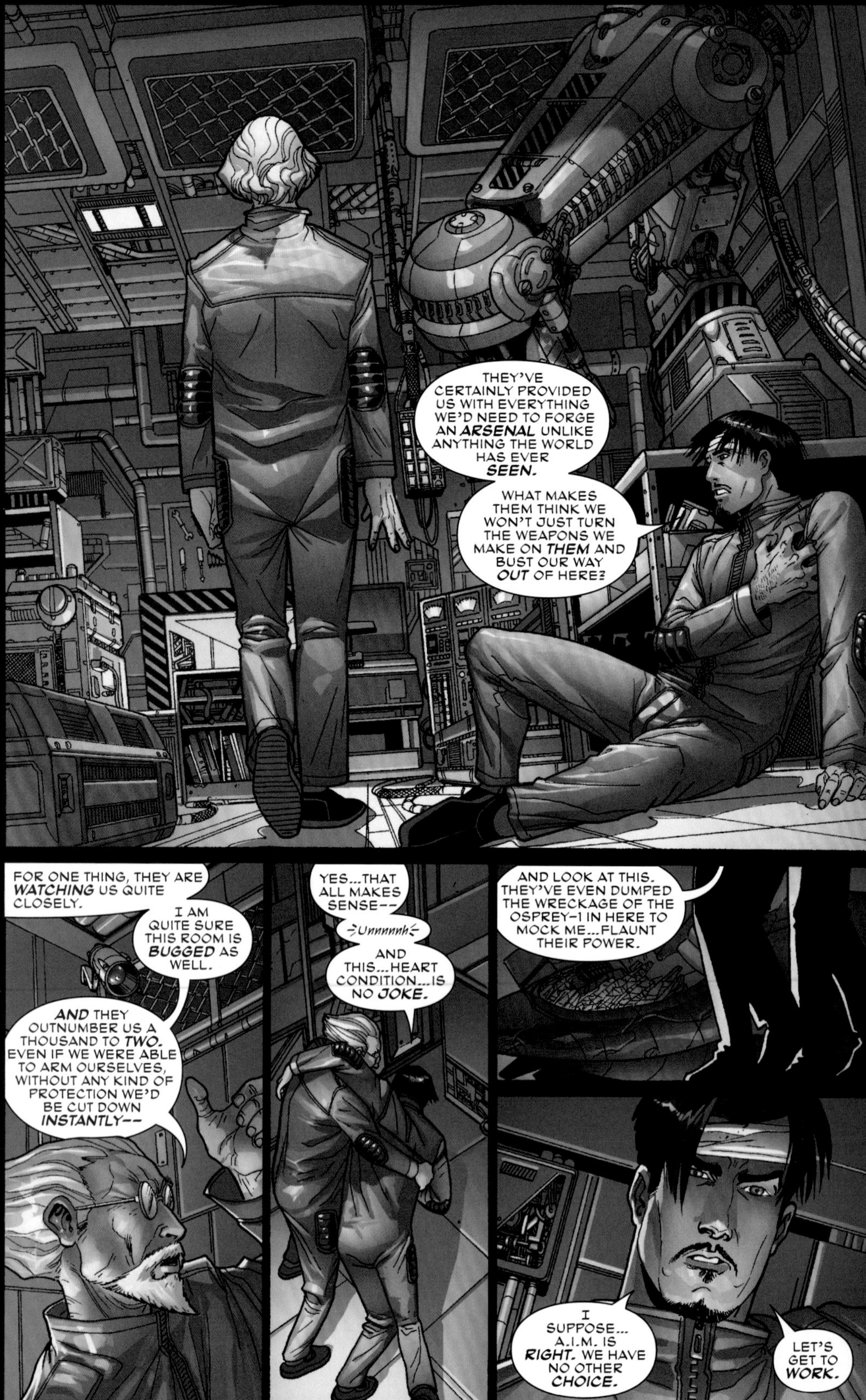
THEY'VE CERTAINLY PROVIDED US WITH EVERYTHING WE'D NEED TO FORGE AN ARSENAL UNLIKE ANYTHING THE WORLD HAS EVER SEEN.
WHAT MAKES THEM THINK WE WON'T JUST TURN THE WEAPONS WE MAKE ON THEM AND BUST OUR WAY OUT OF HERE?
FOR ONE THING, THEY ARE WATCHING US QUITE CLOSELY.
I AM QUITE SURE THIS ROOM IS BUGGED AS WELL.
AND THEY OUTNUMBER US A THOUSAND TO TWO. EVEN IF WE WERE ABLE TO ARM OURSELVES, WITHOUT ANY KIND OF PROTECTION WE'D BE CUT DOWN INSTANTLY--
YES...THAT ALL MAKES SENSE--
Unnnnnh
AND THIS...HEART CONDITION...IS NO JOKE.
AND LOOK AT THIS. THEY'VE EVEN DUMPED THE WRECKAGE OF THE OSPREY-1 IN HERE TO MOCK ME...FLAUNT THEIR POWER.
I SUPPOSE... A.I.M. IS RIGHT. WE HAVE NO OTHER CHOICE.
LET'S GET TO WORK.

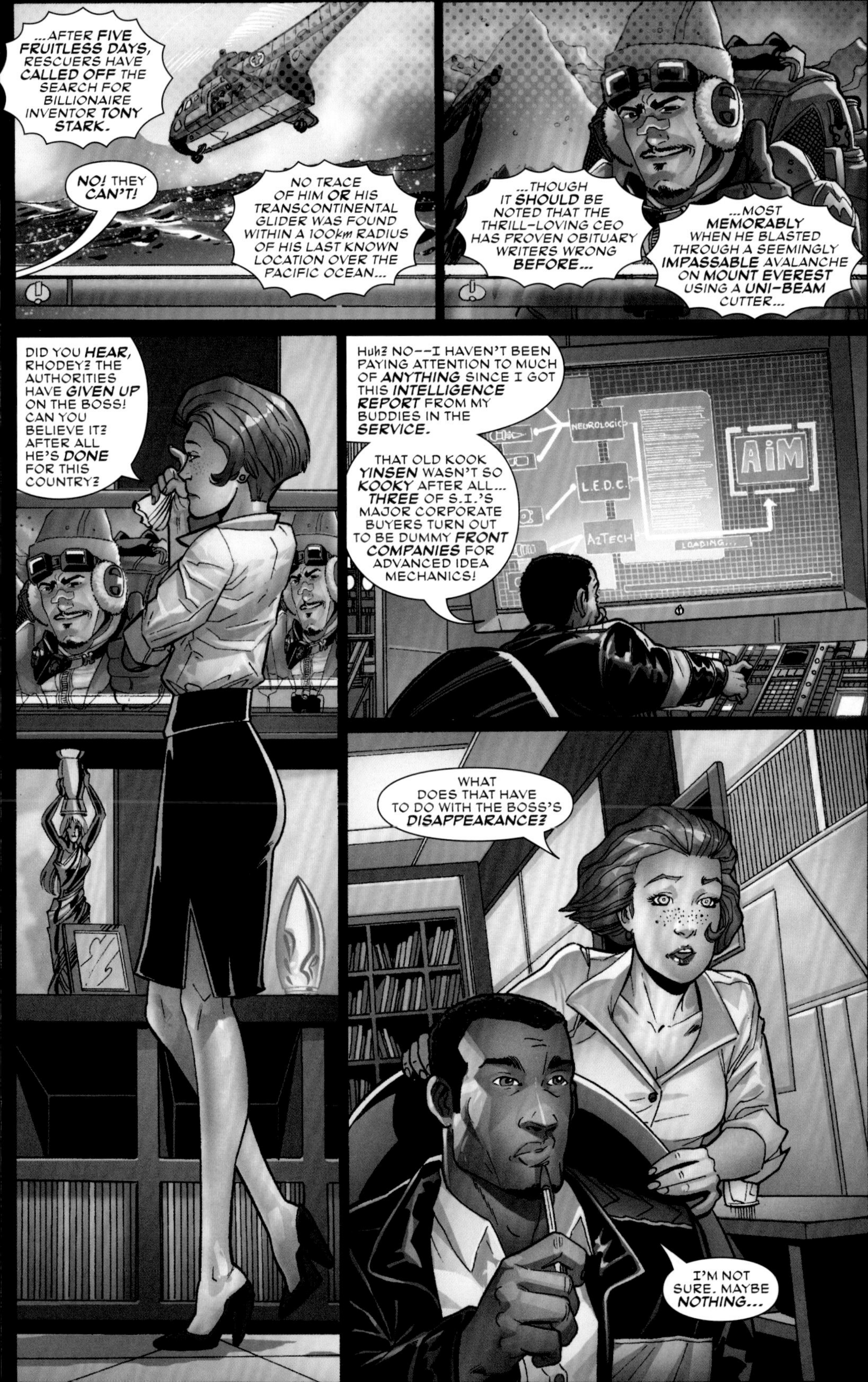
...AFTER FIVE FRUITLESS DAYS, RESCUERS HAVE CALLED OFF THE SEARCH FOR BILLIONAIRE INVENTOR TONY STARK.
NO! THEY CAN'T!
NO TRACE OF HIM OR HIS TRANSCONTINENTAL GLIDER WAS FOUND WITHIN A 100km RADIUS OF HIS LAST KNOWN LOCATION OVER THE PACIFIC OCEAN...
...THOUGH IT SHOULD BE NOTED THAT THE THRILL-LOVING CEO HAS PROVEN OBITUARY WRITERS WRONG BEFORE...
...MOST MEMORABLY WHEN HE BLASTED THROUGH A SEEMINGLY IMPASSABLE AVALANCHE ON MOUNT EVEREST USING A UNI-BEAM CUTTER...
DID YOU HEAR, RHODEY? THE AUTHORITIES HAVE GIVEN UP ON THE BOSS! CAN YOU BELIEVE IT? AFTER ALL HE'S DONE FOR THIS COUNTRY?
HUH? NO--I HAVEN'T BEEN PAYING ATTENTION TO MUCH OF ANYTHING SINCE I GOT THIS INTELLIGENCE REPORT FROM MY BUDDIES IN THE SERVICE.
THAT OLD KOOK YINSEN WASN'T SO KOOKY AFTER ALL... THREE OF S.I.'S MAJOR CORPORATE BUYERS TURN OUT TO BE DUMMY FRONT COMPANIES FOR ADVANCED IDEA MECHANICS!
NEUROLOGIC
L.E.D.C.
AzTECH
AiM
LOADING...
WHAT DOES THAT HAVE TO DO WITH THE BOSS'S DISAPPEARANCE?
I'M NOT SURE. MAYBE NOTHING...

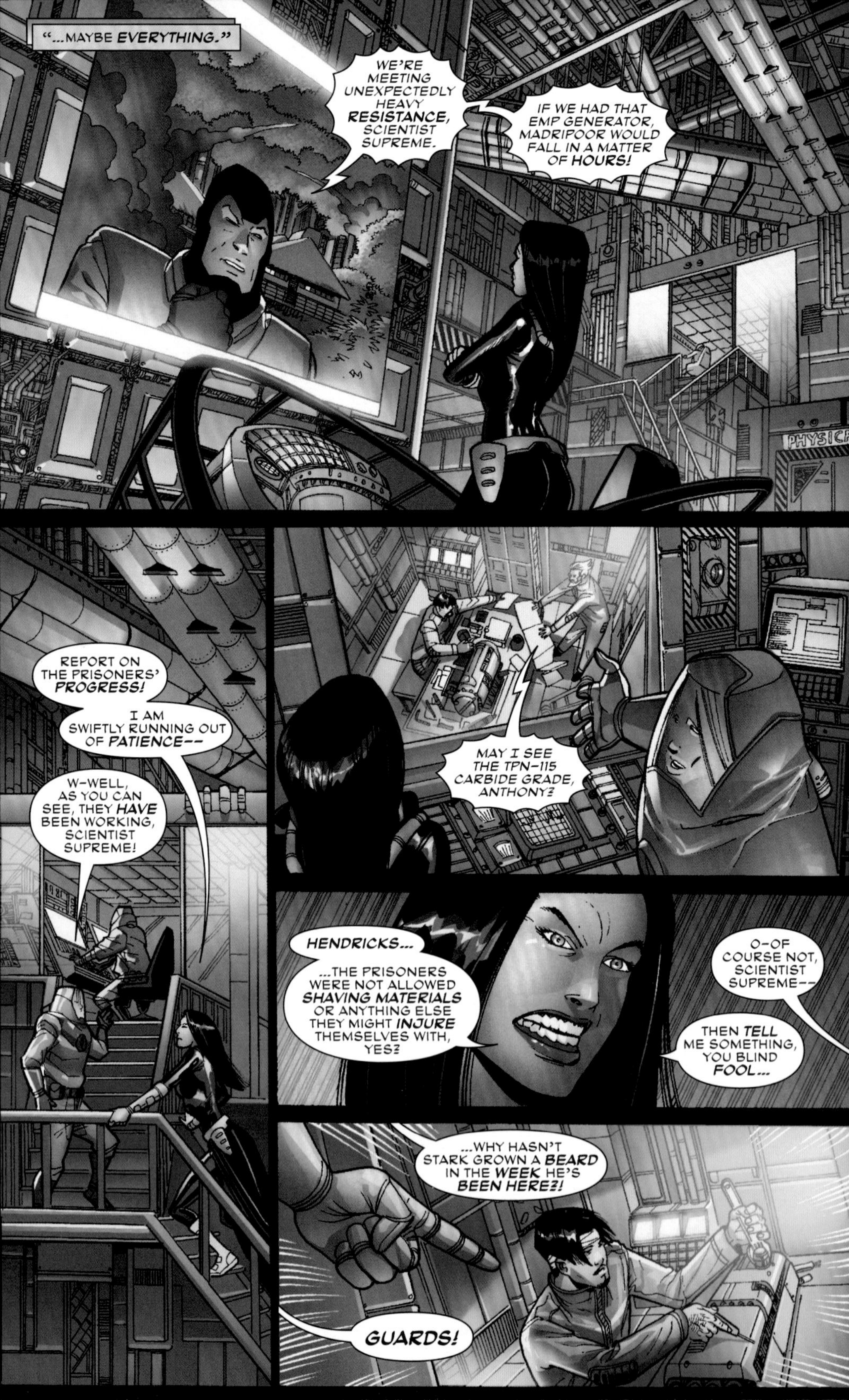
"...MAYBE EVERYTHING."
WE'RE MEETING UNEXPECTEDLY HEAVY RESISTANCE, SCIENTIST SUPREME.
IF WE HAD THAT EMP GENERATOR, MADRIPOOR WOULD FALL IN A MATTER OF HOURS!
PHYSICS
REPORT ON THE PRISONERS' PROGRESS!
I AM SWIFTLY RUNNING OUT OF PATIENCE--
W-WELL, AS YOU CAN SEE, THEY HAVE BEEN WORKING, SCIENTIST SUPREME!
MAY I SEE THE TPN-115 CARBIDE GRADE, ANTHONY?
HENDRICKS...
...THE PRISONERS WERE NOT ALLOWED SHAVING MATERIALS OR ANYTHING ELSE THEY MIGHT INJURE THEMSELVES WITH, YES?
O-OF COURSE NOT, SCIENTIST SUPREME--
THEN TELL ME SOMETHING, YOU BLIND FOOL...
...WHY HASN'T STARK GROWN A BEARD IN THE WEEK HE'S BEEN HERE?!
GUARDS!

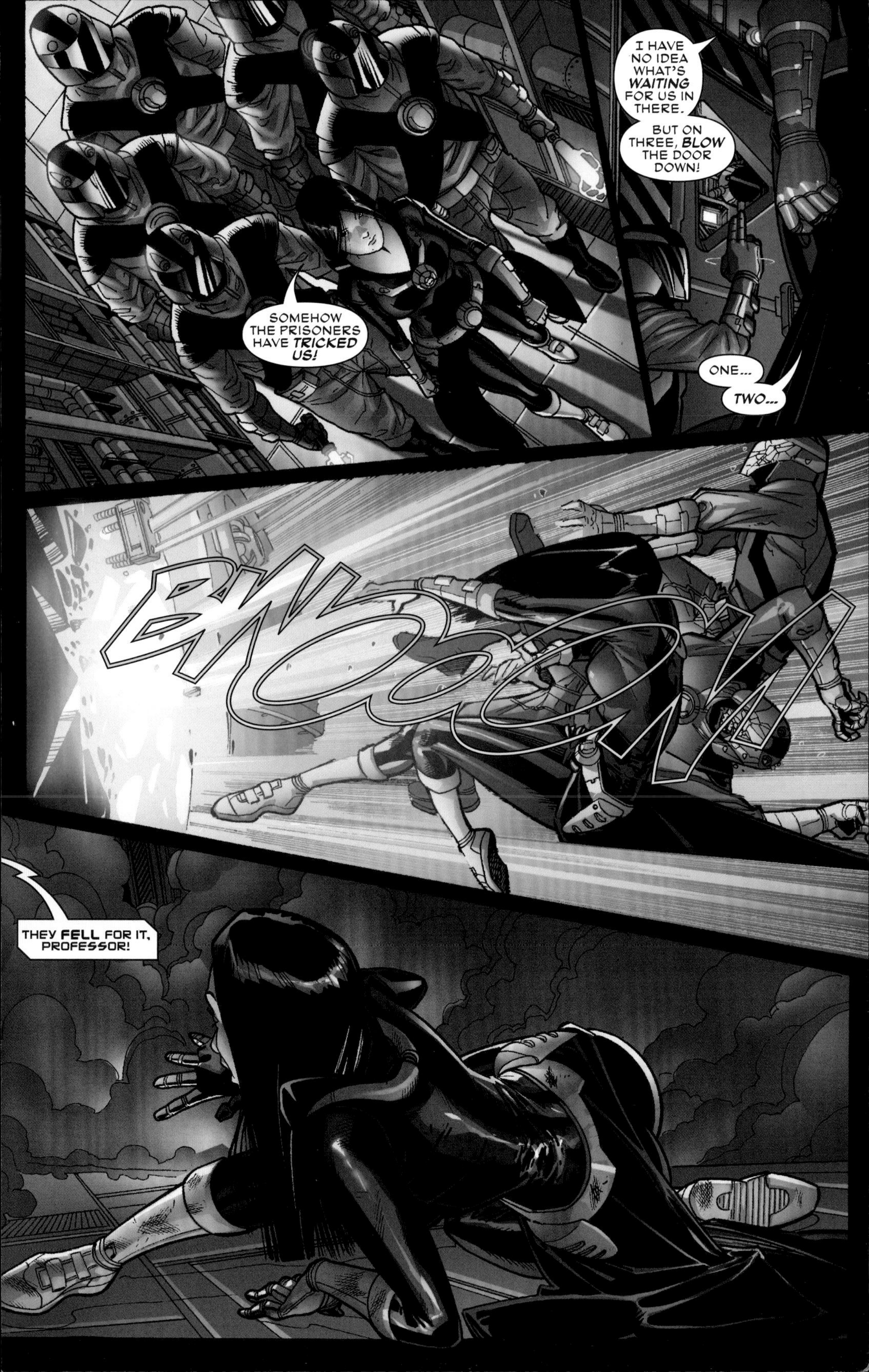
SOMEHOW THE PRISONERS HAVE TRICKED US!
I HAVE NO IDEA WHAT'S WAITING FOR US IN THERE.
BUT ON THREE, BLOW THE DOOR DOWN!
ONE...
TWO...
BWOOOM
THEY FELL FOR IT, PROFESSOR!

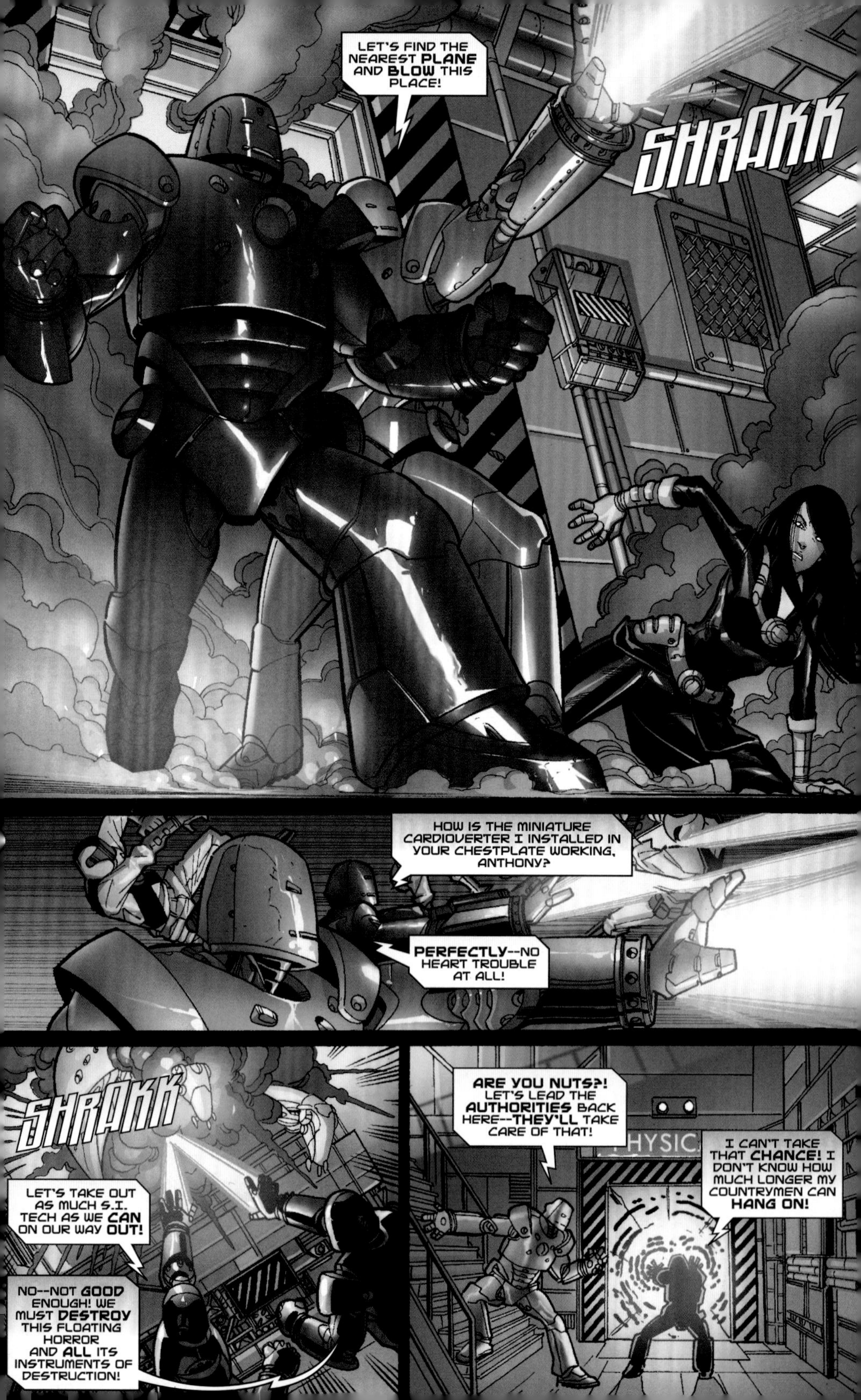
LET'S FIND THE NEAREST PLANE AND BLOW THIS PLACE!
SHRAKK
HOW IS THE MINIATURE CARDIOVERTER I INSTALLED IN YOUR CHESTPLATE WORKING, ANTHONY?
PERFECTLY--NO HEART TROUBLE AT ALL!
SHRAKK
LET'S TAKE OUT AS MUCH S.I. TECH AS WE CAN ON OUR WAY OUT!
NO--NOT GOOD ENOUGH! WE MUST DESTROY THIS FLOATING HORROR AND ALL ITS INSTRUMENTS OF DESTRUCTION!
ARE YOU NUTS?! LET'S LEAD THE AUTHORITIES BACK HERE--THEY'LL TAKE CARE OF THAT!
I CAN'T TAKE THAT CHANCE! I DON'T KNOW HOW MUCH LONGER MY COUNTRYMEN CAN HANG ON!

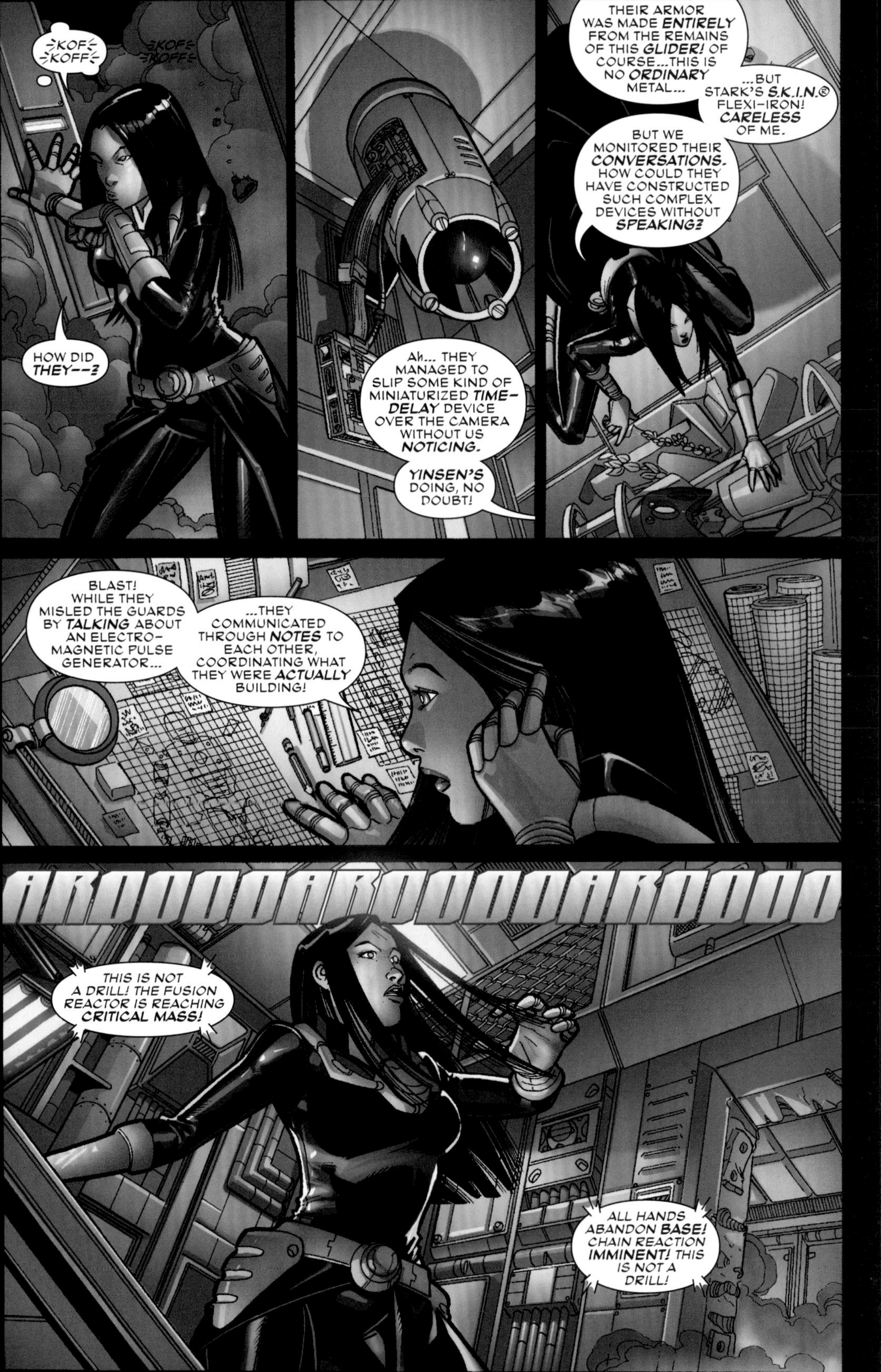

KOF KOFF
KOF KOFF
HOW DID THEY--?
Ah... THEY MANAGED TO SLIP SOME KIND OF MINIATURIZED TIME-DELAY DEVICE OVER THE CAMERA WITHOUT US NOTICING.
YINSEN'S DOING, NO DOUBT!
THEIR ARMOR WAS MADE ENTIRELY FROM THE REMAINS OF THIS GLIDER! OF COURSE... THIS IS NO ORDINARY METAL...
...BUT STARK'S S.K.I.N.® FLEXI-IRON! CARELESS OF ME.
BUT WE MONITORED THEIR CONVERSATIONS. HOW COULD THEY HAVE CONSTRUCTED SUCH COMPLEX DEVICES WITHOUT SPEAKING?
BLAST! WHILE THEY MISLED THE GUARDS BY TALKING ABOUT AN ELECTRO-MAGNETIC PULSE GENERATOR...
...THEY COMMUNICATED THROUGH NOTES TO EACH OTHER, COORDINATING WHAT THEY WERE ACTUALLY BUILDING!
AROOOOAROOOOOAROOOO
THIS IS NOT A DRILL! THE FUSION REACTOR IS REACHING CRITICAL MASS!
ALL HANDS ABANDON BASE! CHAIN REACTION IMMINENT! THIS IS NOT A DRILL!

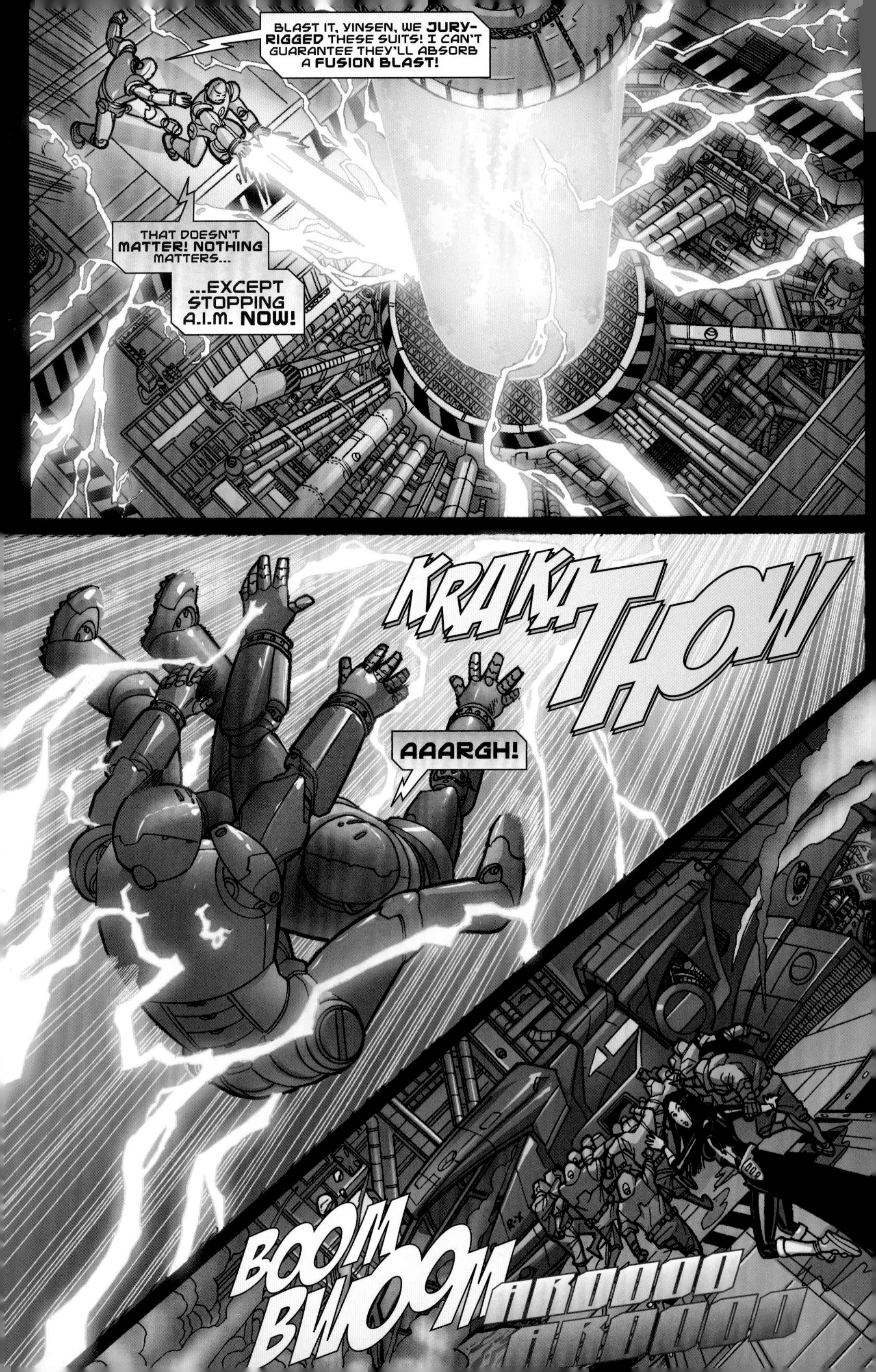
BLAST IT, YINSEN, WE JURY-RIGGED THESE SUITS! I CAN'T GUARANTEE THEY'LL ABSORB A FUSION BLAST!
THAT DOESN'T MATTER! NOTHING MATTERS...
...EXCEPT STOPPING A.I.M. NOW!
KRAKA THOW
AAARGH!
BOOM
BWOOM
AROOOO
AROOOO

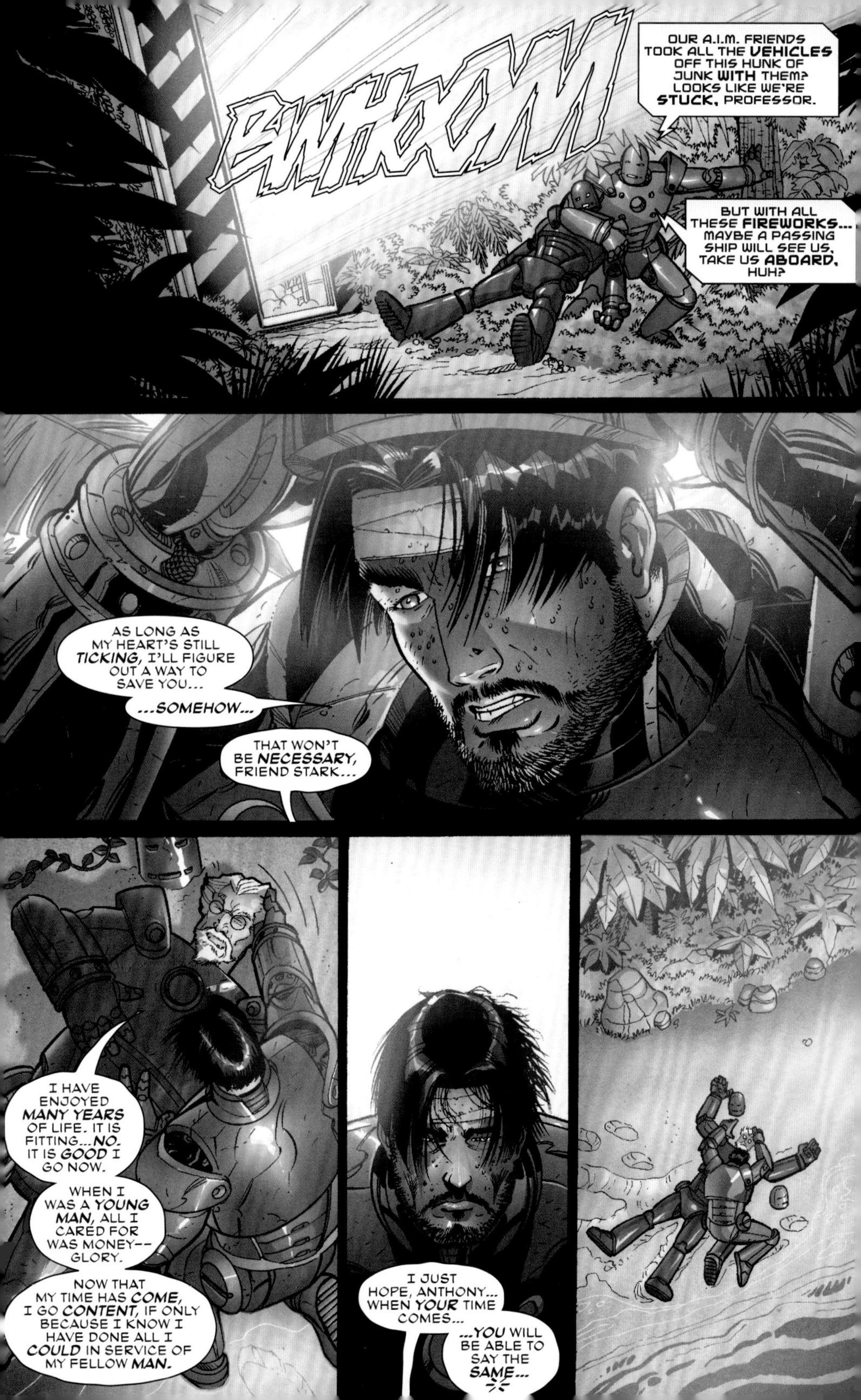
BWHOOM
OUR A.I.M. FRIENDS TOOK ALL THE VEHICLES OFF THIS HUNK OF JUNK WITH THEM? LOOKS LIKE WE'RE STUCK, PROFESSOR.
BUT WITH ALL THESE FIREWORKS... MAYBE A PASSING SHIP WILL SEE US, TAKE US ABOARD, HUH?
AS LONG AS MY HEART'S STILL TICKING, I'LL FIGURE OUT A WAY TO SAVE YOU...
...SOMEHOW...
THAT WON'T BE NECESSARY, FRIEND STARK...
I HAVE ENJOYED MANY YEARS OF LIFE. IT IS FITTING...NO. IT IS GOOD I GO NOW.
WHEN I WAS A YOUNG MAN, ALL I CARED FOR WAS MONEY-- GLORY.
NOW THAT MY TIME HAS COME, I GO CONTENT, IF ONLY BECAUSE I KNOW I HAVE DONE ALL I COULD IN SERVICE OF MY FELLOW MAN.
I JUST HOPE, ANTHONY... WHEN YOUR TIME COMES...
...YOU WILL BE ABLE TO SAY THE SAME...

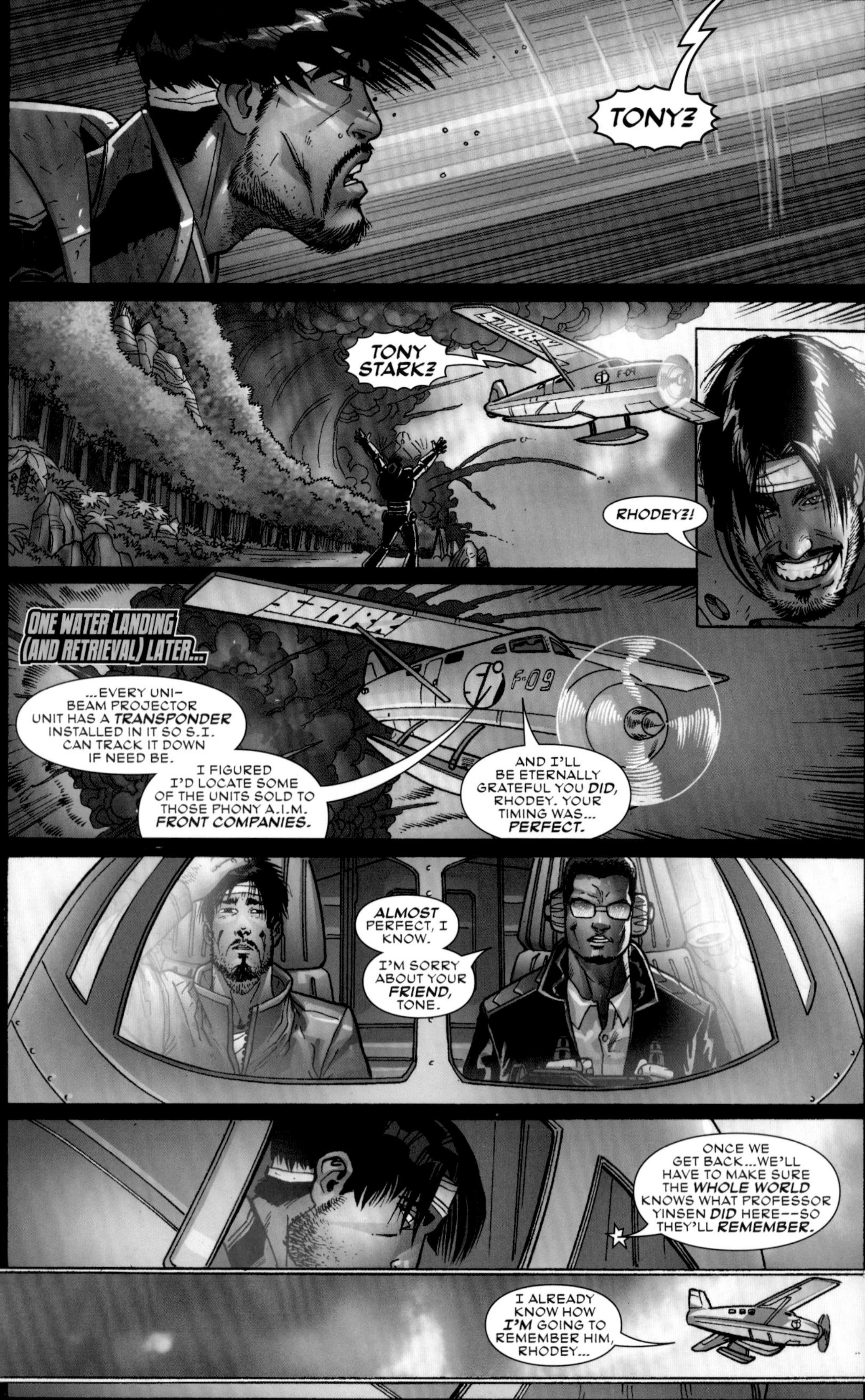
TONY?
TONY STARK?
RHODEY?!
ONE WATER LANDING (AND RETRIEVAL) LATER...
...EVERY UNI-BEAM PROJECTOR UNIT HAS A TRANSPONDER INSTALLED IN IT SO S.I. CAN TRACK IT DOWN IF NEED BE.
I FIGURED I'D LOCATE SOME OF THE UNITS SOLD TO THOSE PHONY A.I.M. FRONT COMPANIES.
AND I'LL BE ETERNALLY GRATEFUL YOU DID, RHODEY. YOUR TIMING WAS... PERFECT.
ALMOST PERFECT, I KNOW.
I'M SORRY ABOUT YOUR FRIEND, TONE.
ONCE WE GET BACK...WE'LL HAVE TO MAKE SURE THE WHOLE WORLD KNOWS WHAT PROFESSOR YINSEN DID HERE--SO THEY'LL REMEMBER.
I ALREADY KNOW HOW I'M GOING TO REMEMBER HIM, RHODEY...

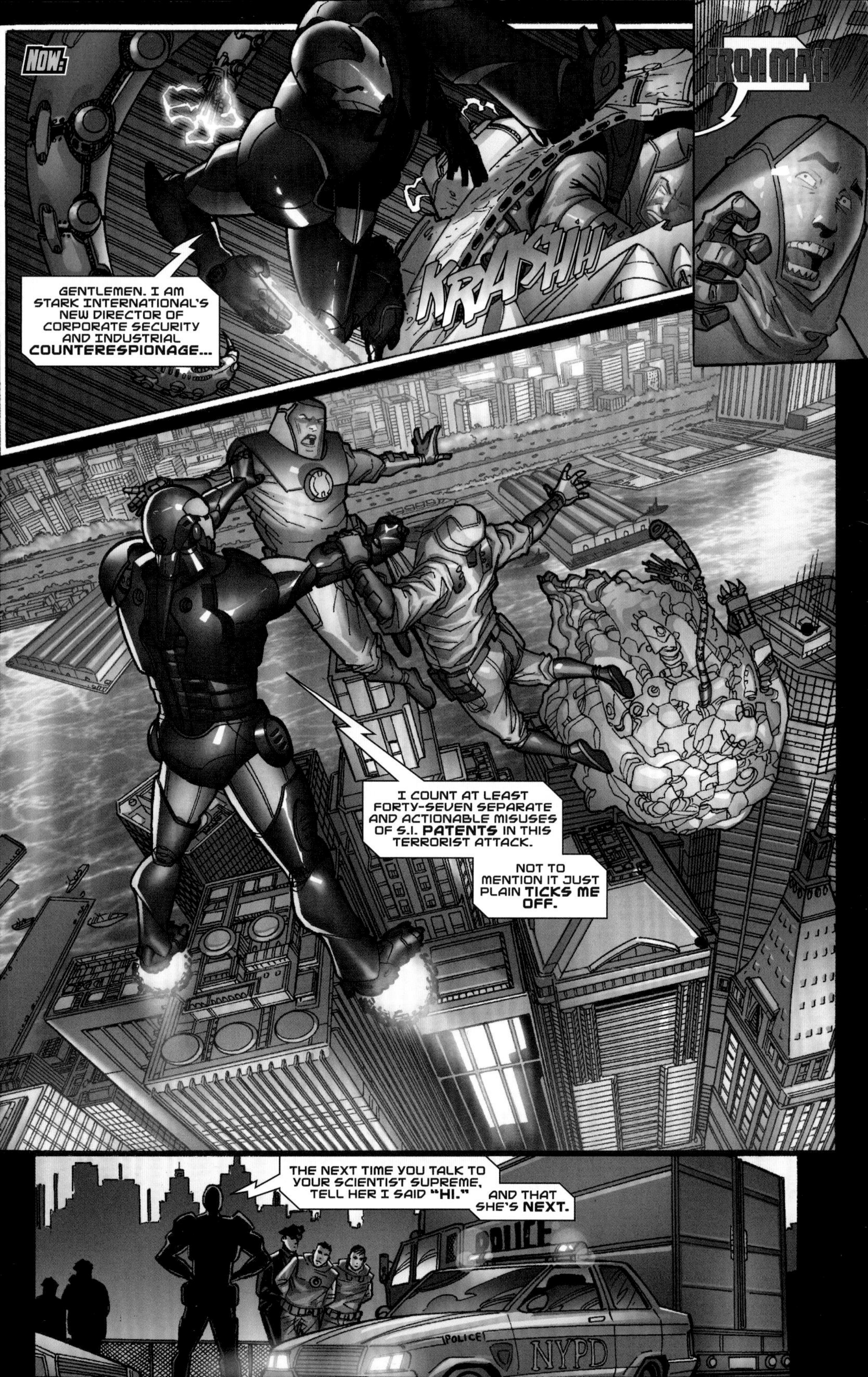
NOW:
IRON MAN!
GENTLEMEN. I AM STARK INTERNATIONAL'S NEW DIRECTOR OF CORPORATE SECURITY AND INDUSTRIAL COUNTERESPIONAGE...
KRASHH
I COUNT AT LEAST FORTY-SEVEN SEPARATE AND ACTIONABLE MISUSES OF S.I. PATENTS IN THIS TERRORIST ATTACK.
NOT TO MENTION IT JUST PLAIN TICKS ME OFF.
THE NEXT TIME YOU TALK TO YOUR SCIENTIST SUPREME, TELL HER I SAID "HI."
AND THAT SHE'S NEXT.
POLICE
NYPD

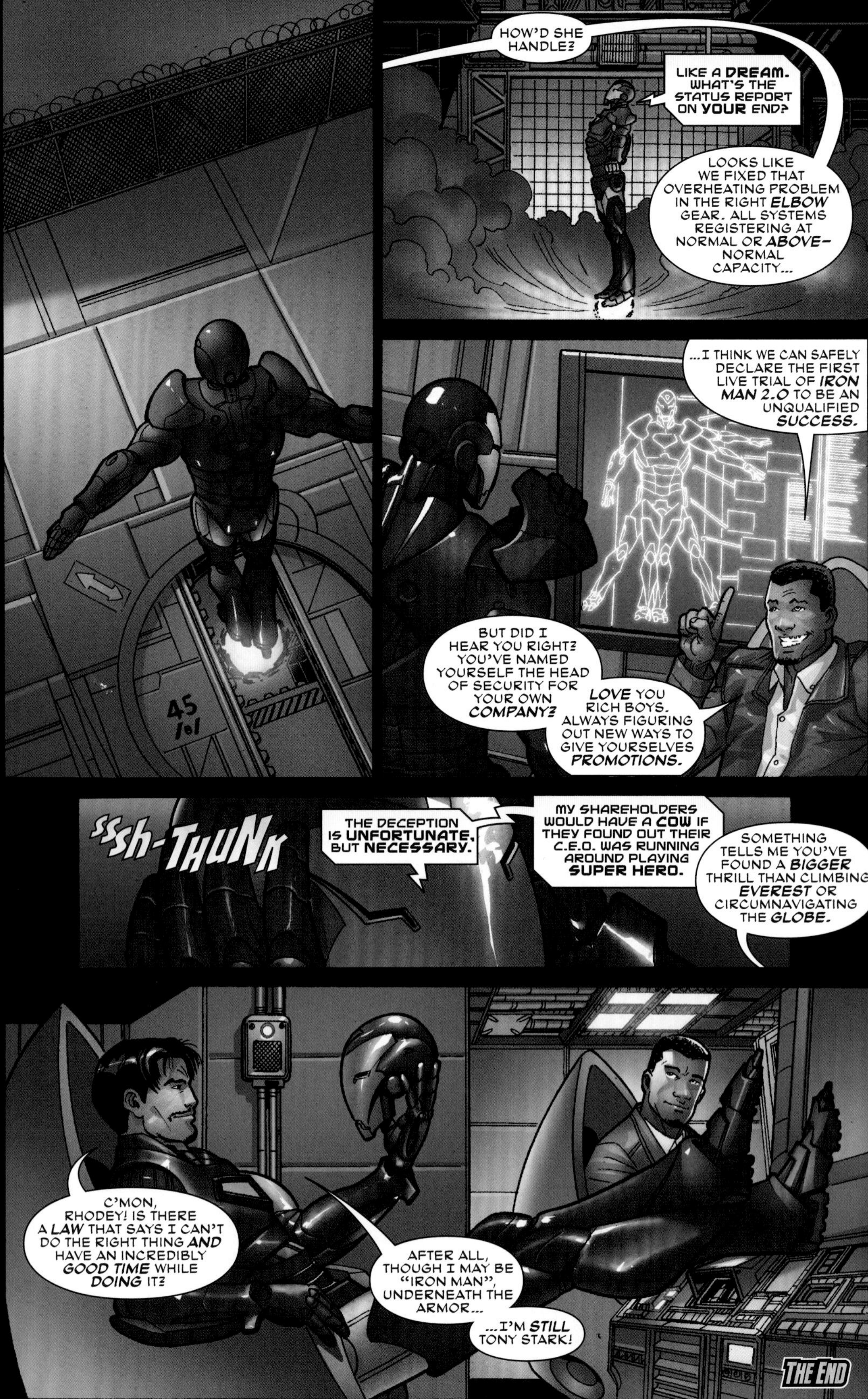
45
HOW'D SHE HANDLE?
LIKE A DREAM. WHAT'S THE STATUS REPORT ON YOUR END?
LOOKS LIKE WE FIXED THAT OVERHEATING PROBLEM IN THE RIGHT ELBOW GEAR. ALL SYSTEMS REGISTERING AT NORMAL OR ABOVE-NORMAL CAPACITY...
...I THINK WE CAN SAFELY DECLARE THE FIRST LIVE TRIAL OF IRON MAN 2.0 TO BE AN UNQUALIFIED SUCCESS.
BUT DID I HEAR YOU RIGHT? YOU'VE NAMED YOURSELF THE HEAD OF SECURITY FOR YOUR OWN COMPANY?
LOVE YOU RICH BOYS. ALWAYS FIGURING OUT NEW WAYS TO GIVE YOURSELVES PROMOTIONS.
SSSH-THUNK
THE DECEPTION IS UNFORTUNATE, BUT NECESSARY.
MY SHAREHOLDERS WOULD HAVE A COW IF THEY FOUND OUT THEIR C.E.O. WAS RUNNING AROUND PLAYING SUPER HERO.
SOMETHING TELLS ME YOU'VE FOUND A BIGGER THRILL THAN CLIMBING EVEREST OR CIRCUMNAVIGATING THE GLOBE.
C'MON, RHODEY! IS THERE A LAW THAT SAYS I CAN'T DO THE RIGHT THING AND HAVE AN INCREDIBLY GOOD TIME WHILE DOING IT?
AFTER ALL, THOUGH I MAY BE "IRON MAN", UNDERNEATH THE ARMOR...
...I'M STILL TONY STARK!
THE END

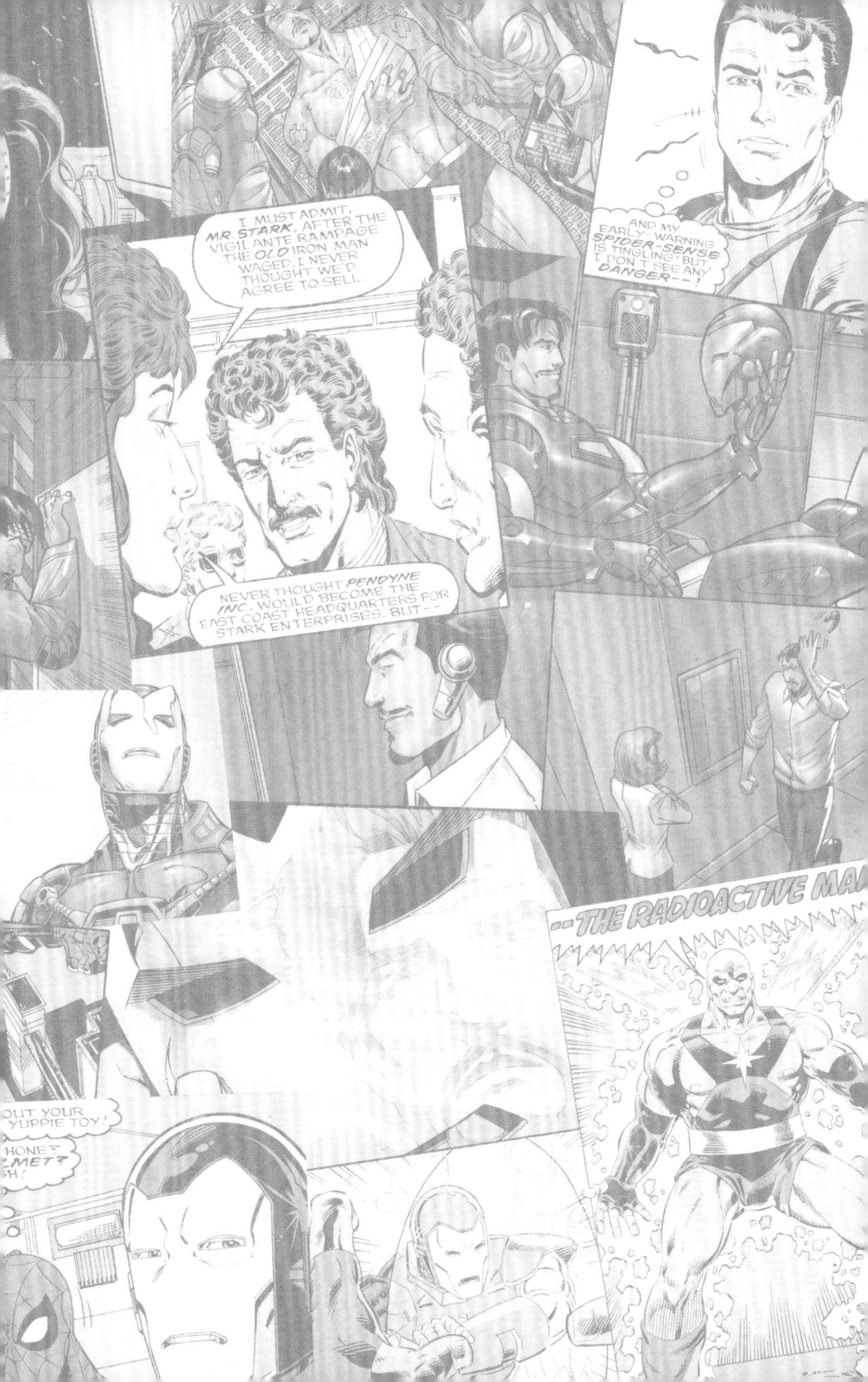
AND MY EARLY-WARNING SPIDER-SENSE IS TINGLING! BUT I DON'T SEE ANY DANGER--!
I MUST ADMIT, MR. STARK, AFTER THE VIGILANTE RAMPAGE THE OLD IRON MAN WAGED, I NEVER THOUGHT WE'D AGREE TO SELL.
NEVER THOUGHT PENDYNE INC. WOULD BECOME THE EAST COAST HEADQUARTERS FOR STARK ENTERPRISES. BUT--
--THE RADIOACTIVE MAN
YUPPIE TOY!

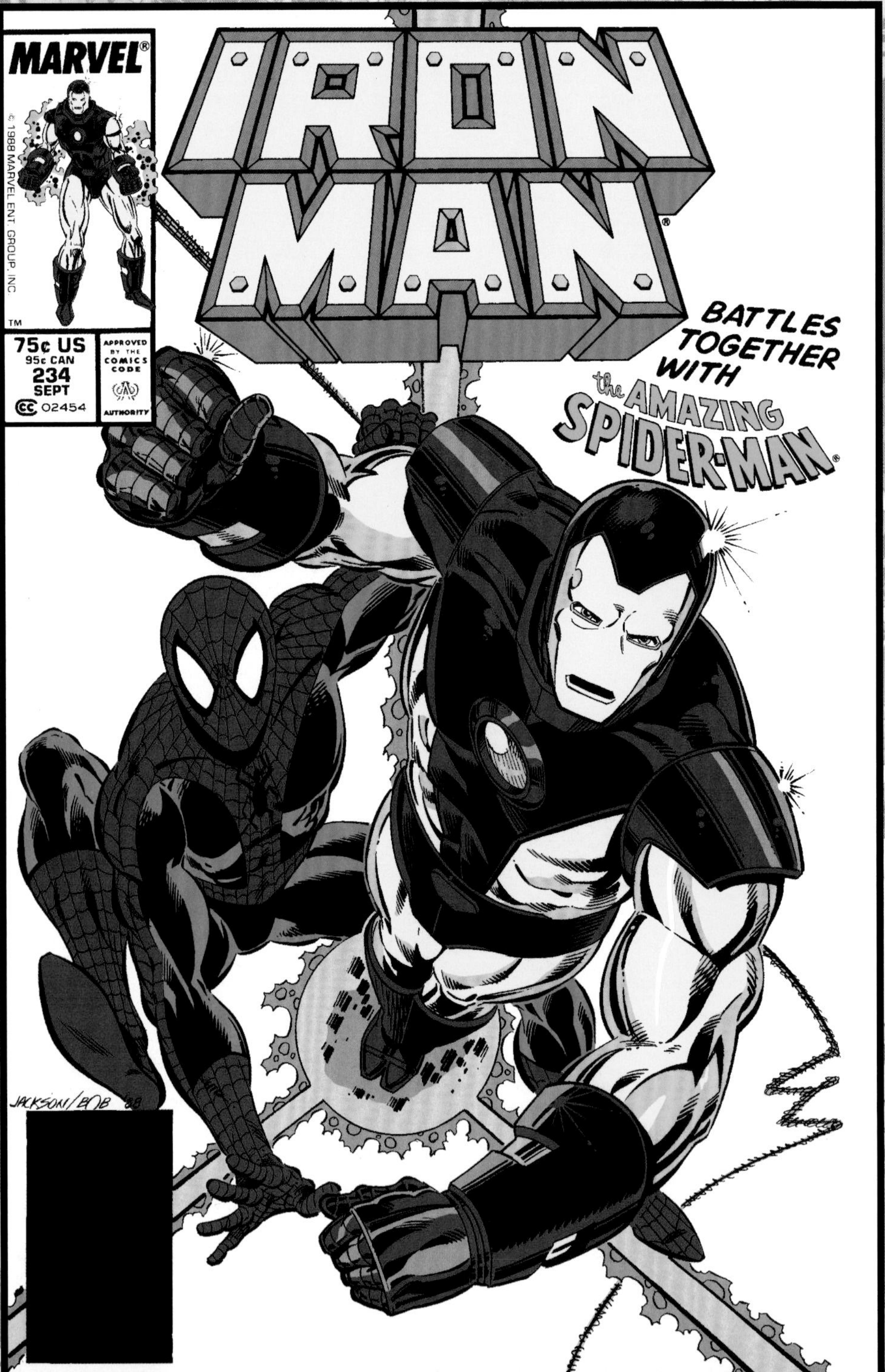
MARVEL
© 1988 MARVEL ENT. GROUP, INC.
IRON MAN
75¢ US
95¢ CAN
234
SEPT
02454
APPROVED BY THE COMICS CODE AUTHORITY
BATTLES TOGETHER WITH
the AMAZING SPIDER-MAN
JACKSON/BOB '88

IRON MAN #234

SPIDER-MAN HAS BEEN CAPTURED BY RADIOACTIVE MAN FOR HIS DEADLY EXPERIMENTS! IT'S UP TO IRON MAN TO RESCUE SPIDEY BEFORE IT'S TOO LATE!

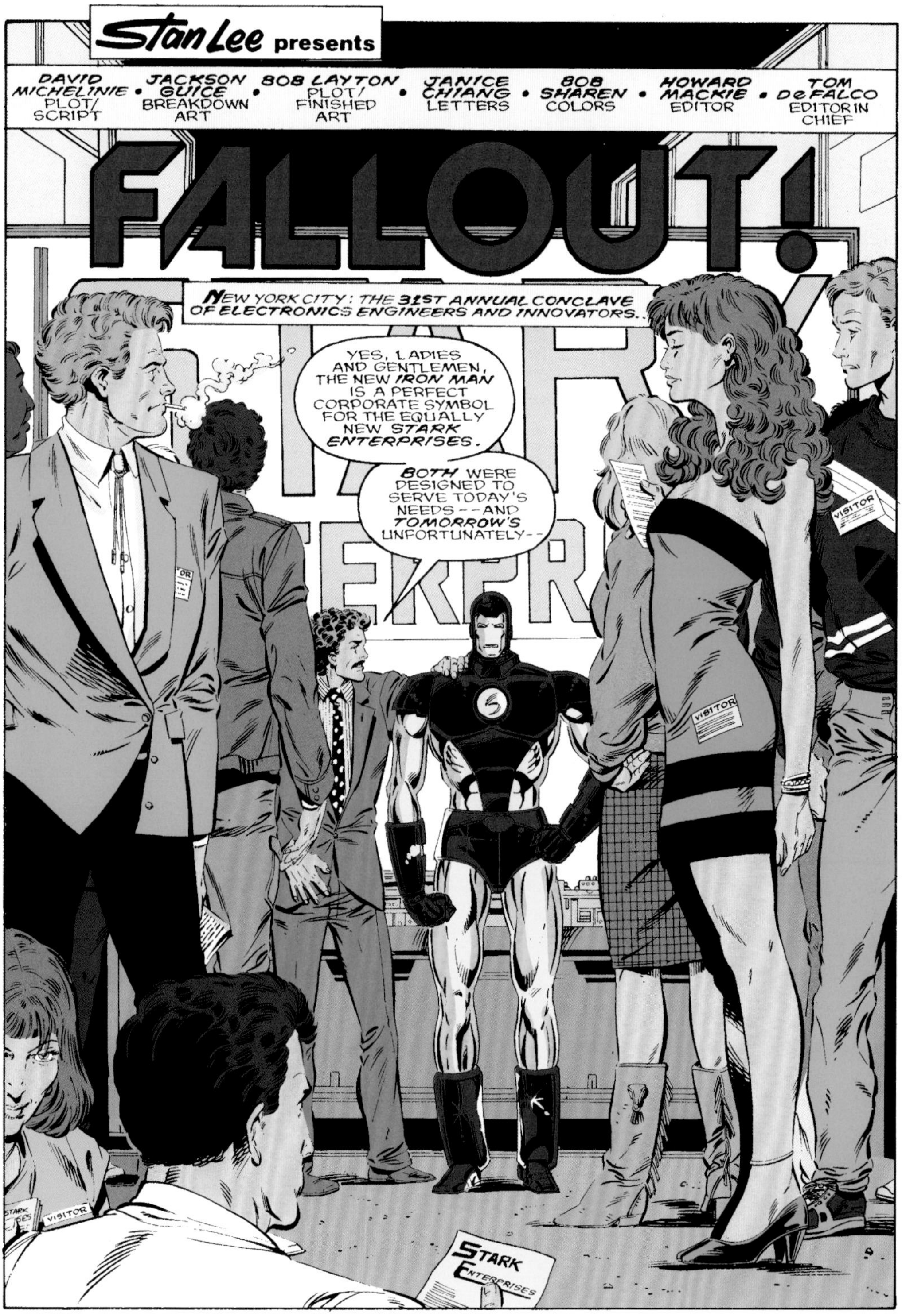
Stan Lee presents
DAVID MICHELINIE • PLOT/SCRIPT
JACKSON GUICE • BREAKDOWN ART
BOB LAYTON • PLOT/ FINISHED ART
JANICE CHIANG • LETTERS
BOB SHAREN • COLORS
HOWARD MACKIE • EDITOR
TOM DeFALCO • EDITOR IN CHIEF
FALLOUT!
NEW YORK CITY: THE 31ST ANNUAL CONCLAVE OF ELECTRONICS ENGINEERS AND INNOVATORS...
YES, LADIES AND GENTLEMEN, THE NEW IRON MAN IS A PERFECT CORPORATE SYMBOL FOR THE EQUALLY NEW STARK ENTERPRISES.
BOTH WERE DESIGNED TO SERVE TODAY'S NEEDS--AND TOMORROW'S UNFORTUNATELY--
VISITOR
VISITOR
VISITOR
STARK ENTERPRISES

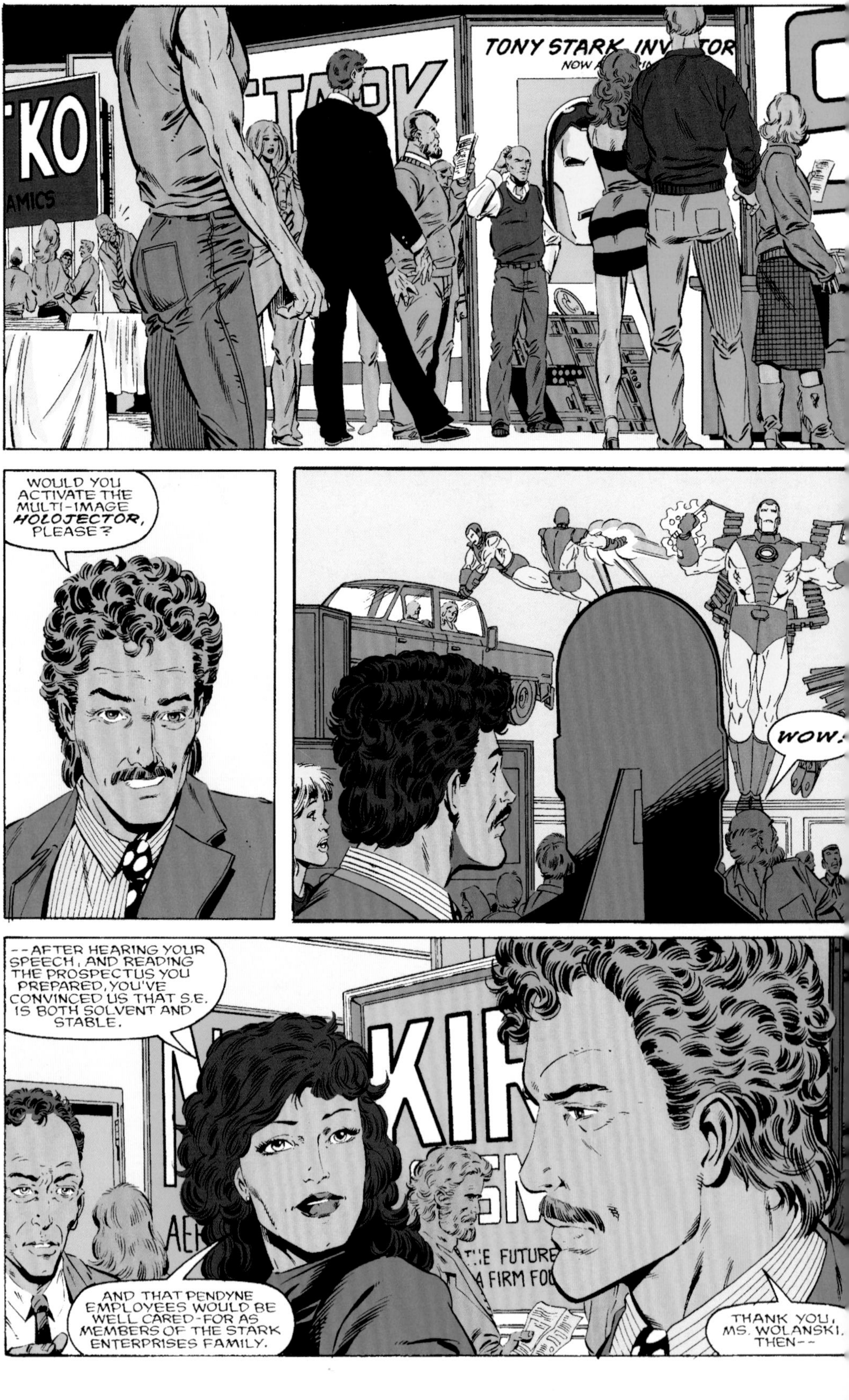

TONY STARK INV TOR
KO
AMICS
STARK
WOULD YOU ACTIVATE THE MULTI-IMAGE HOLOJECTOR, PLEASE?
WOW!
--AFTER HEARING YOUR SPEECH, AND READING THE PROSPECTUS YOU PREPARED, YOU'VE CONVINCED US THAT S.E. IS BOTH SOLVENT AND STABLE.
AND THAT PENDYNE EMPLOYEES WOULD BE WELL CARED-FOR AS MEMBERS OF THE STARK ENTERPRISES FAMILY.
THANK YOU, MS. WOLANSKI, THEN--

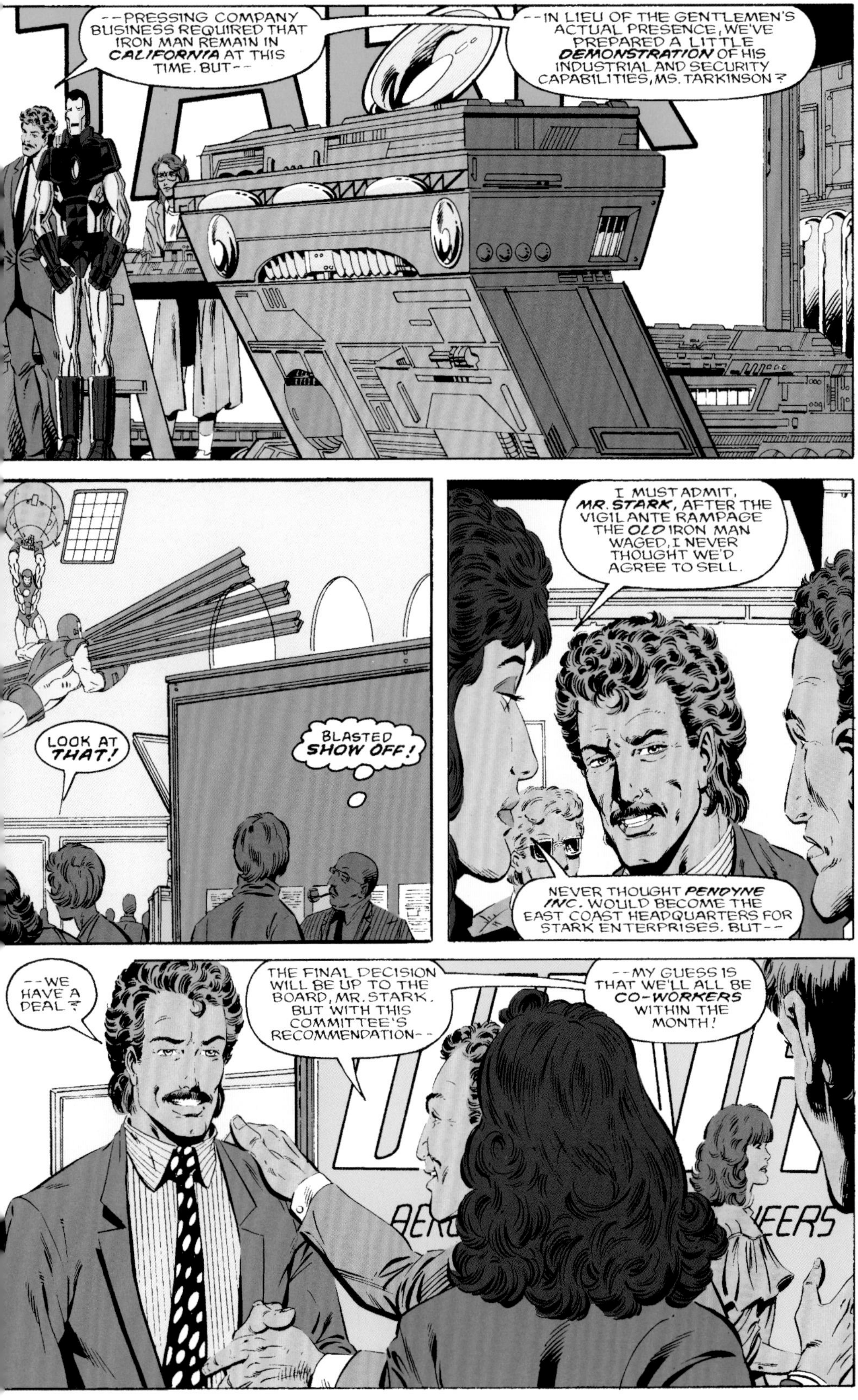
--PRESSING COMPANY BUSINESS REQUIRED THAT IRON MAN REMAIN IN CALIFORNIA AT THIS TIME. BUT--
--IN LIEU OF THE GENTLEMEN'S ACTUAL PRESENCE, WE'VE PREPARED A LITTLE DEMONSTRATION OF HIS INDUSTRIAL AND SECURITY CAPABILITIES, MS. TARKINSON?
LOOK AT THAT!
BLASTED SHOW OFF!
I MUST ADMIT, MR. STARK, AFTER THE VIGILANTE RAMPAGE THE OLD IRON MAN WAGED, I NEVER THOUGHT WE'D AGREE TO SELL.
NEVER THOUGHT PENDYNE INC. WOULD BECOME THE EAST COAST HEADQUARTERS FOR STARK ENTERPRISES. BUT--
--WE HAVE A DEAL?
THE FINAL DECISION WILL BE UP TO THE BOARD, MR. STARK. BUT WITH THIS COMMITTEE'S RECOMMENDATION--
--MY GUESS IS THAT WE'LL ALL BE CO-WORKERS WITHIN THE MONTH!

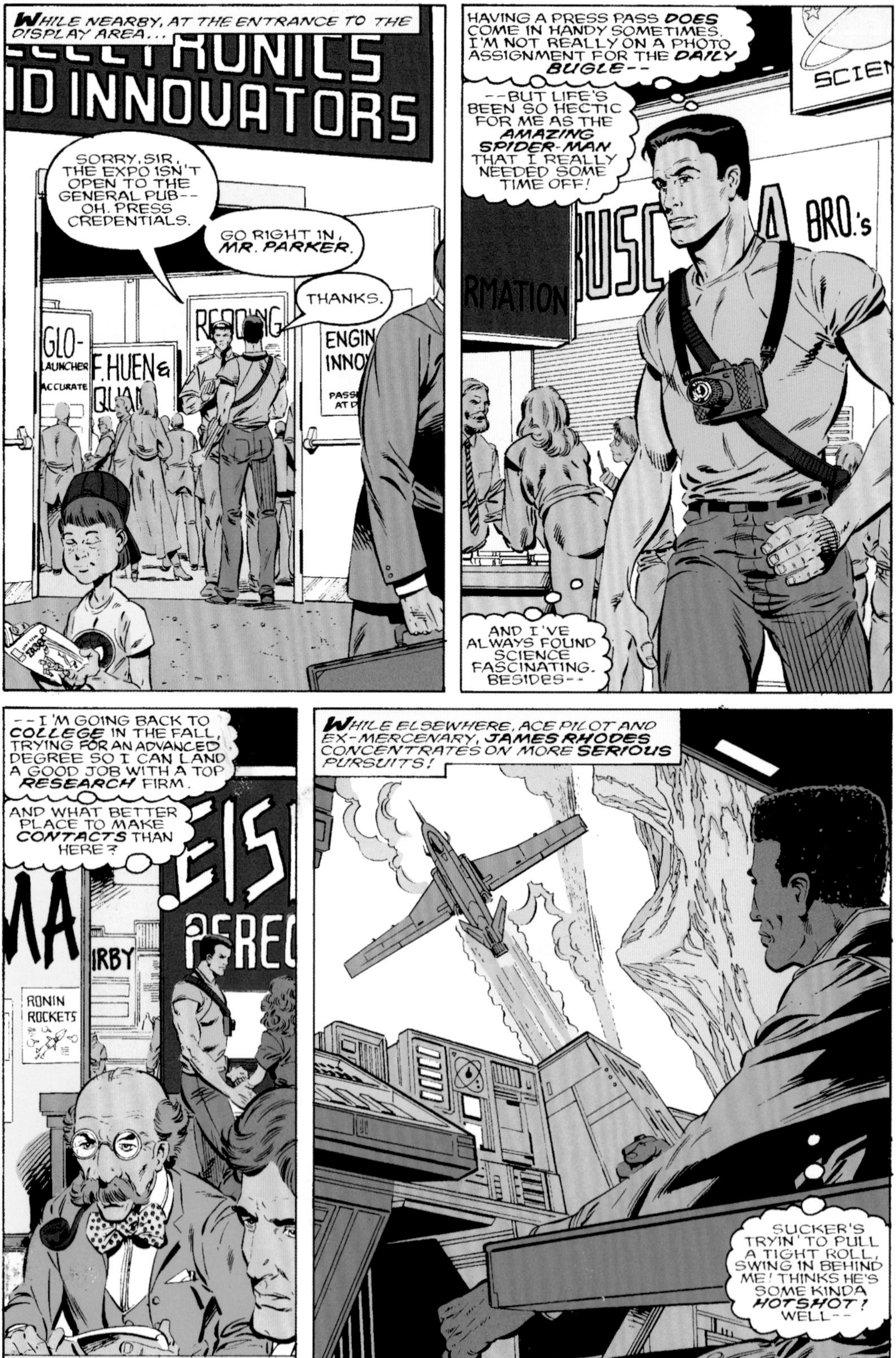
WHILE NEARBY, AT THE ENTRANCE TO THE DISPLAY AREA...
SORRY, SIR, THE EXPO ISN'T OPEN TO THE GENERAL PUB-- OH. PRESS CREDENTIALS.
GO RIGHT IN, MR. PARKER.
THANKS.
HAVING A PRESS PASS DOES COME IN HANDY SOMETIMES. I'M NOT REALLY ON A PHOTO ASSIGNMENT FOR THE DAILY BUGLE--
--BUT LIFE'S BEEN SO HECTIC FOR ME AS THE AMAZING SPIDER-MAN THAT I REALLY NEEDED SOME TIME OFF!
AND I'VE ALWAYS FOUND SCIENCE FASCINATING. BESIDES--
--I'M GOING BACK TO COLLEGE IN THE FALL, TRYING FOR AN ADVANCED DEGREE SO I CAN LAND A GOOD JOB WITH A TOP RESEARCH FIRM.
AND WHAT BETTER PLACE TO MAKE CONTACTS THAN HERE?
PETER PARKER SMILES, AND CONTINUES HIS TOUR.
WHILE ELSEWHERE, ACE PILOT AND EX-MERCENARY, JAMES RHODES CONCENTRATES ON MORE SERIOUS PURSUITS!
SUCKER'S TRYIN' TO PULL A TIGHT ROLL, SWING IN BEHIND ME! THINKS HE'S SOME KINDA HOTSHOT! WELL--

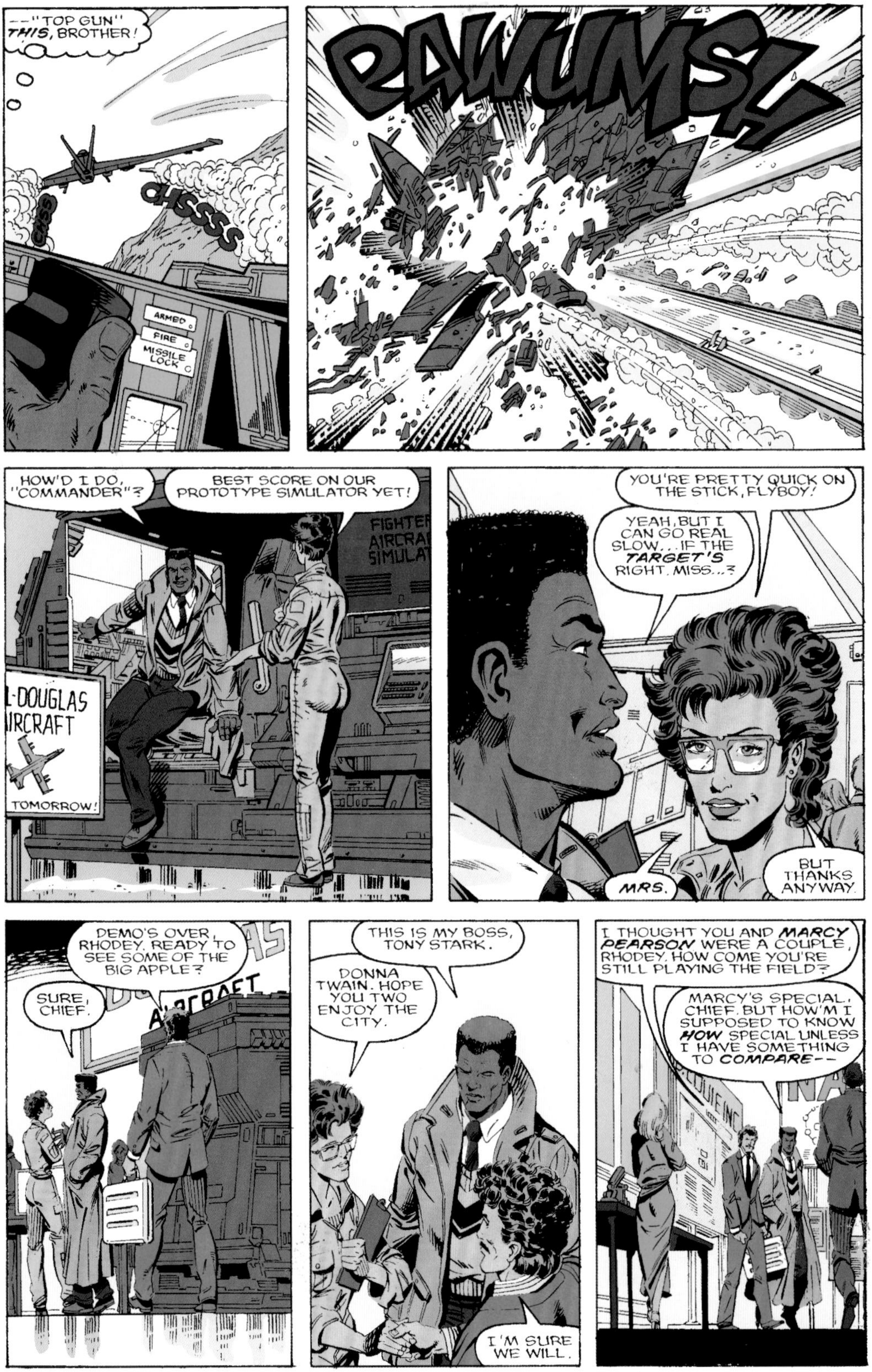
--"TOP GUN" THIS, BROTHER!
CHSS
CHSSSSS
ARMED
FIRE
MISSILE LOCK
RAWUMSH
HOW'D I DO, "COMMANDER"?
BEST SCORE ON OUR PROTOTYPE SIMULATOR YET!
FIGHTER AIRCRA SIMULAT
L-DOUGLAS AIRCRAFT
TOMORROW!
YOU'RE PRETTY QUICK ON THE STICK, FLYBOY!
YEAH, BUT I CAN GO REAL SLOW... IF THE TARGET'S RIGHT. MISS...?
MRS.
BUT THANKS ANYWAY.
DEMO'S OVER, RHODEY. READY TO SEE SOME OF THE BIG APPLE?
SURE, CHIEF.
THIS IS MY BOSS, TONY STARK.
DONNA TWAIN. HOPE YOU TWO ENJOY THE CITY.
I'M SURE WE WILL.
I THOUGHT YOU AND MARCY PEARSON WERE A COUPLE, RHODEY. HOW COME YOU'RE STILL PLAYING THE FIELD?
MARCY'S SPECIAL, CHIEF. BUT HOW'M I SUPPOSED TO KNOW HOW SPECIAL UNLESS I HAVE SOMETHING TO COMPARE--

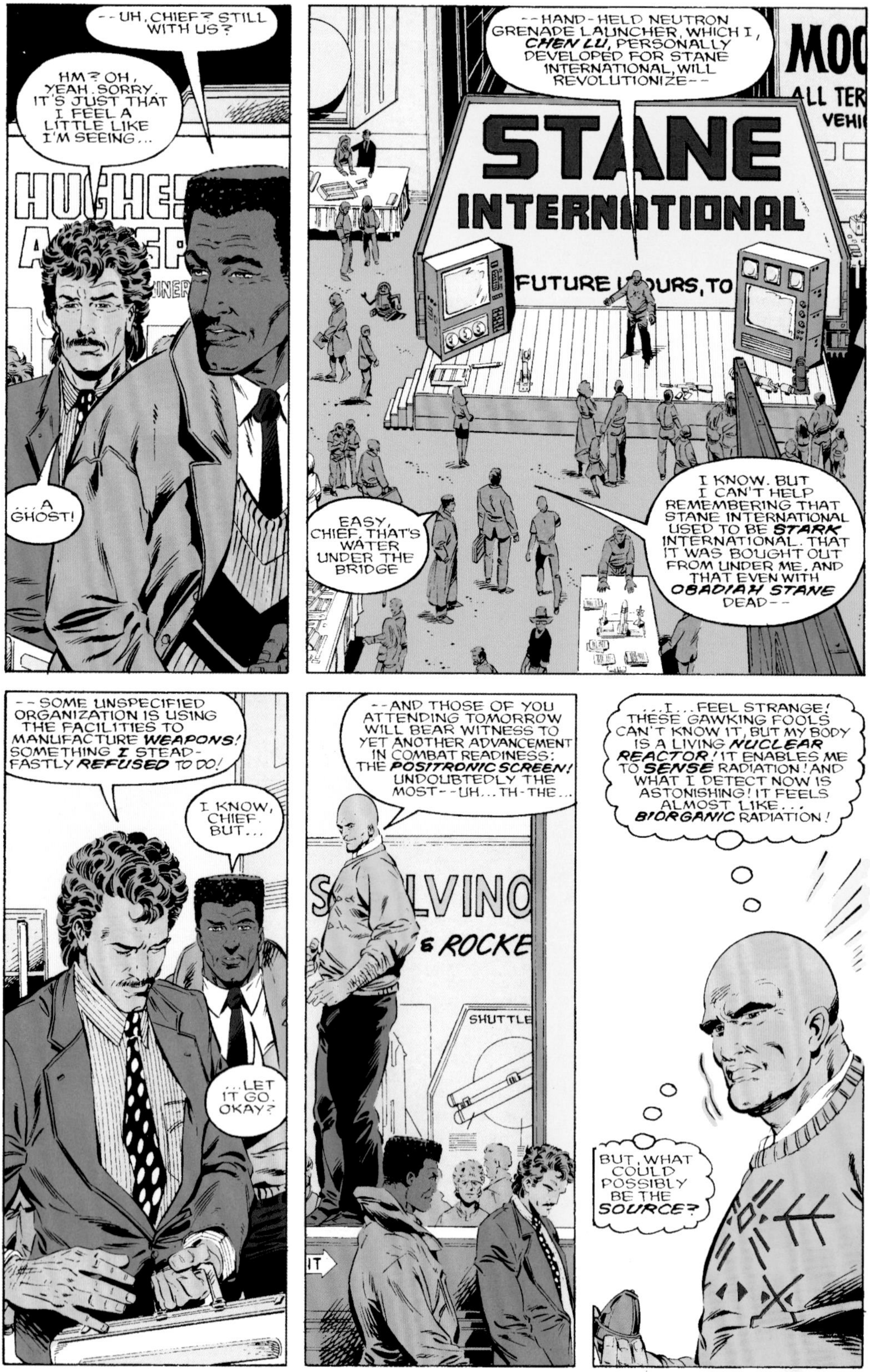
--UH, CHIEF? STILL WITH US?
HM? OH, YEAH. SORRY. IT'S JUST THAT I FEEL A LITTLE LIKE I'M SEEING...
...A GHOST!
--HAND-HELD NEUTRON GRENADE LAUNCHER, WHICH I, CHEN LU, PERSONALLY DEVELOPED FOR STANE INTERNATIONAL, WILL REVOLUTIONIZE--
STANE INTERNATIONAL
FUTURE IS YOURS, TO
EASY, CHIEF. THAT'S WATER UNDER THE BRIDGE
I KNOW. BUT I CAN'T HELP REMEMBERING THAT STANE INTERNATIONAL USED TO BE STARK INTERNATIONAL. THAT IT WAS BOUGHT OUT FROM UNDER ME. AND THAT EVEN WITH OBADIAH STANE DEAD--
--SOME UNSPECIFIED ORGANIZATION IS USING THE FACILITIES TO MANUFACTURE WEAPONS! SOMETHING I STEADFASTLY REFUSED TO DO!
I KNOW, CHIEF. BUT...
...LET IT GO. OKAY?
--AND THOSE OF YOU ATTENDING TOMORROW WILL BEAR WITNESS TO YET ANOTHER ADVANCEMENT IN COMBAT READINESS: THE POSITRONIC SCREEN! UNDOUBTEDLY THE MOST--UH...TH-THE...
...I...FEEL STRANGE! THESE GAWKING FOOLS CAN'T KNOW IT, BUT MY BODY IS A LIVING NUCLEAR REACTOR! IT ENABLES ME TO SENSE RADIATION! AND WHAT I DETECT NOW IS ASTONISHING! IT FEELS ALMOST LIKE... BIORGANIC RADIATION!
BUT, WHAT COULD POSSIBLY BE THE SOURCE?

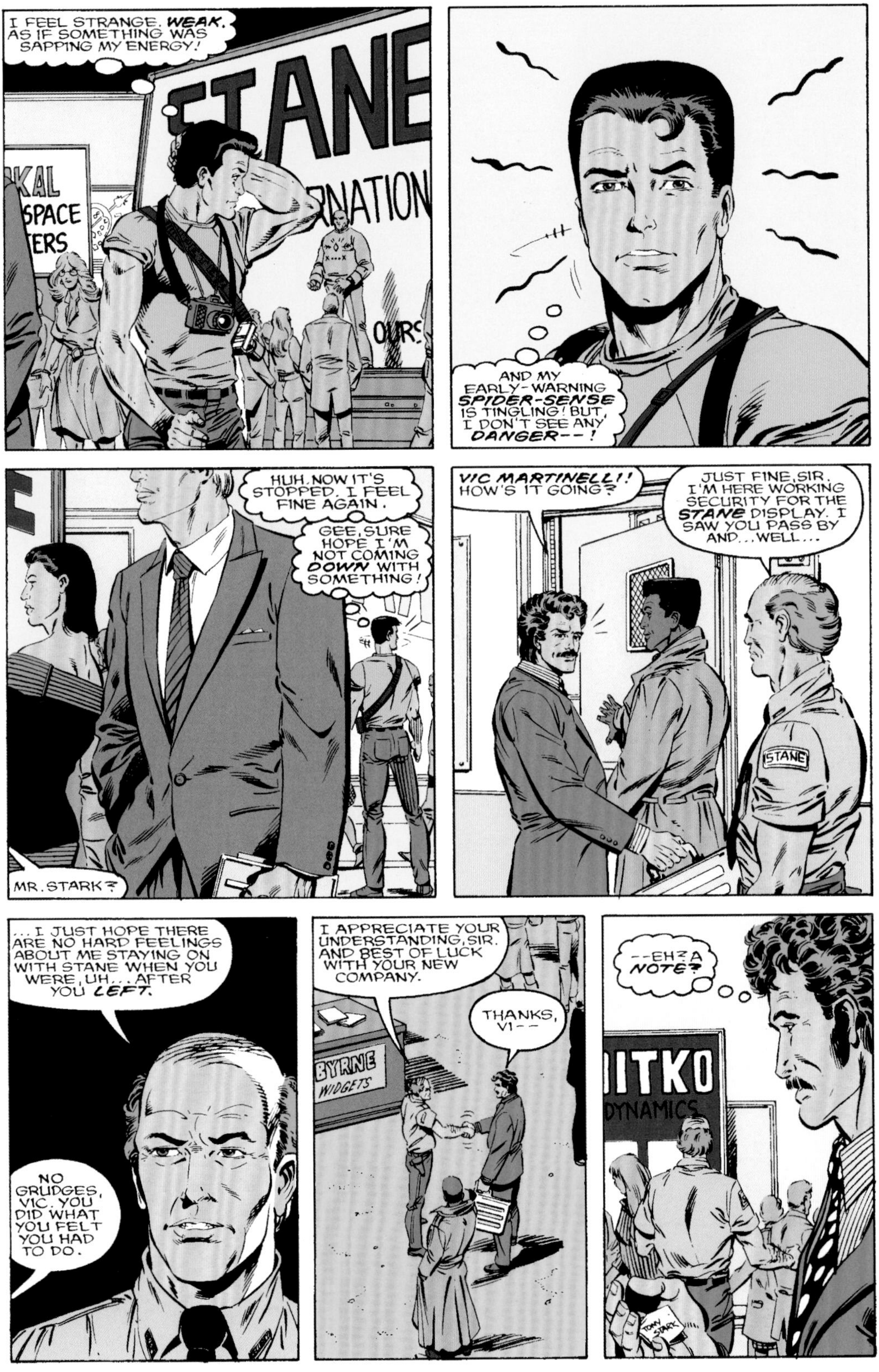
I FEEL STRANGE. WEAK. AS IF SOMETHING WAS SAPPING MY ENERGY!
STANE
RNATION
KAL
SPACE
TERS
OURS
AND MY EARLY-WARNING SPIDER-SENSE IS TINGLING! BUT, I DON'T SEE ANY DANGER--!
HUH. NOW IT'S STOPPED. I FEEL FINE AGAIN.
GEE, SURE HOPE I'M NOT COMING DOWN WITH SOMETHING!
MR. STARK?
VIC MARTINELL!! HOW'S IT GOING?
JUST FINE, SIR. I'M HERE WORKING SECURITY FOR THE STANE DISPLAY. I SAW YOU PASS BY AND... WELL...
STANE
...I JUST HOPE THERE ARE NO HARD FEELINGS ABOUT ME STAYING ON WITH STANE WHEN YOU WERE, UH... AFTER YOU LEFT.
NO GRUDGES, VIC. YOU DID WHAT YOU FELT YOU HAD TO DO.
I APPRECIATE YOUR UNDERSTANDING, SIR. AND BEST OF LUCK WITH YOUR NEW COMPANY.
THANKS, VI--
BYRNE WIDGETS
--EH? A NOTE?
ITKO DYNAMICS
TONY STARK

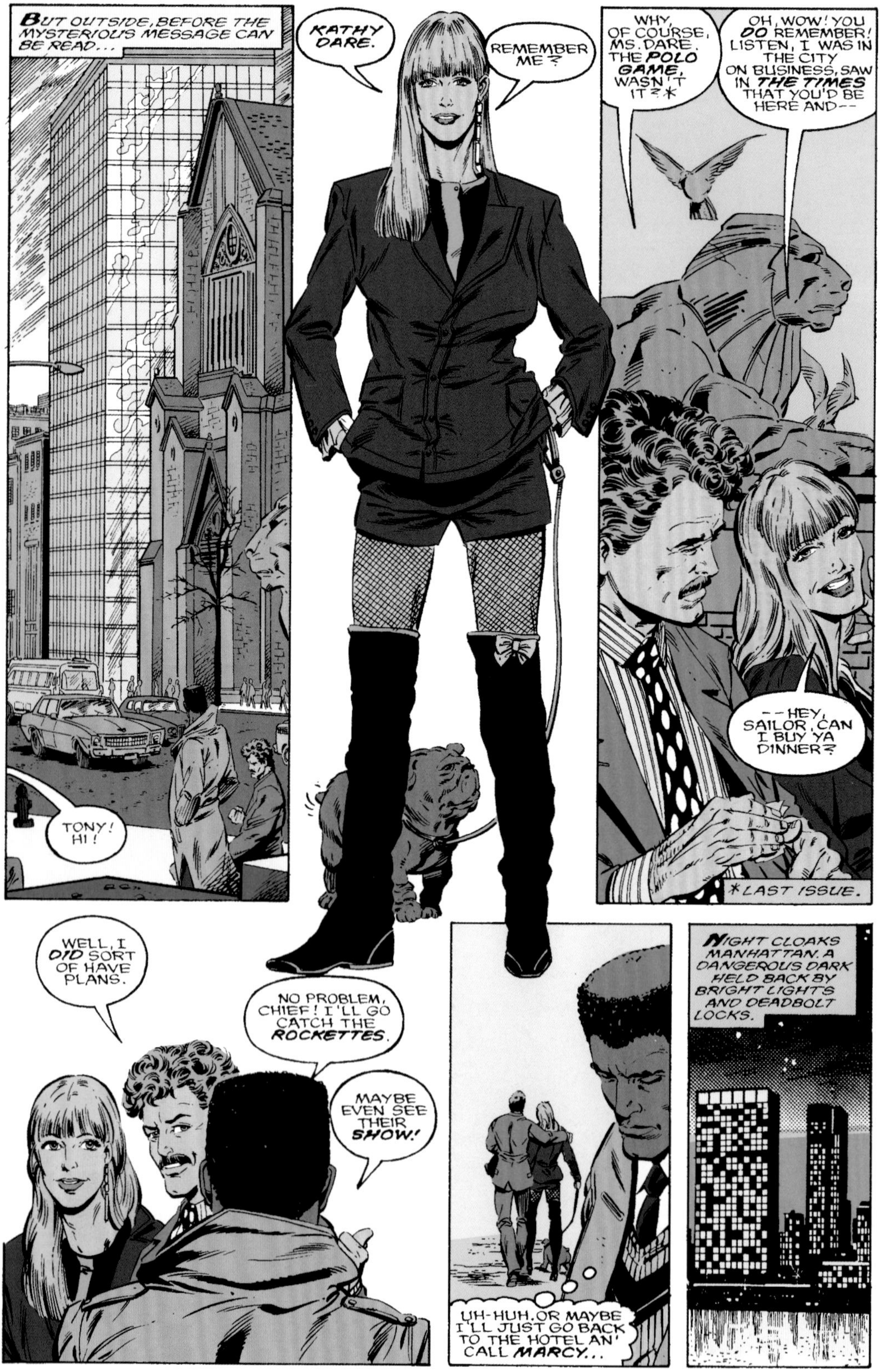

BUT OUTSIDE, BEFORE THE MYSTERIOUS MESSAGE CAN BE READ...
TONY! HI!
KATHY DARE.
REMEMBER ME?
WHY, OF COURSE, MS. DARE. THE POLO GAME, WASN'T IT?*
OH, WOW! YOU DO REMEMBER! LISTEN, I WAS IN THE CITY ON BUSINESS, SAW IN THE TIMES THAT YOU'D BE HERE AND--
--HEY, SAILOR, CAN I BUY YA DINNER?
*LAST ISSUE.
WELL, I DID SORT OF HAVE PLANS.
NO PROBLEM, CHIEF! I'LL GO CATCH THE ROCKETTES.
MAYBE EVEN SEE THEIR SHOW!
UH-HUH. OR MAYBE I'LL JUST GO BACK TO THE HOTEL AN' CALL MARCY...
NIGHT CLOAKS MANHATTAN. A DANGEROUS DARK HELD BACK BY BRIGHT LIGHTS AND DEADBOLT LOCKS.

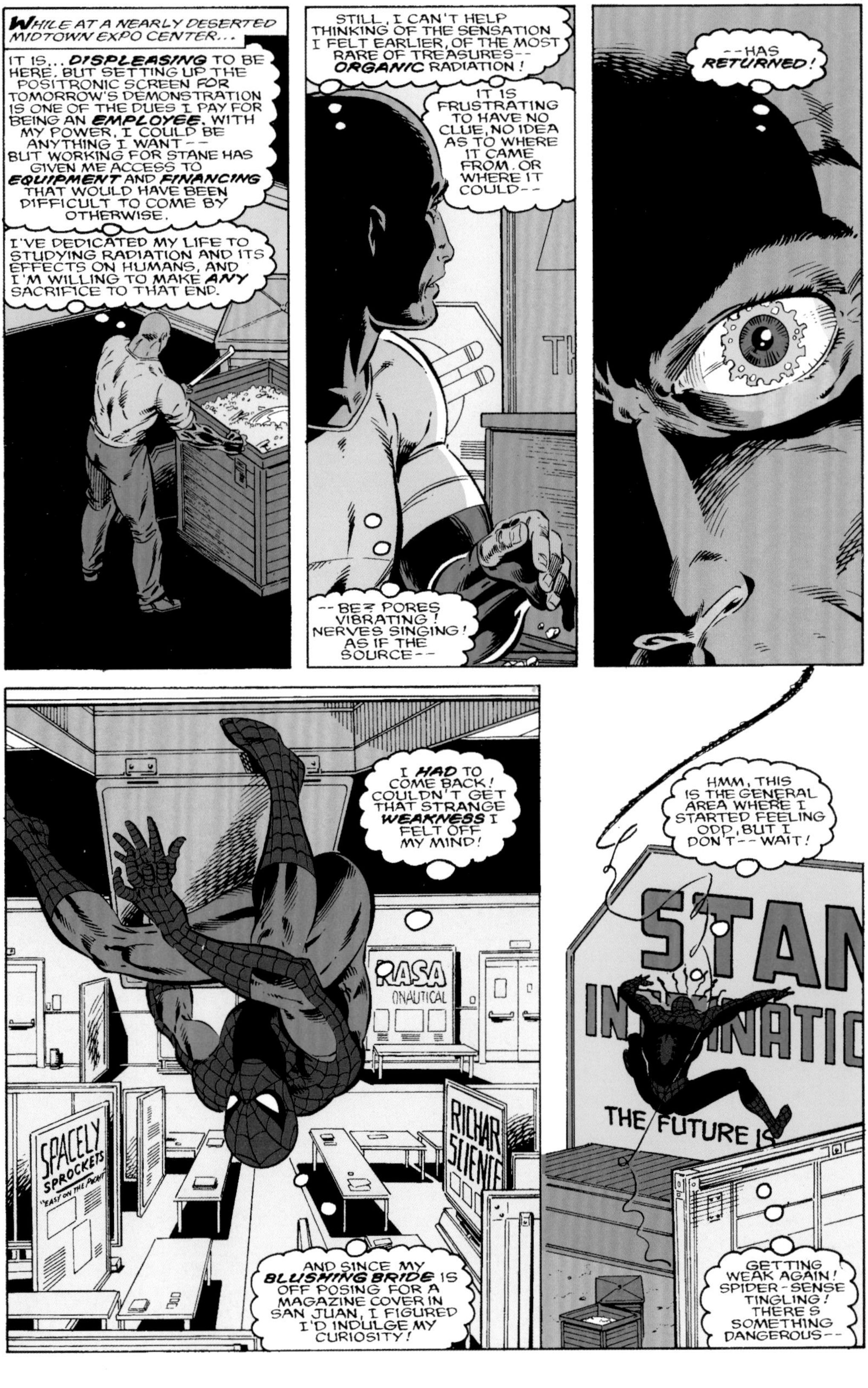
WHILE AT A NEARLY DESERTED MIDTOWN EXPO CENTER...
IT IS... DISPLEASING TO BE HERE, BUT SETTING UP THE POSITRONIC SCREEN FOR TOMORROW'S DEMONSTRATION IS ONE OF THE DUES I PAY FOR BEING AN EMPLOYEE. WITH MY POWER, I COULD BE ANYTHING I WANT-- BUT WORKING FOR STANE HAS GIVEN ME ACCESS TO EQUIPMENT AND FINANCING THAT WOULD HAVE BEEN DIFFICULT TO COME BY OTHERWISE.
I'VE DEDICATED MY LIFE TO STUDYING RADIATION AND ITS EFFECTS ON HUMANS, AND I'M WILLING TO MAKE ANY SACRIFICE TO THAT END.
STILL, I CAN'T HELP THINKING OF THE SENSATION I FELT EARLIER, OF THE MOST RARE OF TREASURES-- ORGANIC RADIATION!
IT IS FRUSTRATING TO HAVE NO CLUE, NO IDEA AS TO WHERE IT CAME FROM. OR WHERE IT COULD--
--BE? PORES VIBRATING! NERVES SINGING! AS IF THE SOURCE--
--HAS RETURNED!
I HAD TO COME BACK! COULDN'T GET THAT STRANGE WEAKNESS I FELT OFF MY MIND!
AND SINCE MY BLUSHING BRIDE IS OFF POSING FOR A MAGAZINE COVER IN SAN JUAN, I FIGURED I'D INDULGE MY CURIOSITY!
SPACELY SPROCKETS "EASY ON THE PLANET"
RASA ONAUTICAL
RICHAR SCIENCE
HMM, THIS IS THE GENERAL AREA WHERE I STARTED FEELING ODD, BUT I DON'T-- WAIT!
STAN IN INATIO
THE FUTURE IS
GETTING WEAK AGAIN! SPIDER-SENSE TINGLING! THERE'S SOMETHING DANGEROUS--

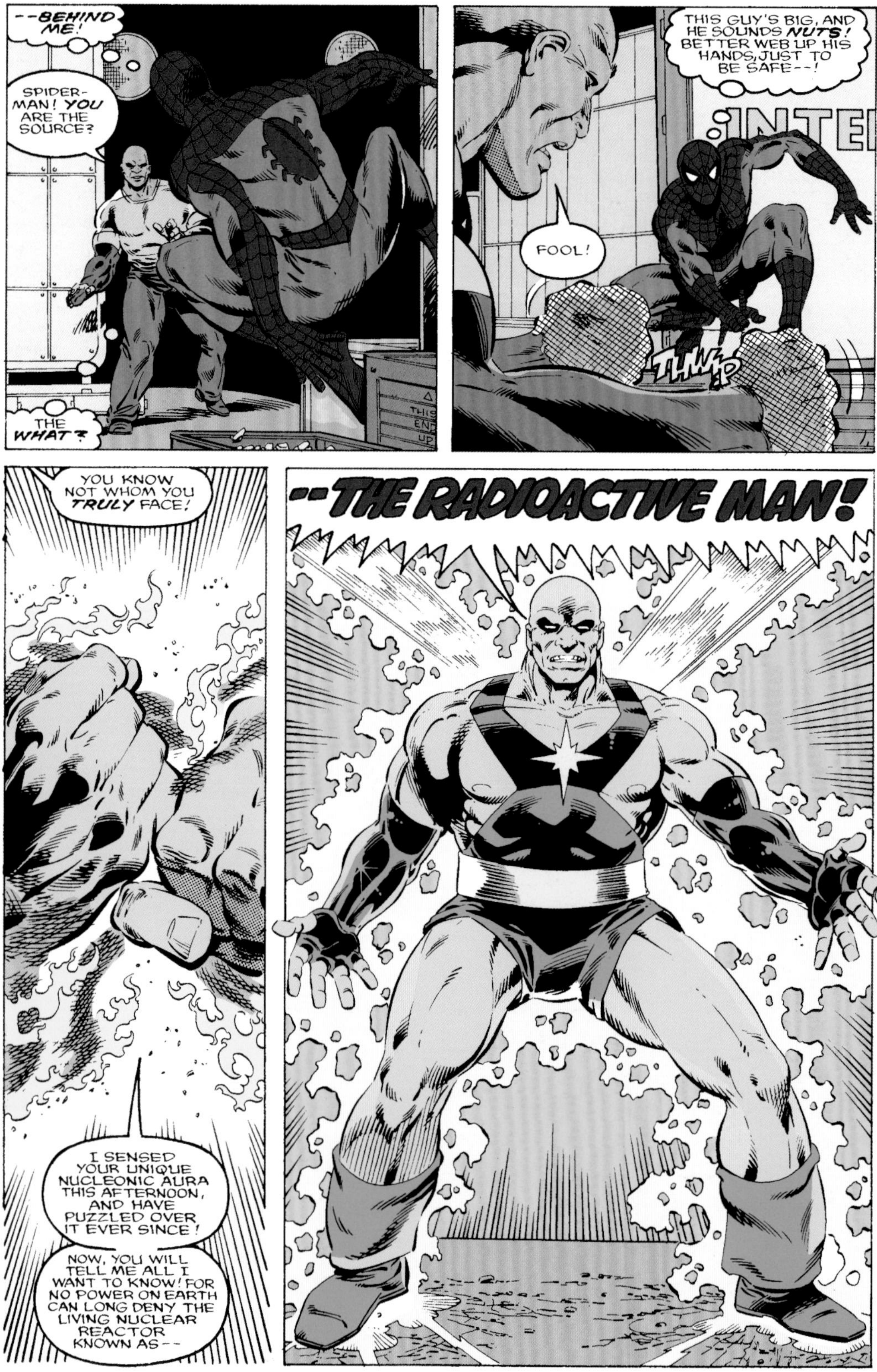
--BEHIND ME!
SPIDER-MAN! YOU ARE THE SOURCE?
THE WHAT?
THIS GUY'S BIG, AND HE SOUNDS NUTS! BETTER WEB UP HIS HANDS, JUST TO BE SAFE--!
FOOL!
THWIP
YOU KNOW NOT WHOM YOU TRULY FACE!
I SENSED YOUR UNIQUE NUCLEONIC AURA THIS AFTERNOON, AND HAVE PUZZLED OVER IT EVER SINCE!
NOW, YOU WILL TELL ME ALL I WANT TO KNOW! FOR NO POWER ON EARTH CAN LONG DENY THE LIVING NUCLEAR REACTOR KNOWN AS--
--THE RADIOACTIVE MAN!

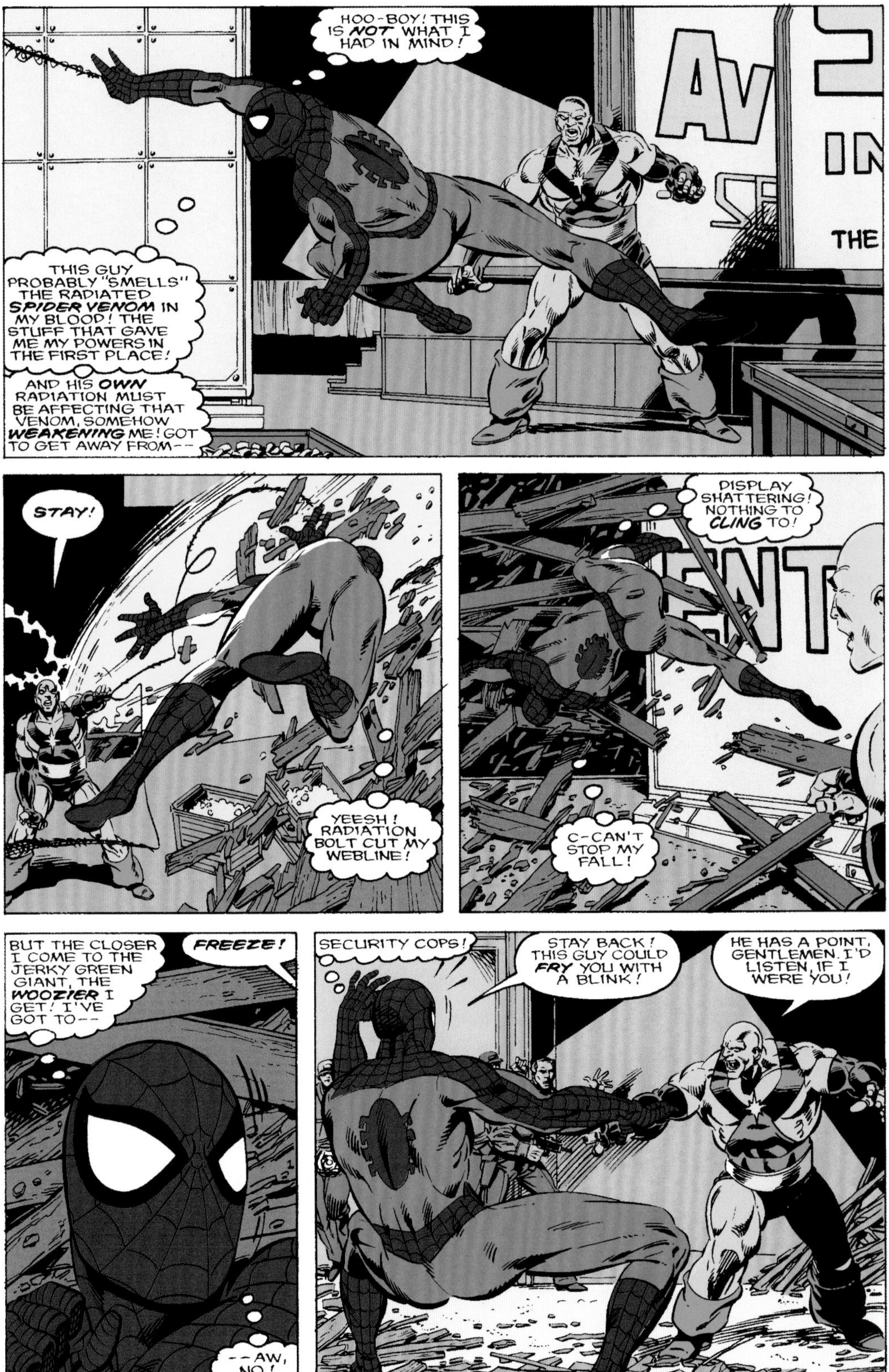
HOO-BOY! THIS IS NOT WHAT I HAD IN MIND!
THIS GUY PROBABLY "SMELLS" THE RADIATED SPIDER VENOM IN MY BLOOD! THE STUFF THAT GAVE ME MY POWERS IN THE FIRST PLACE!
AND HIS OWN RADIATION MUST BE AFFECTING THAT VENOM, SOMEHOW WEAKENING ME! GOT TO GET AWAY FROM--
Av
IN
THE
STAY!
YEESH! RADIATION BOLT CUT MY WEBLINE!
DISPLAY SHATTERING! NOTHING TO CLING TO!
C-CAN'T STOP MY FALL!
BUT THE CLOSER I COME TO THE JERKY GREEN GIANT, THE WOOZIER I GET! I'VE GOT TO--
FREEZE!
--AW, NO!
SECURITY COPS!
STAY BACK! THIS GUY COULD FRY YOU WITH A BLINK!
HE HAS A POINT, GENTLEMEN. I'D LISTEN, IF I WERE YOU!

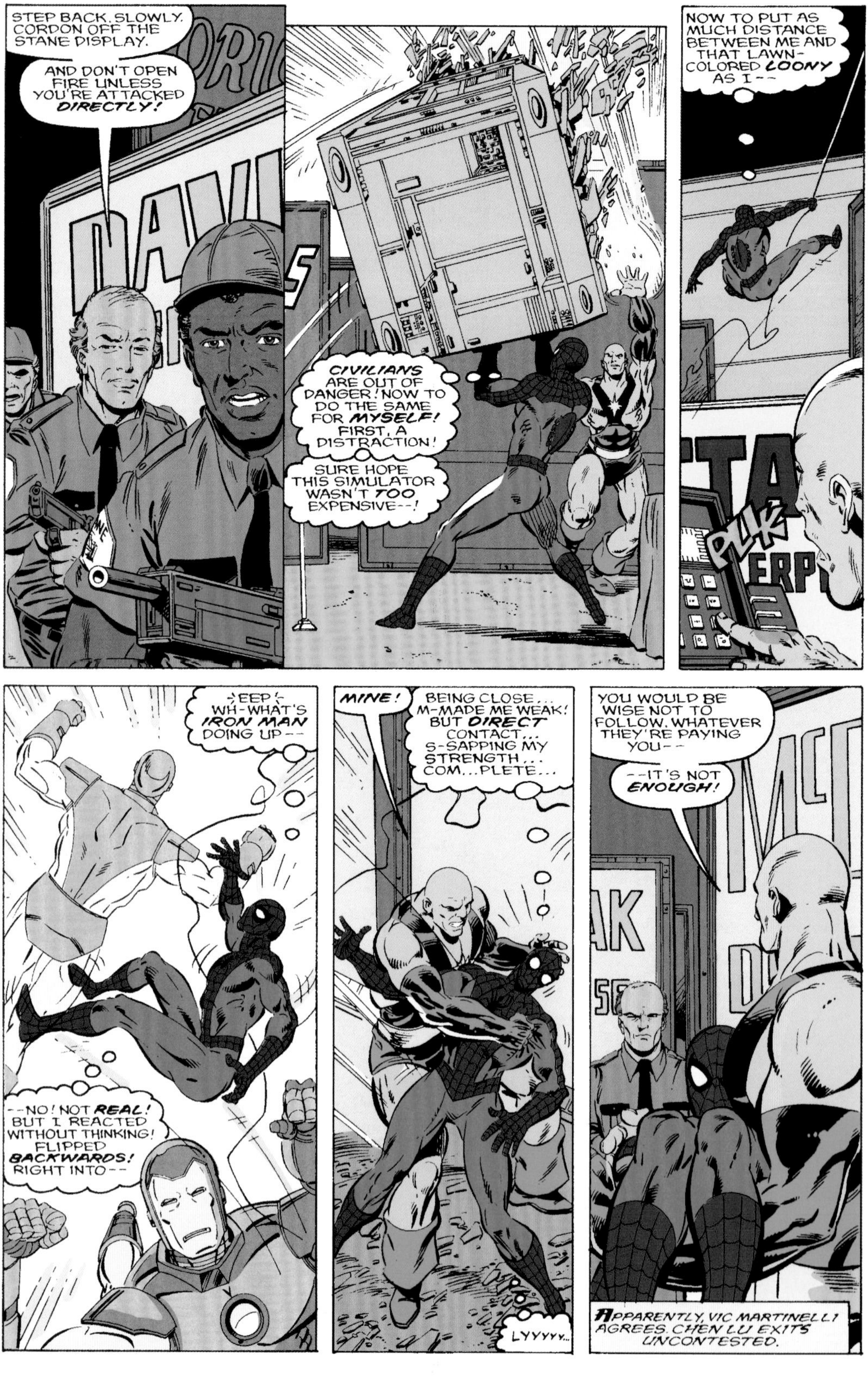
STEP BACK. SLOWLY. CORDON OFF THE STANE DISPLAY.
AND DON'T OPEN FIRE UNLESS YOU'RE ATTACKED DIRECTLY!
CIVILIANS ARE OUT OF DANGER! NOW TO DO THE SAME FOR MYSELF! FIRST, A DISTRACTION!
SURE HOPE THIS SIMULATOR WASN'T TOO EXPENSIVE--!
NOW TO PUT AS MUCH DISTANCE BETWEEN ME AND THAT LAWN-COLORED LOONY AS I--
PLIK
-EEP- WH-WHAT'S IRON MAN DOING UP--
--NO! NOT REAL! BUT I REACTED WITHOUT THINKING! FLIPPED BACKWARDS! RIGHT INTO--
MINE!
BEING CLOSE... M-MADE ME WEAK! BUT DIRECT CONTACT... S-SAPPING MY STRENGTH... COM...PLETE...
LYYYYY...
YOU WOULD BE WISE NOT TO FOLLOW. WHATEVER THEY'RE PAYING YOU--
--IT'S NOT ENOUGH!
APPARENTLY, VIC MARTINELLI AGREES. CHEN LU EXITS UNCONTESTED.

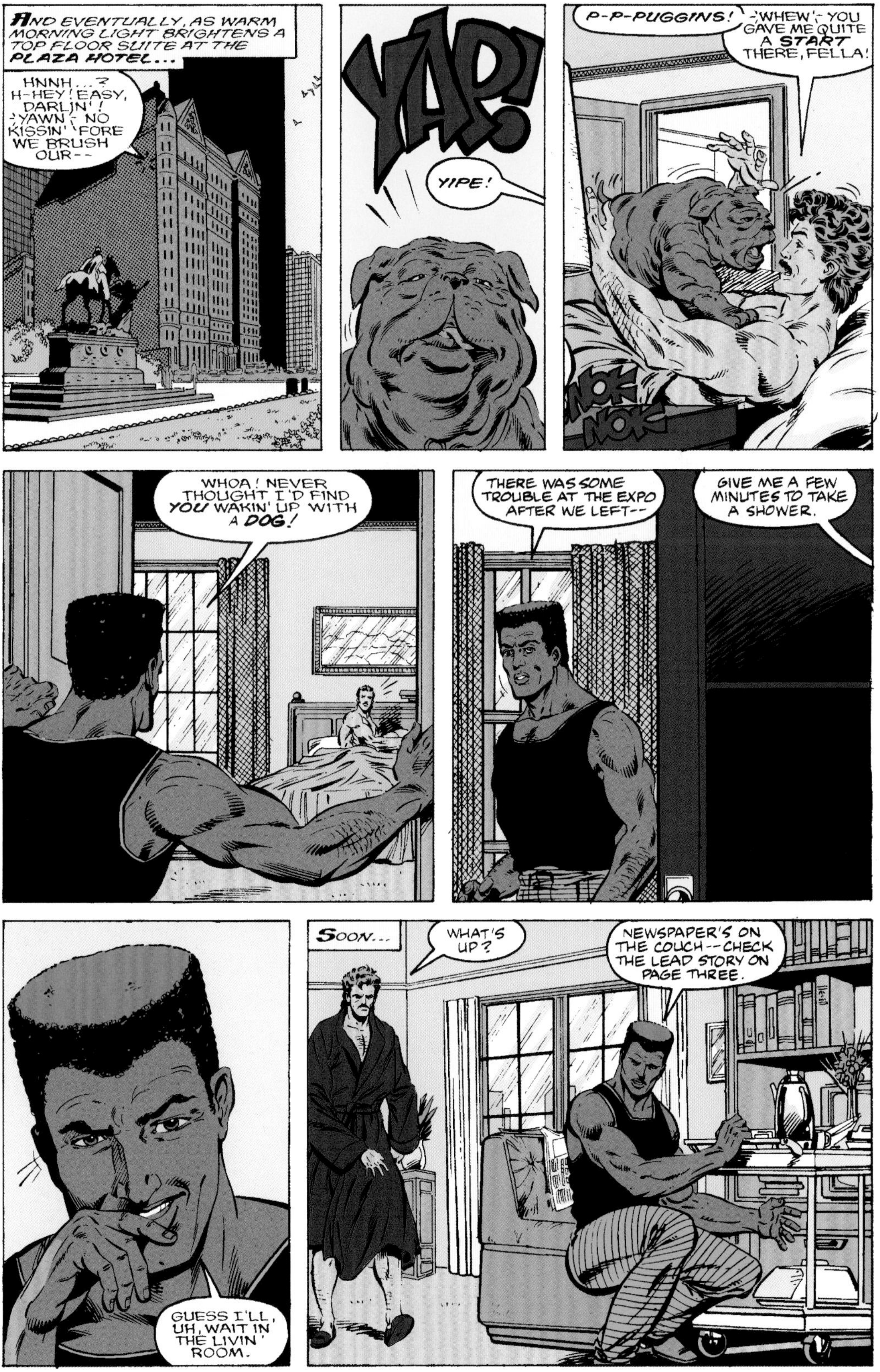
AND EVENTUALLY, AS WARM MORNING LIGHT BRIGHTENS A TOP FLOOR SUITE AT THE PLAZA HOTEL...
HNNH...? H-HEY! EASY, DARLIN'! -YAWN- NO KISSIN' 'FORE WE BRUSH OUR--
YAP!
YIPE!
P-P-PUGGINS!
-WHEW- YOU GAVE ME QUITE A START THERE, FELLA!
NOK NOK
WHOA! NEVER THOUGHT I'D FIND YOU WAKIN' UP WITH A DOG!
THERE WAS SOME TROUBLE AT THE EXPO AFTER WE LEFT--
GIVE ME A FEW MINUTES TO TAKE A SHOWER.
GUESS I'LL, UH, WAIT IN THE LIVIN' ROOM.
SOON...
WHAT'S UP?
NEWSPAPER'S ON THE COUCH--CHECK THE LEAD STORY ON PAGE THREE.

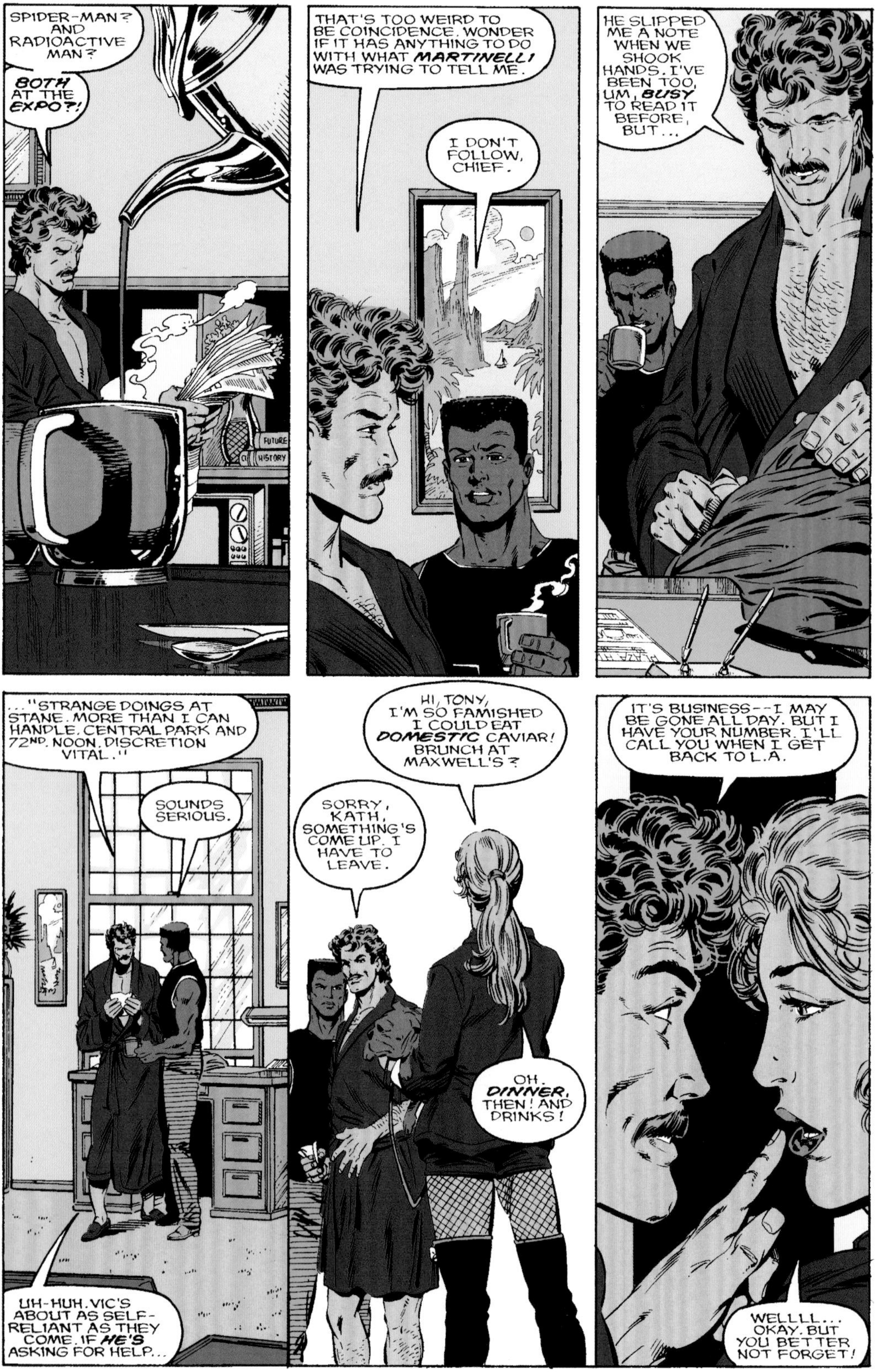
SPIDER-MAN? AND RADIOACTIVE MAN?
BOTH AT THE EXPO?!
THAT'S TOO WEIRD TO BE COINCIDENCE. WONDER IF IT HAS ANYTHING TO DO WITH WHAT MARTINELLI WAS TRYING TO TELL ME.
I DON'T FOLLOW, CHIEF.
HE SLIPPED ME A NOTE WHEN WE SHOOK HANDS. I'VE BEEN TOO, UM, BUSY TO READ IT BEFORE, BUT...
FUTURE
HISTORY
..."STRANGE DOINGS AT STANE. MORE THAN I CAN HANDLE. CENTRAL PARK AND 72ND. NOON. DISCRETION VITAL."
SOUNDS SERIOUS.
UH-HUH. VIC'S ABOUT AS SELF-RELIANT AS THEY COME. IF HE'S ASKING FOR HELP...
HI, TONY, I'M SO FAMISHED I COULD EAT DOMESTIC CAVIAR! BRUNCH AT MAXWELL'S?
SORRY, KATH, SOMETHING'S COME UP. I HAVE TO LEAVE.
OH. DINNER, THEN! AND DRINKS!
IT'S BUSINESS--I MAY BE GONE ALL DAY. BUT I HAVE YOUR NUMBER. I'LL CALL YOU WHEN I GET BACK TO L.A.
WELLLL... OKAY. BUT YOU BETTER NOT FORGET!

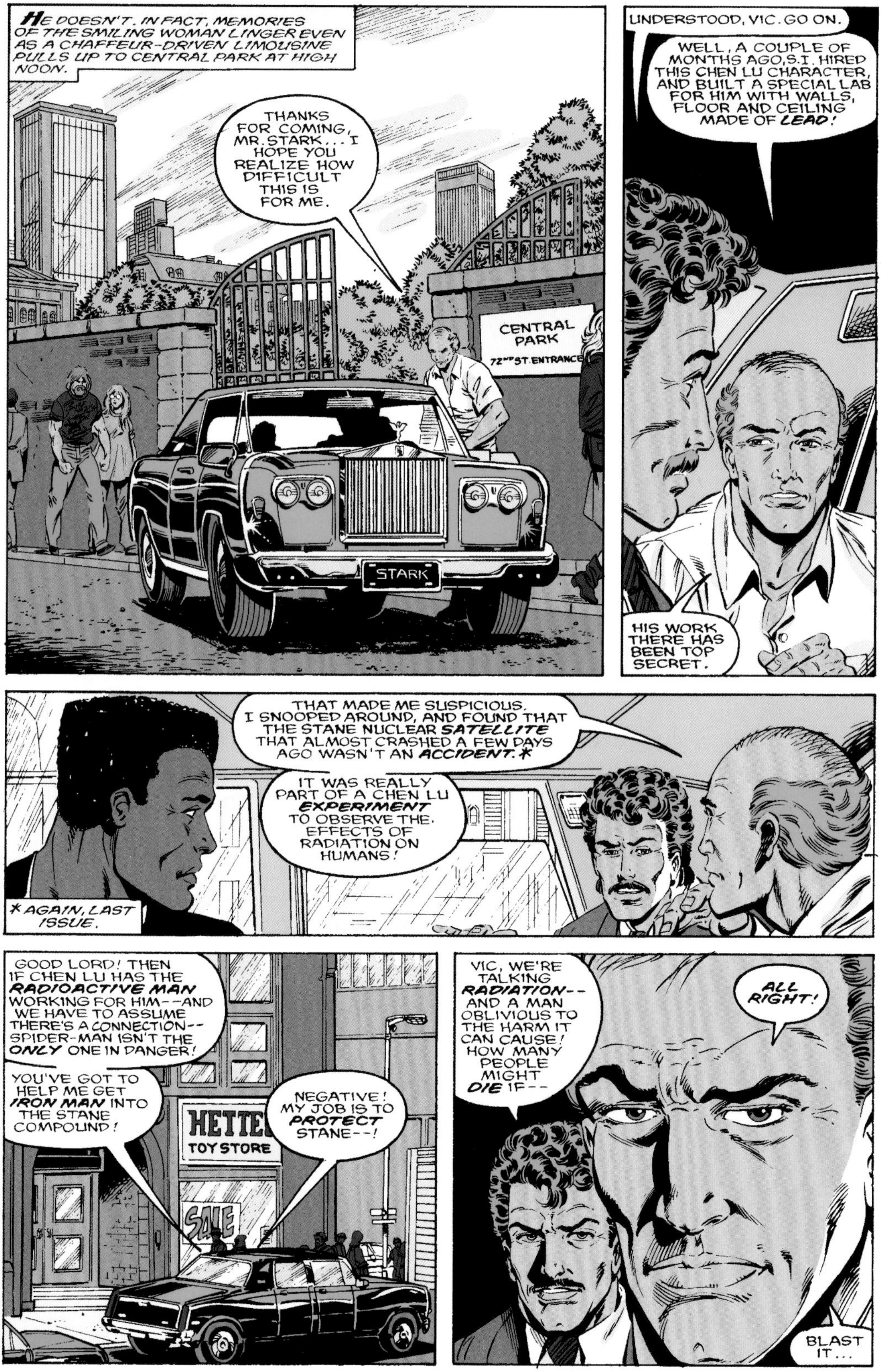

HE DOESN'T. IN FACT, MEMORIES OF THE SMILING WOMAN LINGER EVEN AS A CHAFFEUR-DRIVEN LIMOUSINE PULLS UP TO CENTRAL PARK AT HIGH NOON.
THANKS FOR COMING, MR. STARK... I HOPE YOU REALIZE HOW DIFFICULT THIS IS FOR ME.
CENTRAL PARK
72ND ST. ENTRANCE
STARK
UNDERSTOOD, VIC. GO ON.
WELL, A COUPLE OF MONTHS AGO, S.I. HIRED THIS CHEN LU CHARACTER, AND BUILT A SPECIAL LAB FOR HIM WITH WALLS, FLOOR AND CEILING MADE OF LEAD!
HIS WORK THERE HAS BEEN TOP SECRET.
THAT MADE ME SUSPICIOUS. I SNOOPED AROUND, AND FOUND THAT THE STANE NUCLEAR SATELLITE THAT ALMOST CRASHED A FEW DAYS AGO WASN'T AN ACCIDENT.*
IT WAS REALLY PART OF A CHEN LU EXPERIMENT TO OBSERVE THE EFFECTS OF RADIATION ON HUMANS!
*AGAIN, LAST ISSUE.
GOOD LORD! THEN IF CHEN LU HAS THE RADIOACTIVE MAN WORKING FOR HIM--AND WE HAVE TO ASSUME THERE'S A CONNECTION--SPIDER-MAN ISN'T THE ONLY ONE IN DANGER!
YOU'VE GOT TO HELP ME GET IRON MAN INTO THE STANE COMPOUND!
NEGATIVE! MY JOB IS TO PROTECT STANE--!
TOY STORE
SALE
VIC, WE'RE TALKING RADIATION--AND A MAN OBLIVIOUS TO THE HARM IT CAN CAUSE! HOW MANY PEOPLE MIGHT DIE IF--
ALL RIGHT!
BLAST IT...

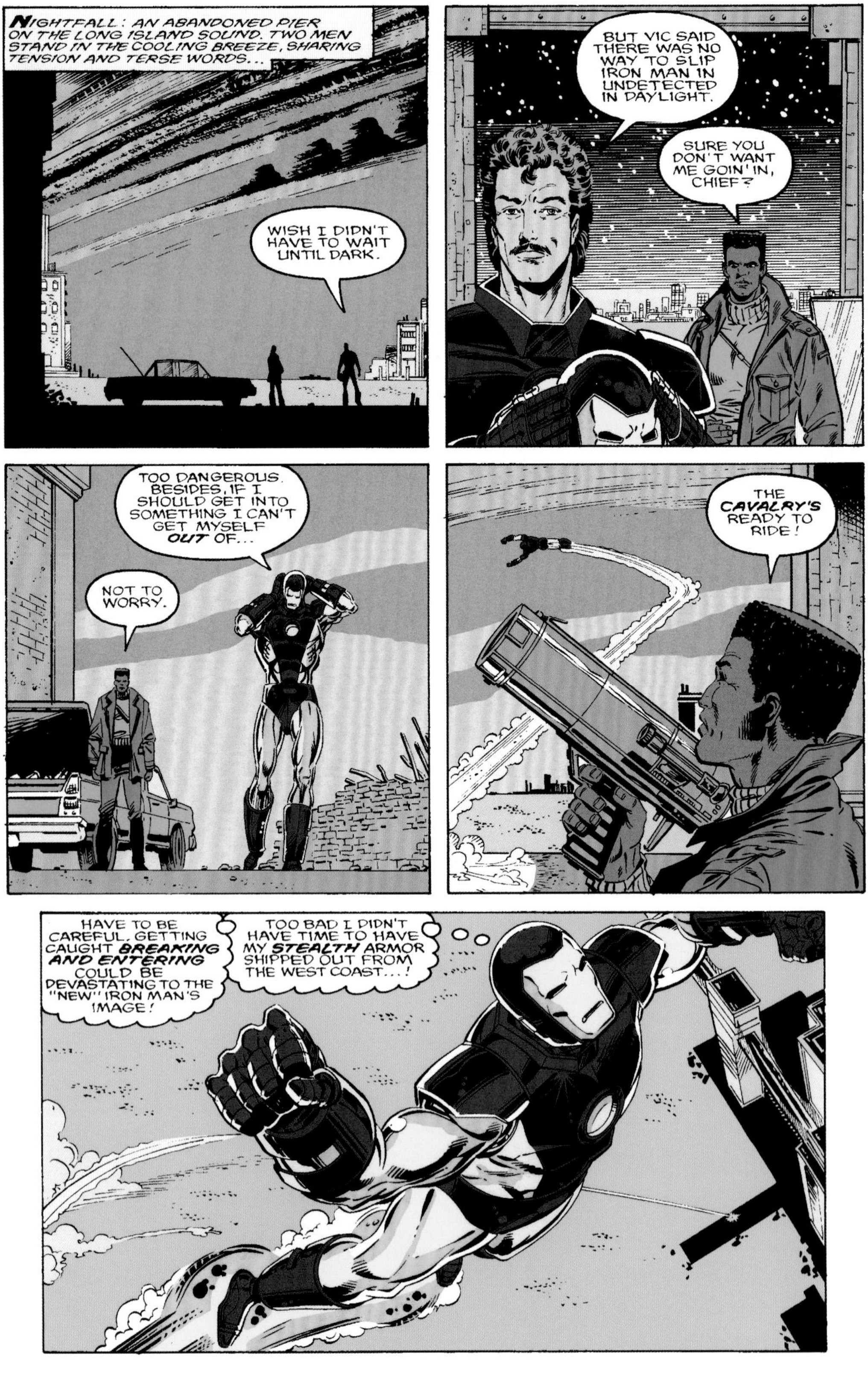
NIGHTFALL: AN ABANDONED PIER ON THE LONG ISLAND SOUND. TWO MEN STAND IN THE COOLING BREEZE, SHARING TENSION AND TERSE WORDS...
WISH I DIDN'T HAVE TO WAIT UNTIL DARK.
BUT VIC SAID THERE WAS NO WAY TO SLIP IRON MAN IN UNDETECTED IN DAYLIGHT.
SURE YOU DON'T WANT ME GOIN' IN, CHIEF?
TOO DANGEROUS. BESIDES, IF I SHOULD GET INTO SOMETHING I CAN'T GET MYSELF OUT OF...
NOT TO WORRY.
THE CAVALRY'S READY TO RIDE!
HAVE TO BE CAREFUL. GETTING CAUGHT BREAKING AND ENTERING COULD BE DEVASTATING TO THE "NEW" IRON MAN'S IMAGE!
TOO BAD I DIDN'T HAVE TIME TO HAVE MY STEALTH ARMOR SHIPPED OUT FROM THE WEST COAST...!

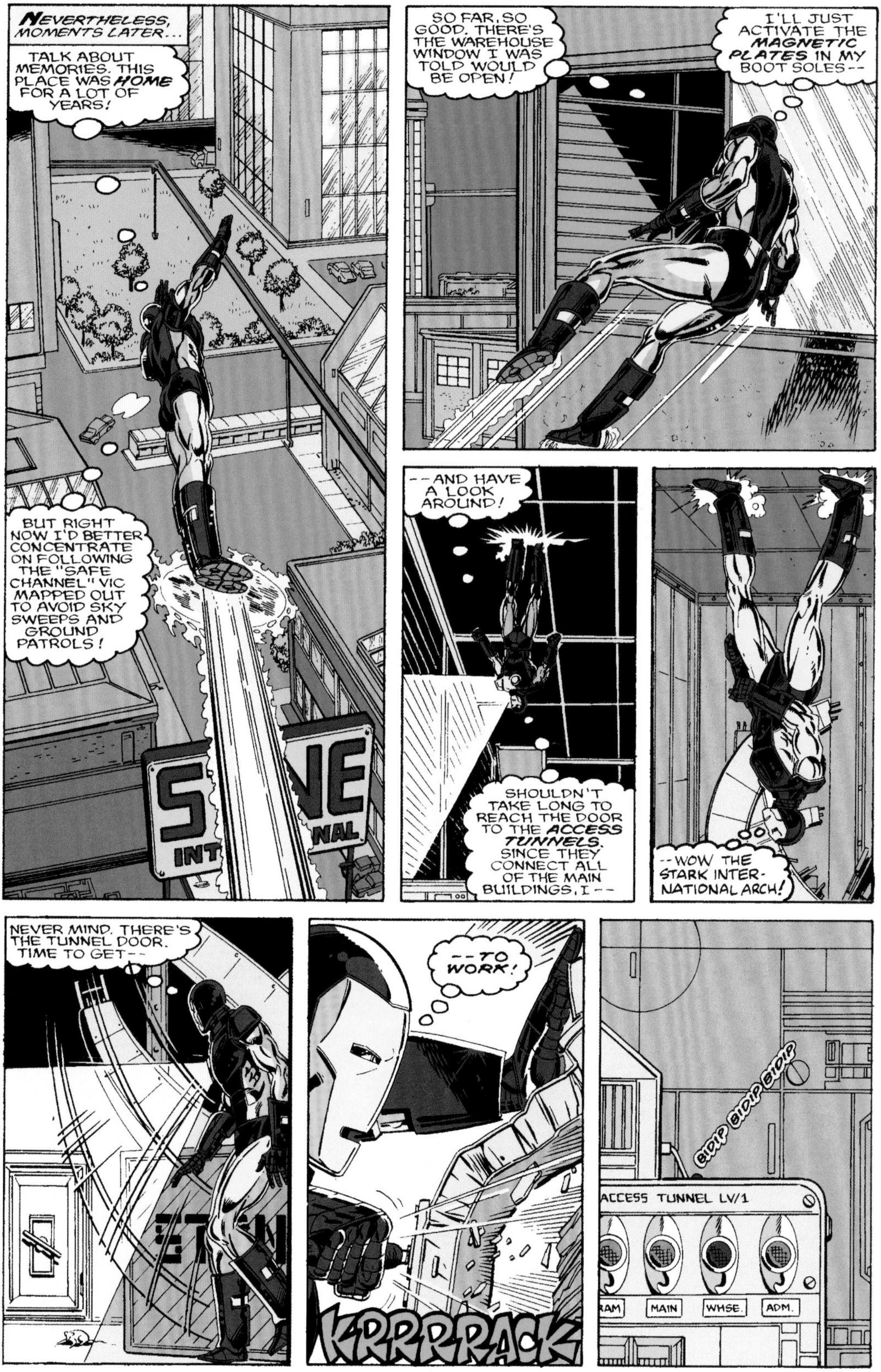
NEVERTHELESS, MOMENTS LATER...
TALK ABOUT MEMORIES. THIS PLACE WAS HOME FOR A LOT OF YEARS!
BUT RIGHT NOW I'D BETTER CONCENTRATE ON FOLLOWING THE "SAFE CHANNEL" VIC MAPPED OUT TO AVOID SKY SWEEPS AND GROUND PATROLS!
S NE
INT NAL
SO FAR, SO GOOD. THERE'S THE WAREHOUSE WINDOW I WAS TOLD WOULD BE OPEN!
I'LL JUST ACTIVATE THE MAGNETIC PLATES IN MY BOOT SOLES--
--AND HAVE A LOOK AROUND!
SHOULDN'T TAKE LONG TO REACH THE DOOR TO THE ACCESS TUNNELS. SINCE THEY CONNECT ALL OF THE MAIN BUILDINGS, I--
--WOW THE STARK INTER-NATIONAL ARCH!
NEVER MIND. THERE'S THE TUNNEL DOOR. TIME TO GET--
--TO WORK!
KRRRRACK
BIDIP BIDIP BIDIP
ACCESS TUNNEL LV/1
RAM
MAIN
WHSE.
ADM.

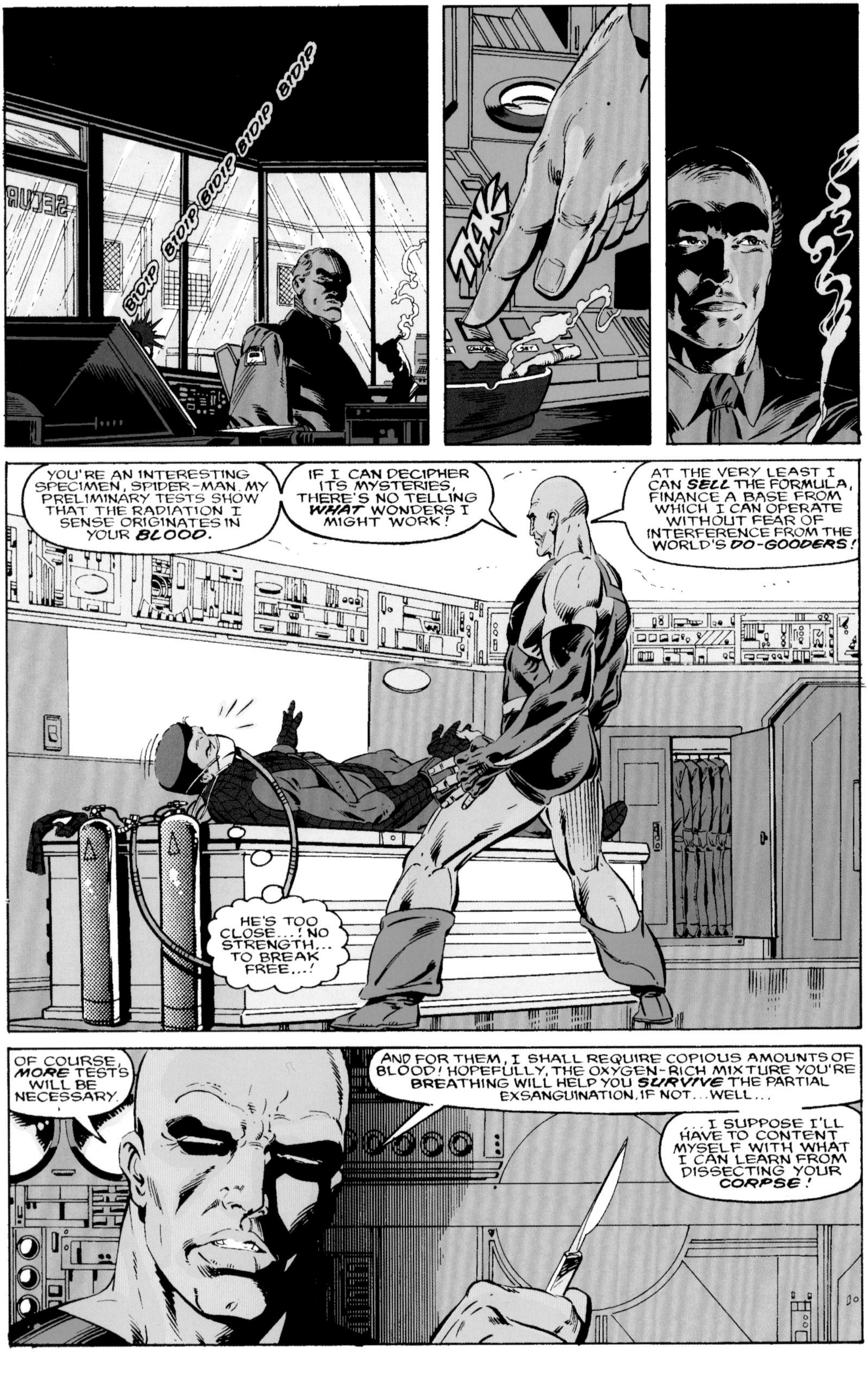
BIDIP BIDIP BIDIP BIDIP BIDIP
TAK
YOU'RE AN INTERESTING SPECIMEN, SPIDER-MAN. MY PRELIMINARY TESTS SHOW THAT THE RADIATION I SENSE ORIGINATES IN YOUR BLOOD.
IF I CAN DECIPHER ITS MYSTERIES, THERE'S NO TELLING WHAT WONDERS I MIGHT WORK!
AT THE VERY LEAST I CAN SELL THE FORMULA, FINANCE A BASE FROM WHICH I CAN OPERATE WITHOUT FEAR OF INTERFERENCE FROM THE WORLD'S DO-GOODERS!
HE'S TOO CLOSE...! NO STRENGTH... TO BREAK FREE...!
OF COURSE, MORE TESTS WILL BE NECESSARY.
AND FOR THEM, I SHALL REQUIRE COPIOUS AMOUNTS OF BLOOD! HOPEFULLY, THE OXYGEN-RICH MIXTURE YOU'RE BREATHING WILL HELP YOU SURVIVE THE PARTIAL EXSANGUINATION. IF NOT... WELL...
...I SUPPOSE I'LL HAVE TO CONTENT MYSELF WITH WHAT I CAN LEARN FROM DISSECTING YOUR CORPSE!

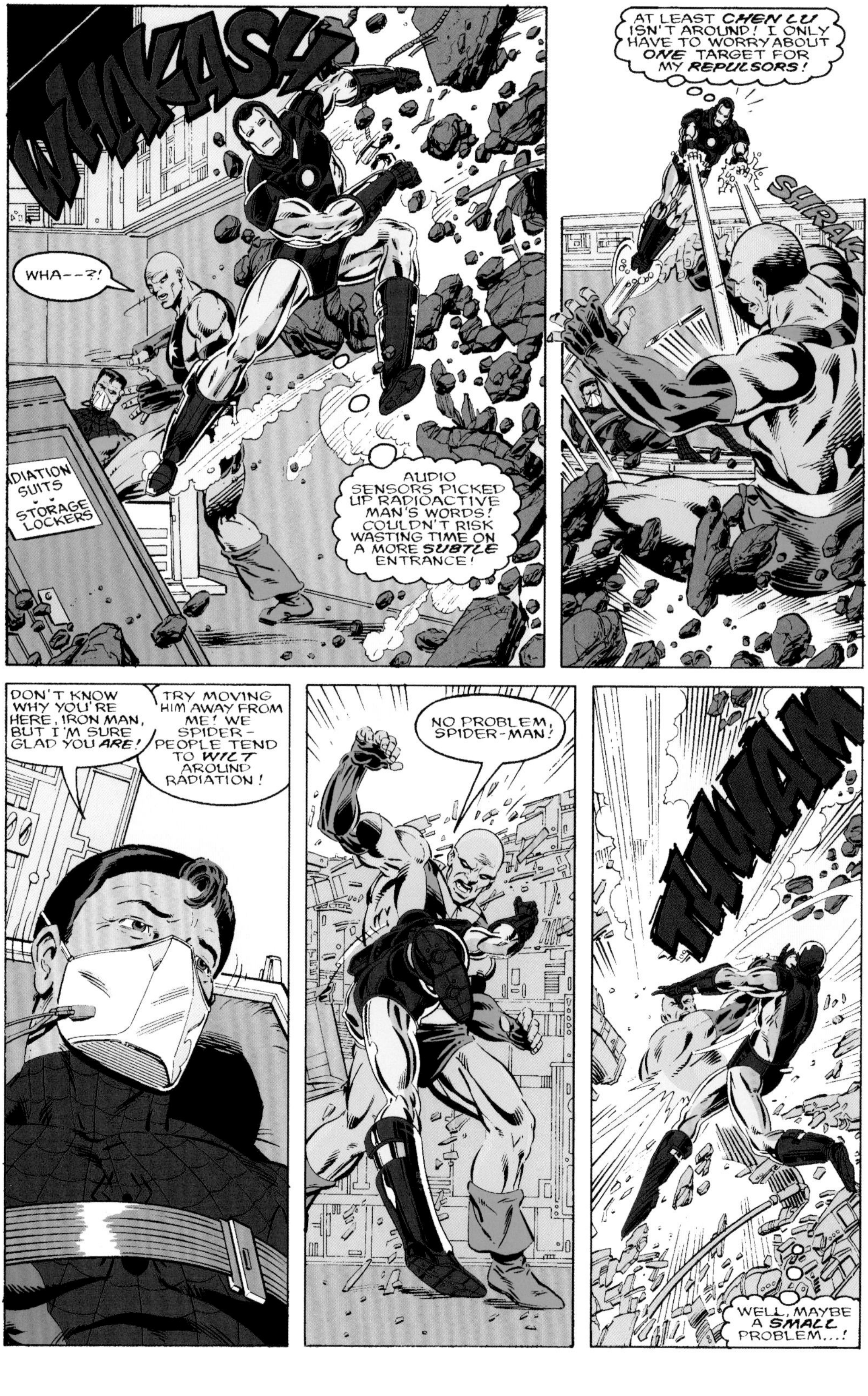
WHAKASH
WHA--?!
AUDIO SENSORS PICKED UP RADIOACTIVE MAN'S WORDS! COULDN'T RISK WASTING TIME ON A MORE SUBTLE ENTRANCE!
ADIATION SUITS • STORAGE LOCKERS
AT LEAST CHEN LU ISN'T AROUND! I ONLY HAVE TO WORRY ABOUT ONE TARGET FOR MY REPULSORS!
SHRAK
DON'T KNOW WHY YOU'RE HERE, IRON MAN, BUT I'M SURE GLAD YOU ARE!
TRY MOVING HIM AWAY FROM ME! WE SPIDER-PEOPLE TEND TO WILT AROUND RADIATION!
NO PROBLEM, SPIDER-MAN!
THWAM
WELL, MAYBE A SMALL PROBLEM...!

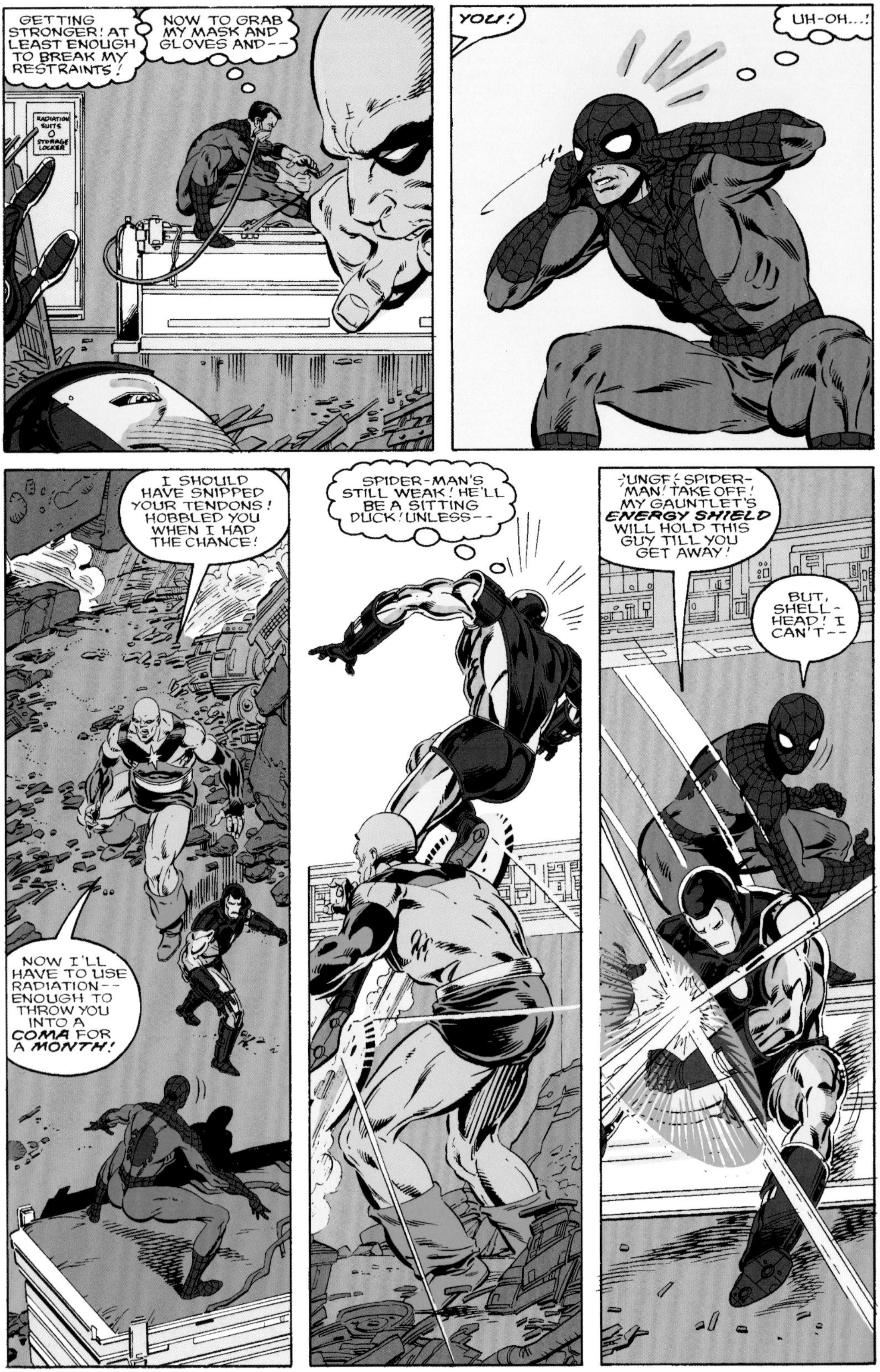
GETTING STRONGER! AT LEAST ENOUGH TO BREAK MY RESTRAINTS!
NOW TO GRAB MY MASK AND GLOVES AND--
RADIATION SUITS STORAGE LOCKER
YOU!
UH-OH...!
I SHOULD HAVE SNIPPED YOUR TENDONS! HOBBLED YOU WHEN I HAD THE CHANCE!
NOW I'LL HAVE TO USE RADIATION-- ENOUGH TO THROW YOU INTO A COMA FOR A MONTH!
SPIDER-MAN'S STILL WEAK! HE'LL BE A SITTING DUCK! UNLESS--
UNGF! SPIDER-MAN! TAKE OFF! MY GAUNTLET'S ENERGY SHIELD WILL HOLD THIS GUY TILL YOU GET AWAY!
BUT, SHELL-HEAD! I CAN'T--

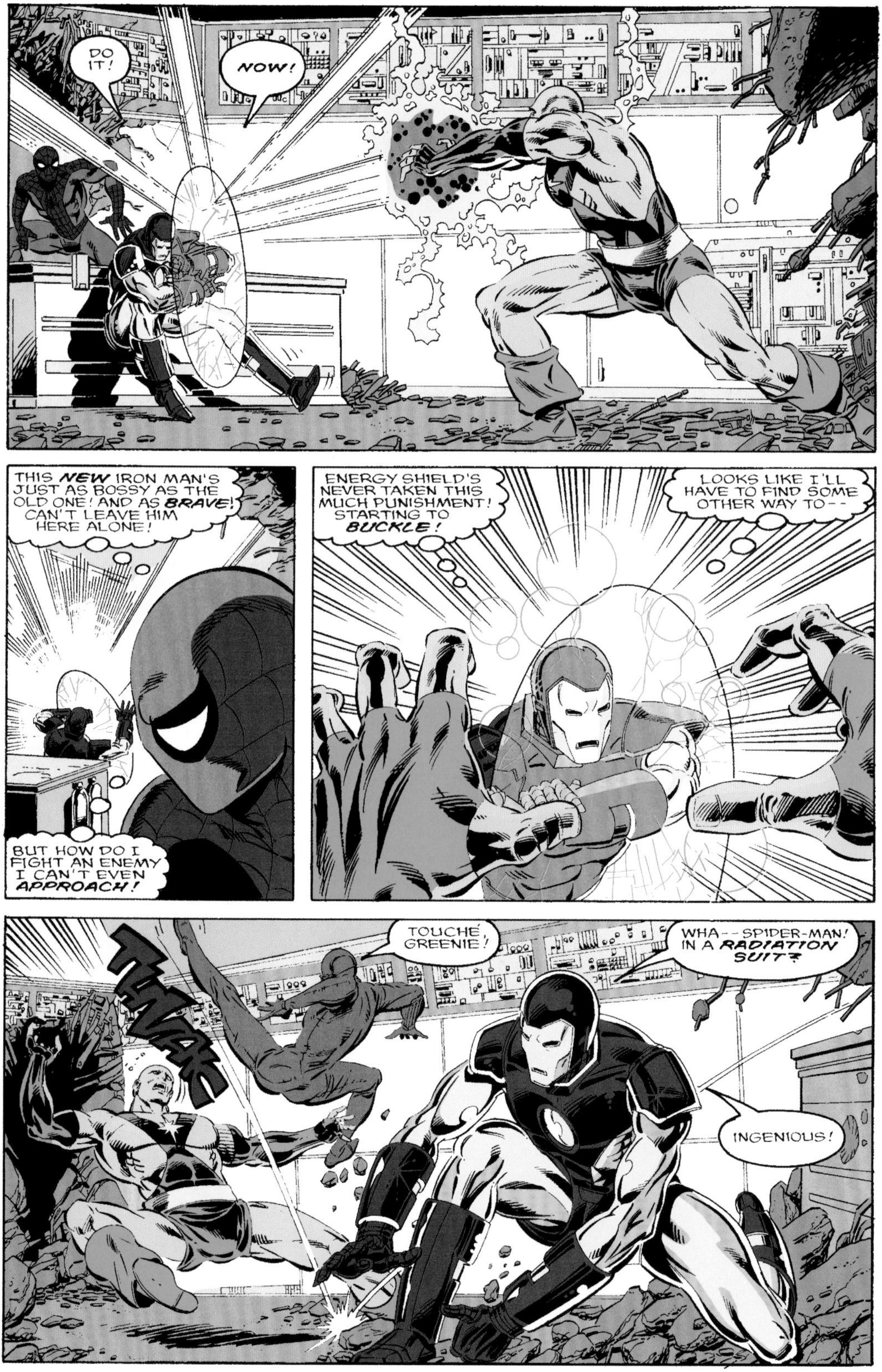
DO IT!
NOW!
THIS NEW IRON MAN'S JUST AS BOSSY AS THE OLD ONE! AND AS BRAVE! CAN'T LEAVE HIM HERE ALONE!
BUT HOW DO I FIGHT AN ENEMY I CAN'T EVEN APPROACH!
ENERGY SHIELD'S NEVER TAKEN THIS MUCH PUNISHMENT! STARTING TO BUCKLE!
LOOKS LIKE I'LL HAVE TO FIND SOME OTHER WAY TO--
THWAK
TOUCHÉ, GREENIE!
WHA--SPIDER-MAN! IN A RADIATION SUIT?
INGENIOUS!

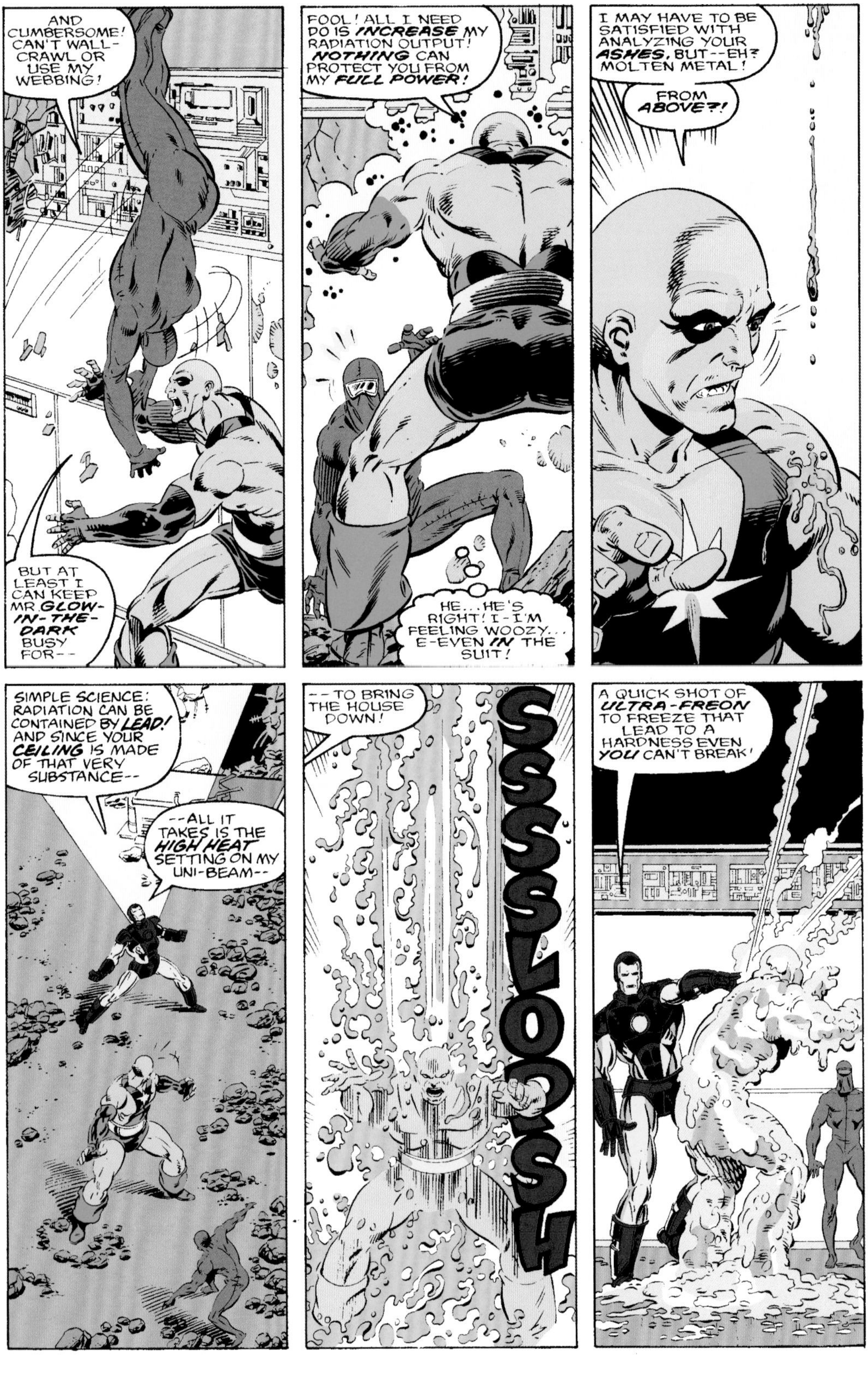
AND CUMBERSOME! CAN'T WALL-CRAWL OR USE MY WEBBING!
BUT AT LEAST I CAN KEEP MR. GLOW-IN-THE-DARK BUSY FOR--
FOOL! ALL I NEED DO IS INCREASE MY RADIATION OUTPUT! NOTHING CAN PROTECT YOU FROM MY FULL POWER!
HE...HE'S RIGHT! I-I'M FEELING WOOZY... E-EVEN IN THE SUIT!
I MAY HAVE TO BE SATISFIED WITH ANALYZING YOUR ASHES. BUT--EH? MOLTEN METAL!
FROM ABOVE?!
SIMPLE SCIENCE: RADIATION CAN BE CONTAINED BY LEAD! AND SINCE YOUR CEILING IS MADE OF THAT VERY SUBSTANCE--
--ALL IT TAKES IS THE HIGH HEAT SETTING ON MY UNI-BEAM--
--TO BRING THE HOUSE DOWN!
SSSSLOOSH
A QUICK SHOT OF ULTRA-FREON TO FREEZE THAT LEAD TO A HARDNESS EVEN YOU CAN'T BREAK!

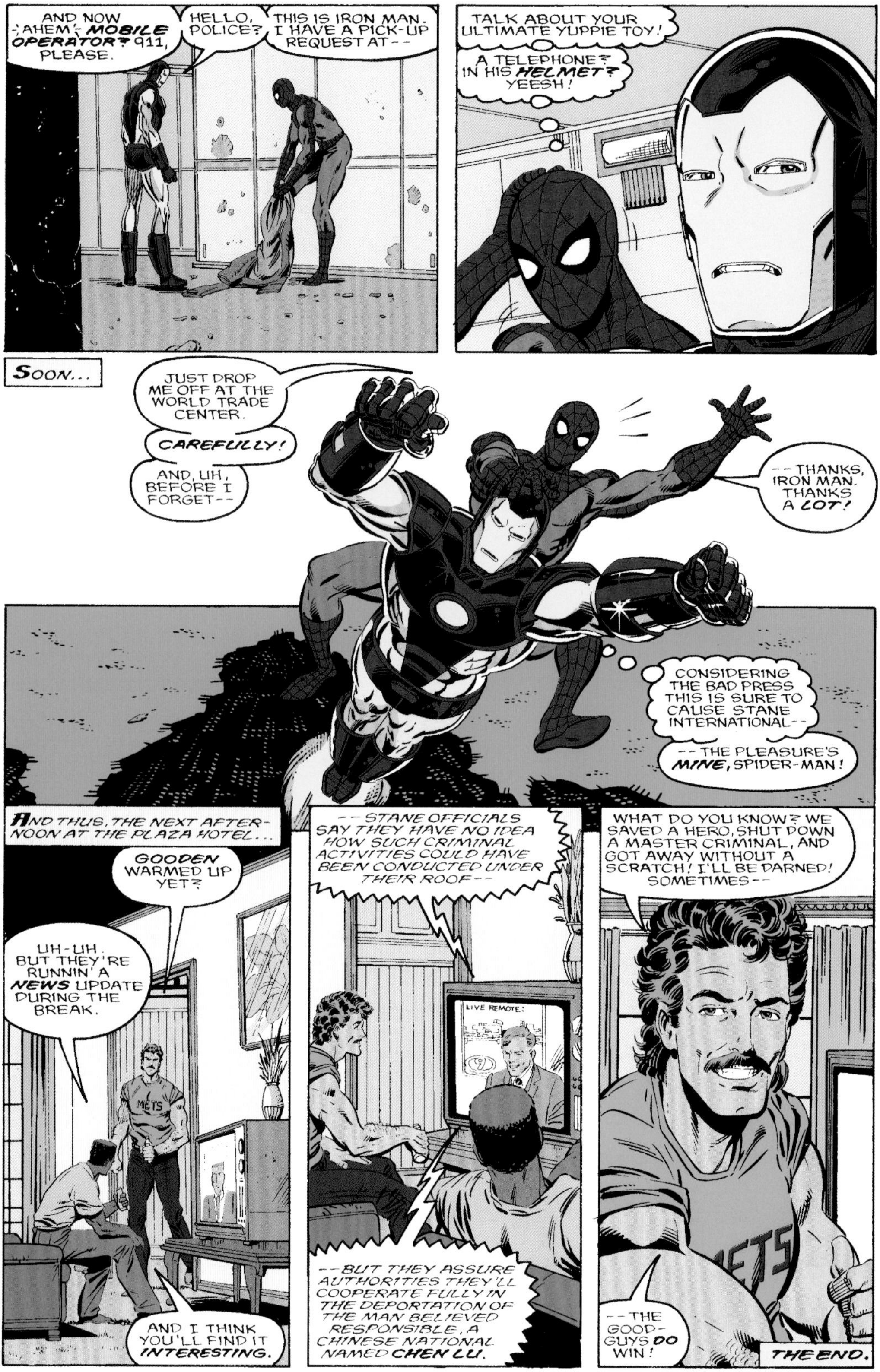

AND NOW -AHEM- MOBILE OPERATOR? 911, PLEASE.
HELLO, POLICE?
THIS IS IRON MAN. I HAVE A PICK-UP REQUEST AT--
TALK ABOUT YOUR ULTIMATE YUPPIE TOY!
A TELEPHONE? IN HIS HELMET? YEESH!
SOON...
JUST DROP ME OFF AT THE WORLD TRADE CENTER.
CAREFULLY!
AND, UH, BEFORE I FORGET--
--THANKS, IRON MAN. THANKS A LOT!
CONSIDERING THE BAD PRESS THIS IS SURE TO CAUSE STANE INTERNATIONAL--
--THE PLEASURE'S MINE, SPIDER-MAN!
AND THUS, THE NEXT AFTERNOON AT THE PLAZA HOTEL...
GOODEN WARMED UP YET?
UH-UH. BUT THEY'RE RUNNIN' A NEWS UPDATE DURING THE BREAK.
AND I THINK YOU'LL FIND IT INTERESTING.
--STANE OFFICIALS SAY THEY HAVE NO IDEA HOW SUCH CRIMINAL ACTIVITIES COULD HAVE BEEN CONDUCTED UNDER THEIR ROOF--
LIVE REMOTE:
--BUT THEY ASSURE AUTHORITIES THEY'LL COOPERATE FULLY IN THE DEPORTATION OF THE MAN BELIEVED RESPONSIBLE, A CHINESE NATIONAL NAMED CHEN LU.
WHAT DO YOU KNOW? WE SAVED A HERO, SHUT DOWN A MASTER CRIMINAL, AND GOT AWAY WITHOUT A SCRATCH! I'LL BE DARNED! SOMETIMES--
--THE GOOD-GUYS DO WIN!
THE END.

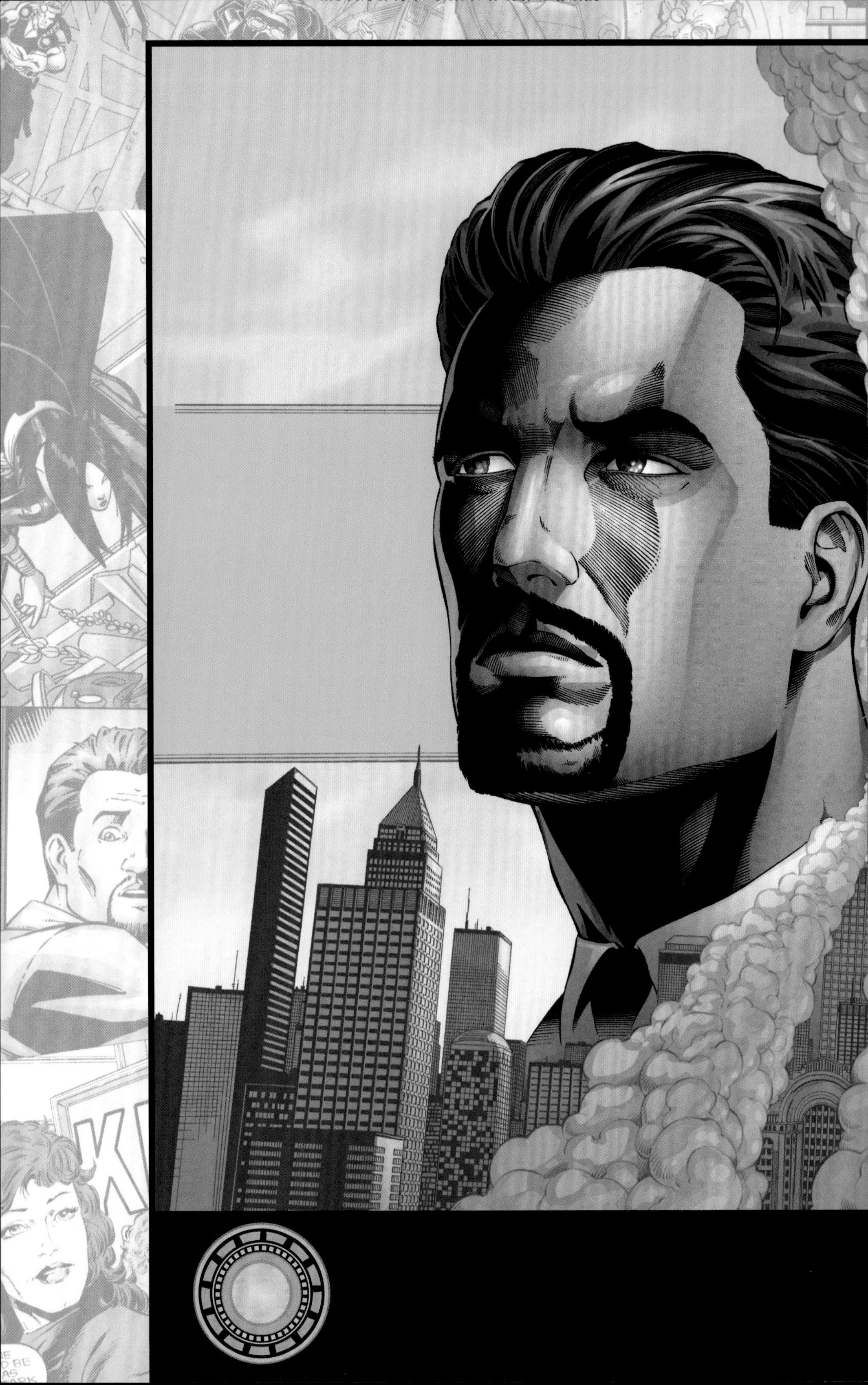

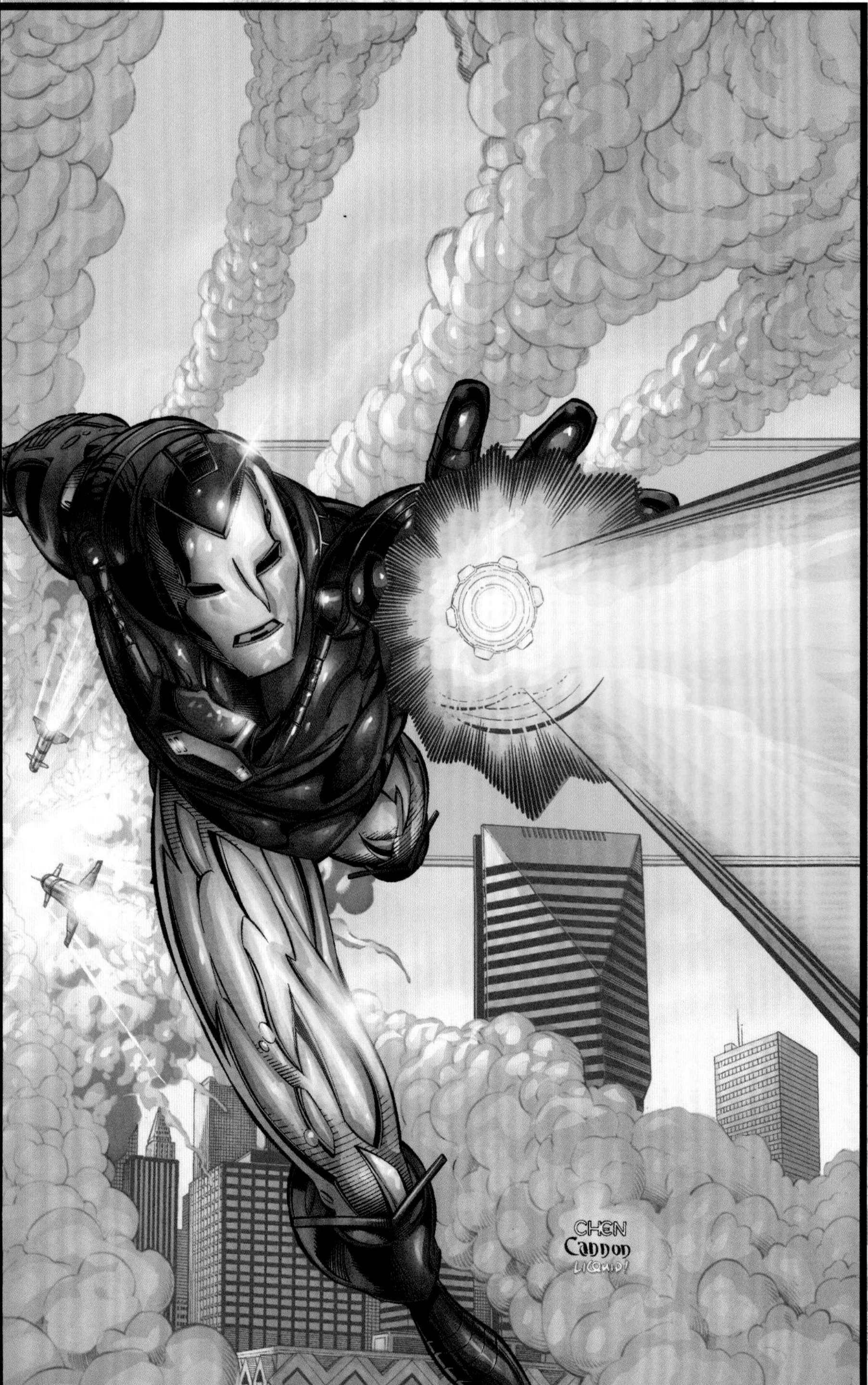
CHEN
Cannon
LIQUID!
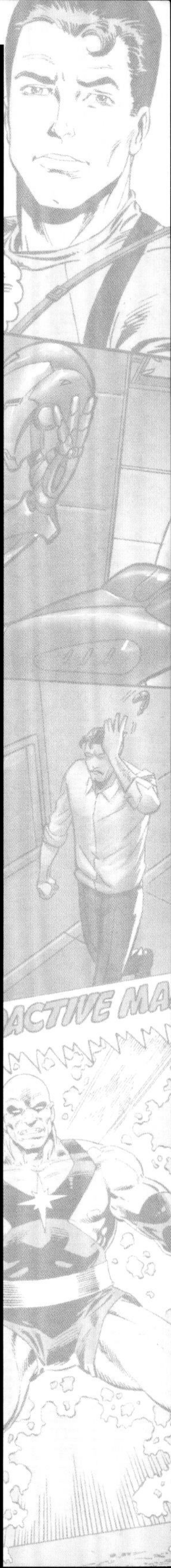

IRON MAN #1

IN DEFEATING THE PSIONIC ENTITY KNOWN AS ONSLAUGHT, TONY STARK AND OTHER HEROES WERE TRANSPORTED TO AN ALTERNATE UNVIERSE. NOW TONY HAS RETURNED AND SEEKS TO RECLAIM HIS LEGACY.

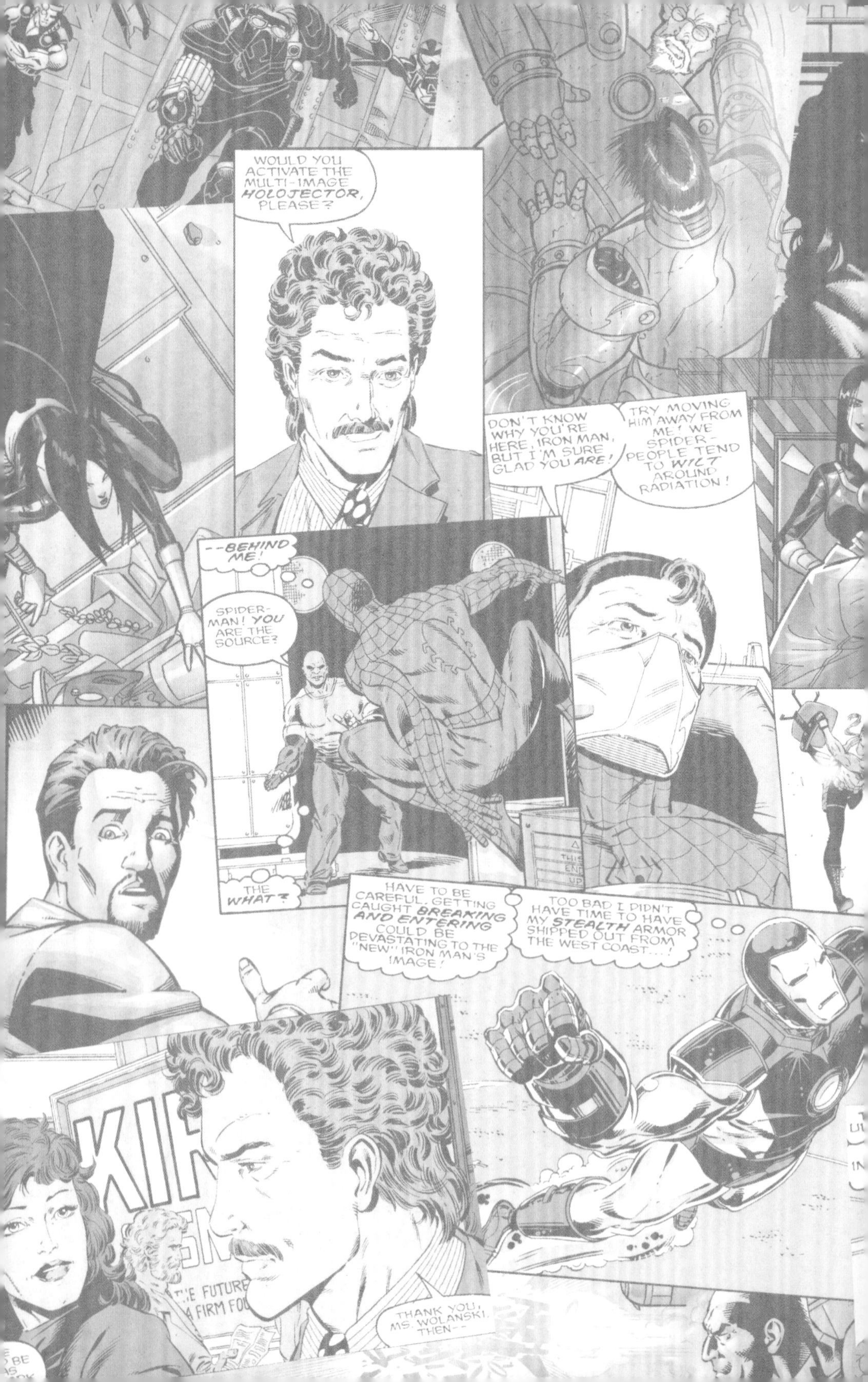
WOULD YOU ACTIVATE THE MULTI-IMAGE HOLOJECTOR, PLEASE?
DON'T KNOW WHY YOU'RE HERE, IRON MAN, BUT I'M SURE GLAD YOU ARE!
TRY MOVING HIM AWAY FROM ME! WE SPIDER-PEOPLE TEND TO WILT AROUND RADIATION!
--BEHIND ME!
SPIDER-MAN! YOU ARE THE SOURCE?
THE WHAT?
HAVE TO BE CAREFUL. GETTING CAUGHT BREAKING AND ENTERING COULD BE DEVASTATING TO THE "NEW" IRON MAN'S IMAGE!
TOO BAD I DIDN'T HAVE TIME TO HAVE MY STEALTH ARMOR SHIPPED OUT FROM THE WEST COAST...!
THE FUTURE
THANK YOU, MS. WOLANSKI. THEN--

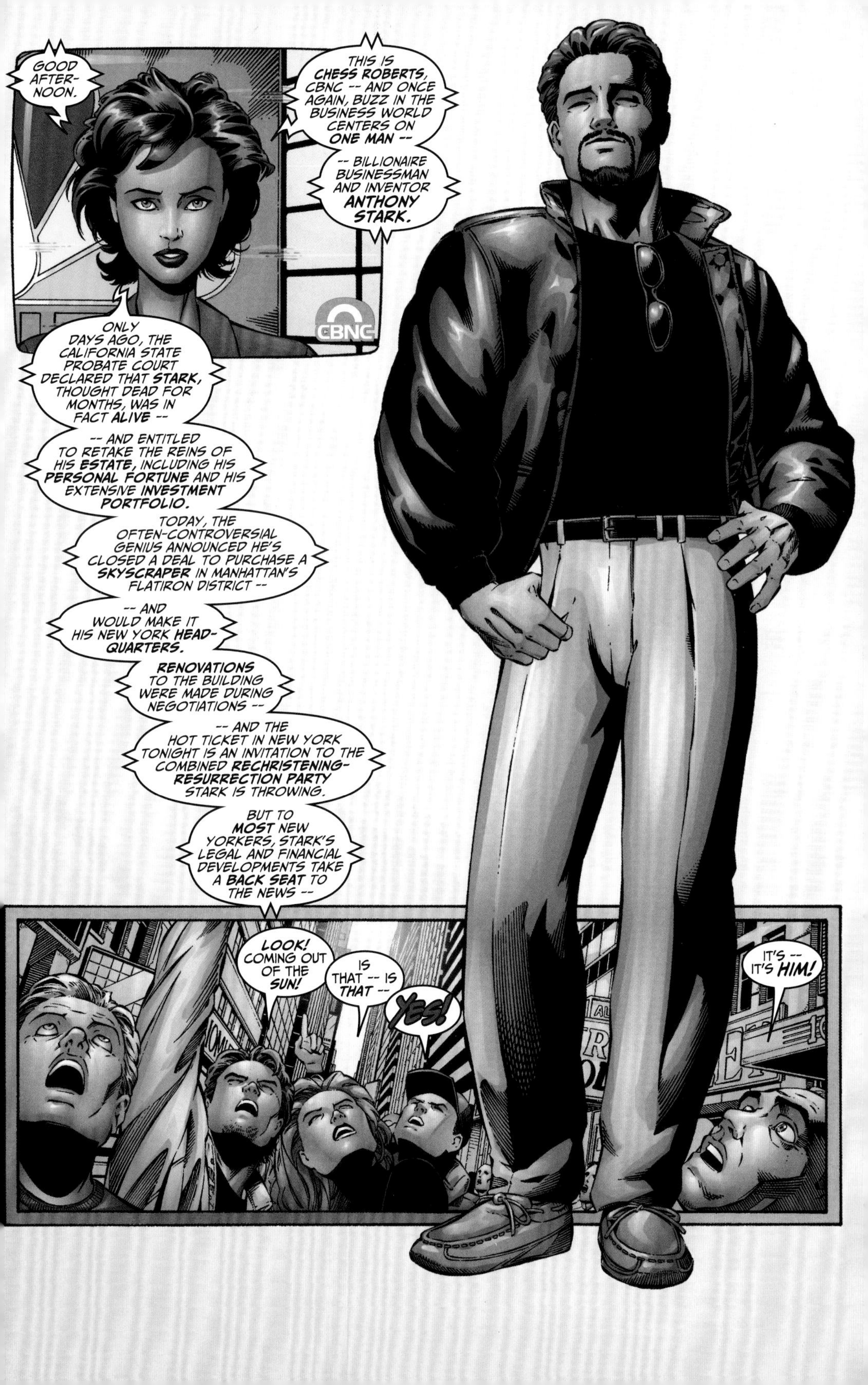
GOOD AFTER-NOON.
THIS IS CHESS ROBERTS, CBNC -- AND ONCE AGAIN, BUZZ IN THE BUSINESS WORLD CENTERS ON ONE MAN --
-- BILLIONAIRE BUSINESSMAN AND INVENTOR ANTHONY STARK.
CBNC
ONLY DAYS AGO, THE CALIFORNIA STATE PROBATE COURT DECLARED THAT STARK, THOUGHT DEAD FOR MONTHS, WAS IN FACT ALIVE --
-- AND ENTITLED TO RETAKE THE REINS OF HIS ESTATE, INCLUDING HIS PERSONAL FORTUNE AND HIS EXTENSIVE INVESTMENT PORTFOLIO.
TODAY, THE OFTEN-CONTROVERSIAL GENIUS ANNOUNCED HE'S CLOSED A DEAL TO PURCHASE A SKYSCRAPER IN MANHATTAN'S FLATIRON DISTRICT --
-- AND WOULD MAKE IT HIS NEW YORK HEAD-QUARTERS.
RENOVATIONS TO THE BUILDING WERE MADE DURING NEGOTIATIONS --
-- AND THE HOT TICKET IN NEW YORK TONIGHT IS AN INVITATION TO THE COMBINED RECHRISTENING-RESURRECTION PARTY STARK IS THROWING.
BUT TO MOST NEW YORKERS, STARK'S LEGAL AND FINANCIAL DEVELOPMENTS TAKE A BACK SEAT TO THE NEWS --
LOOK! COMING OUT OF THE SUN!
IS THAT -- IS THAT --
YES!
IT'S -- IT'S HIM!

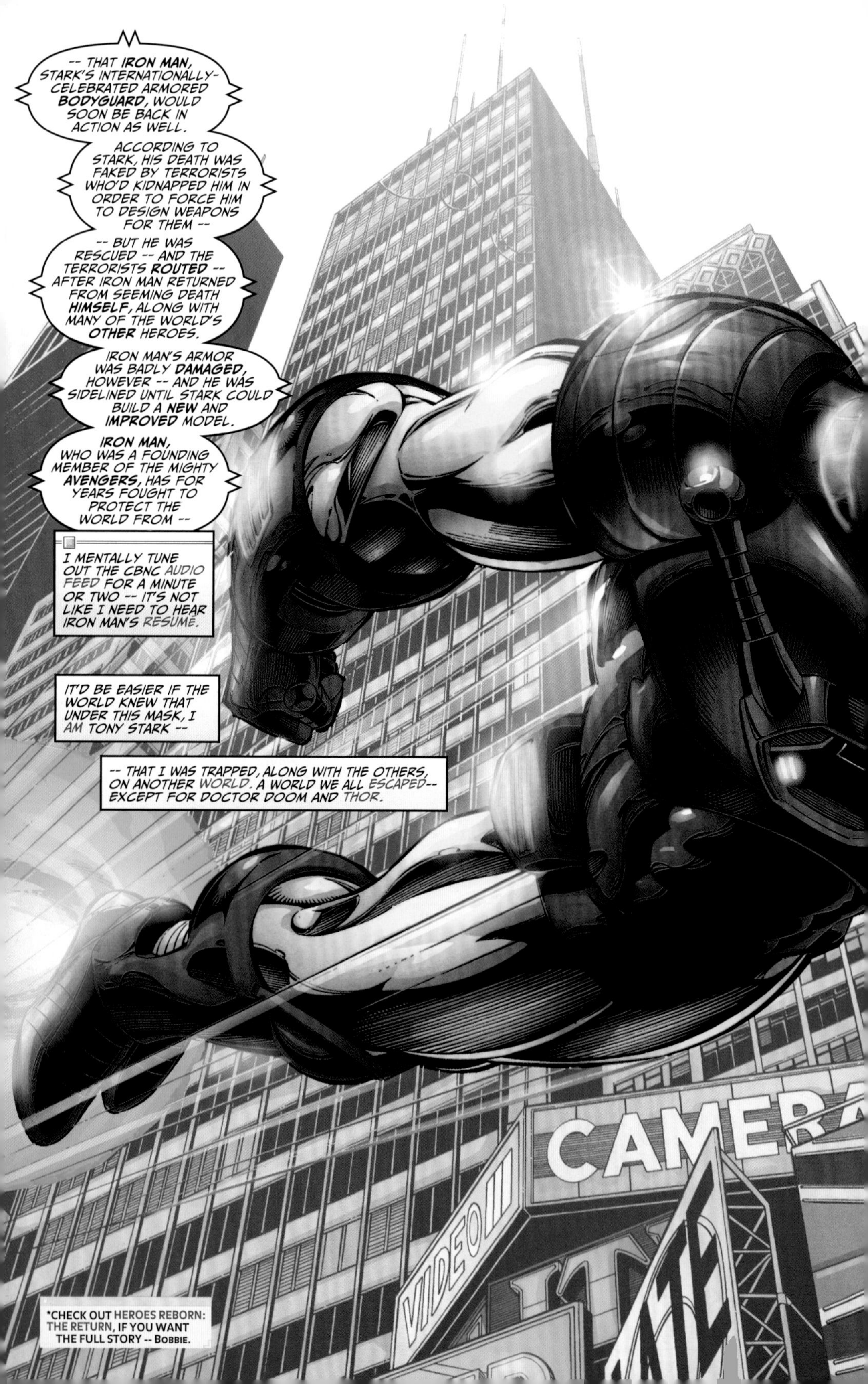
-- THAT IRON MAN, STARK'S INTERNATIONALLY-CELEBRATED ARMORED BODYGUARD, WOULD SOON BE BACK IN ACTION AS WELL.
ACCORDING TO STARK, HIS DEATH WAS FAKED BY TERRORISTS WHO'D KIDNAPPED HIM IN ORDER TO FORCE HIM TO DESIGN WEAPONS FOR THEM --
-- BUT HE WAS RESCUED -- AND THE TERRORISTS ROUTED -- AFTER IRON MAN RETURNED FROM SEEMING DEATH HIMSELF, ALONG WITH MANY OF THE WORLD'S OTHER HEROES.
IRON MAN'S ARMOR WAS BADLY DAMAGED, HOWEVER -- AND HE WAS SIDELINED UNTIL STARK COULD BUILD A NEW AND IMPROVED MODEL.
IRON MAN, WHO WAS A FOUNDING MEMBER OF THE MIGHTY AVENGERS, HAS FOR YEARS FOUGHT TO PROTECT THE WORLD FROM --
I MENTALLY TUNE OUT THE CBNC AUDIO FEED FOR A MINUTE OR TWO -- IT'S NOT LIKE I NEED TO HEAR IRON MAN'S RESUME.
IT'D BE EASIER IF THE WORLD KNEW THAT UNDER THIS MASK, I AM TONY STARK --
-- THAT I WAS TRAPPED, ALONG WITH THE OTHERS, ON ANOTHER WORLD. A WORLD WE ALL ESCAPED-- EXCEPT FOR DOCTOR DOOM AND THOR.
CAMERA
VIDEO
*CHECK OUT HEROES REBORN: THE RETURN, IF YOU WANT THE FULL STORY -- BOBBIE.

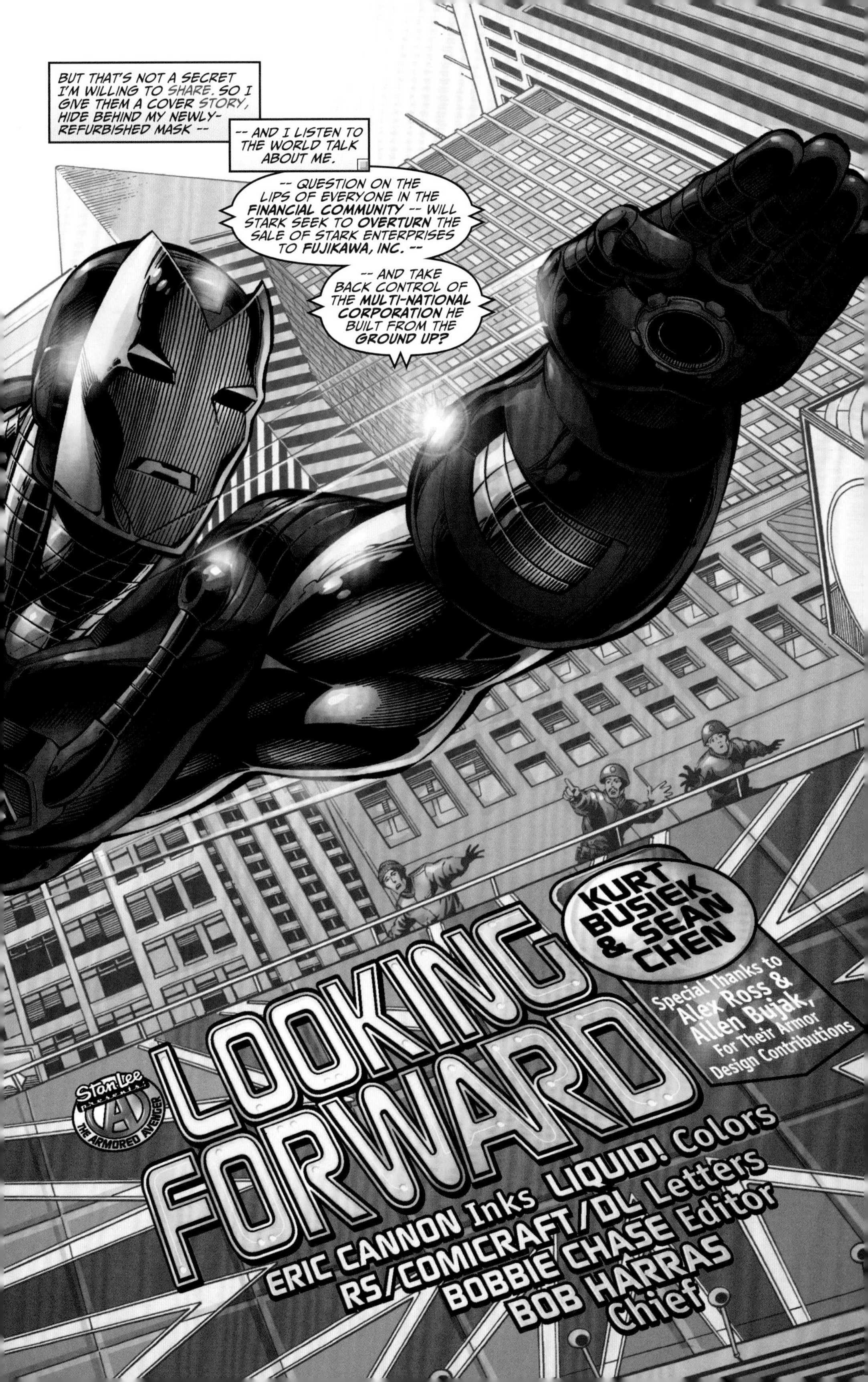
BUT THAT'S NOT A SECRET I'M WILLING TO SHARE. SO I GIVE THEM A COVER STORY, HIDE BEHIND MY NEWLY-REFURBISHED MASK --
-- AND I LISTEN TO THE WORLD TALK ABOUT ME.
-- QUESTION ON THE LIPS OF EVERYONE IN THE FINANCIAL COMMUNITY -- WILL STARK SEEK TO OVERTURN THE SALE OF STARK ENTERPRISES TO FUJIKAWA, INC. --
-- AND TAKE BACK CONTROL OF THE MULTI-NATIONAL CORPORATION HE BUILT FROM THE GROUND UP?
LOOKING FORWARD
KURT BUSIEK & SEAN CHEN
Special Thanks to Alex Ross & Allen Bujak, For Their Armor Design Contributions
Stan Lee PRESENTS
THE ARMORED AVENGER
ERIC CANNON Inks LIQUID! Colors
RS/COMICRAFT/DL Letters
BOBBIE CHASE Editor
BOB HARRAS Chief

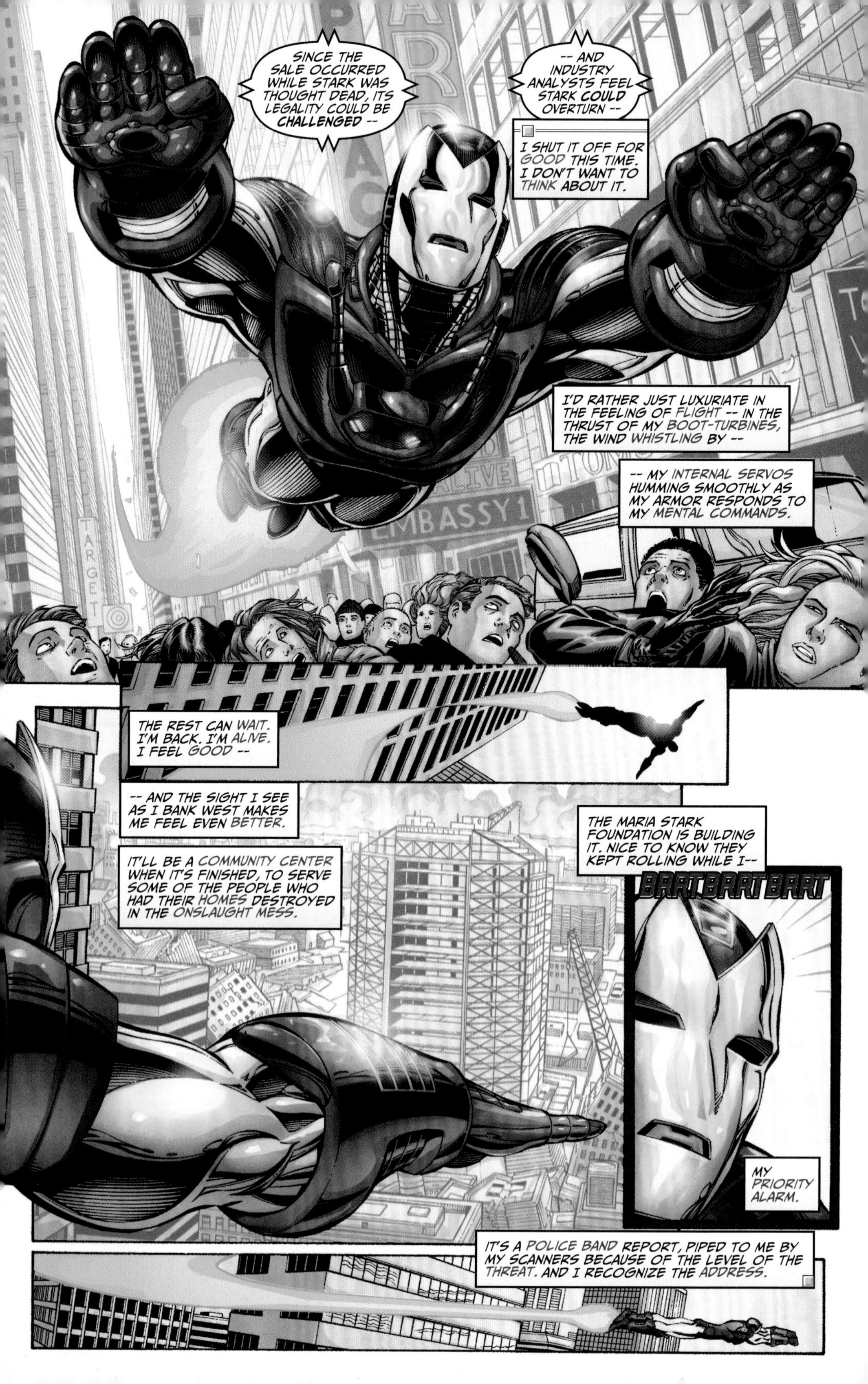
SINCE THE SALE OCCURRED WHILE STARK WAS THOUGHT DEAD, ITS LEGALITY COULD BE CHALLENGED --
-- AND INDUSTRY ANALYSTS FEEL STARK COULD OVERTURN --
I SHUT IT OFF FOR GOOD THIS TIME. I DON'T WANT TO THINK ABOUT IT.
I'D RATHER JUST LUXURIATE IN THE FEELING OF FLIGHT -- IN THE THRUST OF MY BOOT-TURBINES, THE WIND WHISTLING BY --
-- MY INTERNAL SERVOS HUMMING SMOOTHLY AS MY ARMOR RESPONDS TO MY MENTAL COMMANDS.
EMBASSY 1
TARGET
THE REST CAN WAIT. I'M BACK. I'M ALIVE. I FEEL GOOD --
-- AND THE SIGHT I SEE AS I BANK WEST MAKES ME FEEL EVEN BETTER.
IT'LL BE A COMMUNITY CENTER WHEN IT'S FINISHED, TO SERVE SOME OF THE PEOPLE WHO HAD THEIR HOMES DESTROYED IN THE ONSLAUGHT MESS.
THE MARIA STARK FOUNDATION IS BUILDING IT. NICE TO KNOW THEY KEPT ROLLING WHILE I--
BRRT BRRT BRRT
MY PRIORITY ALARM.
IT'S A POLICE BAND REPORT, PIPED TO ME BY MY SCANNERS BECAUSE OF THE LEVEL OF THE THREAT. AND I RECOGNIZE THE ADDRESS.

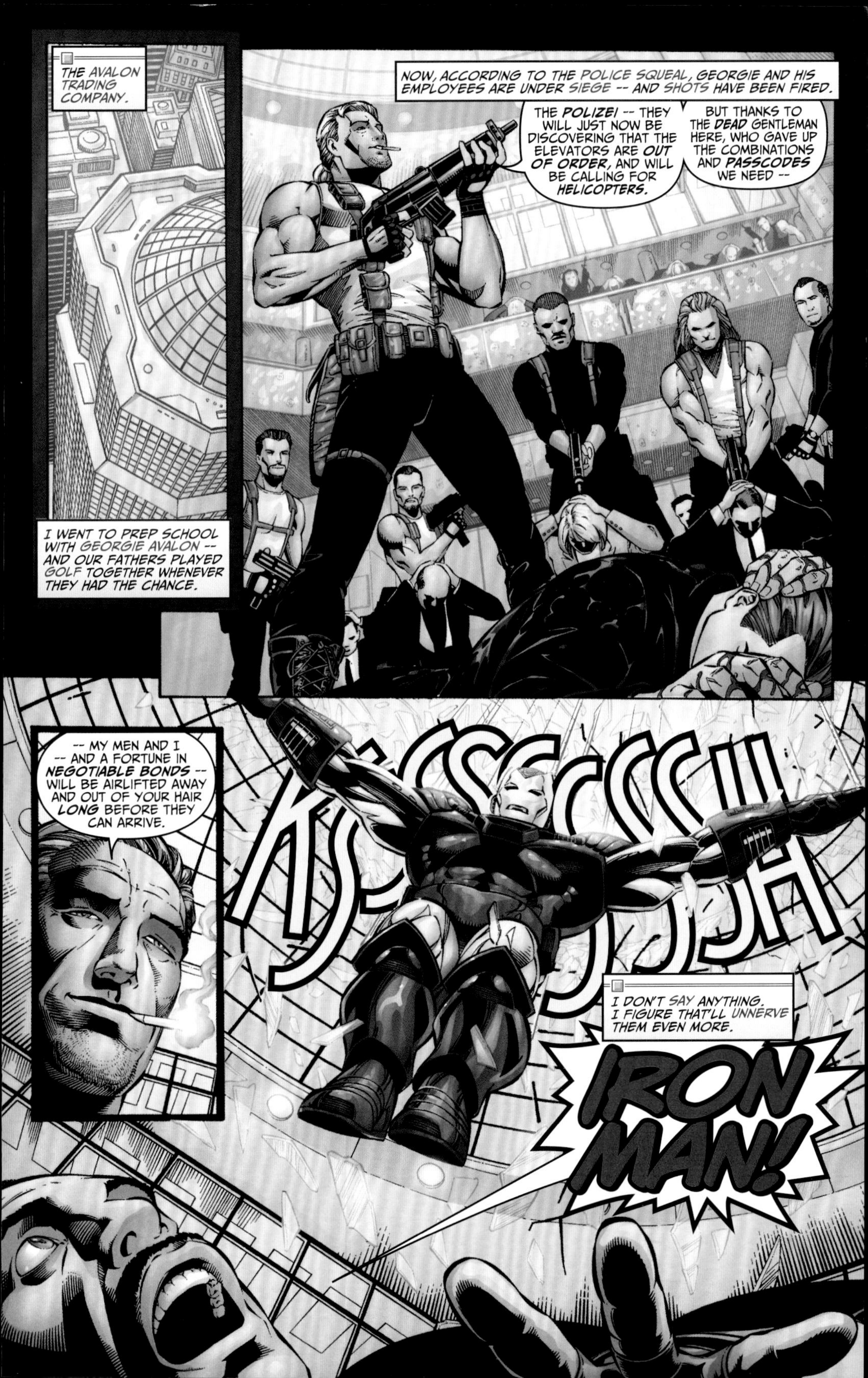
THE AVALON TRADING COMPANY.
NOW, ACCORDING TO THE POLICE SQUEAL, GEORGIE AND HIS EMPLOYEES ARE UNDER SIEGE -- AND SHOTS HAVE BEEN FIRED.
THE POLIZEI -- THEY WILL JUST NOW BE DISCOVERING THAT THE ELEVATORS ARE OUT OF ORDER, AND WILL BE CALLING FOR HELICOPTERS.
BUT THANKS TO THE DEAD GENTLEMAN HERE, WHO GAVE UP THE COMBINATIONS AND PASSCODES WE NEED --
I WENT TO PREP SCHOOL WITH GEORGIE AVALON -- AND OUR FATHERS PLAYED GOLF TOGETHER WHENEVER THEY HAD THE CHANCE.
-- MY MEN AND I -- AND A FORTUNE IN NEGOTIABLE BONDS -- WILL BE AIRLIFTED AWAY AND OUT OF YOUR HAIR LONG BEFORE THEY CAN ARRIVE.
KSSSSSSH
I DON'T SAY ANYTHING. I FIGURE THAT'LL UNNERVE THEM EVEN MORE.
IRON MAN!

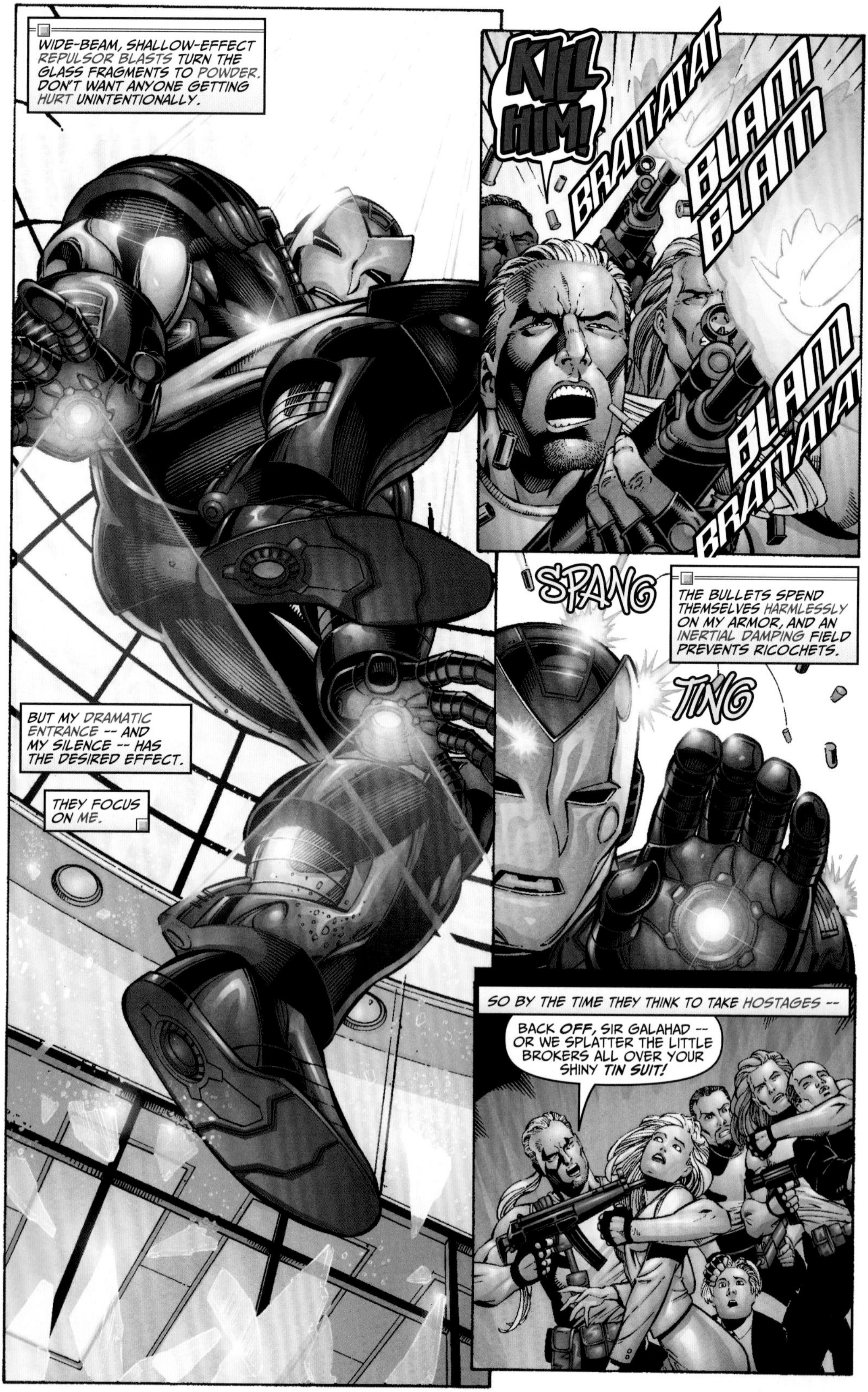
WIDE-BEAM, SHALLOW-EFFECT REPULSOR BLASTS TURN THE GLASS FRAGMENTS TO POWDER. DON'T WANT ANYONE GETTING HURT UNINTENTIONALLY.
BUT MY DRAMATIC ENTRANCE -- AND MY SILENCE -- HAS THE DESIRED EFFECT.
THEY FOCUS ON ME.
KILL HIM!
BRATTATAT
BLAM
BLAM
BLAM
BRATTATAT
SPANG
THE BULLETS SPEND THEMSELVES HARMLESSLY ON MY ARMOR, AND AN INERTIAL DAMPING FIELD PREVENTS RICOCHETS.
TING
SO BY THE TIME THEY THINK TO TAKE HOSTAGES --
BACK OFF, SIR GALAHAD -- OR WE SPLATTER THE LITTLE BROKERS ALL OVER YOUR SHINY TIN SUIT!

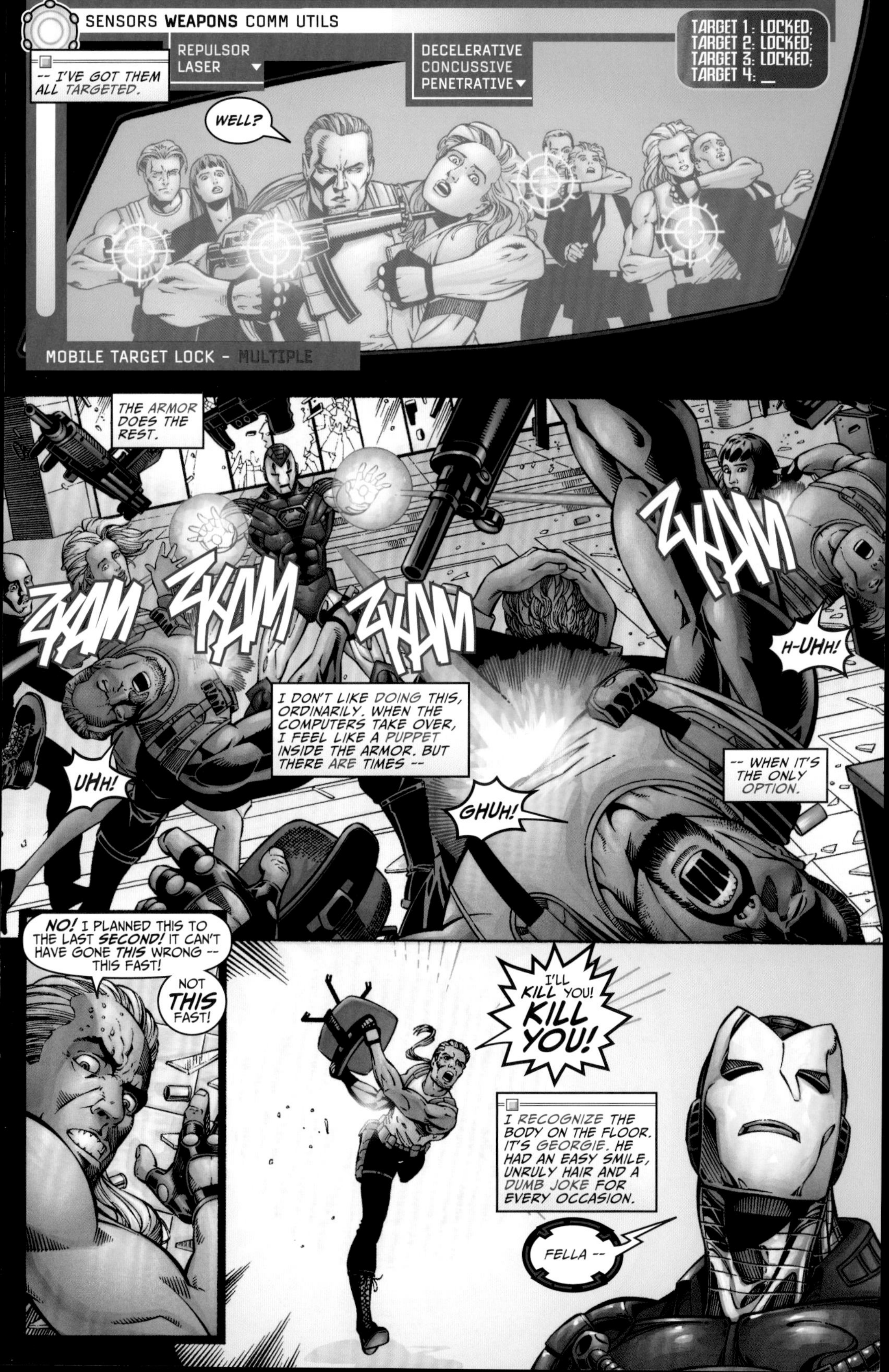
SENSORS WEAPONS COMM UTILS
REPULSOR
LASER
DECELERATIVE
CONCUSSIVE
PENETRATIVE
TARGET 1: LOCKED;
TARGET 2: LOCKED;
TARGET 3: LOCKED;
TARGET 4: _
-- I'VE GOT THEM ALL TARGETED.
WELL?
MOBILE TARGET LOCK - MULTIPLE
THE ARMOR DOES THE REST.
ZKAM
ZKAM
ZKAM
ZKAM
I DON'T LIKE DOING THIS, ORDINARILY. WHEN THE COMPUTERS TAKE OVER, I FEEL LIKE A PUPPET INSIDE THE ARMOR. BUT THERE ARE TIMES --
H-UHH!
UHH!
GHUH!
-- WHEN IT'S THE ONLY OPTION.
NO! I PLANNED THIS TO THE LAST SECOND! IT CAN'T HAVE GONE THIS WRONG -- THIS FAST!
NOT THIS FAST!
I'LL KILL YOU! KILL YOU!
I RECOGNIZE THE BODY ON THE FLOOR. IT'S GEORGIE. HE HAD AN EASY SMILE, UNRULY HAIR AND A DUMB JOKE FOR EVERY OCCASION.
FELLA --

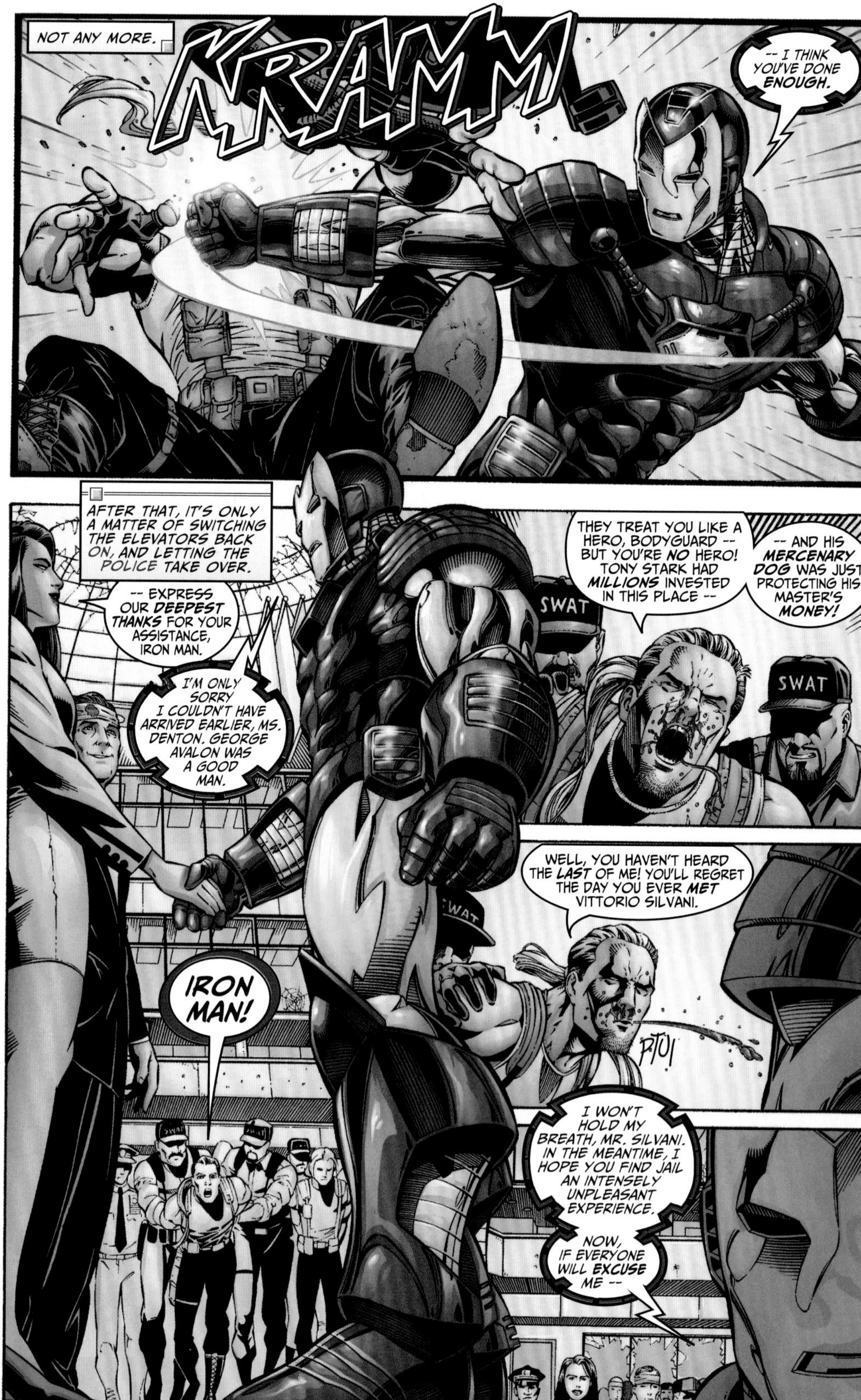
NOT ANY MORE.
KRAMM
-- I THINK YOU'VE DONE ENOUGH.
AFTER THAT, IT'S ONLY A MATTER OF SWITCHING THE ELEVATORS BACK ON, AND LETTING THE POLICE TAKE OVER.
-- EXPRESS OUR DEEPEST THANKS FOR YOUR ASSISTANCE, IRON MAN.
I'M ONLY SORRY I COULDN'T HAVE ARRIVED EARLIER, MS. DENTON. GEORGE AVALON WAS A GOOD MAN.
IRON MAN!
THEY TREAT YOU LIKE A HERO, BODYGUARD -- BUT YOU'RE NO HERO! TONY STARK HAD MILLIONS INVESTED IN THIS PLACE --
-- AND HIS MERCENARY DOG WAS JUST PROTECTING HIS MASTER'S MONEY!
SWAT
SWAT
WELL, YOU HAVEN'T HEARD THE LAST OF ME! YOU'LL REGRET THE DAY YOU EVER MET VITTORIO SILVANI.
PTUI
I WON'T HOLD MY BREATH, MR. SILVANI. IN THE MEANTIME, I HOPE YOU FIND JAIL AN INTENSELY UNPLEASANT EXPERIENCE.
NOW, IF EVERYONE WILL EXCUSE ME --

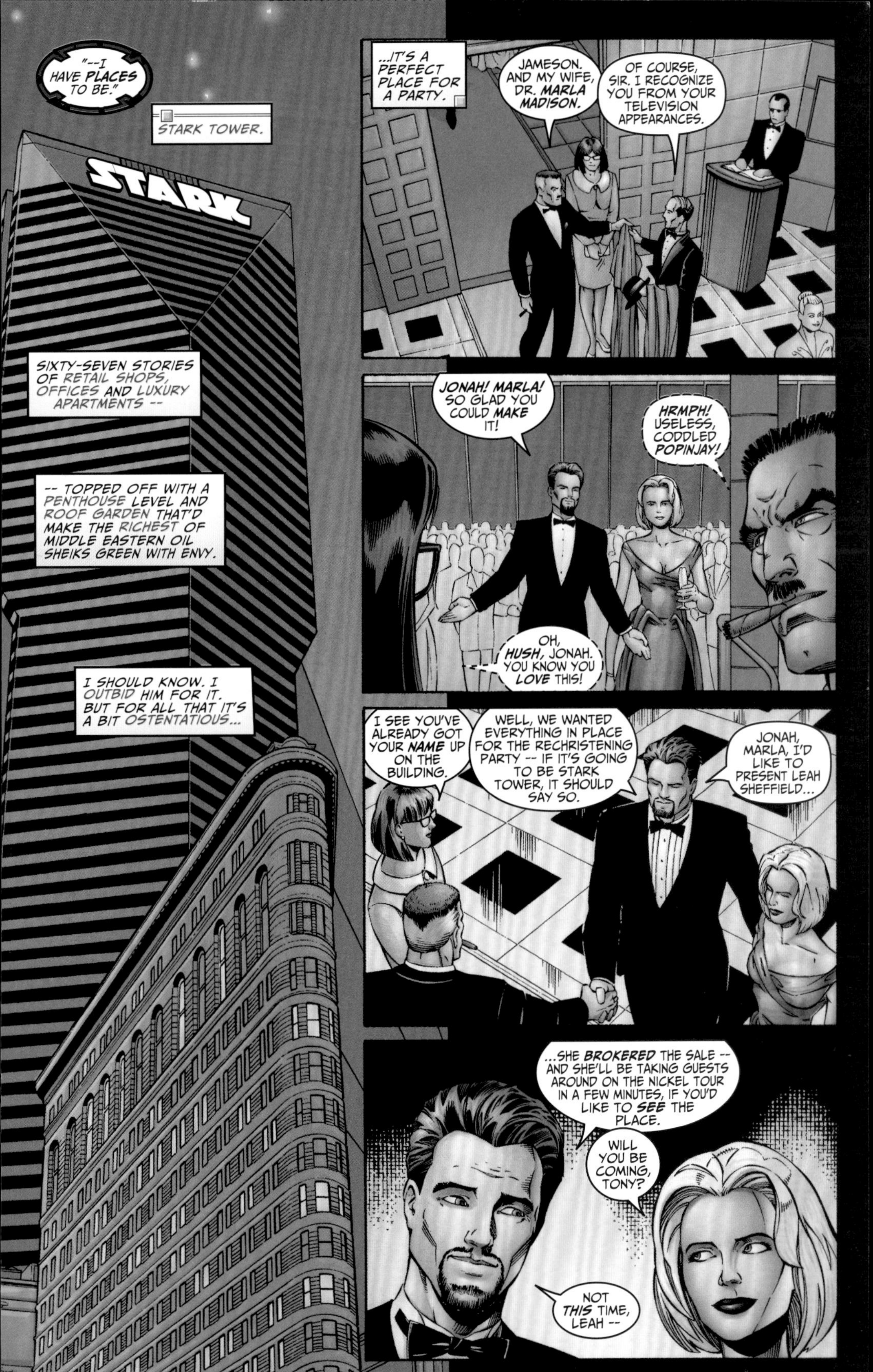
"--I HAVE PLACES TO BE."
STARK TOWER.
STARK
SIXTY-SEVEN STORIES OF RETAIL SHOPS, OFFICES AND LUXURY APARTMENTS --
-- TOPPED OFF WITH A PENTHOUSE LEVEL AND ROOF GARDEN THAT'D MAKE THE RICHEST OF MIDDLE EASTERN OIL SHEIKS GREEN WITH ENVY.
I SHOULD KNOW. I OUTBID HIM FOR IT. BUT FOR ALL THAT IT'S A BIT OSTENTATIOUS...
...IT'S A PERFECT PLACE FOR A PARTY.
JAMESON. AND MY WIFE, DR. MARLA MADISON.
OF COURSE, SIR. I RECOGNIZE YOU FROM YOUR TELEVISION APPEARANCES.
JONAH! MARLA! SO GLAD YOU COULD MAKE IT!
HRMPH! USELESS, CODDLED POPINJAY!
OH, HUSH, JONAH. YOU KNOW YOU LOVE THIS!
I SEE YOU'VE ALREADY GOT YOUR NAME UP ON THE BUILDING.
WELL, WE WANTED EVERYTHING IN PLACE FOR THE RECHRISTENING PARTY -- IF IT'S GOING TO BE STARK TOWER, IT SHOULD SAY SO.
JONAH, MARLA, I'D LIKE TO PRESENT LEAH SHEFFIELD...
...SHE BROKERED THE SALE -- AND SHE'LL BE TAKING GUESTS AROUND ON THE NICKEL TOUR IN A FEW MINUTES, IF YOU'D LIKE TO SEE THE PLACE.
WILL YOU BE COMING, TONY?
NOT THIS TIME, LEAH --

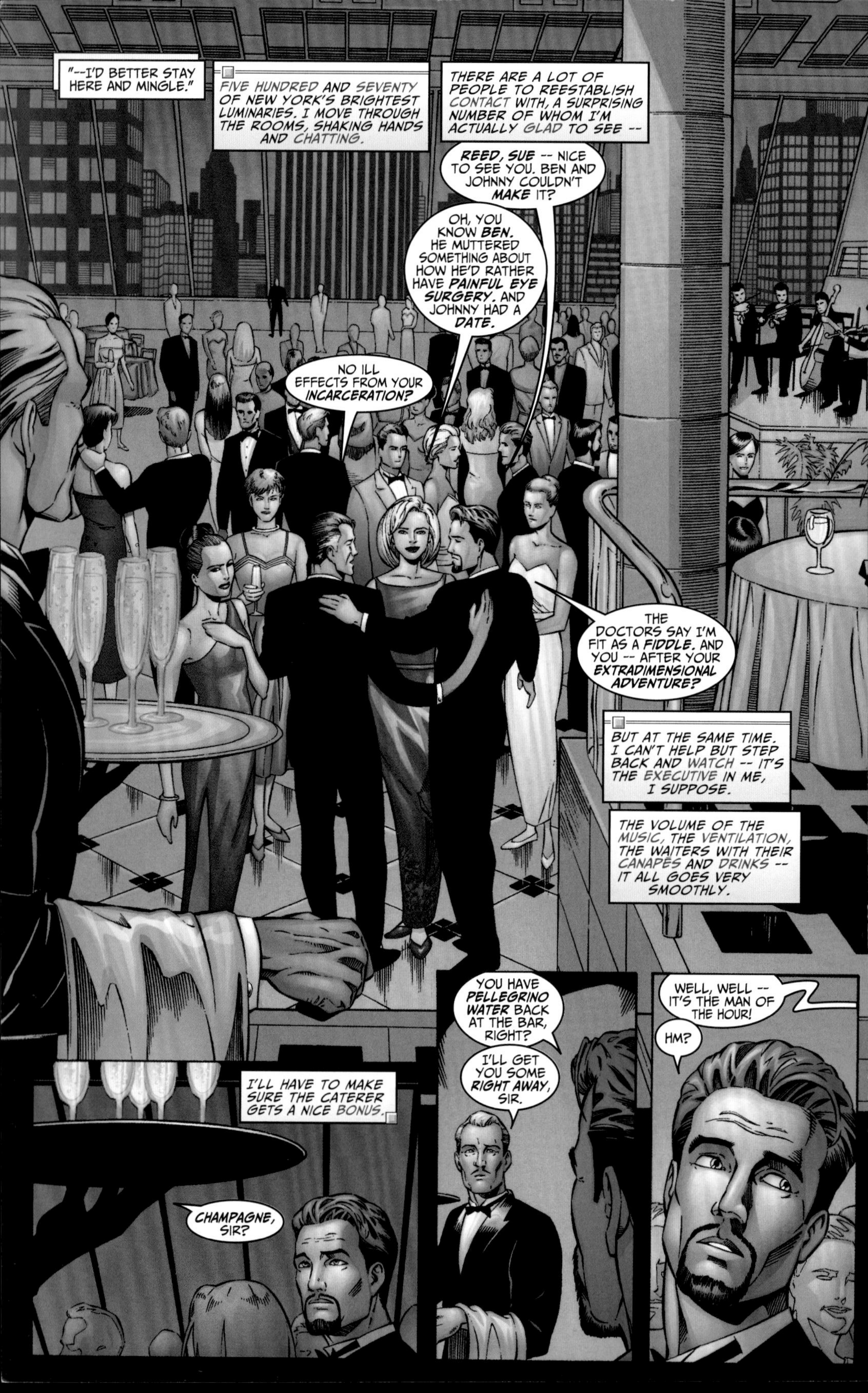
"--I'D BETTER STAY HERE AND MINGLE."
FIVE HUNDRED AND SEVENTY OF NEW YORK'S BRIGHTEST LUMINARIES. I MOVE THROUGH THE ROOMS, SHAKING HANDS AND CHATTING.
THERE ARE A LOT OF PEOPLE TO REESTABLISH CONTACT WITH, A SURPRISING NUMBER OF WHOM I'M ACTUALLY GLAD TO SEE --
REED, SUE -- NICE TO SEE YOU. BEN AND JOHNNY COULDN'T MAKE IT?
OH, YOU KNOW BEN. HE MUTTERED SOMETHING ABOUT HOW HE'D RATHER HAVE PAINFUL EYE SURGERY. AND JOHNNY HAD A DATE.
NO ILL EFFECTS FROM YOUR INCARCERATION?
THE DOCTORS SAY I'M FIT AS A FIDDLE. AND YOU -- AFTER YOUR EXTRADIMENSIONAL ADVENTURE?
BUT AT THE SAME TIME. I CAN'T HELP BUT STEP BACK AND WATCH -- IT'S THE EXECUTIVE IN ME, I SUPPOSE.
THE VOLUME OF THE MUSIC, THE VENTILATION, THE WAITERS WITH THEIR CANAPÉS AND DRINKS -- IT ALL GOES VERY SMOOTHLY.
I'LL HAVE TO MAKE SURE THE CATERER GETS A NICE BONUS.
CHAMPAGNE, SIR?
YOU HAVE PELLEGRINO WATER BACK AT THE BAR, RIGHT?
I'LL GET YOU SOME RIGHT AWAY, SIR.
WELL, WELL -- IT'S THE MAN OF THE HOUR!
HM?

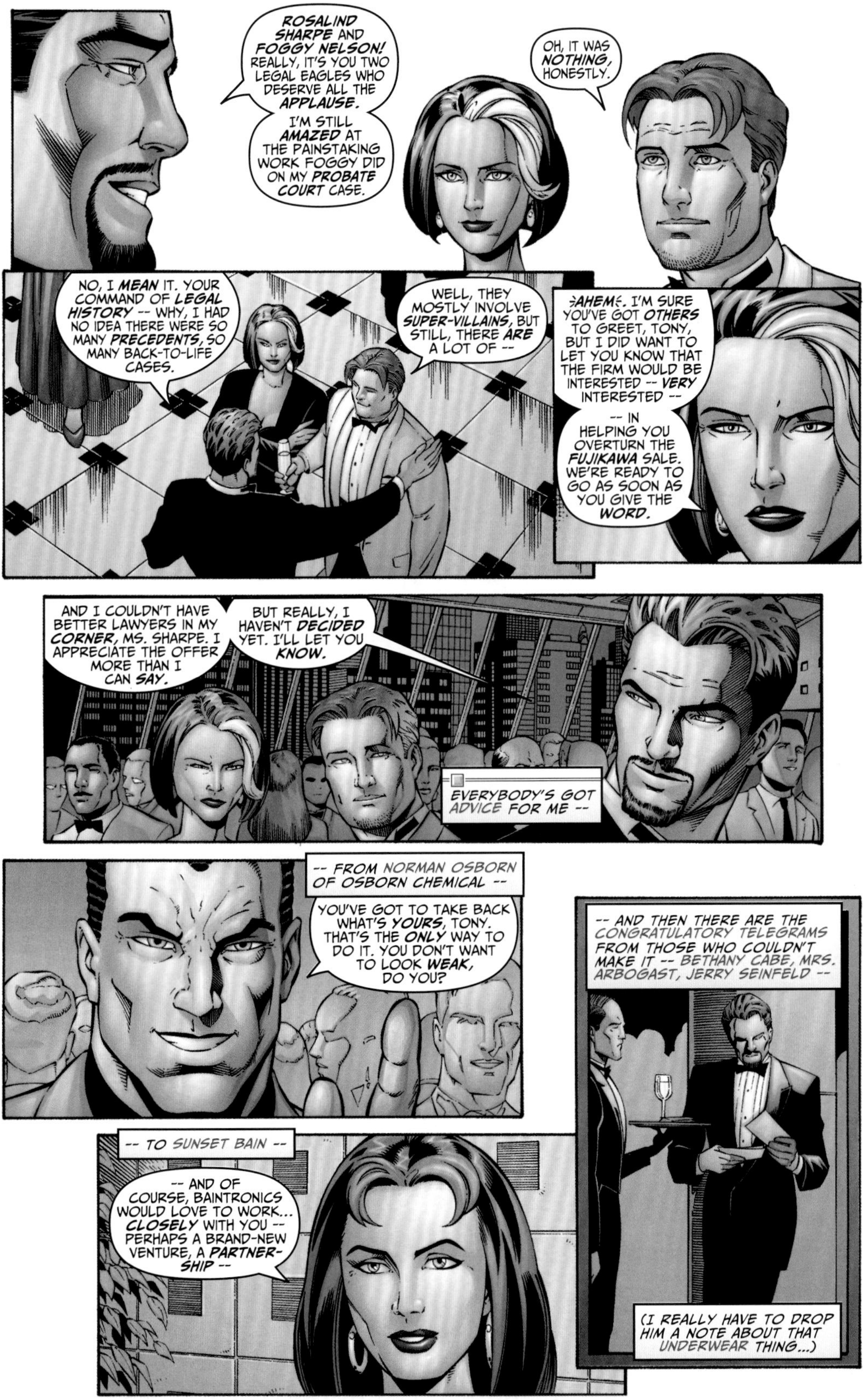
ROSALIND SHARPE AND FOGGY NELSON! REALLY, IT'S YOU TWO LEGAL EAGLES WHO DESERVE ALL THE APPLAUSE.
I'M STILL AMAZED AT THE PAINSTAKING WORK FOGGY DID ON MY PROBATE COURT CASE.
OH, IT WAS NOTHING, HONESTLY.
NO, I MEAN IT. YOUR COMMAND OF LEGAL HISTORY -- WHY, I HAD NO IDEA THERE WERE SO MANY PRECEDENTS, SO MANY BACK-TO-LIFE CASES.
WELL, THEY MOSTLY INVOLVE SUPER-VILLAINS, BUT STILL, THERE ARE A LOT OF --
AHEM. I'M SURE YOU'VE GOT OTHERS TO GREET, TONY, BUT I DID WANT TO LET YOU KNOW THAT THE FIRM WOULD BE INTERESTED -- VERY INTERESTED --
-- IN HELPING YOU OVERTURN THE FUJIKAWA SALE. WE'RE READY TO GO AS SOON AS YOU GIVE THE WORD.
AND I COULDN'T HAVE BETTER LAWYERS IN MY CORNER, MS. SHARPE. I APPRECIATE THE OFFER MORE THAN I CAN SAY.
BUT REALLY, I HAVEN'T DECIDED YET. I'LL LET YOU KNOW.
EVERYBODY'S GOT ADVICE FOR ME --
-- FROM NORMAN OSBORN OF OSBORN CHEMICAL --
YOU'VE GOT TO TAKE BACK WHAT'S YOURS, TONY. THAT'S THE ONLY WAY TO DO IT. YOU DON'T WANT TO LOOK WEAK, DO YOU?
-- AND THEN THERE ARE THE CONGRATULATORY TELEGRAMS FROM THOSE WHO COULDN'T MAKE IT -- BETHANY CABE, MRS. ARBOGAST, JERRY SEINFELD --
(I REALLY HAVE TO DROP HIM A NOTE ABOUT THAT UNDERWEAR THING...)
-- TO SUNSET BAIN --
-- AND OF COURSE, BAINTRONICS WOULD LOVE TO WORK... CLOSELY WITH YOU -- PERHAPS A BRAND-NEW VENTURE, A PARTNER-SHIP --

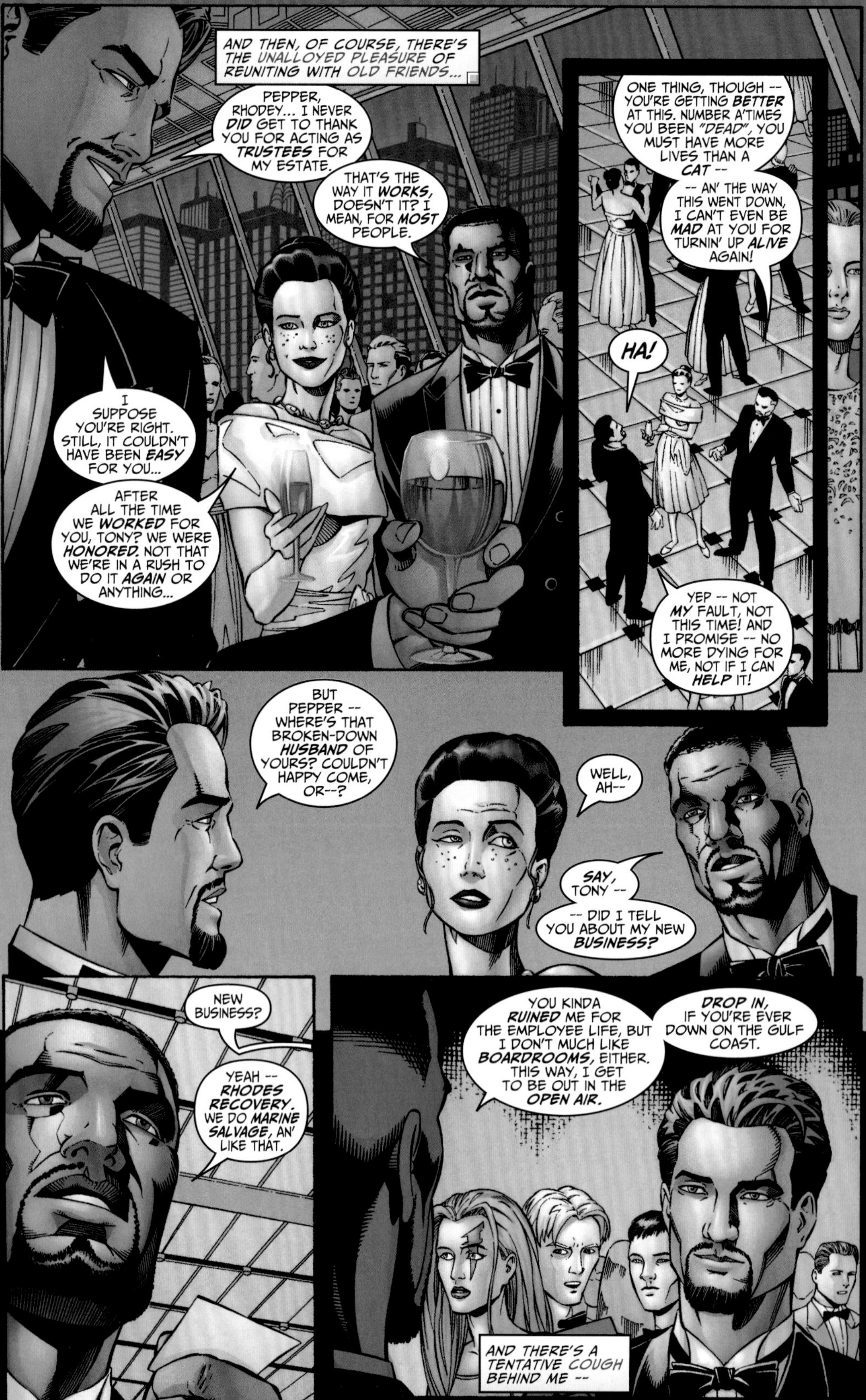
AND THEN, OF COURSE, THERE'S THE UNALLOYED PLEASURE OF REUNITING WITH OLD FRIENDS...
PEPPER, RHODEY... I NEVER DID GET TO THANK YOU FOR ACTING AS TRUSTEES FOR MY ESTATE.
THAT'S THE WAY IT WORKS, DOESN'T IT? I MEAN, FOR MOST PEOPLE.
I SUPPOSE YOU'RE RIGHT. STILL, IT COULDN'T HAVE BEEN EASY FOR YOU...
AFTER ALL THE TIME WE WORKED FOR YOU, TONY? WE WERE HONORED. NOT THAT WE'RE IN A RUSH TO DO IT AGAIN OR ANYTHING...
ONE THING, THOUGH -- YOU'RE GETTING BETTER AT THIS. NUMBER A'TIMES YOU BEEN "DEAD", YOU MUST HAVE MORE LIVES THAN A CAT --
-- AN' THE WAY THIS WENT DOWN, I CAN'T EVEN BE MAD AT YOU FOR TURNIN' UP ALIVE AGAIN!
HA!
YEP -- NOT MY FAULT, NOT THIS TIME! AND I PROMISE -- NO MORE DYING FOR ME, NOT IF I CAN HELP IT!
BUT PEPPER -- WHERE'S THAT BROKEN-DOWN HUSBAND OF YOURS? COULDN'T HAPPY COME, OR--?
WELL, AH--
SAY, TONY --
-- DID I TELL YOU ABOUT MY NEW BUSINESS?
NEW BUSINESS?
YEAH -- RHODES RECOVERY. WE DO MARINE SALVAGE, AN' LIKE THAT.
YOU KINDA RUINED ME FOR THE EMPLOYEE LIFE, BUT I DON'T MUCH LIKE BOARDROOMS, EITHER. THIS WAY, I GET TO BE OUT IN THE OPEN AIR.
DROP IN, IF YOU'RE EVER DOWN ON THE GULF COAST.
AND THERE'S A TENTATIVE COUGH BEHIND ME --

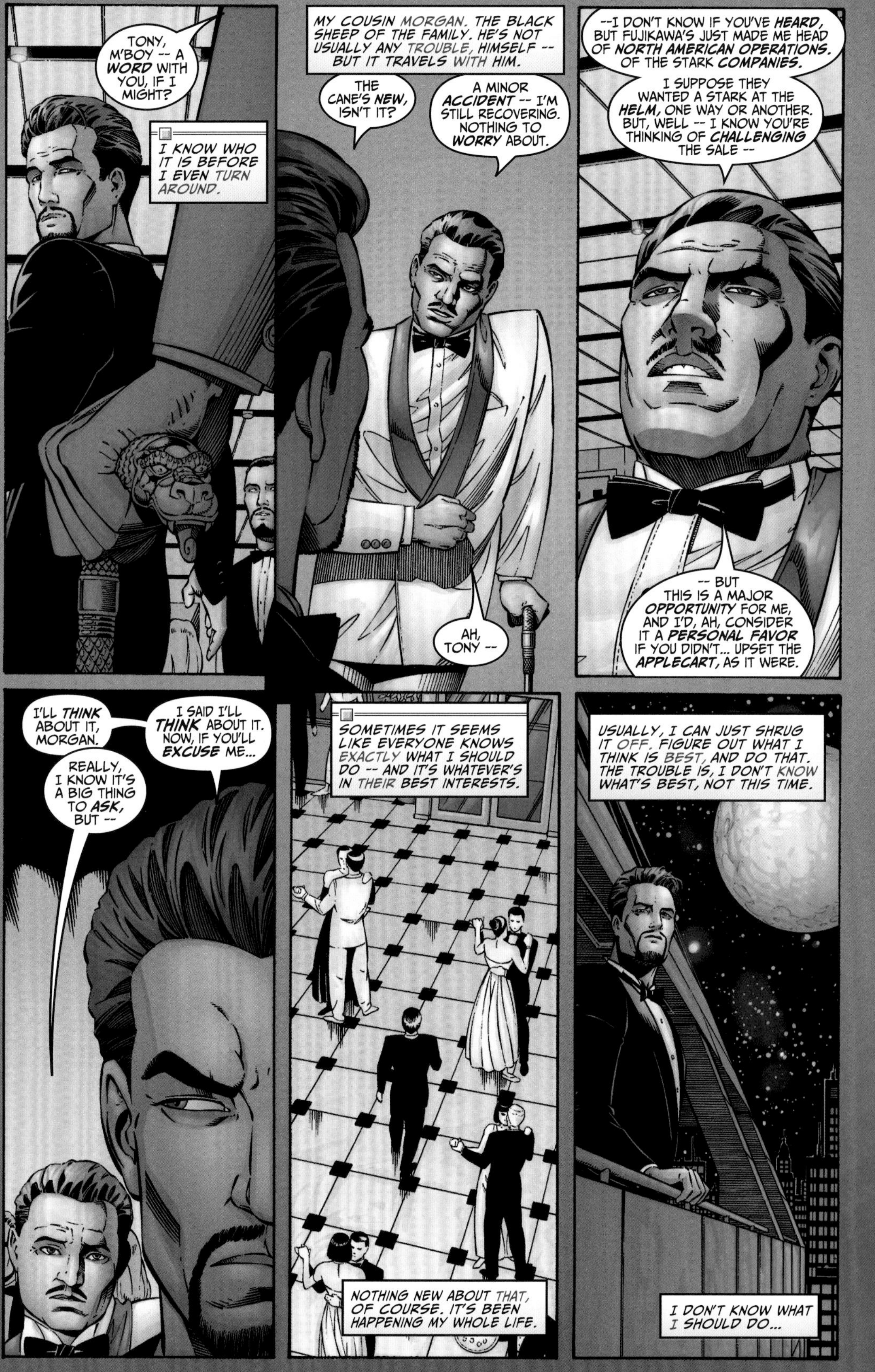
TONY, M'BOY -- A WORD WITH YOU, IF I MIGHT?
I KNOW WHO IT IS BEFORE I EVEN TURN AROUND.
MY COUSIN MORGAN. THE BLACK SHEEP OF THE FAMILY. HE'S NOT USUALLY ANY TROUBLE, HIMSELF -- BUT IT TRAVELS WITH HIM.
THE CANE'S NEW, ISN'T IT?
A MINOR ACCIDENT -- I'M STILL RECOVERING. NOTHING TO WORRY ABOUT.
AH, TONY --
--I DON'T KNOW IF YOU'VE HEARD, BUT FUJIKAWA'S JUST MADE ME HEAD OF NORTH AMERICAN OPERATIONS. OF THE STARK COMPANIES.
I SUPPOSE THEY WANTED A STARK AT THE HELM, ONE WAY OR ANOTHER. BUT, WELL -- I KNOW YOU'RE THINKING OF CHALLENGING THE SALE --
-- BUT THIS IS A MAJOR OPPORTUNITY FOR ME, AND I'D, AH, CONSIDER IT A PERSONAL FAVOR IF YOU DIDN'T... UPSET THE APPLECART, AS IT WERE.
I'LL THINK ABOUT IT, MORGAN.
REALLY, I KNOW IT'S A BIG THING TO ASK, BUT --
I SAID I'LL THINK ABOUT IT. NOW, IF YOU'LL EXCUSE ME...
SOMETIMES IT SEEMS LIKE EVERYONE KNOWS EXACTLY WHAT I SHOULD DO -- AND IT'S WHATEVER'S IN THEIR BEST INTERESTS.
NOTHING NEW ABOUT THAT, OF COURSE. IT'S BEEN HAPPENING MY WHOLE LIFE.
USUALLY, I CAN JUST SHRUG IT OFF. FIGURE OUT WHAT I THINK IS BEST, AND DO THAT. THE TROUBLE IS, I DON'T KNOW WHAT'S BEST, NOT THIS TIME.
I DON'T KNOW WHAT I SHOULD DO...

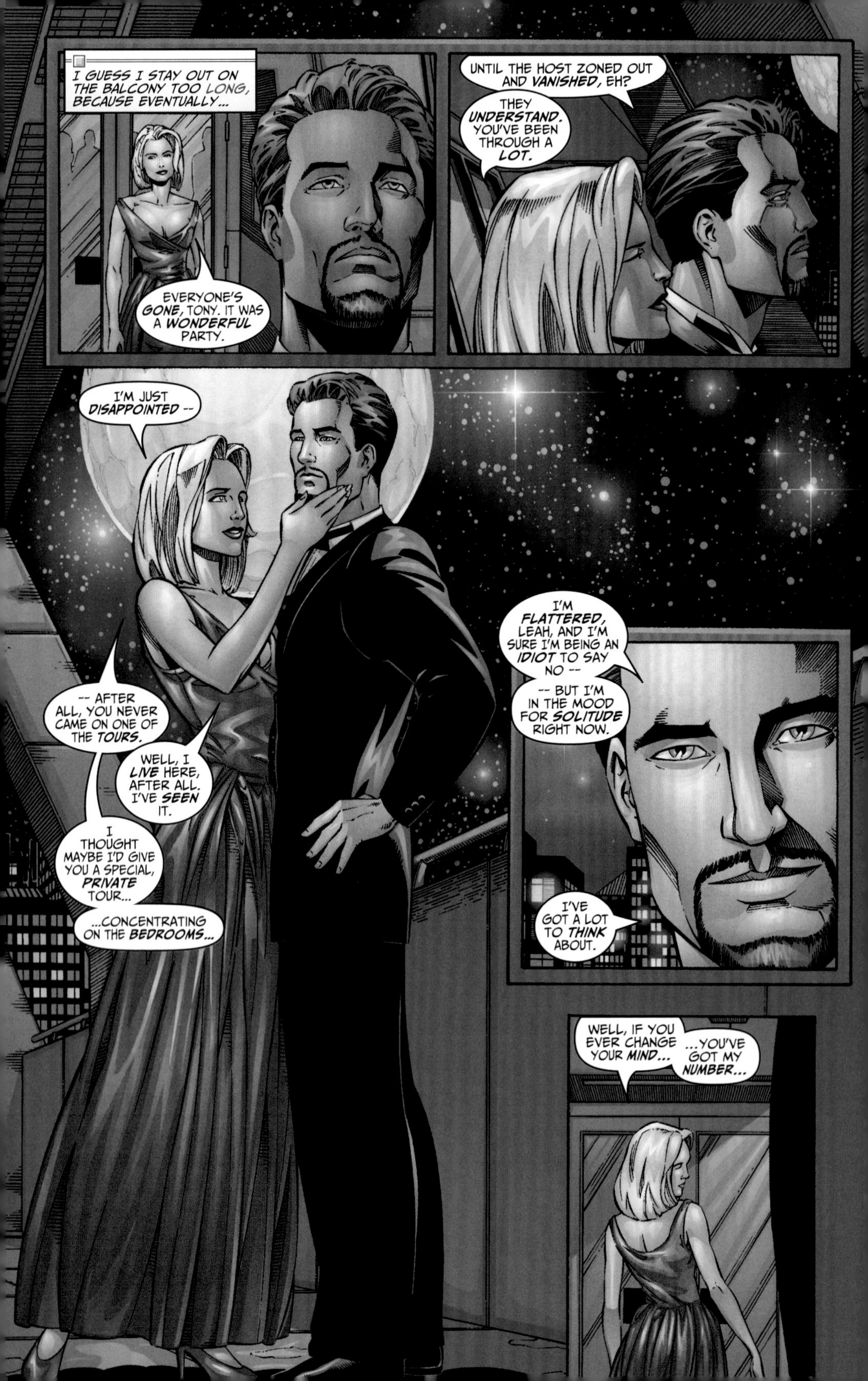
I GUESS I STAY OUT ON THE BALCONY TOO LONG, BECAUSE EVENTUALLY...
EVERYONE'S GONE, TONY. IT WAS A WONDERFUL PARTY.
UNTIL THE HOST ZONED OUT AND VANISHED, EH?
THEY UNDERSTAND. YOU'VE BEEN THROUGH A LOT.
I'M JUST DISAPPOINTED --
-- AFTER ALL, YOU NEVER CAME ON ONE OF THE TOURS.
WELL, I LIVE HERE, AFTER ALL. I'VE SEEN IT.
I THOUGHT MAYBE I'D GIVE YOU A SPECIAL, PRIVATE TOUR...
...CONCENTRATING ON THE BEDROOMS...
I'M FLATTERED, LEAH, AND I'M SURE I'M BEING AN IDIOT TO SAY NO --
-- BUT I'M IN THE MOOD FOR SOLITUDE RIGHT NOW.
I'VE GOT A LOT TO THINK ABOUT.
WELL, IF YOU EVER CHANGE YOUR MIND...
...YOU'VE GOT MY NUMBER...

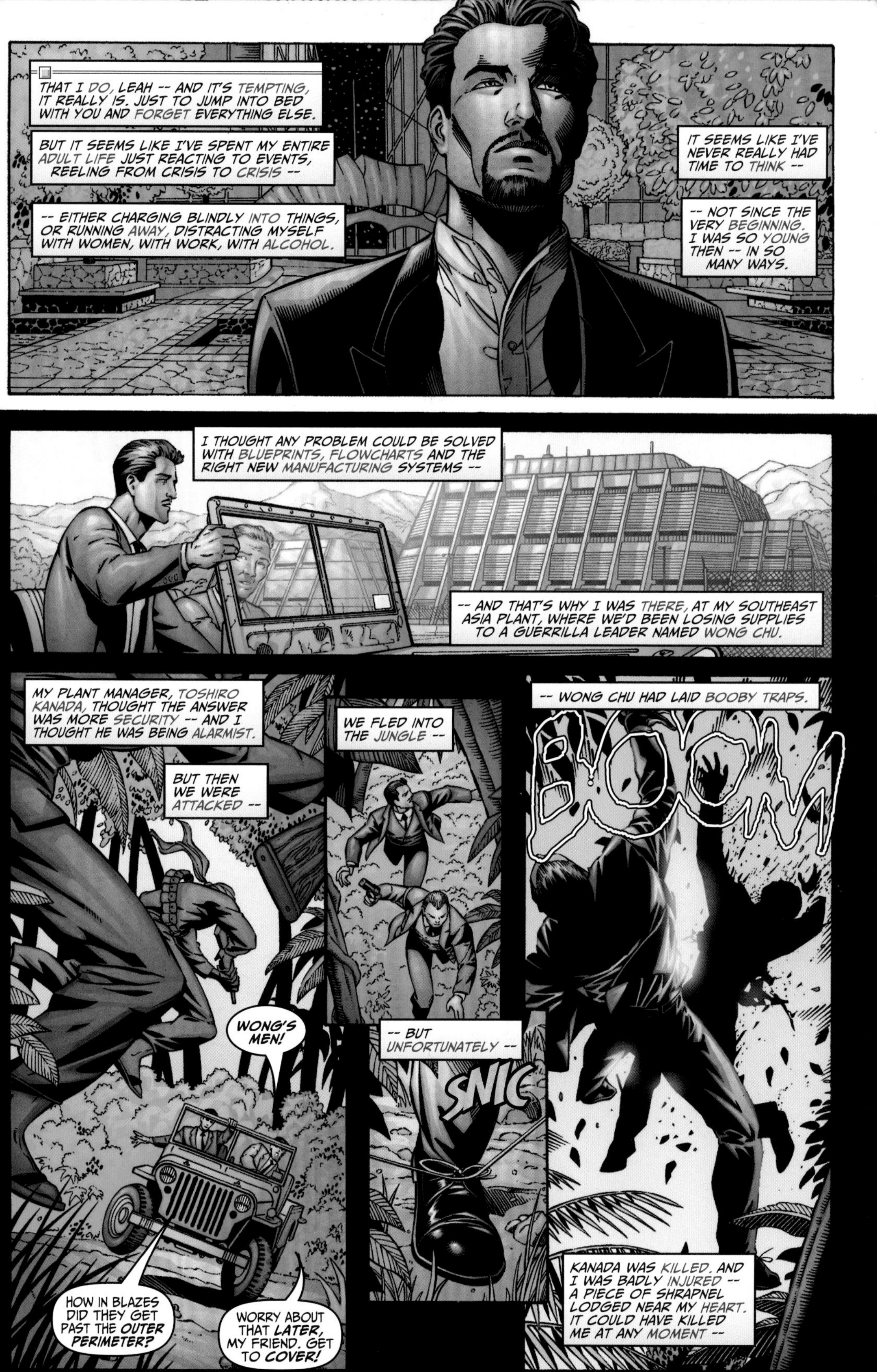
THAT I DO, LEAH -- AND IT'S TEMPTING, IT REALLY IS. JUST TO JUMP INTO BED WITH YOU AND FORGET EVERYTHING ELSE.
BUT IT SEEMS LIKE I'VE SPENT MY ENTIRE ADULT LIFE JUST REACTING TO EVENTS, REELING FROM CRISIS TO CRISIS --
-- EITHER CHARGING BLINDLY INTO THINGS, OR RUNNING AWAY, DISTRACTING MYSELF WITH WOMEN, WITH WORK, WITH ALCOHOL.
IT SEEMS LIKE I'VE NEVER REALLY HAD TIME TO THINK --
-- NOT SINCE THE VERY BEGINNING. I WAS SO YOUNG THEN -- IN SO MANY WAYS.
I THOUGHT ANY PROBLEM COULD BE SOLVED WITH BLUEPRINTS, FLOWCHARTS AND THE RIGHT NEW MANUFACTURING SYSTEMS --
-- AND THAT'S WHY I WAS THERE, AT MY SOUTHEAST ASIA PLANT, WHERE WE'D BEEN LOSING SUPPLIES TO A GUERRILLA LEADER NAMED WONG CHU.
MY PLANT MANAGER, TOSHIRO KANADA, THOUGHT THE ANSWER WAS MORE SECURITY -- AND I THOUGHT HE WAS BEING ALARMIST.
BUT THEN WE WERE ATTACKED --
WONG'S MEN!
HOW IN BLAZES DID THEY GET PAST THE OUTER PERIMETER?
WORRY ABOUT THAT LATER, MY FRIEND. GET TO COVER!
WE FLED INTO THE JUNGLE --
-- BUT UNFORTUNATELY --
SNIC
-- WONG CHU HAD LAID BOOBY TRAPS.
BOOM
KANADA WAS KILLED. AND I WAS BADLY INJURED -- A PIECE OF SHRAPNEL LODGED NEAR MY HEART. IT COULD HAVE KILLED ME AT ANY MOMENT --

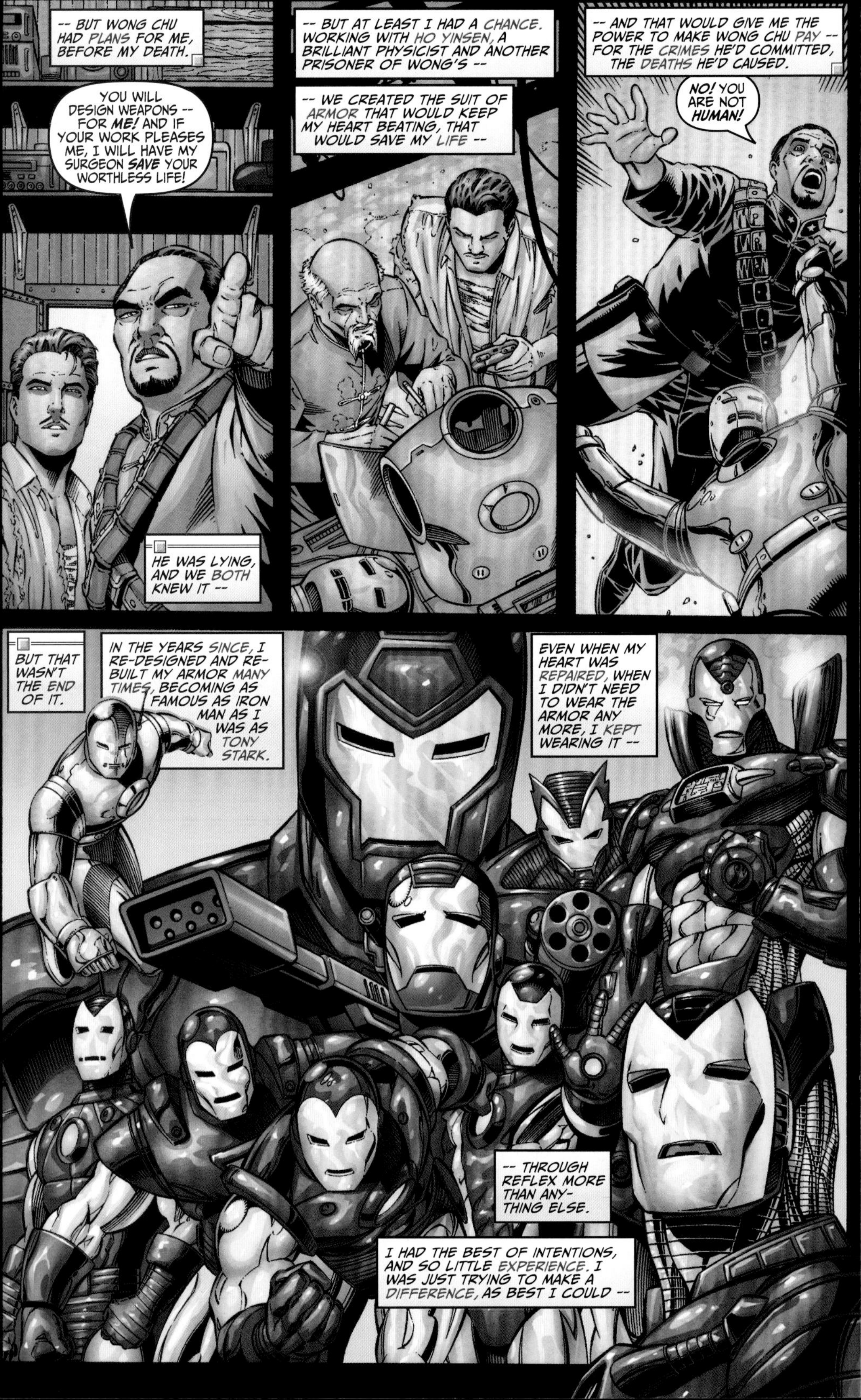
-- BUT WONG CHU HAD PLANS FOR ME, BEFORE MY DEATH.
YOU WILL DESIGN WEAPONS -- FOR ME! AND IF YOUR WORK PLEASES ME, I WILL HAVE MY SURGEON SAVE YOUR WORTHLESS LIFE!
HE WAS LYING, AND WE BOTH KNEW IT --
-- BUT AT LEAST I HAD A CHANCE. WORKING WITH HO YINSEN, A BRILLIANT PHYSICIST AND ANOTHER PRISONER OF WONG'S --
-- WE CREATED THE SUIT OF ARMOR THAT WOULD KEEP MY HEART BEATING, THAT WOULD SAVE MY LIFE --
-- AND THAT WOULD GIVE ME THE POWER TO MAKE WONG CHU PAY -- FOR THE CRIMES HE'D COMMITTED, THE DEATHS HE'D CAUSED.
NO! YOU ARE NOT HUMAN!
BUT THAT WASN'T THE END OF IT.
IN THE YEARS SINCE, I RE-DESIGNED AND RE-BUILT MY ARMOR MANY TIMES, BECOMING AS FAMOUS AS IRON MAN AS I WAS AS TONY STARK.
EVEN WHEN MY HEART WAS REPAIRED, WHEN I DIDN'T NEED TO WEAR THE ARMOR ANY MORE, I KEPT WEARING IT --
-- THROUGH REFLEX MORE THAN ANY-THING ELSE.
I HAD THE BEST OF INTENTIONS, AND SO LITTLE EXPERIENCE. I WAS JUST TRYING TO MAKE A DIFFERENCE, AS BEST I COULD --

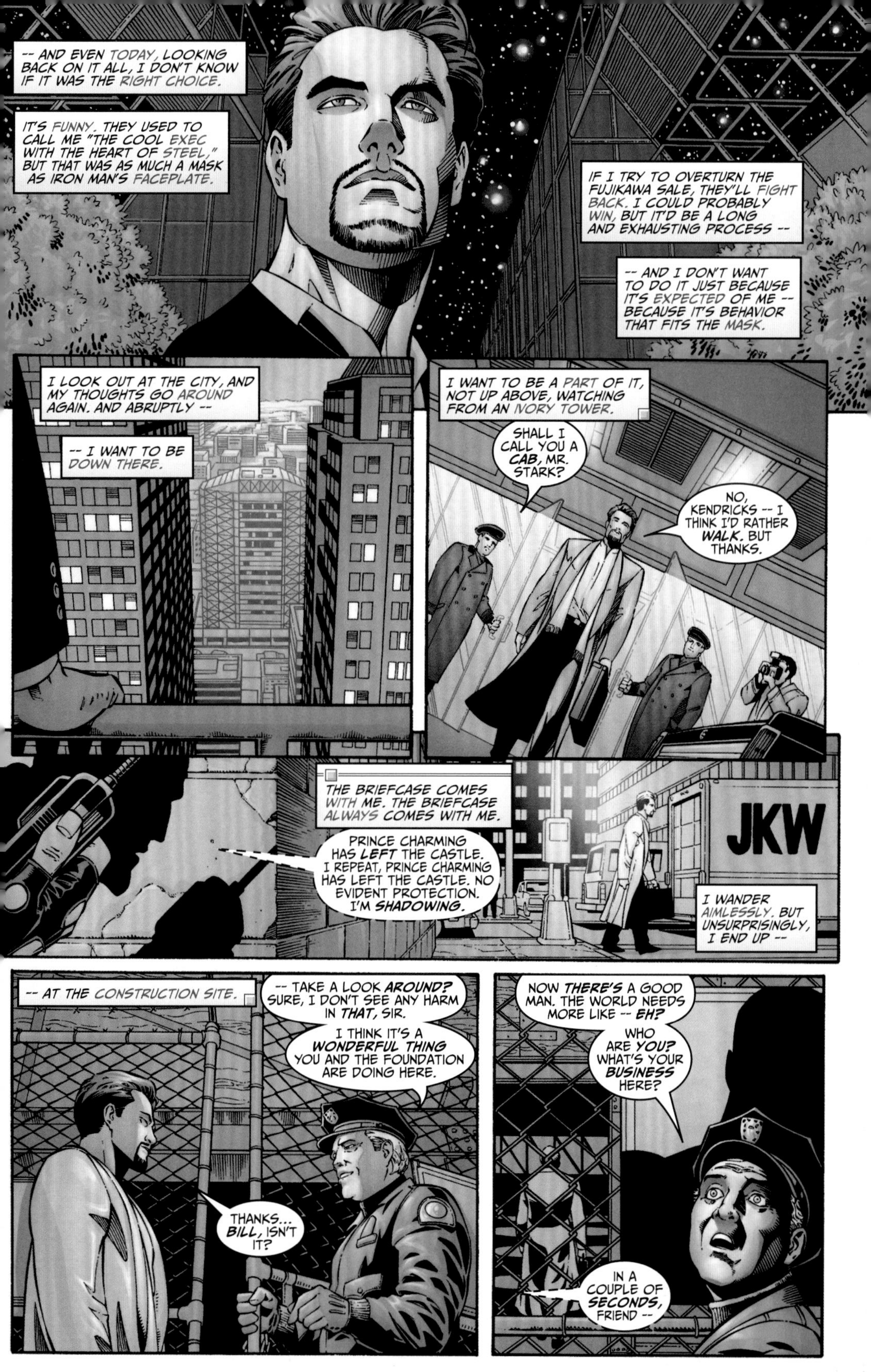

-- AND EVEN TODAY, LOOKING BACK ON IT ALL, I DON'T KNOW IF IT WAS THE RIGHT CHOICE.
IT'S FUNNY. THEY USED TO CALL ME "THE COOL EXEC WITH THE HEART OF STEEL," BUT THAT WAS AS MUCH A MASK AS IRON MAN'S FACEPLATE.
IF I TRY TO OVERTURN THE FUJIKAWA SALE, THEY'LL FIGHT BACK. I COULD PROBABLY WIN, BUT IT'D BE A LONG AND EXHAUSTING PROCESS --
-- AND I DON'T WANT TO DO IT JUST BECAUSE IT'S EXPECTED OF ME -- BECAUSE IT'S BEHAVIOR THAT FITS THE MASK.
I LOOK OUT AT THE CITY, AND MY THOUGHTS GO AROUND AGAIN. AND ABRUPTLY --
-- I WANT TO BE DOWN THERE.
I WANT TO BE A PART OF IT, NOT UP ABOVE, WATCHING FROM AN IVORY TOWER.
SHALL I CALL YOU A CAB, MR. STARK?
NO, KENDRICKS -- I THINK I'D RATHER WALK. BUT THANKS.
THE BRIEFCASE COMES WITH ME. THE BRIEFCASE ALWAYS COMES WITH ME.
PRINCE CHARMING HAS LEFT THE CASTLE. I REPEAT, PRINCE CHARMING HAS LEFT THE CASTLE. NO EVIDENT PROTECTION. I'M SHADOWING.
JKW
I WANDER AIMLESSLY. BUT UNSURPRISINGLY, I END UP --
-- AT THE CONSTRUCTION SITE.
-- TAKE A LOOK AROUND? SURE, I DON'T SEE ANY HARM IN THAT, SIR.
I THINK IT'S A WONDERFUL THING YOU AND THE FOUNDATION ARE DOING HERE.
THANKS... BILL, ISN'T IT?
NOW THERE'S A GOOD MAN. THE WORLD NEEDS MORE LIKE -- EH?
WHO ARE YOU? WHAT'S YOUR BUSINESS HERE?
IN A COUPLE OF SECONDS, FRIEND --

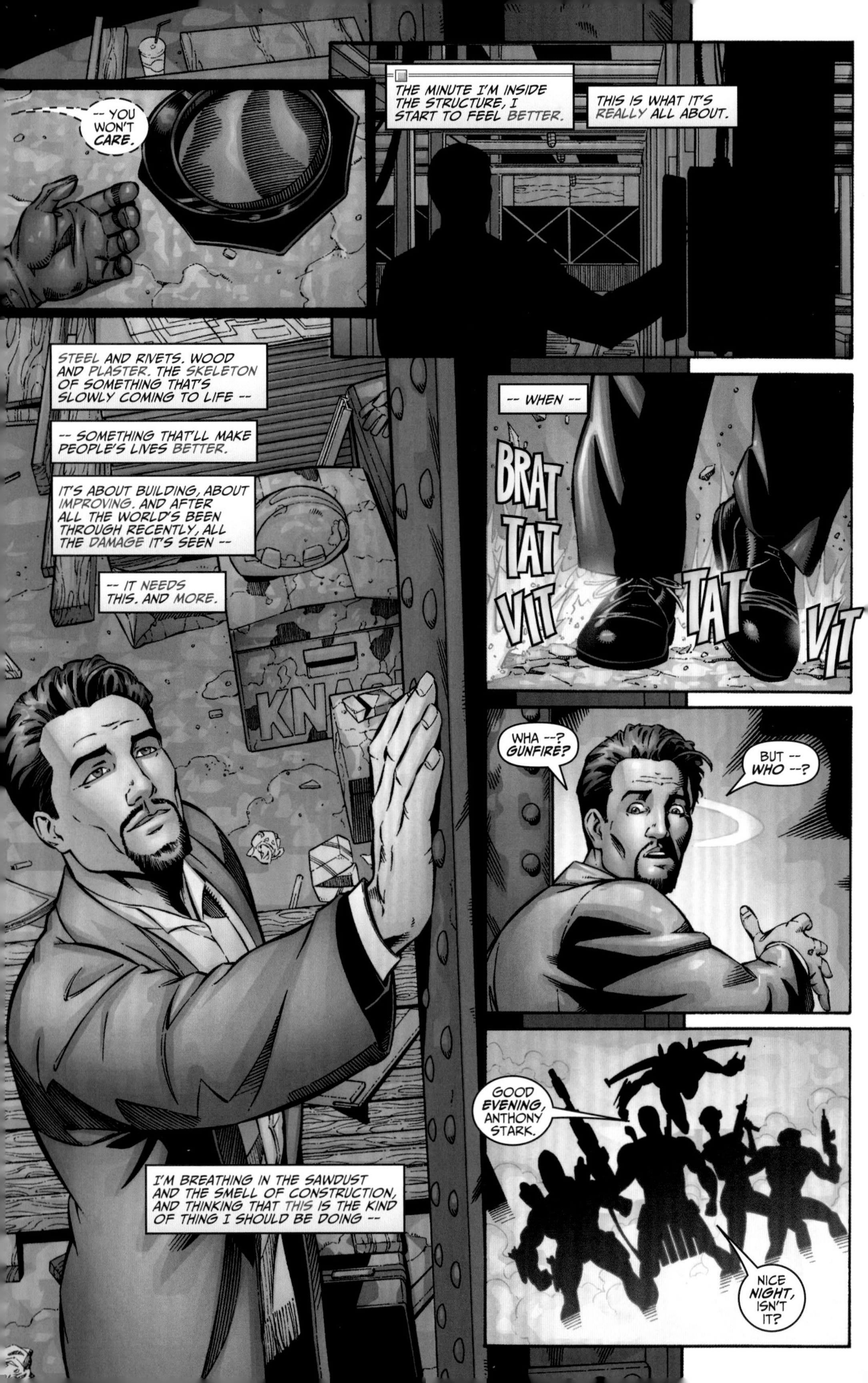
-- YOU WON'T CARE.
THE MINUTE I'M INSIDE THE STRUCTURE, I START TO FEEL BETTER.
THIS IS WHAT IT'S REALLY ALL ABOUT.
STEEL AND RIVETS. WOOD AND PLASTER. THE SKELETON OF SOMETHING THAT'S SLOWLY COMING TO LIFE --
-- SOMETHING THAT'LL MAKE PEOPLE'S LIVES BETTER.
IT'S ABOUT BUILDING, ABOUT IMPROVING. AND AFTER ALL THE WORLD'S BEEN THROUGH RECENTLY, ALL THE DAMAGE IT'S SEEN --
-- IT NEEDS THIS. AND MORE.
I'M BREATHING IN THE SAWDUST AND THE SMELL OF CONSTRUCTION, AND THINKING THAT THIS IS THE KIND OF THING I SHOULD BE DOING --
-- WHEN --
BRAT TAT VIT
TAT
VIT
WHA --? GUNFIRE?
BUT -- WHO --?
GOOD EVENING, ANTHONY STARK.
NICE NIGHT, ISN'T IT?

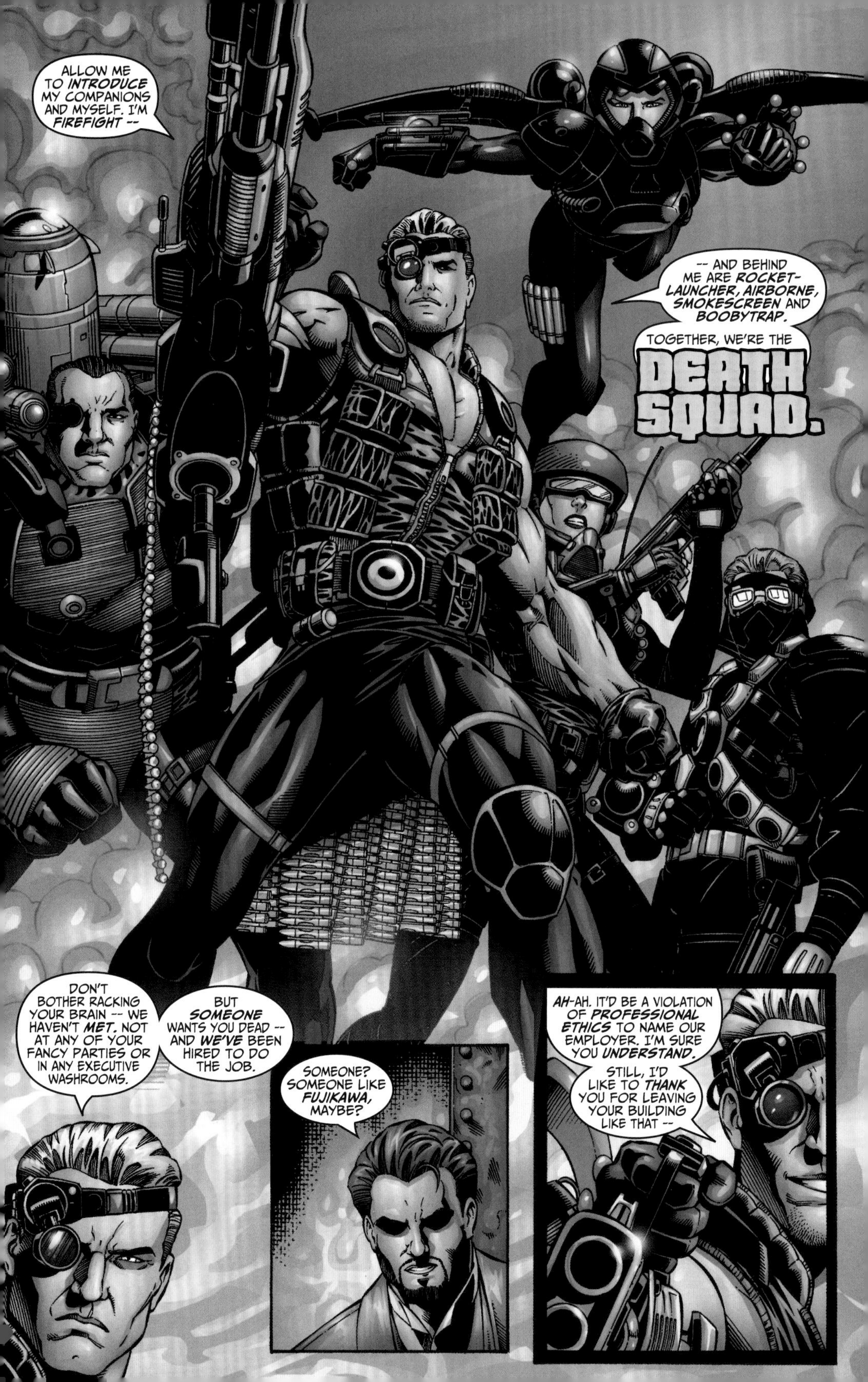
ALLOW ME TO INTRODUCE MY COMPANIONS AND MYSELF. I'M FIREFIGHT --
-- AND BEHIND ME ARE ROCKET-LAUNCHER, AIRBORNE, SMOKESCREEN AND BOOBYTRAP.
TOGETHER, WE'RE THE
DEATH SQUAD.
DON'T BOTHER RACKING YOUR BRAIN -- WE HAVEN'T MET. NOT AT ANY OF YOUR FANCY PARTIES OR IN ANY EXECUTIVE WASHROOMS.
BUT SOMEONE WANTS YOU DEAD -- AND WE'VE BEEN HIRED TO DO THE JOB.
SOMEONE? SOMEONE LIKE FUJIKAWA, MAYBE?
AH-AH. IT'D BE A VIOLATION OF PROFESSIONAL ETHICS TO NAME OUR EMPLOYER. I'M SURE YOU UNDERSTAND.
STILL, I'D LIKE TO THANK YOU FOR LEAVING YOUR BUILDING LIKE THAT --

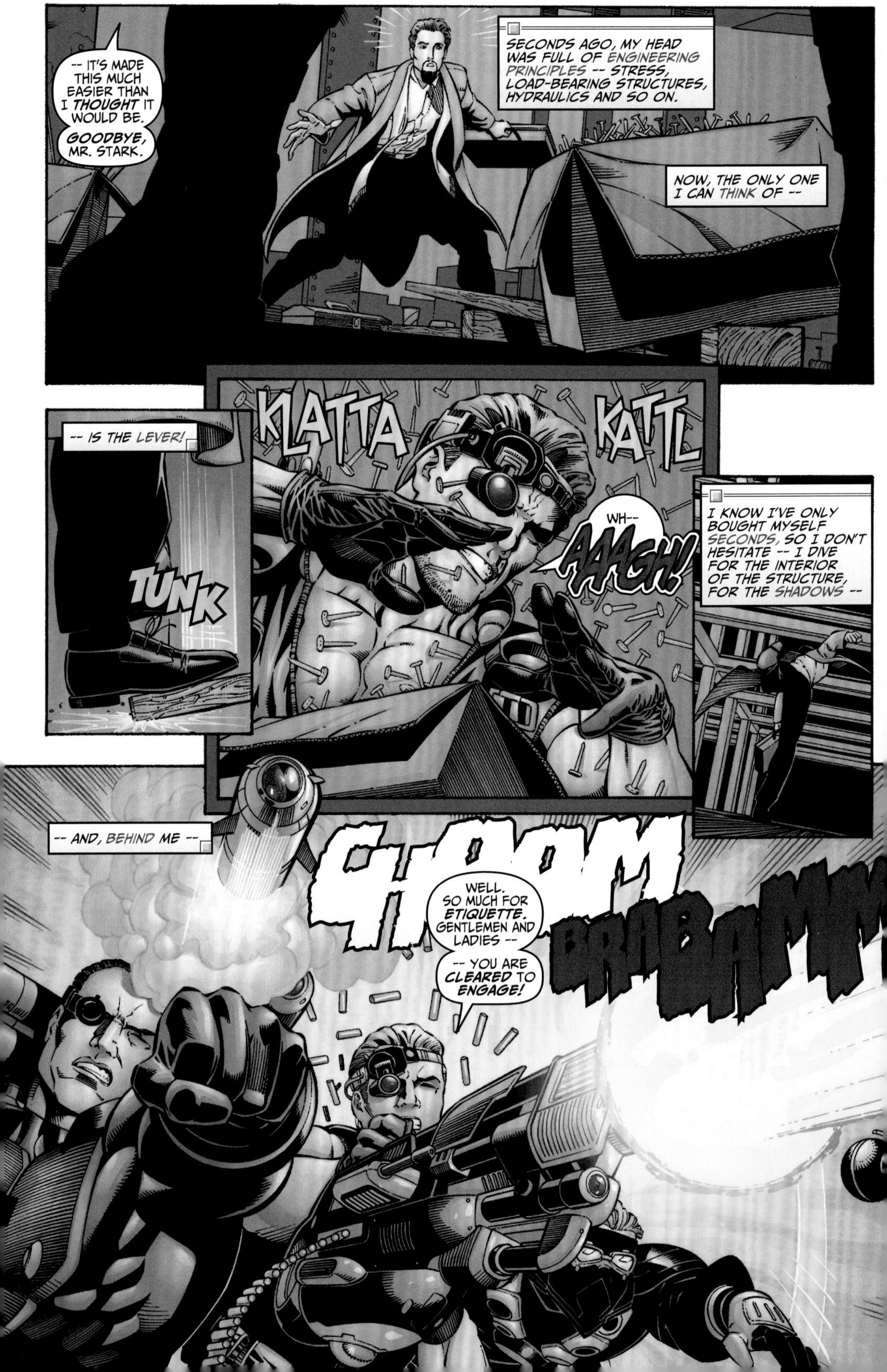
-- IT'S MADE THIS MUCH EASIER THAN I THOUGHT IT WOULD BE.
GOODBYE, MR. STARK.
SECONDS AGO, MY HEAD WAS FULL OF ENGINEERING PRINCIPLES -- STRESS, LOAD-BEARING STRUCTURES, HYDRAULICS AND SO ON.
NOW, THE ONLY ONE I CAN THINK OF --
-- IS THE LEVER!
TUNK
KLATTA
KATTL
WH--
AAAGH!
I KNOW I'VE ONLY BOUGHT MYSELF SECONDS, SO I DON'T HESITATE -- I DIVE FOR THE INTERIOR OF THE STRUCTURE, FOR THE SHADOWS --
-- AND, BEHIND ME --
WELL. SO MUCH FOR ETIQUETTE. GENTLEMEN AND LADIES --
-- YOU ARE CLEARED TO ENGAGE!

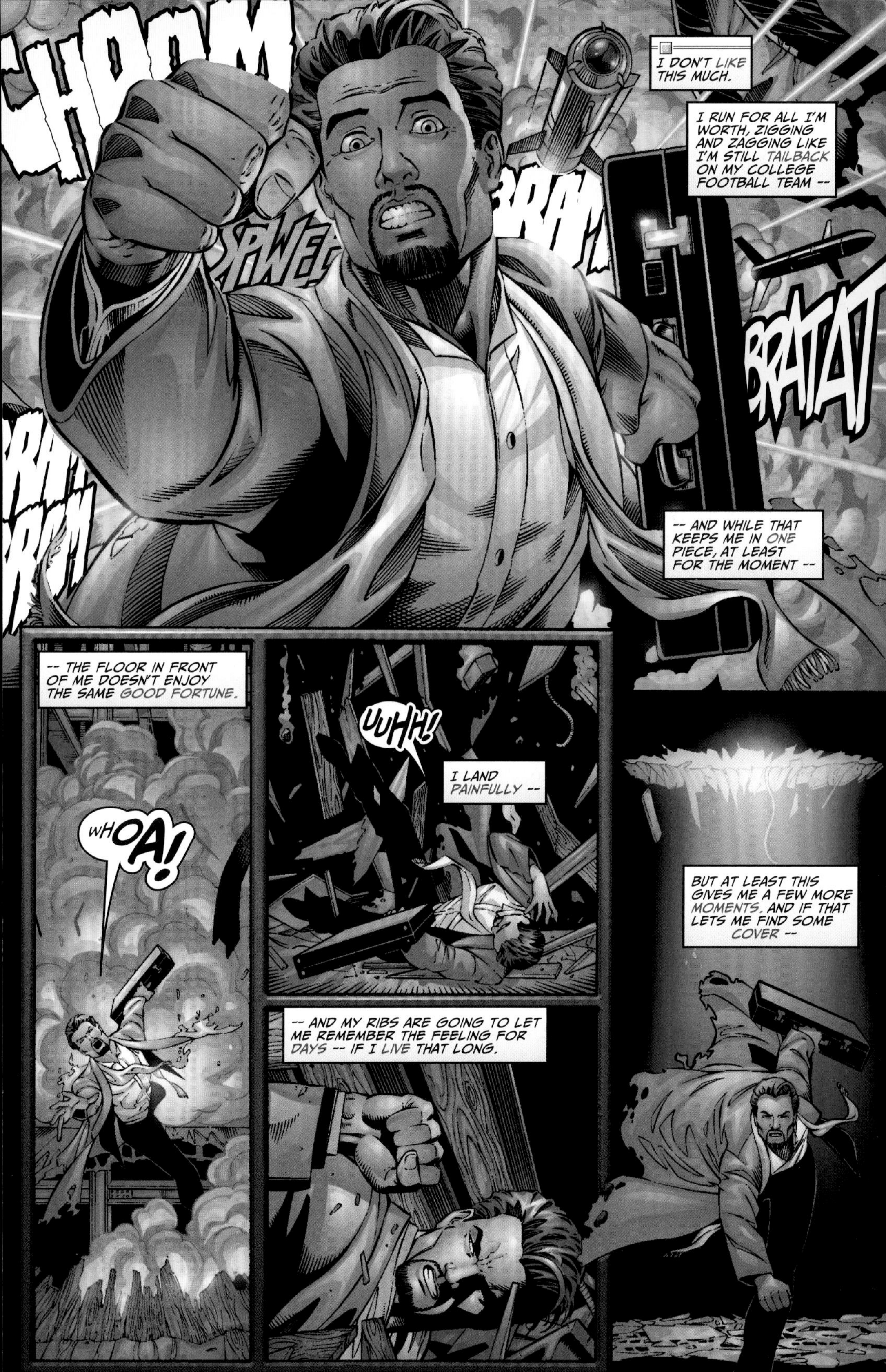
CHOOM
I DON'T LIKE THIS MUCH.
I RUN FOR ALL I'M WORTH, ZIGGING AND ZAGGING LIKE I'M STILL TAILBACK ON MY COLLEGE FOOTBALL TEAM --
BRATAT
-- AND WHILE THAT KEEPS ME IN ONE PIECE, AT LEAST FOR THE MOMENT --
-- THE FLOOR IN FRONT OF ME DOESN'T ENJOY THE SAME GOOD FORTUNE.
WHOA!
UUHH!
I LAND PAINFULLY --
-- AND MY RIBS ARE GOING TO LET ME REMEMBER THE FEELING FOR DAYS -- IF I LIVE THAT LONG.
BUT AT LEAST THIS GIVES ME A FEW MORE MOMENTS. AND IF THAT LETS ME FIND SOME COVER --

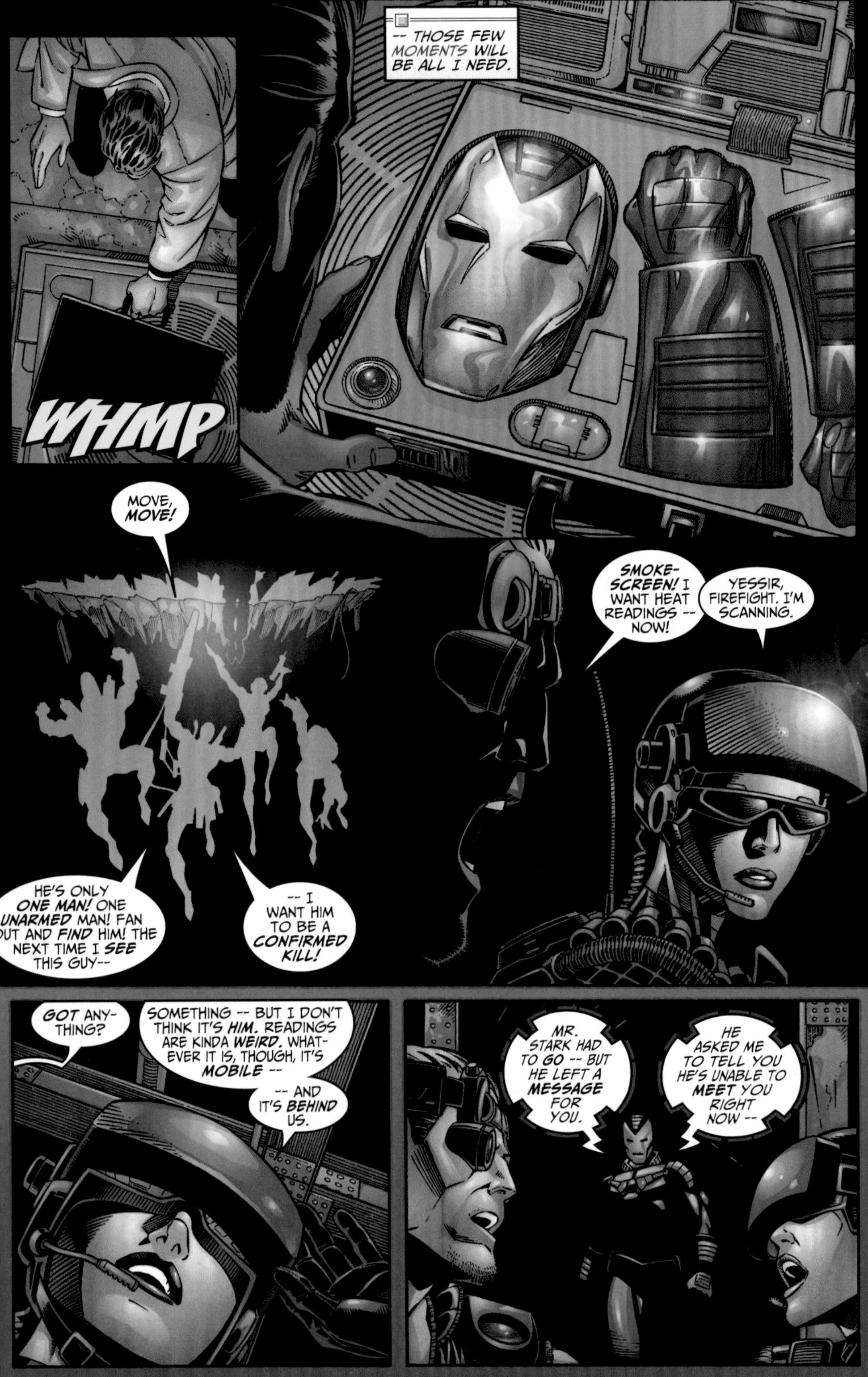
-- THOSE FEW MOMENTS WILL BE ALL I NEED.
WHMP
MOVE, MOVE!
HE'S ONLY ONE MAN! ONE UNARMED MAN! FAN OUT AND FIND HIM! THE NEXT TIME I SEE THIS GUY--
-- I WANT HIM TO BE A CONFIRMED KILL!
SMOKE-SCREEN! I WANT HEAT READINGS -- NOW!
YESSIR, FIREFIGHT. I'M SCANNING.
GOT ANY-THING?
SOMETHING -- BUT I DON'T THINK IT'S HIM. READINGS ARE KINDA WEIRD. WHAT-EVER IT IS, THOUGH, IT'S MOBILE --
-- AND IT'S BEHIND US.
MR. STARK HAD TO GO -- BUT HE LEFT A MESSAGE FOR YOU.
HE ASKED ME TO TELL YOU HE'S UNABLE TO MEET YOU RIGHT NOW --

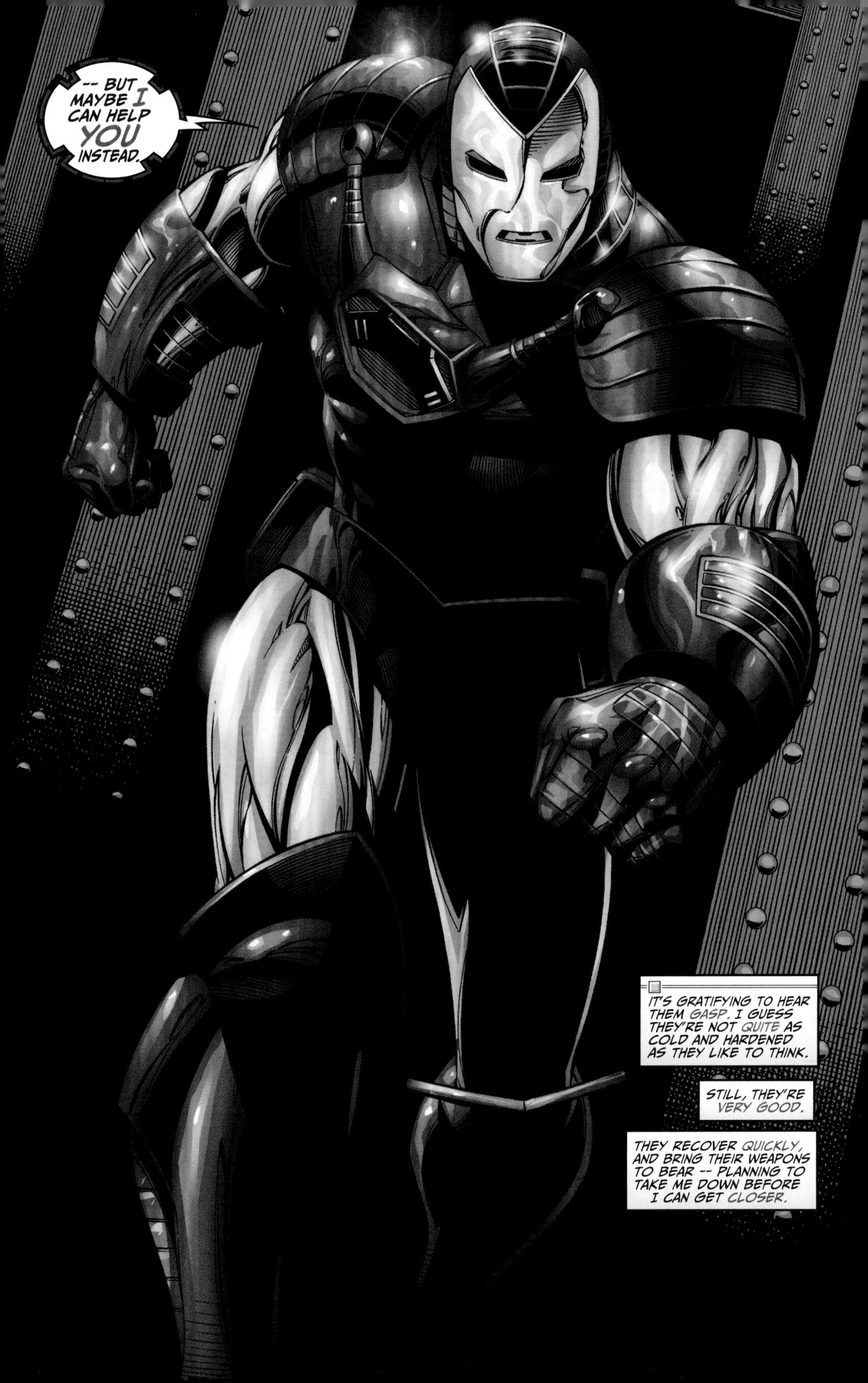
-- BUT MAYBE I CAN HELP YOU INSTEAD.
IT'S GRATIFYING TO HEAR THEM GASP. I GUESS THEY'RE NOT QUITE AS COLD AND HARDENED AS THEY LIKE TO THINK.
STILL, THEY'RE VERY GOOD.
THEY RECOVER QUICKLY, AND BRING THEIR WEAPONS TO BEAR -- PLANNING TO TAKE ME DOWN BEFORE I CAN GET CLOSER.

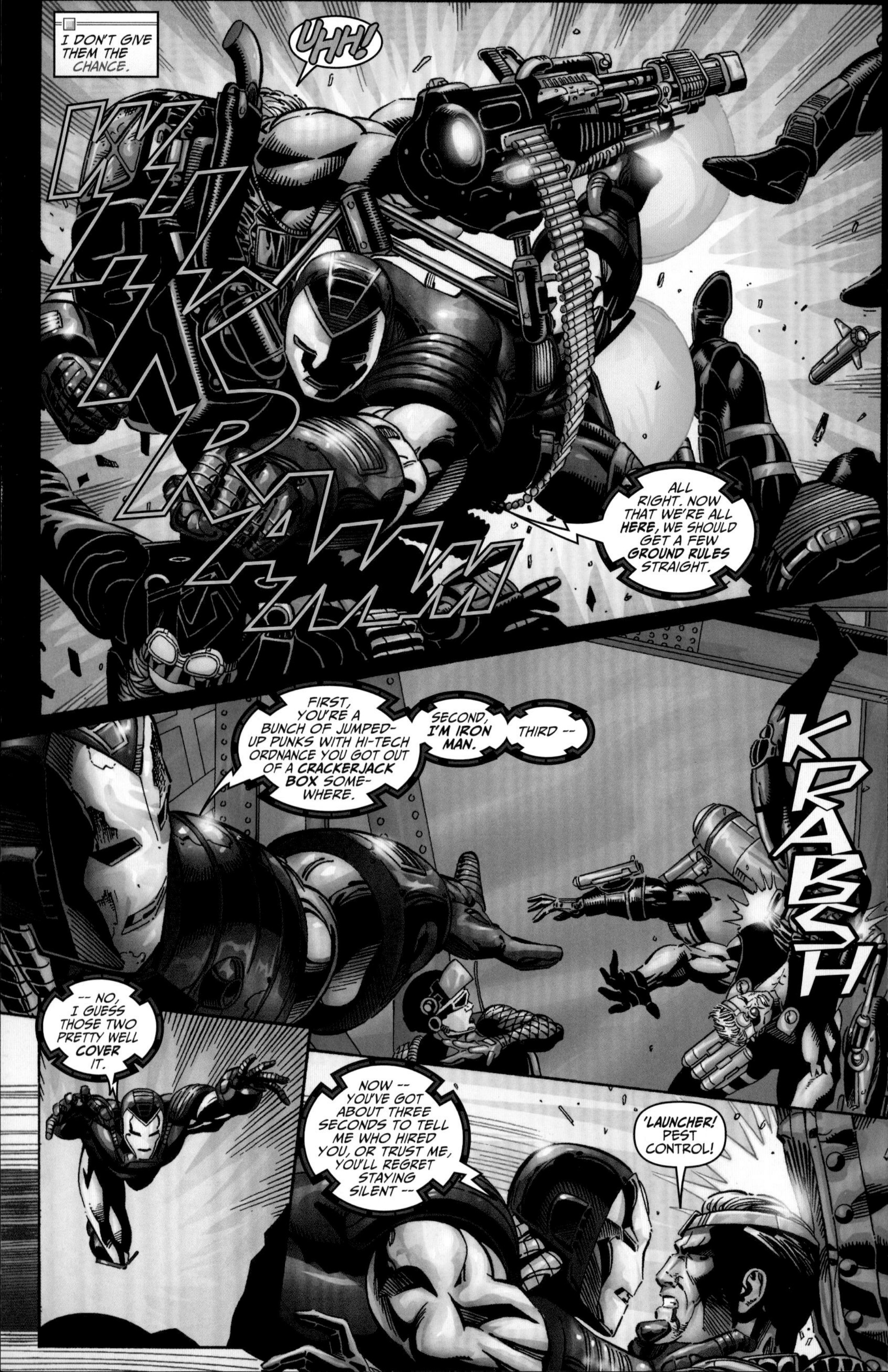
I DON'T GIVE THEM THE CHANCE.
UHH!
WHHRAMM
ALL RIGHT. NOW THAT WE'RE ALL HERE, WE SHOULD GET A FEW GROUND RULES STRAIGHT.
FIRST, YOU'RE A BUNCH OF JUMPED-UP PUNKS WITH HI-TECH ORDNANCE YOU GOT OUT OF A CRACKERJACK BOX SOME-WHERE.
SECOND, I'M IRON MAN.
THIRD --
KRABSH
-- NO, I GUESS THOSE TWO PRETTY WELL COVER IT.
NOW -- YOU'VE GOT ABOUT THREE SECONDS TO TELL ME WHO HIRED YOU, OR TRUST ME, YOU'LL REGRET STAYING SILENT --
'LAUNCHER! PEST CONTROL!

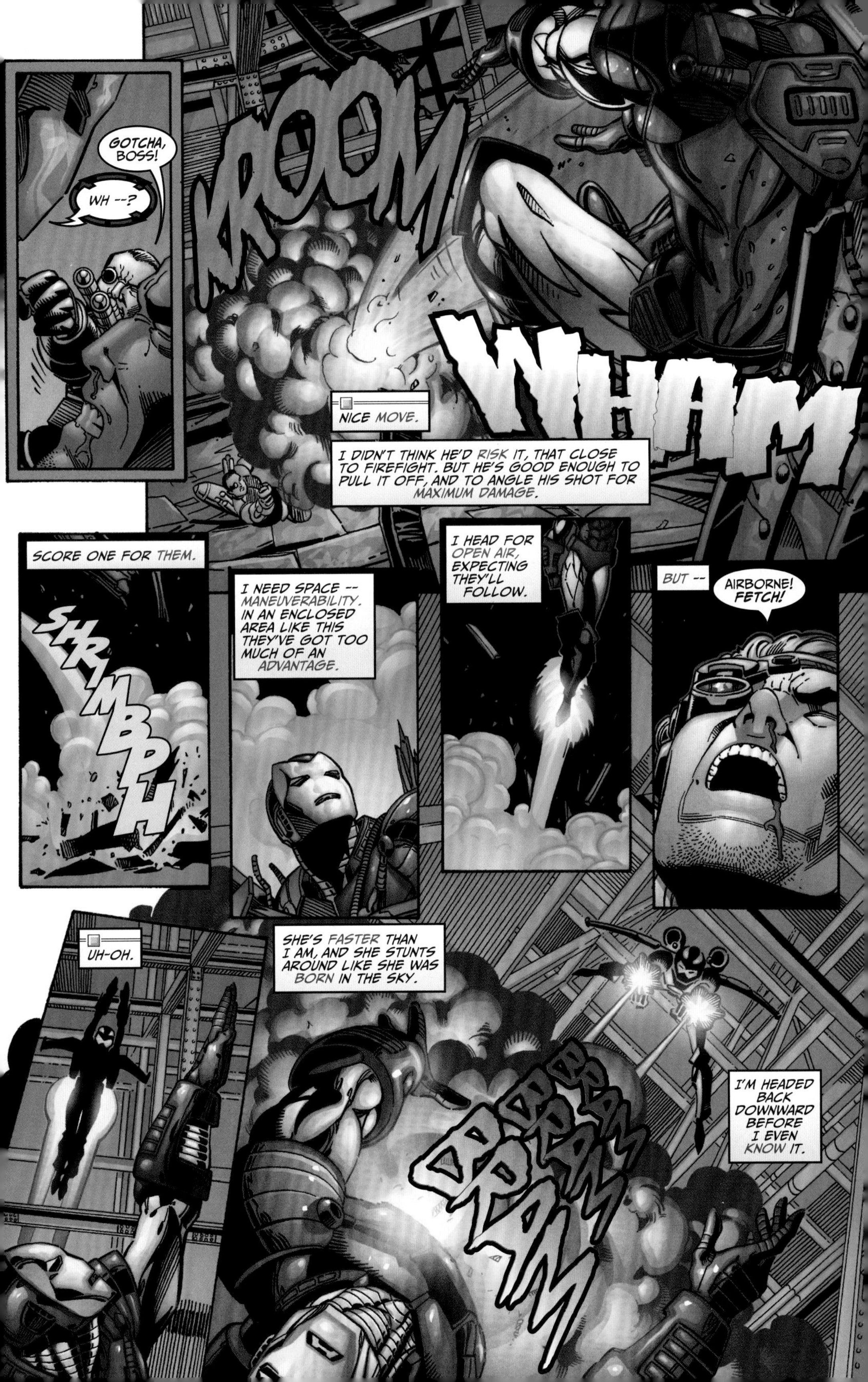
GOTCHA, BOSS!
WH --?
KROOM
WHAM
NICE MOVE.
I DIDN'T THINK HE'D RISK IT, THAT CLOSE TO FIREFIGHT. BUT HE'S GOOD ENOUGH TO PULL IT OFF, AND TO ANGLE HIS SHOT FOR MAXIMUM DAMAGE.
SCORE ONE FOR THEM.
SHRIMBDH
I NEED SPACE -- MANEUVERABILITY. IN AN ENCLOSED AREA LIKE THIS THEY'VE GOT TOO MUCH OF AN ADVANTAGE.
I HEAD FOR OPEN AIR, EXPECTING THEY'LL FOLLOW.
BUT --
AIRBORNE! FETCH!
UH-OH.
SHE'S FASTER THAN I AM, AND SHE STUNTS AROUND LIKE SHE WAS BORN IN THE SKY.
BRAM BRAM BRAM
I'M HEADED BACK DOWNWARD BEFORE I EVEN KNOW IT.

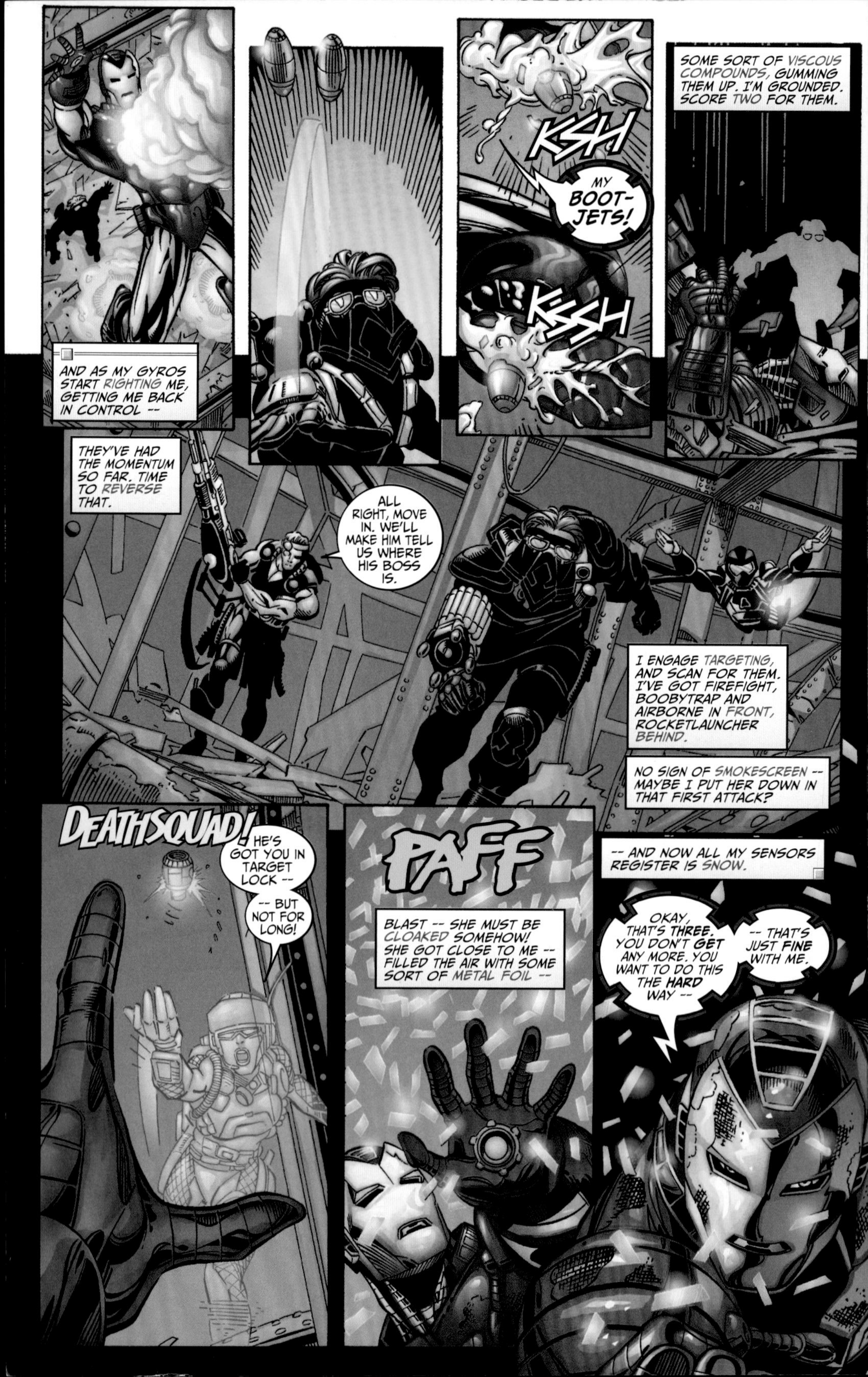
AND AS MY GYROS START RIGHTING ME, GETTING ME BACK IN CONTROL --
KSH
MY BOOT-JETS!
KSSH
SOME SORT OF VISCOUS COMPOUNDS, GUMMING THEM UP. I'M GROUNDED. SCORE TWO FOR THEM.
THEY'VE HAD THE MOMENTUM SO FAR. TIME TO REVERSE THAT.
ALL RIGHT, MOVE IN. WE'LL MAKE HIM TELL US WHERE HIS BOSS IS.
I ENGAGE TARGETING, AND SCAN FOR THEM. I'VE GOT FIREFIGHT, BOOBYTRAP AND AIRBORNE IN FRONT, ROCKETLAUNCHER BEHIND.
NO SIGN OF SMOKESCREEN -- MAYBE I PUT HER DOWN IN THAT FIRST ATTACK?
DEATHSQUAD!
HE'S GOT YOU IN TARGET LOCK --
-- BUT NOT FOR LONG!
PAFF
BLAST -- SHE MUST BE CLOAKED SOMEHOW! SHE GOT CLOSE TO ME -- FILLED THE AIR WITH SOME SORT OF METAL FOIL --
-- AND NOW ALL MY SENSORS REGISTER IS SNOW.
OKAY, THAT'S THREE. YOU DON'T GET ANY MORE. YOU WANT TO DO THIS THE HARD WAY --
-- THAT'S JUST FINE WITH ME.

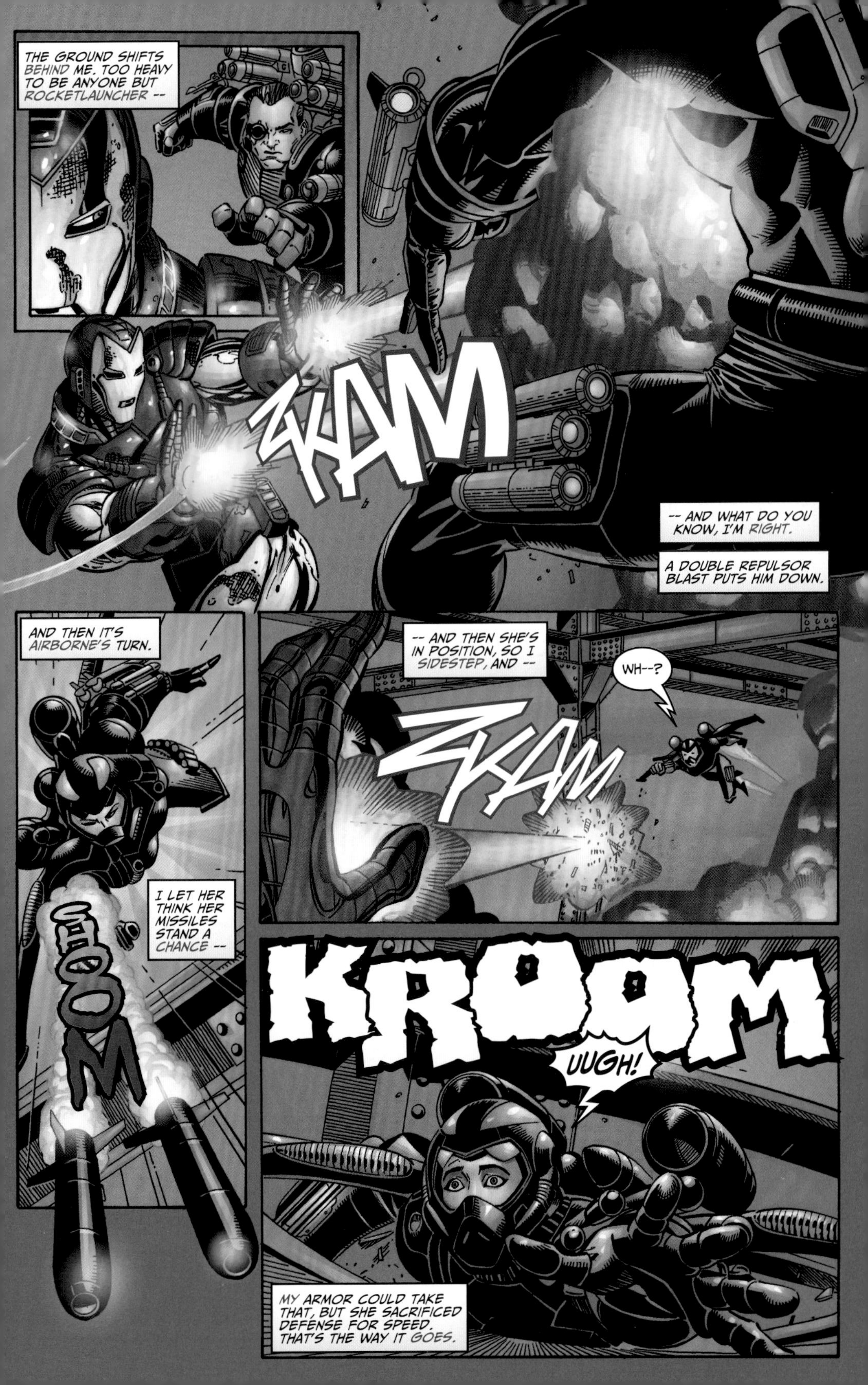
THE GROUND SHIFTS BEHIND ME. TOO HEAVY TO BE ANYONE BUT ROCKETLAUNCHER --
ZKAM
-- AND WHAT DO YOU KNOW, I'M RIGHT.
A DOUBLE REPULSOR BLAST PUTS HIM DOWN.
AND THEN IT'S AIRBORNE'S TURN.
I LET HER THINK HER MISSILES STAND A CHANCE --
-- AND THEN SHE'S IN POSITION, SO I SIDESTEP, AND --
WH--?
ZKAM
KROOM
UUGH!
MY ARMOR COULD TAKE THAT, BUT SHE SACRIFICED DEFENSE FOR SPEED. THAT'S THE WAY IT GOES.

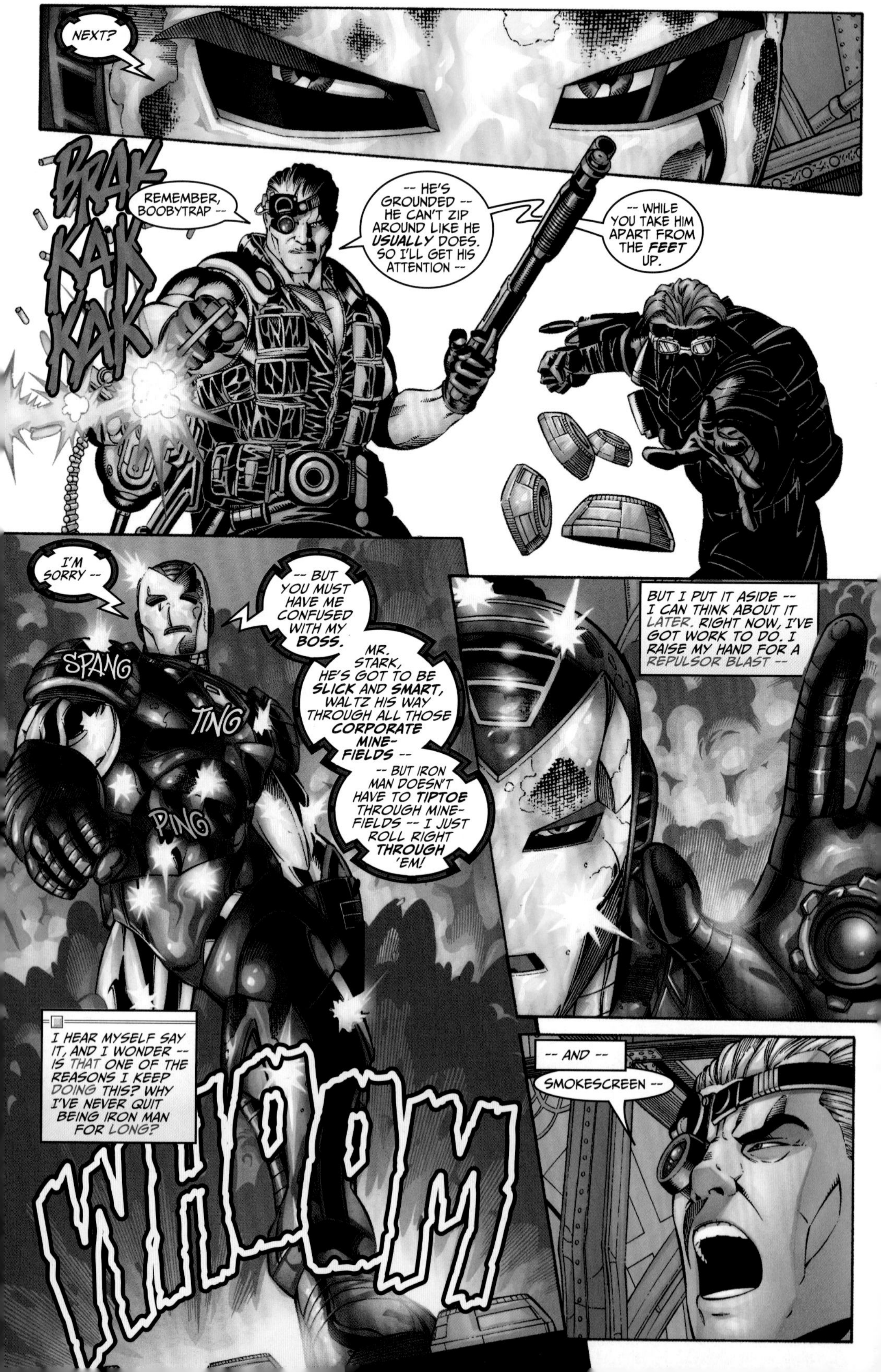
NEXT?
BRAK KAK KAK
REMEMBER, BOOBYTRAP --
-- HE'S GROUNDED -- HE CAN'T ZIP AROUND LIKE HE USUALLY DOES. SO I'LL GET HIS ATTENTION --
-- WHILE YOU TAKE HIM APART FROM THE FEET UP.
I'M SORRY --
-- BUT YOU MUST HAVE ME CONFUSED WITH MY BOSS.
SPANG
TING
PING
MR. STARK, HE'S GOT TO BE SLICK AND SMART, WALTZ HIS WAY THROUGH ALL THOSE CORPORATE MINE-FIELDS --
-- BUT IRON MAN DOESN'T HAVE TO TIPTOE THROUGH MINE-FIELDS -- I JUST ROLL RIGHT THROUGH 'EM!
I HEAR MYSELF SAY IT, AND I WONDER -- IS THAT ONE OF THE REASONS I KEEP DOING THIS? WHY I'VE NEVER QUIT BEING IRON MAN FOR LONG?
BUT I PUT IT ASIDE -- I CAN THINK ABOUT IT LATER. RIGHT NOW, I'VE GOT WORK TO DO. I RAISE MY HAND FOR A REPULSOR BLAST --
WHOOM
-- AND --
SMOKESCREEN --

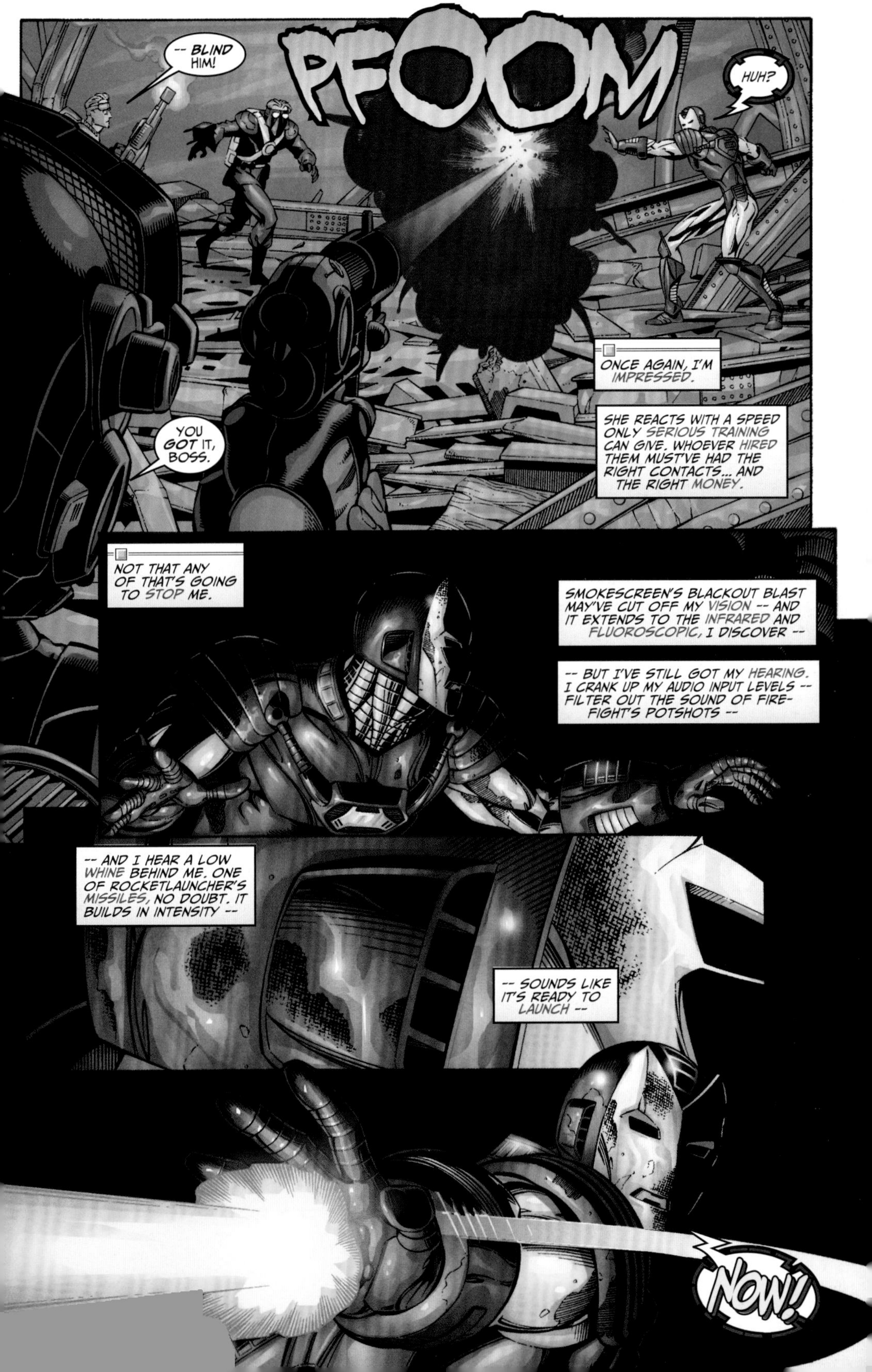

-- BLIND HIM!
PFOOM
HUH?
YOU GOT IT, BOSS.
ONCE AGAIN, I'M IMPRESSED.
SHE REACTS WITH A SPEED ONLY SERIOUS TRAINING CAN GIVE. WHOEVER HIRED THEM MUST'VE HAD THE RIGHT CONTACTS... AND THE RIGHT MONEY.
NOT THAT ANY OF THAT'S GOING TO STOP ME.
SMOKESCREEN'S BLACKOUT BLAST MAY'VE CUT OFF MY VISION -- AND IT EXTENDS TO THE INFRARED AND FLUOROSCOPIC, I DISCOVER --
-- BUT I'VE STILL GOT MY HEARING. I CRANK UP MY AUDIO INPUT LEVELS -- FILTER OUT THE SOUND OF FIRE-FIGHT'S POTSHOTS --
-- AND I HEAR A LOW WHINE BEHIND ME. ONE OF ROCKETLAUNCHER'S MISSILES, NO DOUBT. IT BUILDS IN INTENSITY --
-- SOUNDS LIKE IT'S READY TO LAUNCH --
NOW!

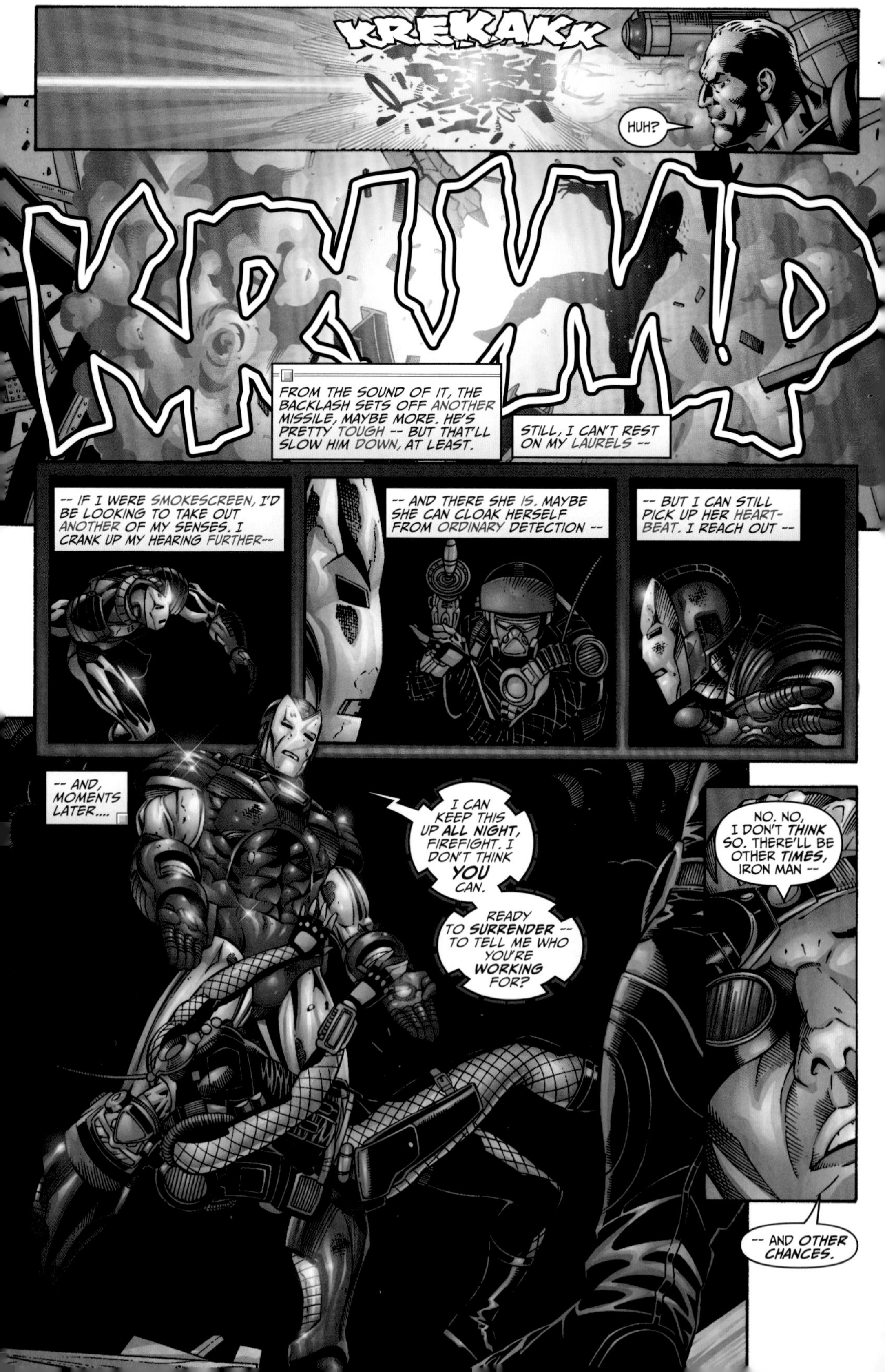
KREKAKK
HUH?
FROM THE SOUND OF IT, THE BACKLASH SETS OFF ANOTHER MISSILE, MAYBE MORE. HE'S PRETTY TOUGH -- BUT THAT'LL SLOW HIM DOWN, AT LEAST.
STILL, I CAN'T REST ON MY LAURELS --
-- IF I WERE SMOKESCREEN, I'D BE LOOKING TO TAKE OUT ANOTHER OF MY SENSES. I CRANK UP MY HEARING FURTHER--
-- AND THERE SHE IS. MAYBE SHE CAN CLOAK HERSELF FROM ORDINARY DETECTION --
-- BUT I CAN STILL PICK UP HER HEART-BEAT. I REACH OUT --
-- AND, MOMENTS LATER....
I CAN KEEP THIS UP ALL NIGHT, FIREFIGHT. I DON'T THINK YOU CAN.
READY TO SURRENDER -- TO TELL ME WHO YOU'RE WORKING FOR?
NO. NO, I DON'T THINK SO. THERE'LL BE OTHER TIMES, IRON MAN --
-- AND OTHER CHANCES.

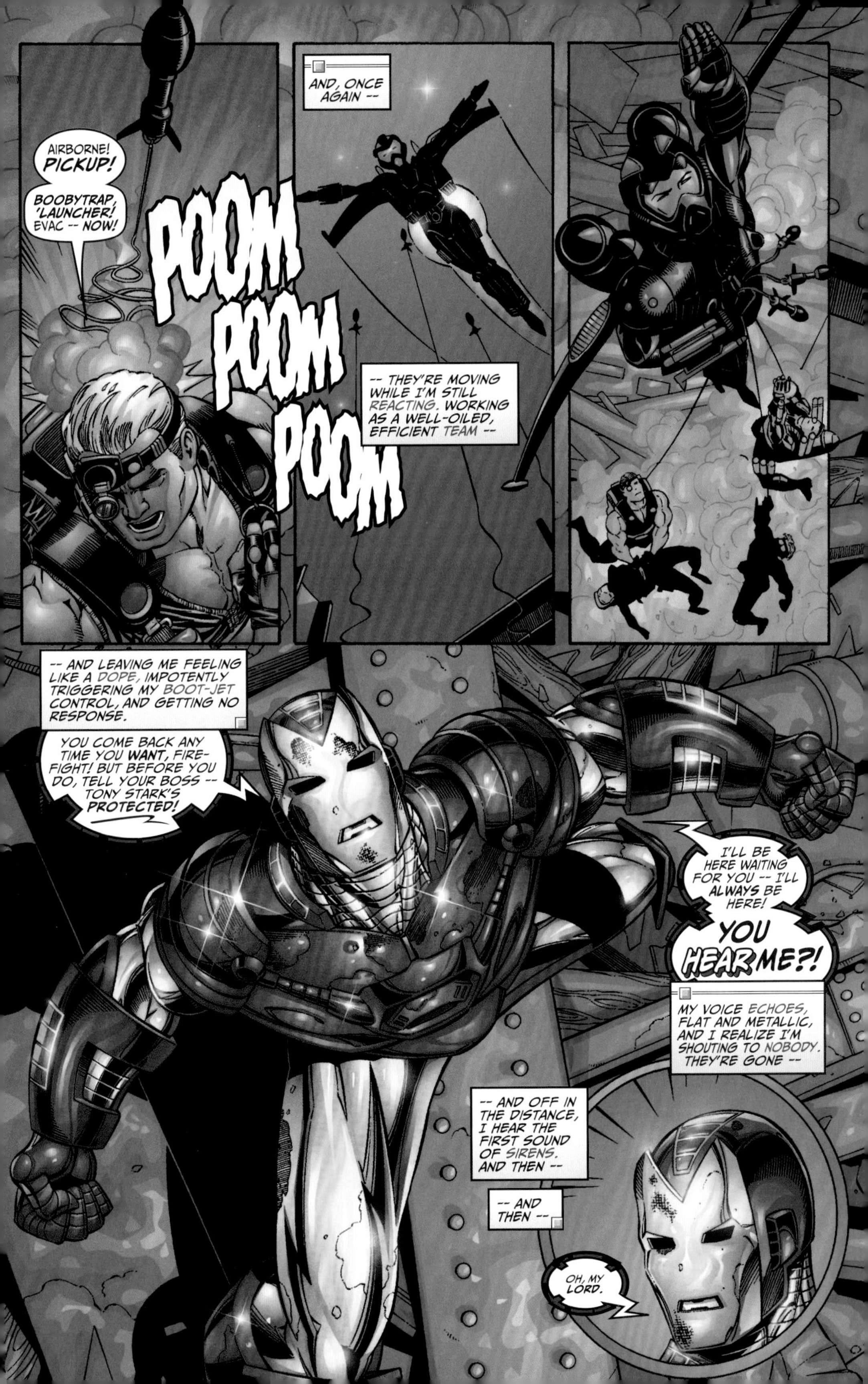
AIRBORNE! PICKUP!
BOOBYTRAP, 'LAUNCHER! EVAC -- NOW!
POOM POOM POOM
AND, ONCE AGAIN --
-- THEY'RE MOVING WHILE I'M STILL REACTING. WORKING AS A WELL-OILED, EFFICIENT TEAM --
-- AND LEAVING ME FEELING LIKE A DOPE, IMPOTENTLY TRIGGERING MY BOOT-JET CONTROL, AND GETTING NO RESPONSE.
YOU COME BACK ANY TIME YOU WANT, FIRE-FIGHT! BUT BEFORE YOU DO, TELL YOUR BOSS -- TONY STARK'S PROTECTED!
I'LL BE HERE WAITING FOR YOU -- I'LL ALWAYS BE HERE!
YOU HEAR ME?!
MY VOICE ECHOES, FLAT AND METALLIC, AND I REALIZE I'M SHOUTING TO NOBODY. THEY'RE GONE --
-- AND OFF IN THE DISTANCE, I HEAR THE FIRST SOUND OF SIRENS. AND THEN --
-- AND THEN --
OH, MY LORD.

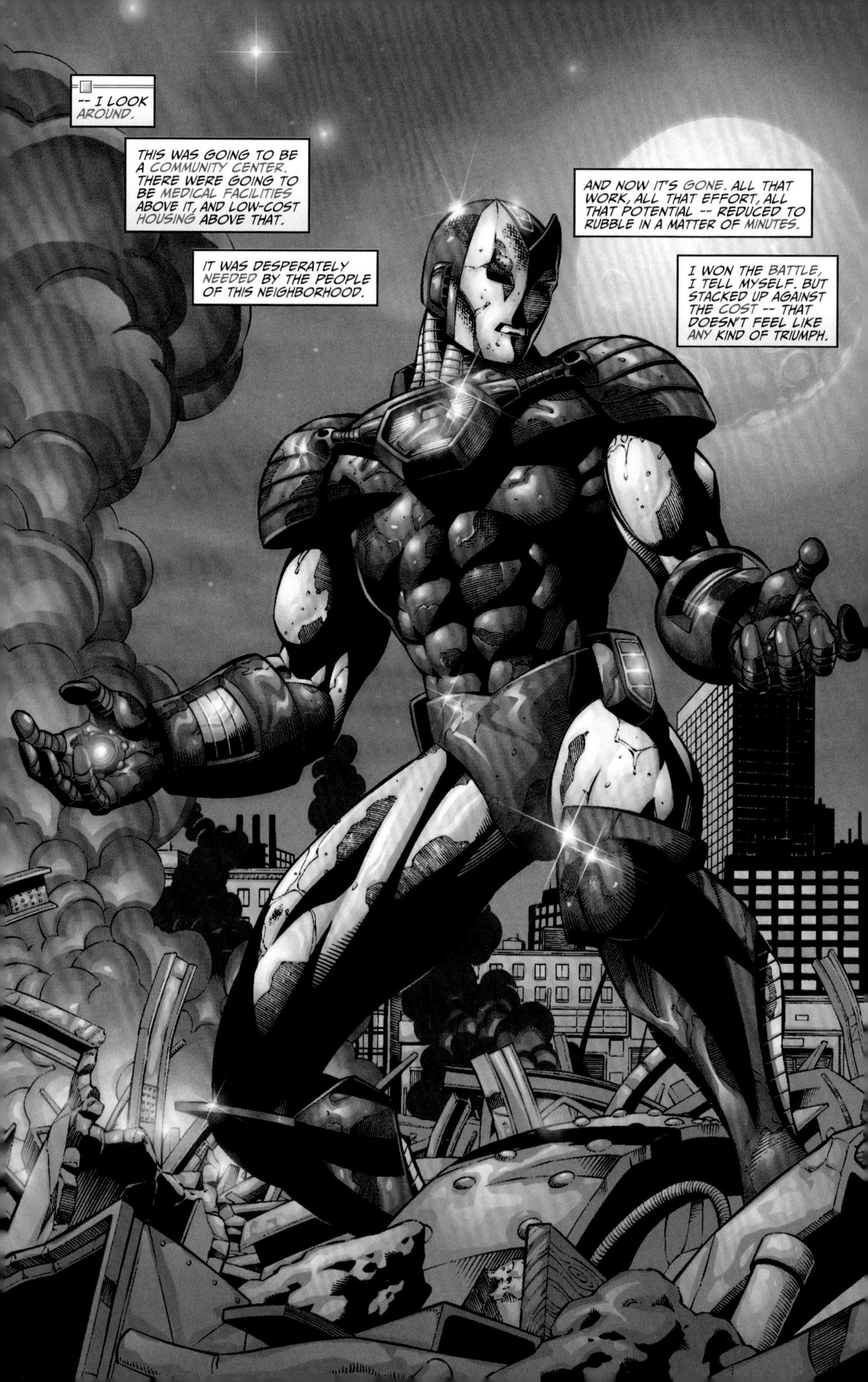
-- I LOOK AROUND.
THIS WAS GOING TO BE A COMMUNITY CENTER. THERE WERE GOING TO BE MEDICAL FACILITIES ABOVE IT, AND LOW-COST HOUSING ABOVE THAT.
IT WAS DESPERATELY NEEDED BY THE PEOPLE OF THIS NEIGHBORHOOD.
AND NOW IT'S GONE. ALL THAT WORK, ALL THAT EFFORT, ALL THAT POTENTIAL -- REDUCED TO RUBBLE IN A MATTER OF MINUTES.
I WON THE BATTLE, I TELL MYSELF. BUT STACKED UP AGAINST THE COST -- THAT DOESN'T FEEL LIKE ANY KIND OF TRIUMPH.

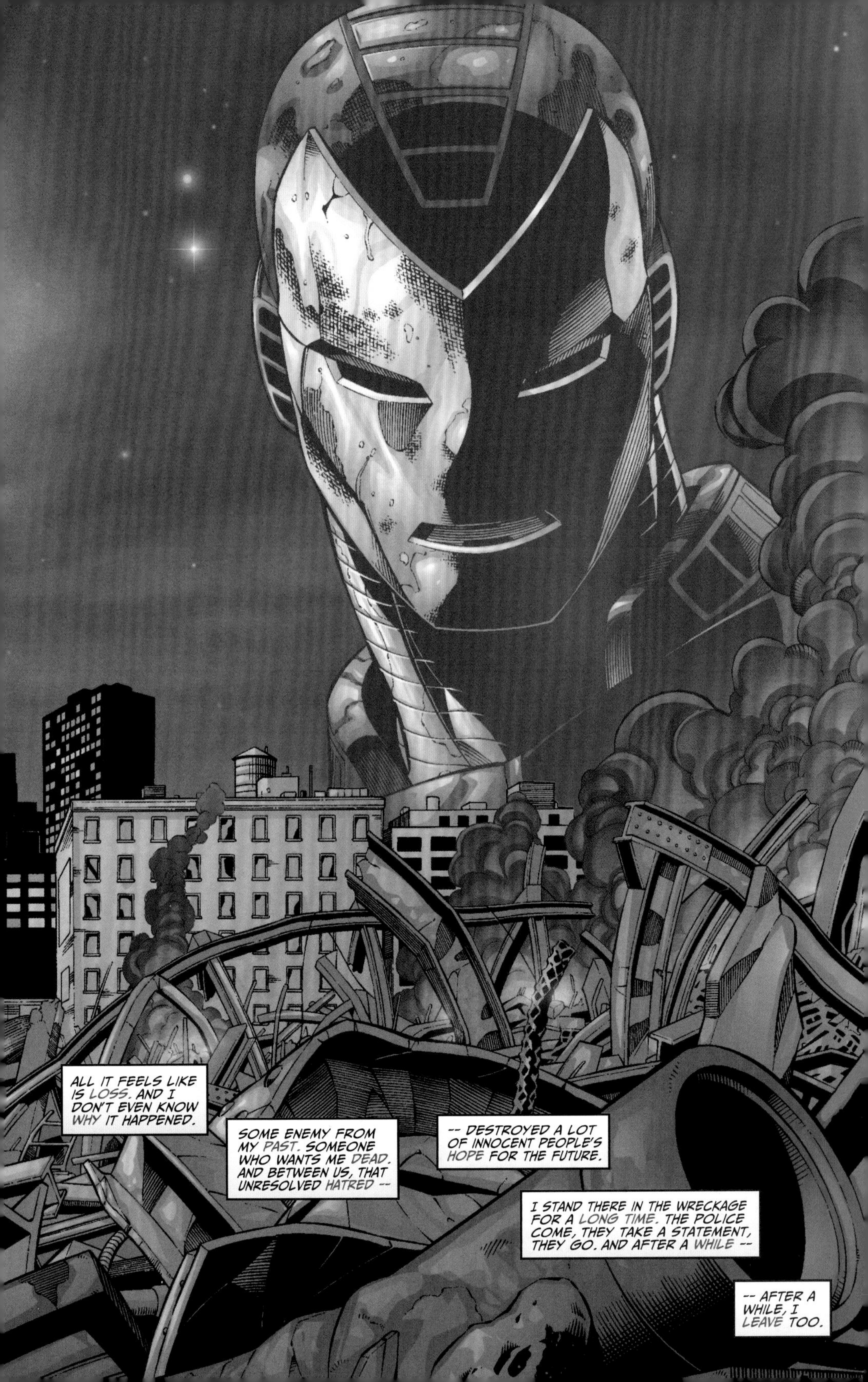
ALL IT FEELS LIKE IS LOSS. AND I DON'T EVEN KNOW WHY IT HAPPENED.
SOME ENEMY FROM MY PAST. SOMEONE WHO WANTS ME DEAD. AND BETWEEN US, THAT UNRESOLVED HATRED --
-- DESTROYED A LOT OF INNOCENT PEOPLE'S HOPE FOR THE FUTURE.
I STAND THERE IN THE WRECKAGE FOR A LONG TIME. THE POLICE COME, THEY TAKE A STATEMENT, THEY GO. AND AFTER A WHILE --
-- AFTER A WHILE, I LEAVE TOO.

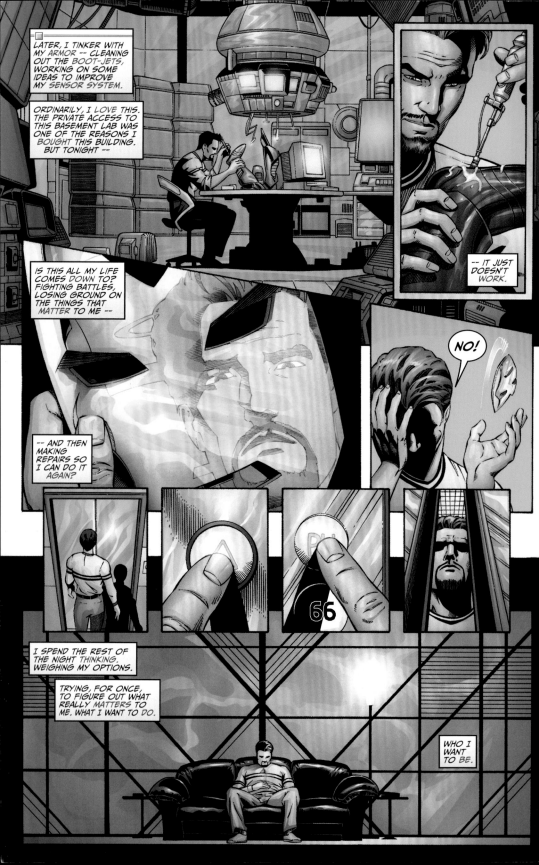

LATER, I TINKER WITH MY ARMOR -- CLEANING OUT THE BOOT-JETS, WORKING ON SOME IDEAS TO IMPROVE MY SENSOR SYSTEM.

ORDINARILY, I LOVE THIS. THE PRIVATE ACCESS TO THIS BASEMENT LAB WAS ONE OF THE REASONS I BOUGHT THIS BUILDING. BUT TONIGHT --

-- IT JUST DOESN'T WORK.

IS THIS ALL MY LIFE COMES DOWN TO? FIGHTING BATTLES, LOSING GROUND ON THE THINGS THAT MATTER TO ME --

NO!

-- AND THEN MAKING REPAIRS SO I CAN DO IT AGAIN?

66

I SPEND THE REST OF THE NIGHT THINKING. WEIGHING MY OPTIONS.

TRYING, FOR ONCE, TO FIGURE OUT WHAT REALLY MATTERS TO ME. WHAT I WANT TO DO.

WHO I WANT TO BE.

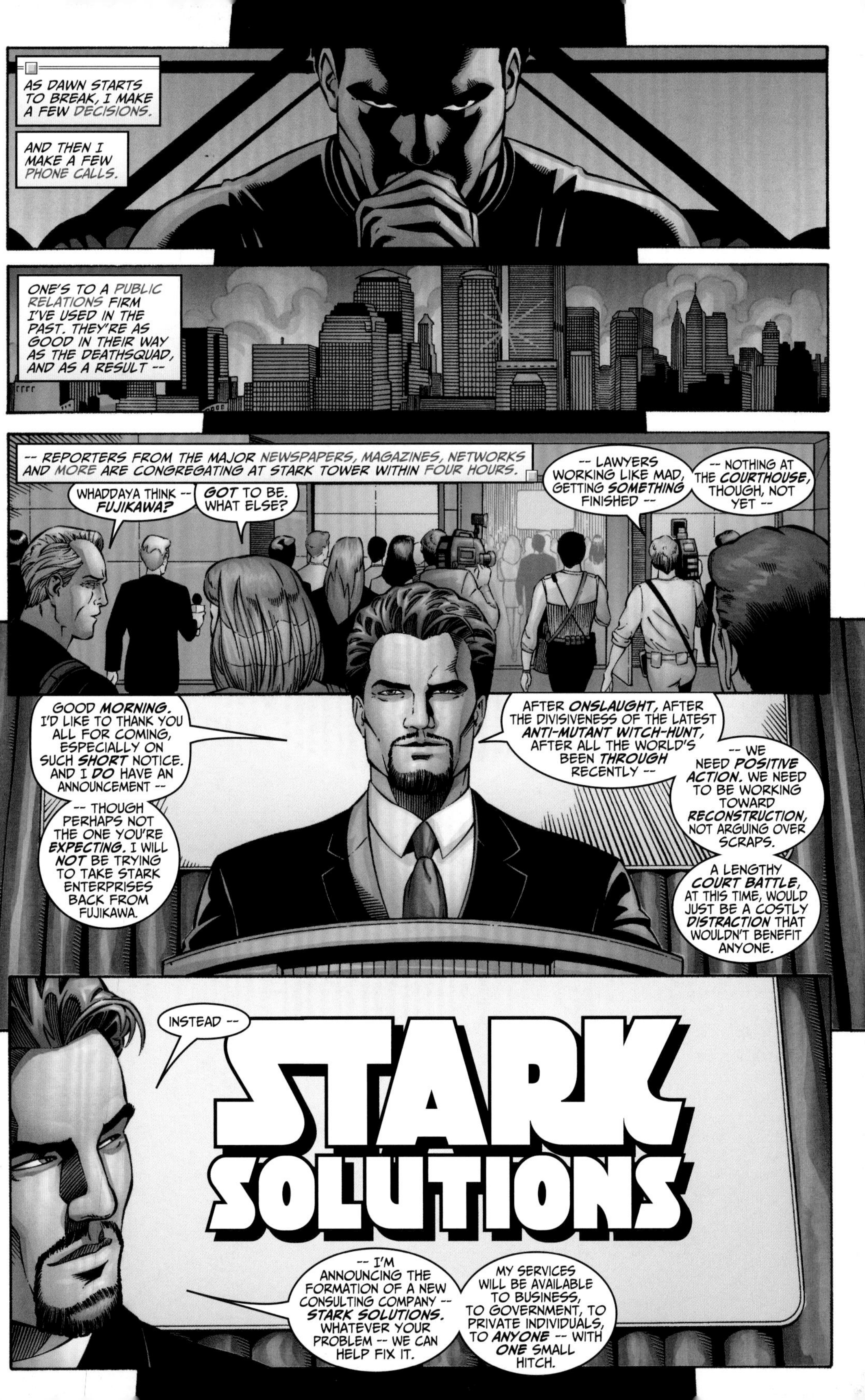

AS DAWN STARTS TO BREAK, I MAKE A FEW DECISIONS.
AND THEN I MAKE A FEW PHONE CALLS.
ONE'S TO A PUBLIC RELATIONS FIRM I'VE USED IN THE PAST. THEY'RE AS GOOD IN THEIR WAY AS THE DEATHSQUAD, AND AS A RESULT --
-- REPORTERS FROM THE MAJOR NEWSPAPERS, MAGAZINES, NETWORKS AND MORE ARE CONGREGATING AT STARK TOWER WITHIN FOUR HOURS.
WHADDAYA THINK -- FUJIKAWA?
GOT TO BE. WHAT ELSE?
-- LAWYERS WORKING LIKE MAD, GETTING SOMETHING FINISHED --
-- NOTHING AT THE COURTHOUSE, THOUGH, NOT YET --
GOOD MORNING. I'D LIKE TO THANK YOU ALL FOR COMING, ESPECIALLY ON SUCH SHORT NOTICE. AND I DO HAVE AN ANNOUNCEMENT --
-- THOUGH PERHAPS NOT THE ONE YOU'RE EXPECTING. I WILL NOT BE TRYING TO TAKE STARK ENTERPRISES BACK FROM FUJIKAWA.
AFTER ONSLAUGHT, AFTER THE DIVISIVENESS OF THE LATEST ANTI-MUTANT WITCH-HUNT, AFTER ALL THE WORLD'S BEEN THROUGH RECENTLY --
-- WE NEED POSITIVE ACTION. WE NEED TO BE WORKING TOWARD RECONSTRUCTION, NOT ARGUING OVER SCRAPS.
A LENGTHY COURT BATTLE, AT THIS TIME, WOULD JUST BE A COSTLY DISTRACTION THAT WOULDN'T BENEFIT ANYONE.
INSTEAD --
STARK SOLUTIONS
-- I'M ANNOUNCING THE FORMATION OF A NEW CONSULTING COMPANY -- STARK SOLUTIONS. WHATEVER YOUR PROBLEM -- WE CAN HELP FIX IT.
MY SERVICES WILL BE AVAILABLE TO BUSINESS, TO GOVERNMENT, TO PRIVATE INDIVIDUALS, TO ANYONE -- WITH ONE SMALL HITCH.

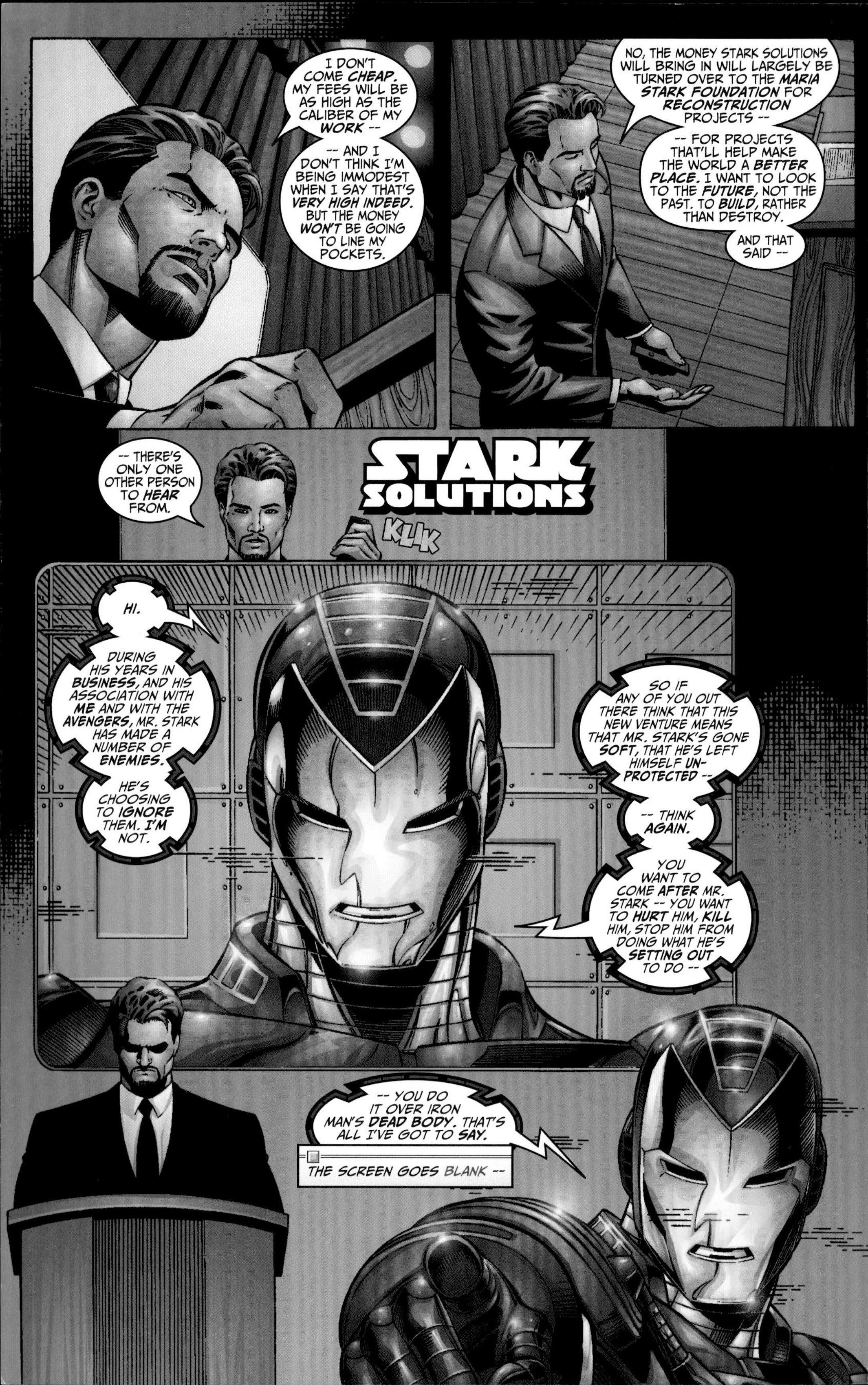
I DON'T COME CHEAP. MY FEES WILL BE AS HIGH AS THE CALIBER OF MY WORK --
-- AND I DON'T THINK I'M BEING IMMODEST WHEN I SAY THAT'S VERY HIGH INDEED. BUT THE MONEY WON'T BE GOING TO LINE MY POCKETS.
NO, THE MONEY STARK SOLUTIONS WILL BRING IN WILL LARGELY BE TURNED OVER TO THE MARIA STARK FOUNDATION FOR RECONSTRUCTION PROJECTS --
-- FOR PROJECTS THAT'LL HELP MAKE THE WORLD A BETTER PLACE. I WANT TO LOOK TO THE FUTURE, NOT THE PAST. TO BUILD, RATHER THAN DESTROY.
AND THAT SAID --
-- THERE'S ONLY ONE OTHER PERSON TO HEAR FROM.
STARK SOLUTIONS
KLIK
HI.
DURING HIS YEARS IN BUSINESS, AND HIS ASSOCIATION WITH ME AND WITH THE AVENGERS, MR. STARK HAS MADE A NUMBER OF ENEMIES.
HE'S CHOOSING TO IGNORE THEM. I'M NOT.
SO IF ANY OF YOU OUT THERE THINK THAT THIS NEW VENTURE MEANS THAT MR. STARK'S GONE SOFT, THAT HE'S LEFT HIMSELF UN-PROTECTED --
-- THINK AGAIN.
YOU WANT TO COME AFTER MR. STARK -- YOU WANT TO HURT HIM, KILL HIM, STOP HIM FROM DOING WHAT HE'S SETTING OUT TO DO --
-- YOU DO IT OVER IRON MAN'S DEAD BODY. THAT'S ALL I'VE GOT TO SAY.
THE SCREEN GOES BLANK --

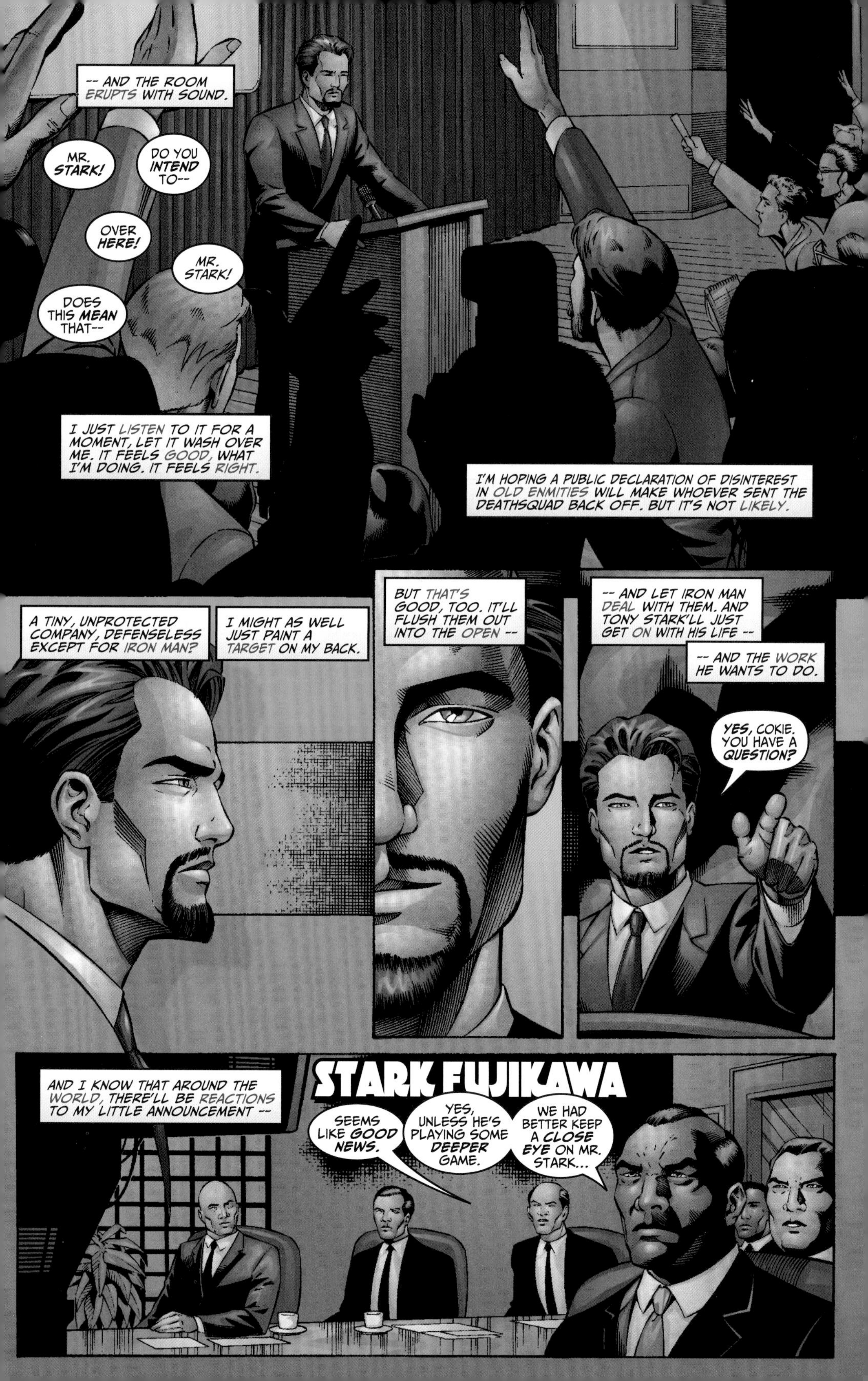
-- AND THE ROOM ERUPTS WITH SOUND.
MR. STARK!
DO YOU INTEND TO--
OVER HERE!
MR. STARK!
DOES THIS MEAN THAT--
I JUST LISTEN TO IT FOR A MOMENT, LET IT WASH OVER ME. IT FEELS GOOD, WHAT I'M DOING. IT FEELS RIGHT.
I'M HOPING A PUBLIC DECLARATION OF DISINTEREST IN OLD ENMITIES WILL MAKE WHOEVER SENT THE DEATHSQUAD BACK OFF. BUT IT'S NOT LIKELY.
A TINY, UNPROTECTED COMPANY, DEFENSELESS EXCEPT FOR IRON MAN?
I MIGHT AS WELL JUST PAINT A TARGET ON MY BACK.
BUT THAT'S GOOD, TOO. IT'LL FLUSH THEM OUT INTO THE OPEN --
-- AND LET IRON MAN DEAL WITH THEM. AND TONY STARK'LL JUST GET ON WITH HIS LIFE --
-- AND THE WORK HE WANTS TO DO.
YES, COKIE. YOU HAVE A QUESTION?
AND I KNOW THAT AROUND THE WORLD, THERE'LL BE REACTIONS TO MY LITTLE ANNOUNCEMENT --
STARK FUJIKAWA
SEEMS LIKE GOOD NEWS.
YES, UNLESS HE'S PLAYING SOME DEEPER GAME.
WE HAD BETTER KEEP A CLOSE EYE ON MR. STARK...

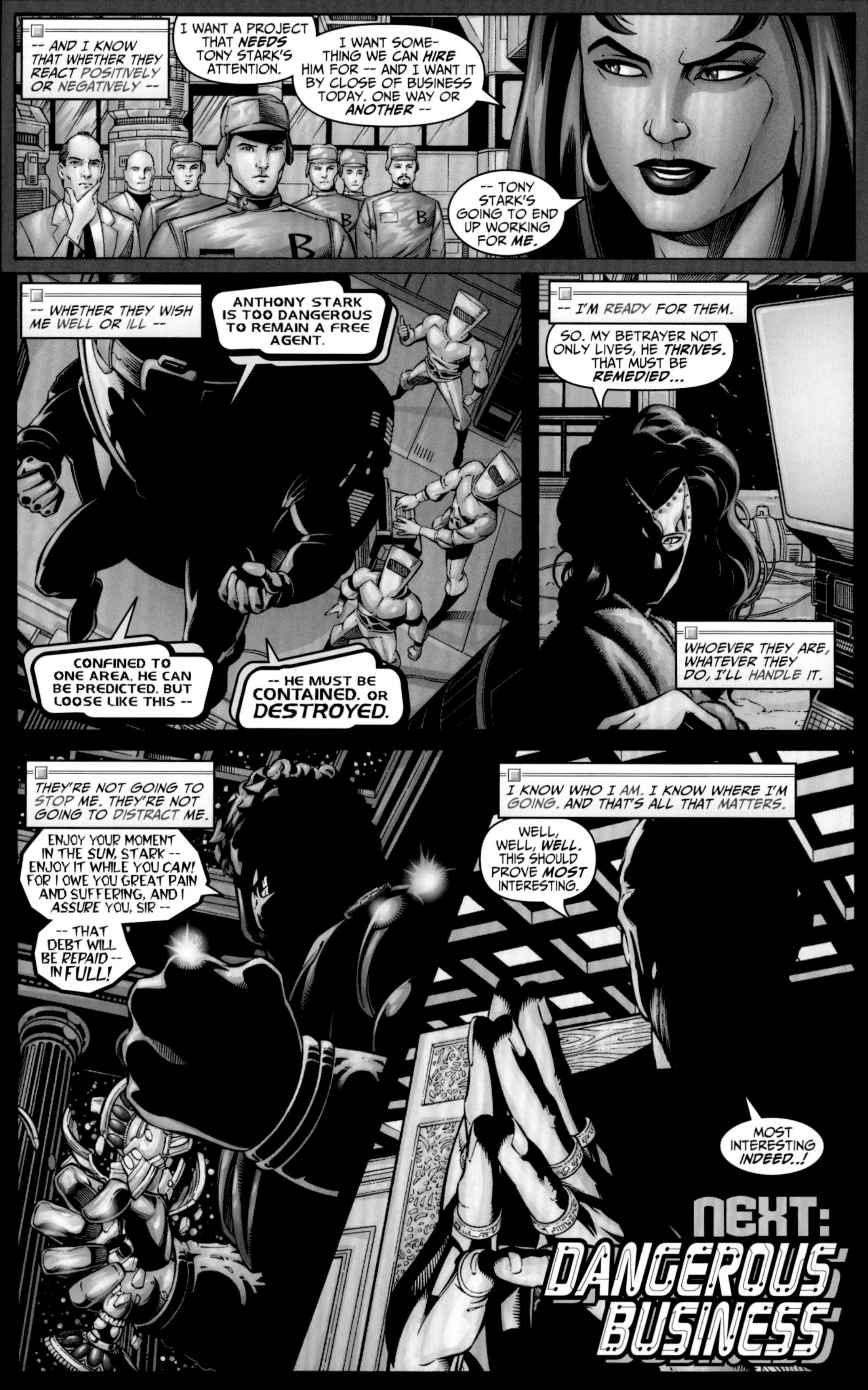
-- AND I KNOW THAT WHETHER THEY REACT POSITIVELY OR NEGATIVELY --
I WANT A PROJECT THAT NEEDS TONY STARK'S ATTENTION.
I WANT SOME-THING WE CAN HIRE HIM FOR -- AND I WANT IT BY CLOSE OF BUSINESS TODAY. ONE WAY OR ANOTHER --
-- TONY STARK'S GOING TO END UP WORKING FOR ME.
-- WHETHER THEY WISH ME WELL OR ILL --
ANTHONY STARK IS TOO DANGEROUS TO REMAIN A FREE AGENT.
CONFINED TO ONE AREA, HE CAN BE PREDICTED. BUT LOOSE LIKE THIS --
-- HE MUST BE CONTAINED. OR DESTROYED.
-- I'M READY FOR THEM.
SO. MY BETRAYER NOT ONLY LIVES, HE THRIVES. THAT MUST BE REMEDIED...
WHOEVER THEY ARE, WHATEVER THEY DO, I'LL HANDLE IT.
THEY'RE NOT GOING TO STOP ME. THEY'RE NOT GOING TO DISTRACT ME.
ENJOY YOUR MOMENT IN THE SUN, STARK -- ENJOY IT WHILE YOU CAN! FOR I OWE YOU GREAT PAIN AND SUFFERING, AND I ASSURE YOU, SIR --
-- THAT DEBT WILL BE REPAID -- IN FULL!
I KNOW WHO I AM. I KNOW WHERE I'M GOING. AND THAT'S ALL THAT MATTERS.
WELL, WELL, WELL. THIS SHOULD PROVE MOST INTERESTING.
MOST INTERESTING INDEED..!
NEXT:
DANGEROUS BUSINESS

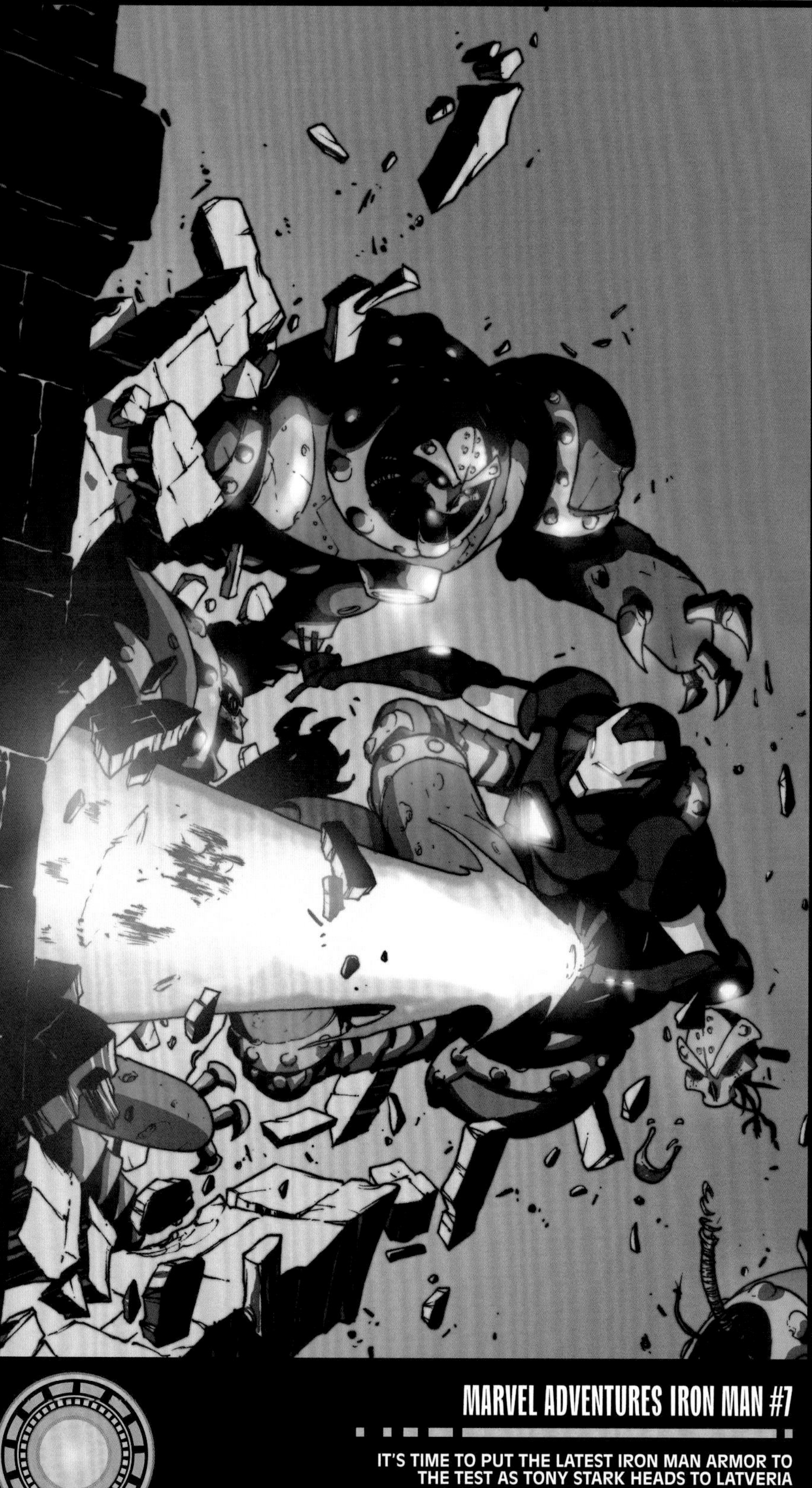

MARVEL ADVENTURES IRON MAN #7

IT'S TIME TO PUT THE LATEST IRON MAN ARMOR TO THE TEST AS TONY STARK HEADS TO LATVERIA TO SAVE HIS FRIENDS FROM DOCTOR DOOM!

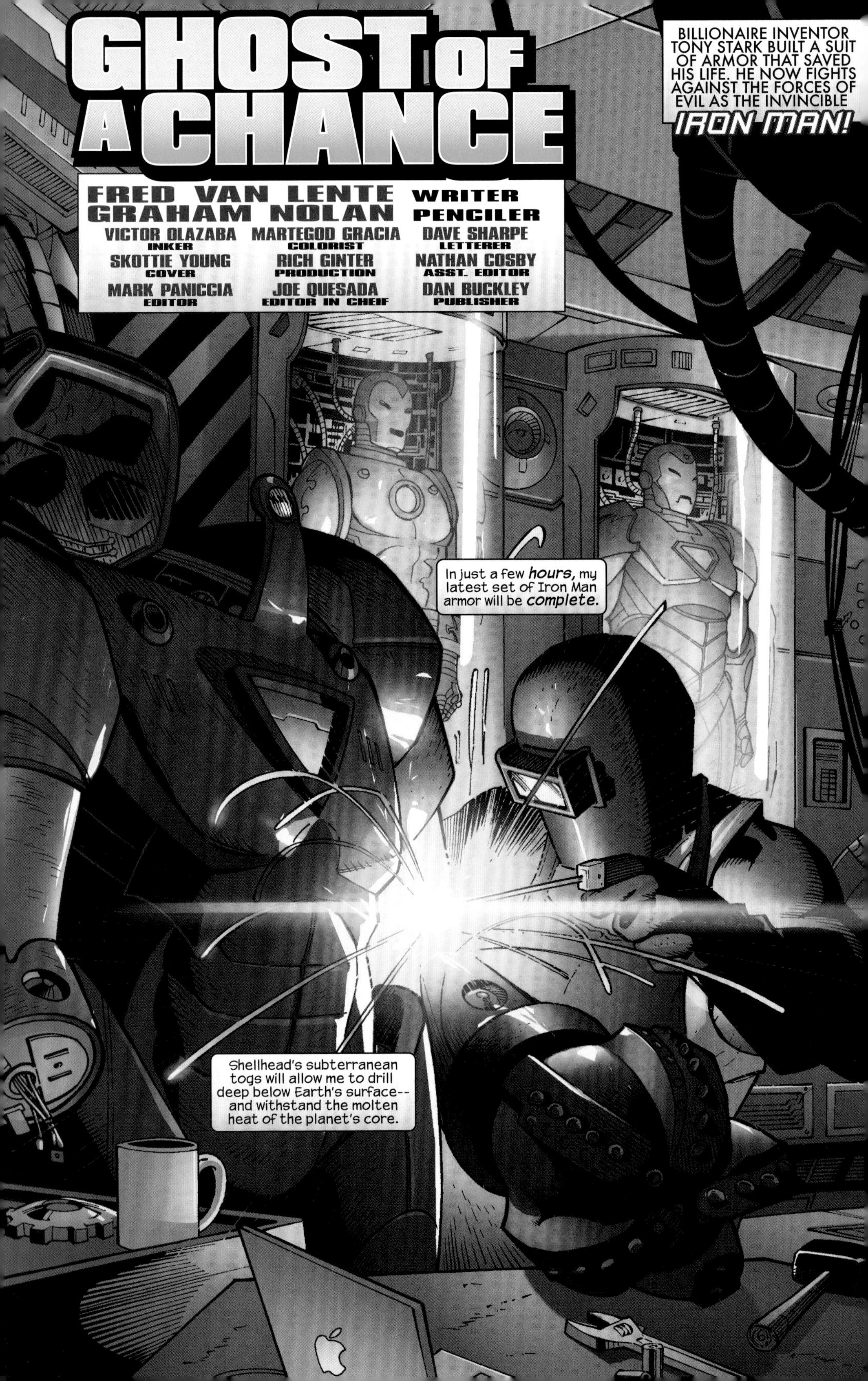
GHOST OF A CHANCE
FRED VAN LENTE WRITER
GRAHAM NOLAN PENCILER
VICTOR OLAZABA INKER
MARTEGOD GRACIA COLORIST
DAVE SHARPE LETTERER
SKOTTIE YOUNG COVER
RICH GINTER PRODUCTION
NATHAN COSBY ASST. EDITOR
MARK PANICCIA EDITOR
JOE QUESADA EDITOR IN CHEIF
DAN BUCKLEY PUBLISHER
BILLIONAIRE INVENTOR TONY STARK BUILT A SUIT OF ARMOR THAT SAVED HIS LIFE. HE NOW FIGHTS AGAINST THE FORCES OF EVIL AS THE INVINCIBLE IRON MAN!
In just a few hours, my latest set of Iron Man armor will be complete.
Shellhead's subterranean togs will allow me to drill deep below Earth's surface--and withstand the molten heat of the planet's core.

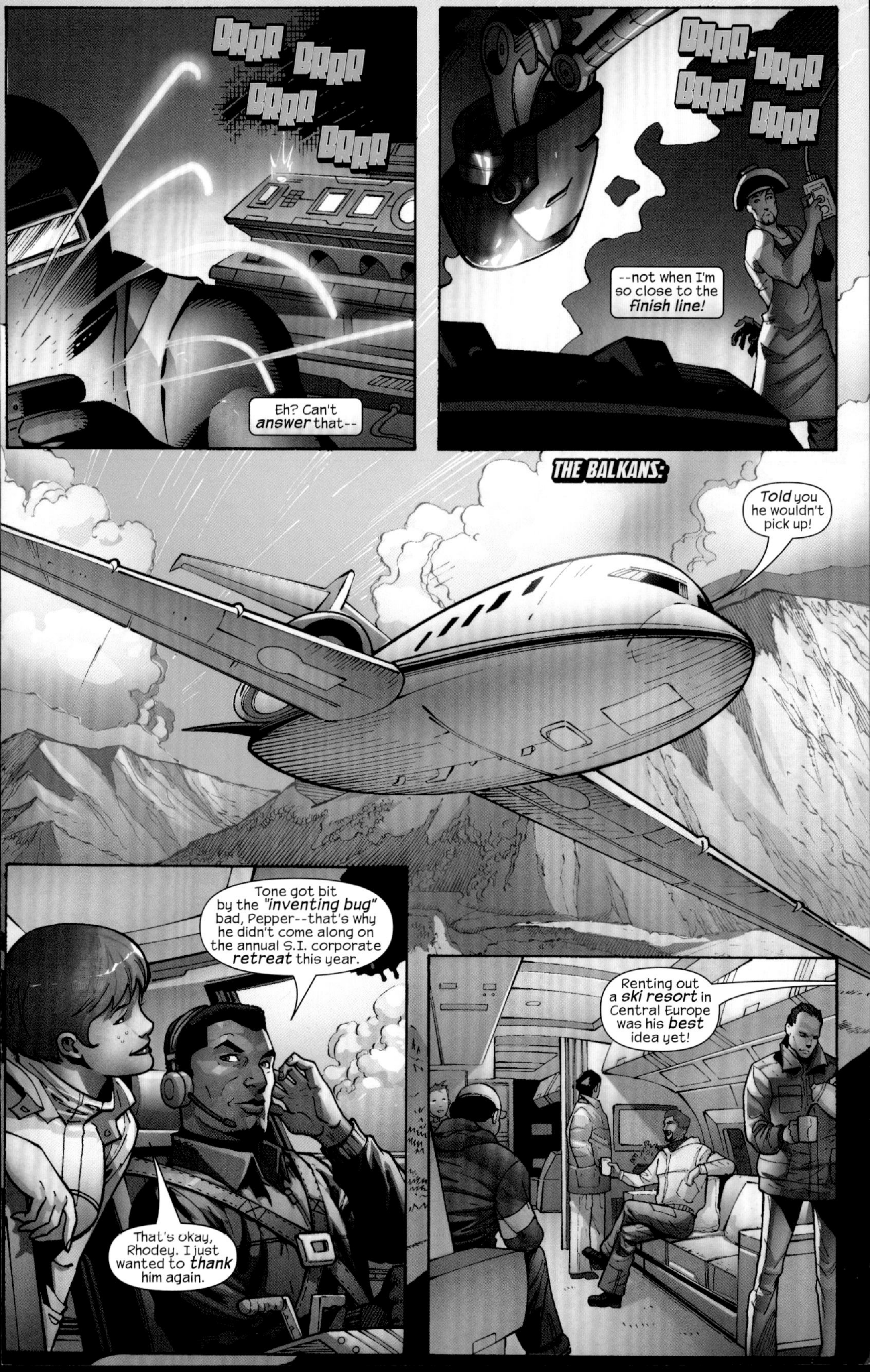
BRRR BRRR BRRR BRRR
Eh? Can't answer that--
BRRR BRRR BRRR BRRR
--not when I'm so close to the finish line!
THE BALKANS:
Told you he wouldn't pick up!
Tone got bit by the "inventing bug" bad, Pepper--that's why he didn't come along on the annual S.I. corporate retreat this year.
That's okay, Rhodey. I just wanted to thank him again.
Renting out a ski resort in Central Europe was his best idea yet!

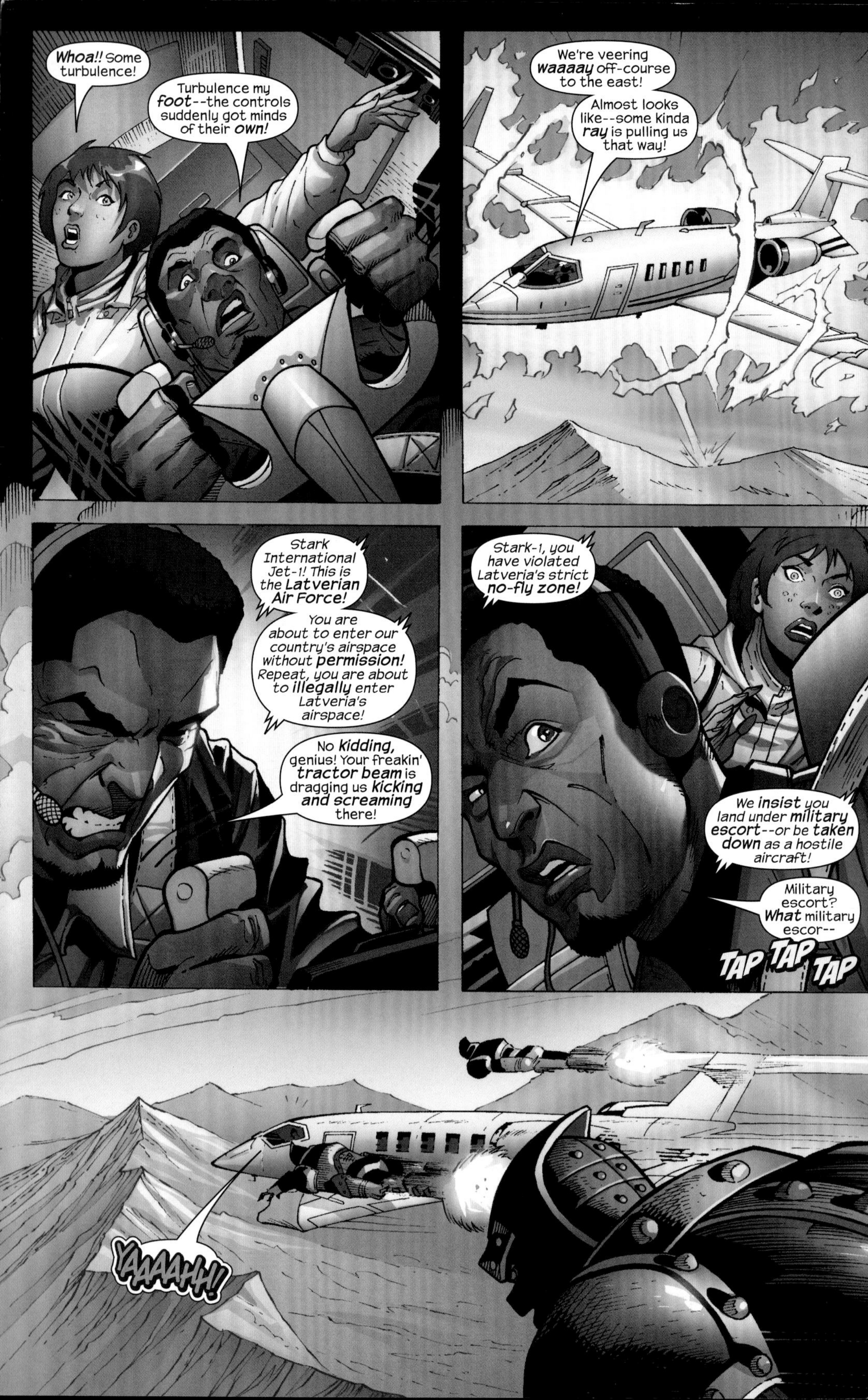

Whoa!! Some turbulence!
Turbulence my foot--the controls suddenly got minds of their own!
We're veering waaaay off-course to the east!
Almost looks like--some kinda ray is pulling us that way!
Stark International Jet-1! This is the Latverian Air Force!
You are about to enter our country's airspace without permission! Repeat, you are about to illegally enter Latveria's airspace!
No kidding, genius! Your freakin' tractor beam is dragging us kicking and screaming there!
Stark-1, you have violated Latveria's strict no-fly zone!
We insist you land under military escort--or be taken down as a hostile aircraft!
Military escort? What military escor--
TAP TAP TAP
YAAAAHH!!

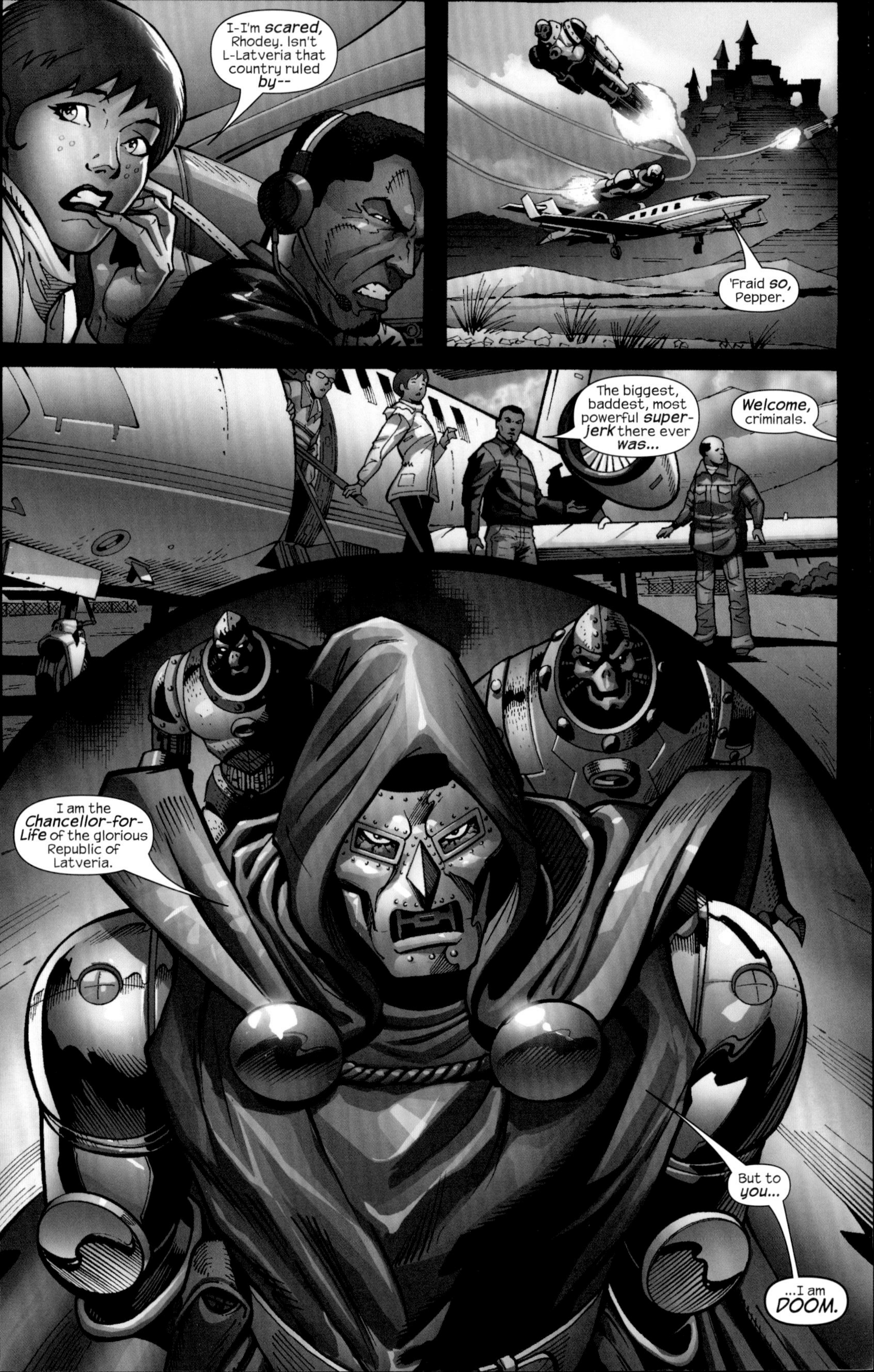

I-I'm scared, Rhodey. Isn't L-Latveria that country ruled by--
'Fraid so, Pepper.
The biggest, baddest, most powerful super-jerk there ever was...
Welcome, criminals.
I am the Chancellor-for-Life of the glorious Republic of Latveria.
But to you...
...I am DOOM.

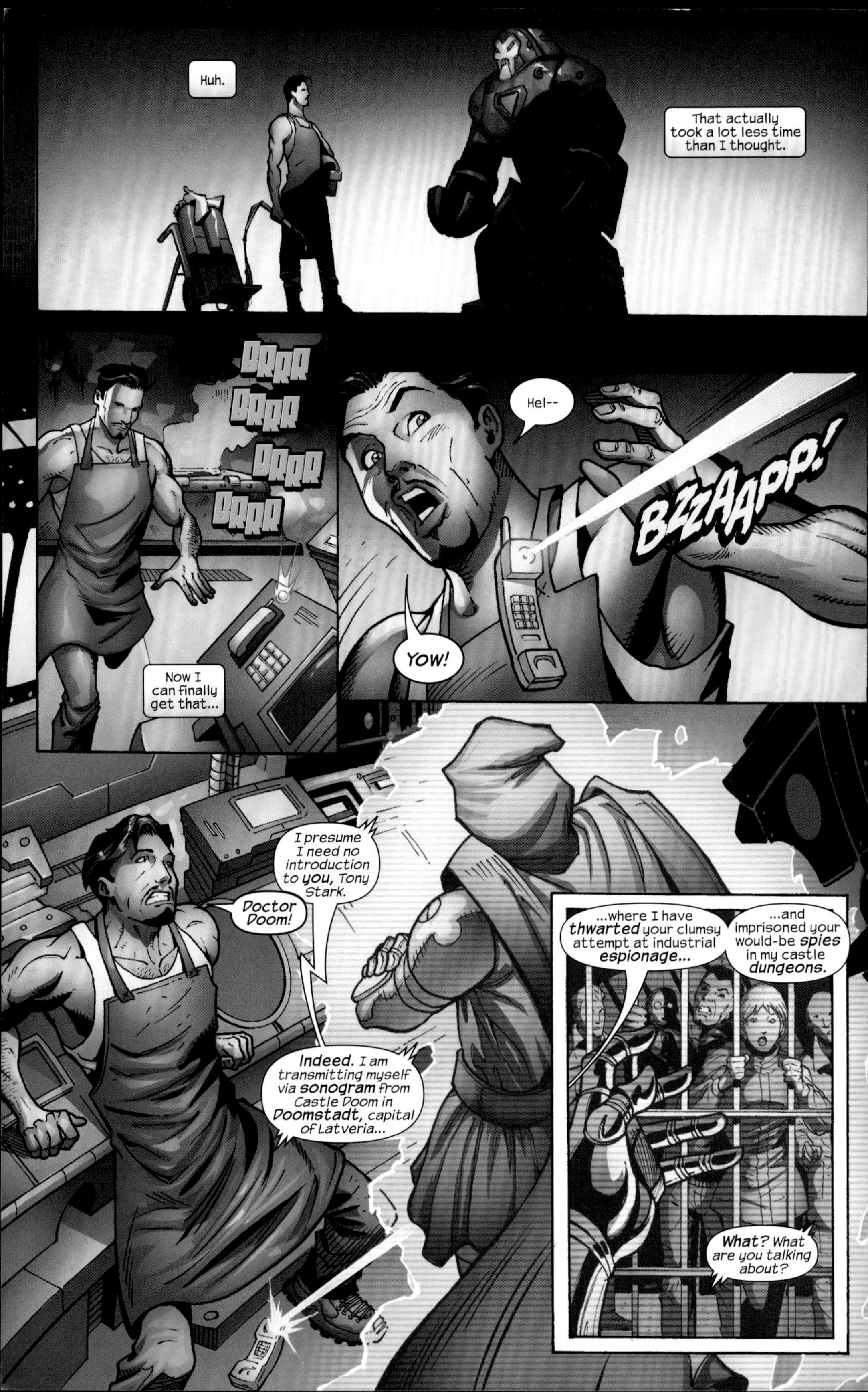
Huh.
That actually took a lot less time than I thought.
BRRR BRRR BRRR BRRR
Now I can finally get that...
Hel--
BZZAAPP!
YOW!
Doctor Doom!
I presume I need no introduction to you, Tony Stark.
Indeed. I am transmitting myself via sonogram from Castle Doom in Doomstadt, capital of Latveria...
...where I have thwarted your clumsy attempt at industrial espionage...
...and imprisoned your would-be spies in my castle dungeons.
What? What are you talking about?

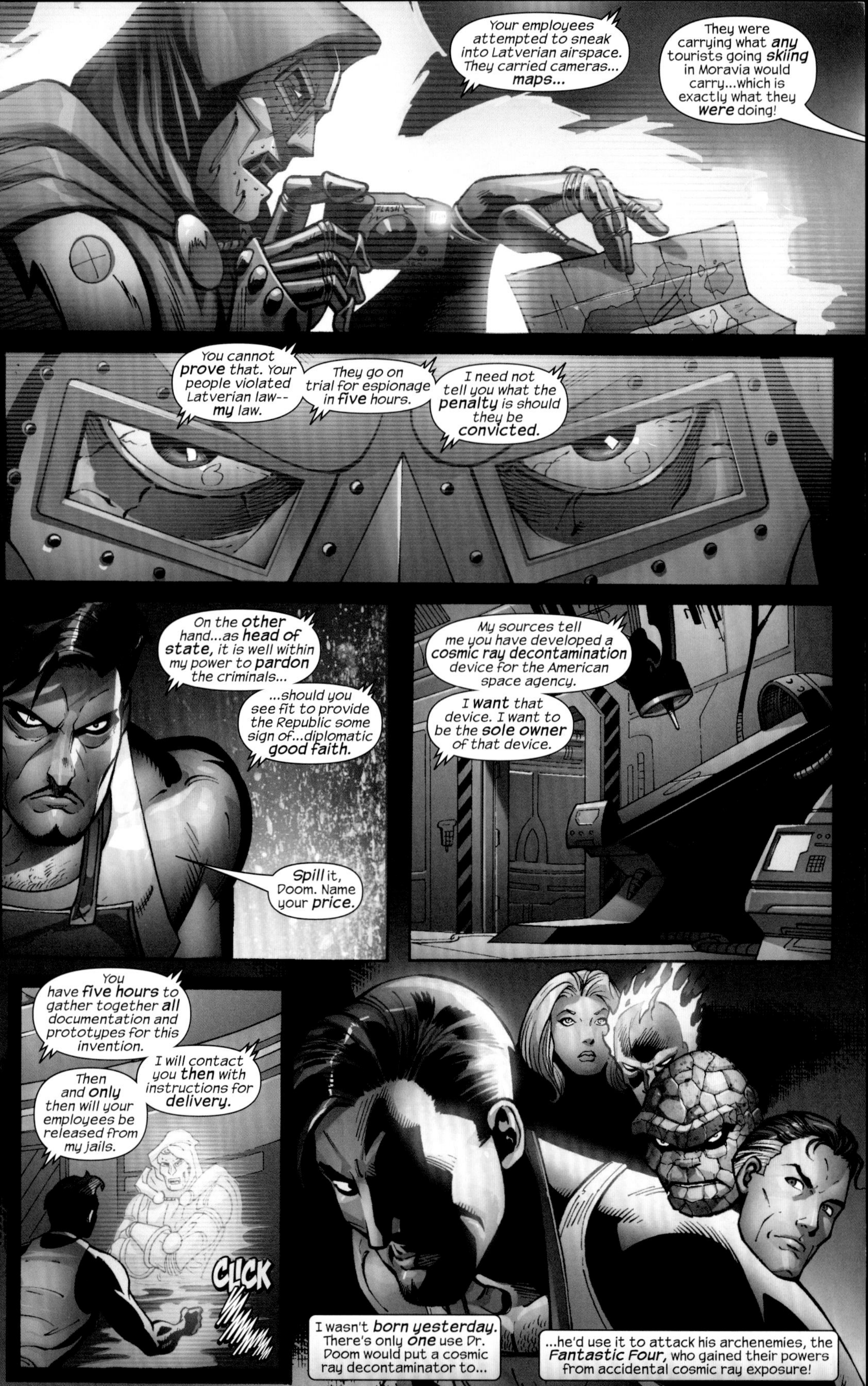

Your employees attempted to sneak into Latverian airspace. They carried cameras... maps...
They were carrying what any tourists going skiing in Moravia would carry...which is exactly what they were doing!
You cannot prove that. Your people violated Latverian law-- my law.
They go on trial for espionage in five hours.
I need not tell you what the penalty is should they be convicted.
On the other hand...as head of state, it is well within my power to pardon the criminals...
...should you see fit to provide the Republic some sign of...diplomatic good faith.
Spill it, Doom. Name your price.
My sources tell me you have developed a cosmic ray decontamination device for the American space agency.
I want that device. I want to be the sole owner of that device.
You have five hours to gather together all documentation and prototypes for this invention.
I will contact you then with instructions for delivery.
Then and only then will your employees be released from my jails.
CLICK
I wasn't born yesterday. There's only one use Dr. Doom would put a cosmic ray decontaminator to...
...he'd use it to attack his archenemies, the Fantastic Four, who gained their powers from accidental cosmic ray exposure!

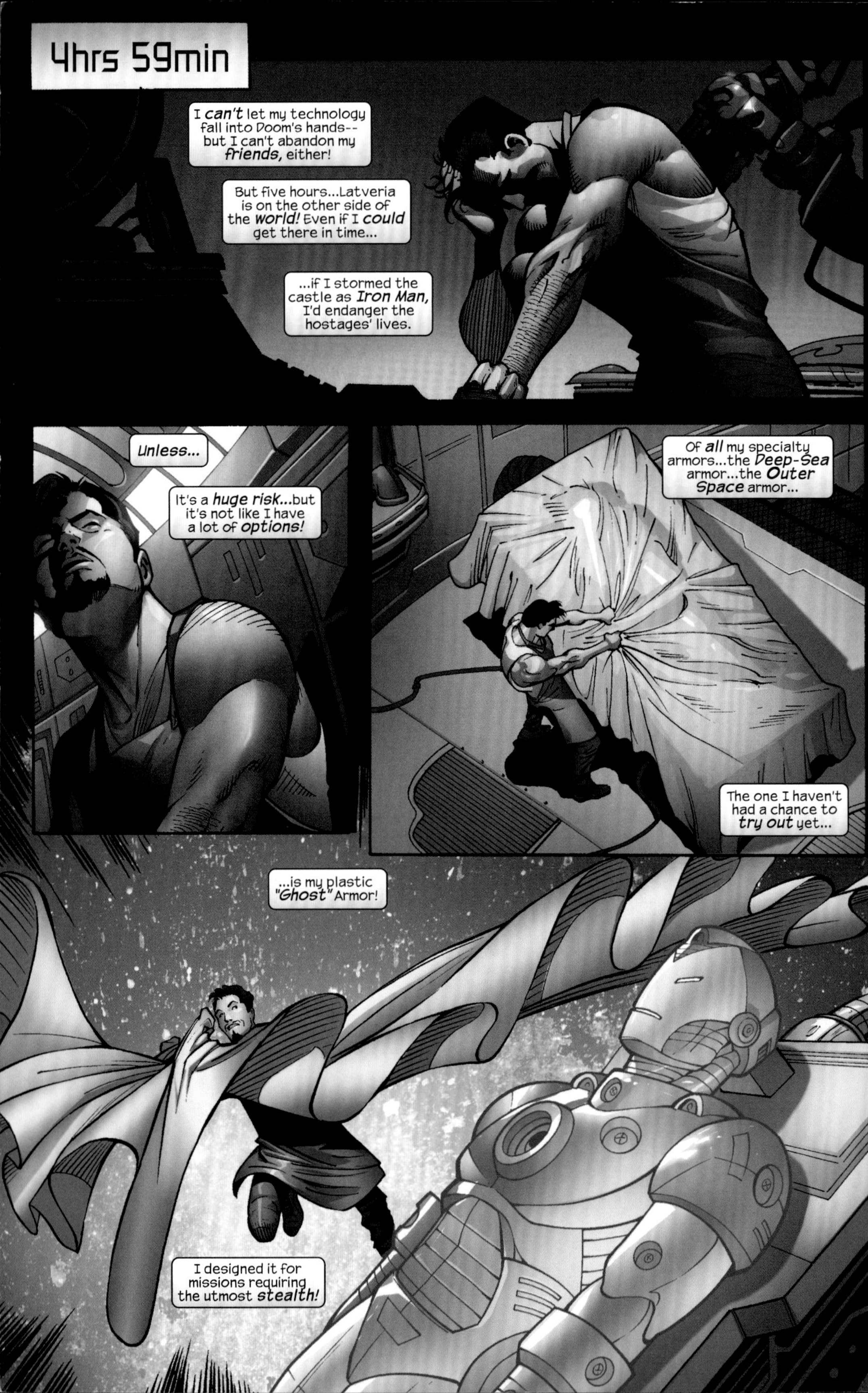
4hrs 59min
I can't let my technology fall into Doom's hands--but I can't abandon my friends, either!
But five hours...Latveria is on the other side of the world! Even if I could get there in time...
...if I stormed the castle as Iron Man, I'd endanger the hostages' lives.
Unless...
It's a huge risk...but it's not like I have a lot of options!
Of all my specialty armors...the Deep-Sea armor...the Outer Space armor...
The one I haven't had a chance to try out yet...
...is my plastic "Ghost" Armor!
I designed it for missions requiring the utmost stealth!

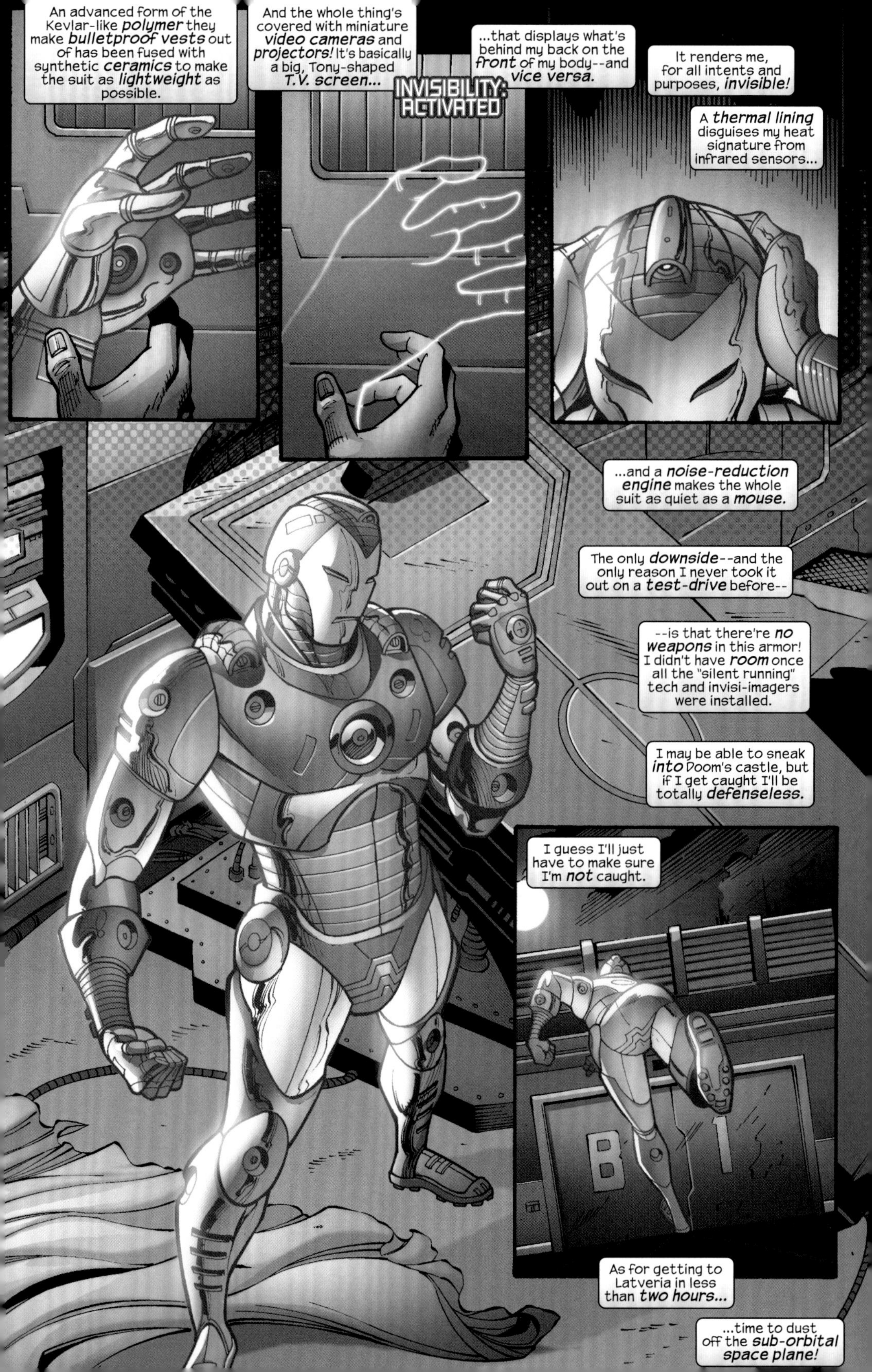
An advanced form of the Kevlar-like polymer they make bulletproof vests out of has been fused with synthetic ceramics to make the suit as lightweight as possible.
And the whole thing's covered with miniature video cameras and projectors! It's basically a big, Tony-shaped T.V. screen...
INVISIBILITY: ACTIVATED
...that displays what's behind my back on the front of my body--and vice versa.
It renders me, for all intents and purposes, invisible!
A thermal lining disguises my heat signature from infrared sensors...
...and a noise-reduction engine makes the whole suit as quiet as a mouse.
The only downside--and the only reason I never took it out on a test-drive before--
--is that there're no weapons in this armor! I didn't have room once all the "silent running" tech and invisi-imagers were installed.
I may be able to sneak into Doom's castle, but if I get caught I'll be totally defenseless.
I guess I'll just have to make sure I'm not caught.
B 1
As for getting to Latveria in less than two hours...
...time to dust off the sub-orbital space plane!

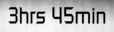

This experimental jet shoots *straight up* into outer space at a *kilometer a second...*

...literally *hopping* between continents before dropping back down to its intended destination.

The autopilot will take over from *here*.

Before Doom's flying robots can catch *up* with it--or even *identify* it--the space plane will be *far* outside Latverian airspace.

Without *me*, though.

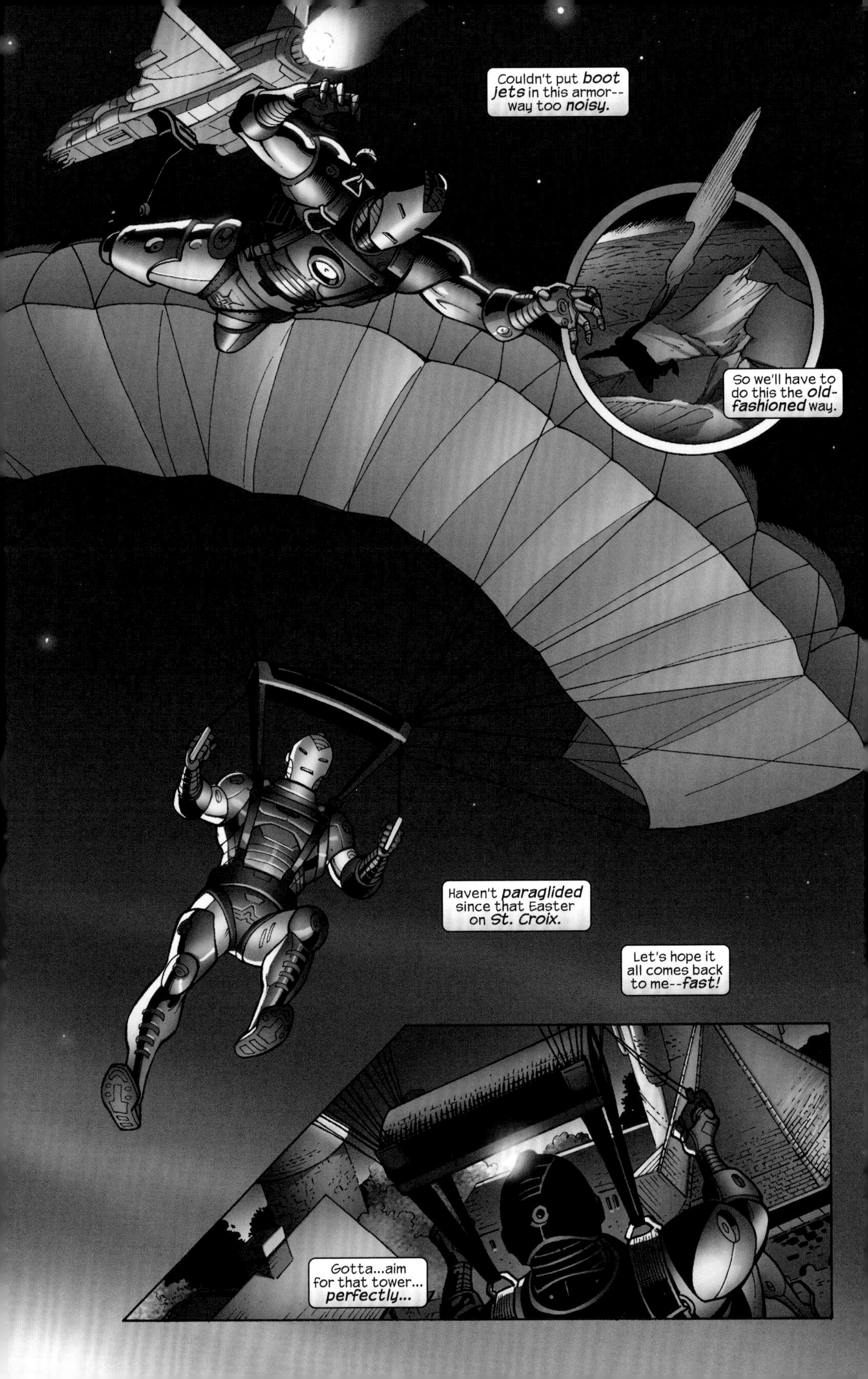
Couldn't put boot jets in this armor--way too noisy.
So we'll have to do this the old-fashioned way.
Haven't paraglided since that Easter on St. Croix.
Let's hope it all comes back to me--fast!
Gotta...aim for that tower... perfectly...

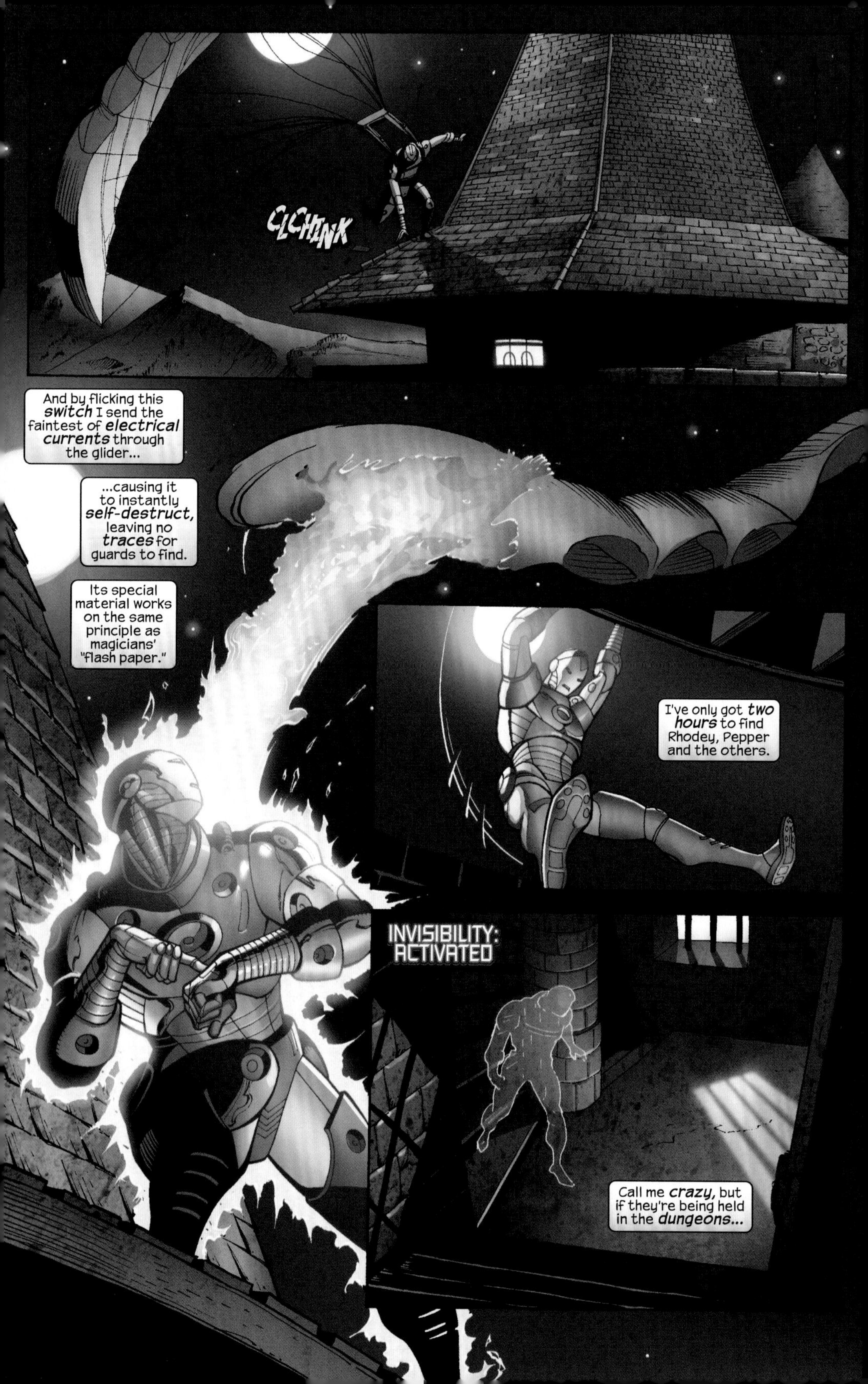

CLCHINK
And by flicking this switch I send the faintest of electrical currents through the glider...
...causing it to instantly self-destruct, leaving no traces for guards to find.
Its special material works on the same principle as magicians' "flash paper."
I've only got two hours to find Rhodey, Pepper and the others.
INVISIBILITY: ACTIVATED
Call me crazy, but if they're being held in the dungeons...

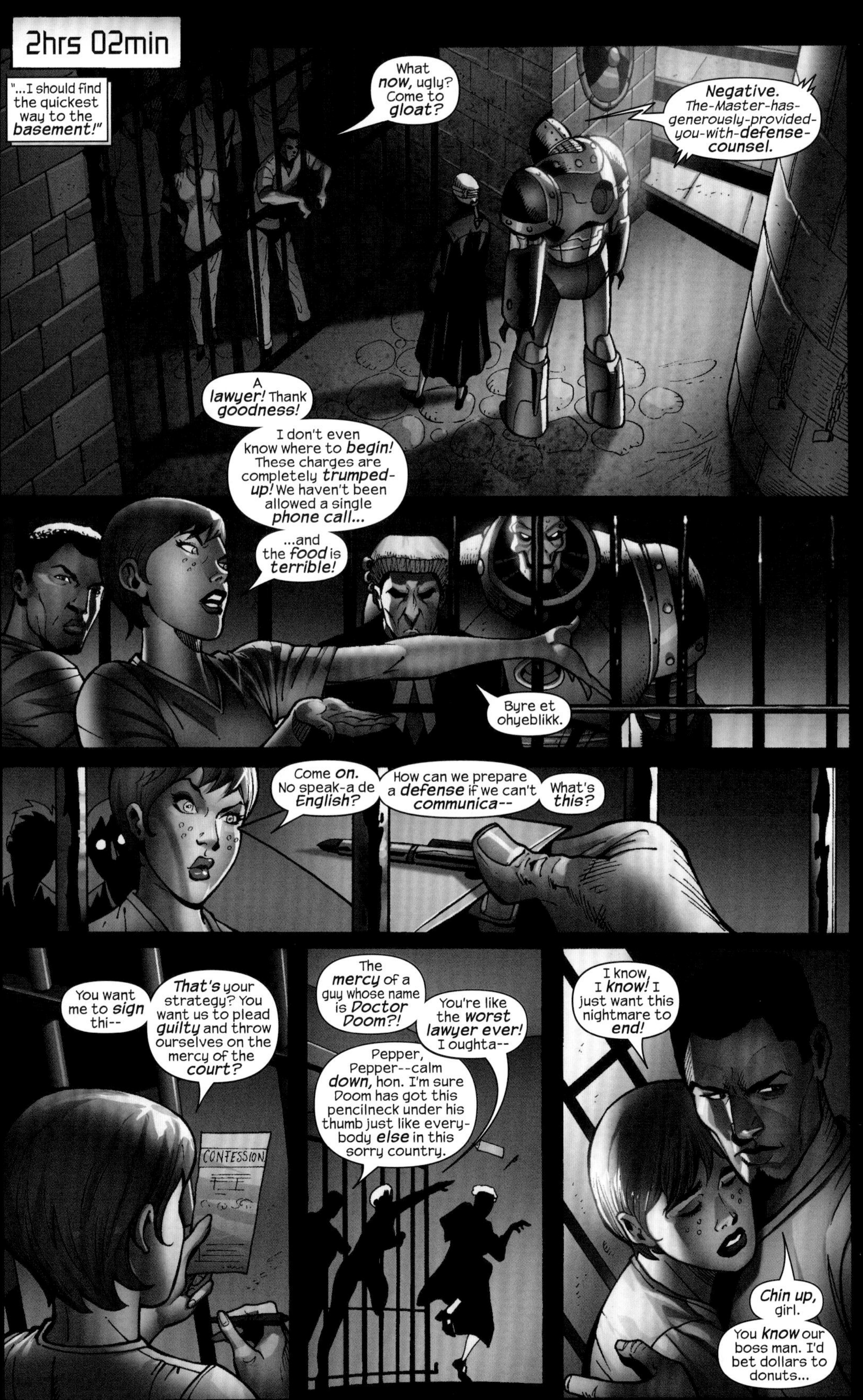
2hrs 02min
"...I should find the quickest way to the basement!"
What now, ugly? Come to gloat?
Negative. The-Master-has-generously-provided-you-with-defense-counsel.
A lawyer! Thank goodness!
I don't even know where to begin! These charges are completely trumped-up! We haven't been allowed a single phone call...
...and the food is terrible!
Byre et ohyeblikk.
Come on. No speak-a de English?
How can we prepare a defense if we can't communica--
What's this?
You want me to sign thi--
That's your strategy? You want us to plead guilty and throw ourselves on the mercy of the court?
CONFESSION
The mercy of a guy whose name is Doctor Doom?!
You're like the worst lawyer ever! I oughta--
Pepper, Pepper--calm down, hon. I'm sure Doom has got this pencilneck under his thumb just like every-body else in this sorry country.
I know, I know! I just want this nightmare to end!
Chin up, girl.
You know our boss man. I'd bet dollars to donuts...

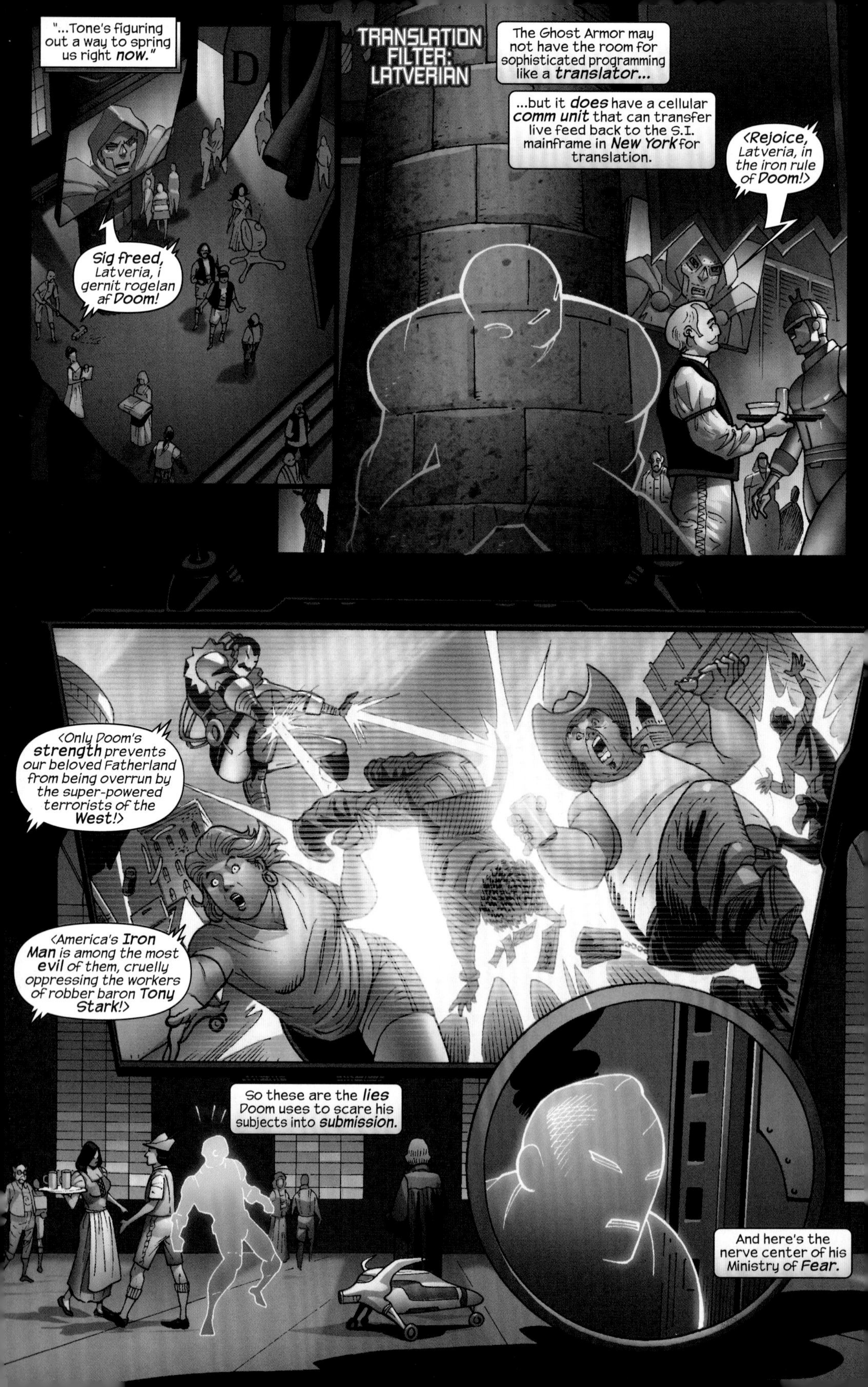
"...Tone's figuring out a way to spring us right now."
TRANSLATION FILTER: LATVERIAN
The Ghost Armor may not have the room for sophisticated programming like a translator...
...but it does have a cellular comm unit that can transfer live feed back to the S.I. mainframe in New York for translation.
Sig freed, Latveria, i gernit rogelan af Doom!
<Rejoice, Latveria, in the iron rule of Doom!>
<Only Doom's strength prevents our beloved Fatherland from being overrun by the super-powered terrorists of the West!>
<America's Iron Man is among the most evil of them, cruelly oppressing the workers of robber baron Tony Stark!>
So these are the lies Doom uses to scare his subjects into submission.
And here's the nerve center of his Ministry of Fear.

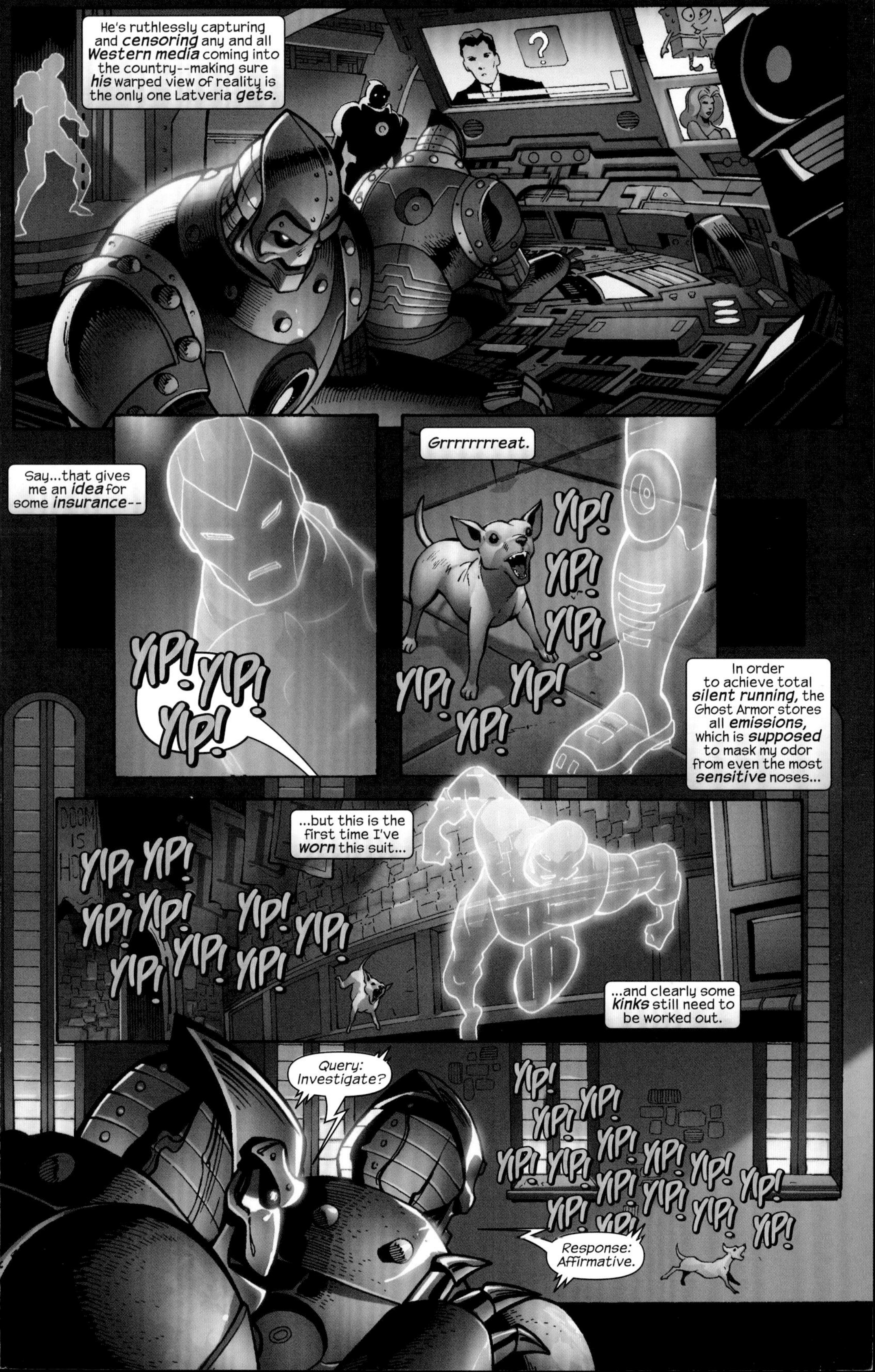
He's ruthlessly capturing and censoring any and all Western media coming into the country--making sure his warped view of reality is the only one Latveria gets.
Say...that gives me an idea for some insurance--
YIP! YIP! YIP!
Grrrrrrrreat.
YIP! YIP! YIP! YIP! YIP! YIP!
In order to achieve total silent running, the Ghost Armor stores all emissions, which is supposed to mask my odor from even the most sensitive noses...
...but this is the first time I've worn this suit...
YIP! YIP! YIP! YIP! YIP! YIP! YIP! YIP! YIP!
...and clearly some kinks still need to be worked out.
Query: Investigate?
YIP! YIP! YIP! YIP! YIP! YIP! YIP! YIP! YIP! YIP! YIP! YIP! YIP! YIP!
Response: Affirmative.

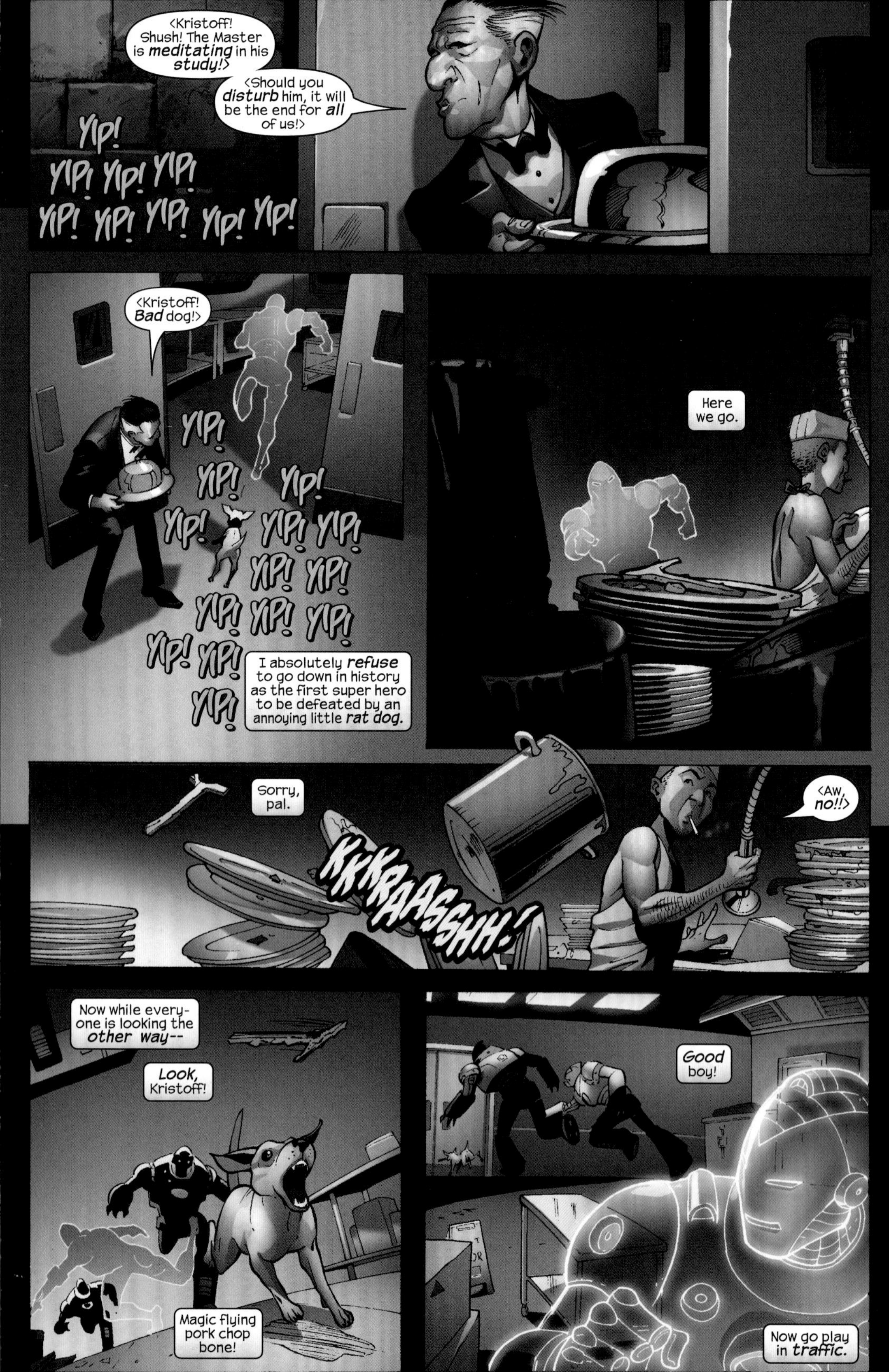
<Kristoff! Shush! The Master is *meditating* in his *study!*>
<Should you *disturb* him, it will be the end for *all* of us!>
YIP! YIP! YIP! YIP! YIP! YIP! YIP! YIP! YIP!
<Kristoff! *Bad* dog!>
YIP! YIP! YIP! YIP! YIP! YIP! YIP! YIP! YIP! YIP! YIP! YIP! YIP!
I absolutely *refuse* to go down in history as the first super hero to be defeated by an annoying little *rat dog.*
Here we go.
Sorry, pal.
KKKRAASSHH!
<Aw, *no!!*>
Now while every-one is looking the *other way*--
Look, Kristoff!
Magic flying pork chop bone!
Good boy!
Now go play in *traffic.*

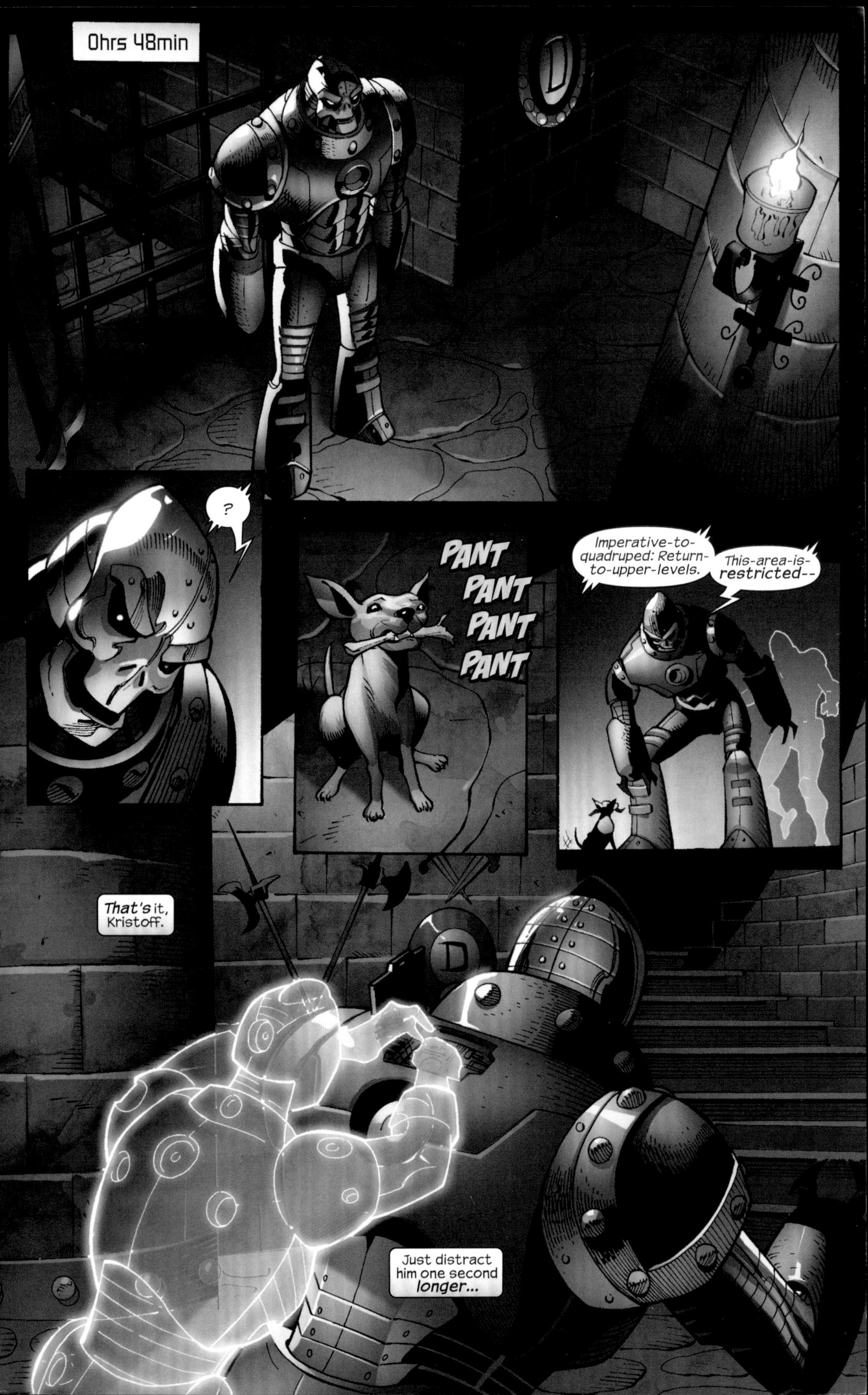
0hrs 48min
?
PANT PANT PANT PANT
Imperative-to-quadruped: Return-to-upper-levels.
This-area-is-restricted--
That's it, Kristoff.
Just distract him one second longer...

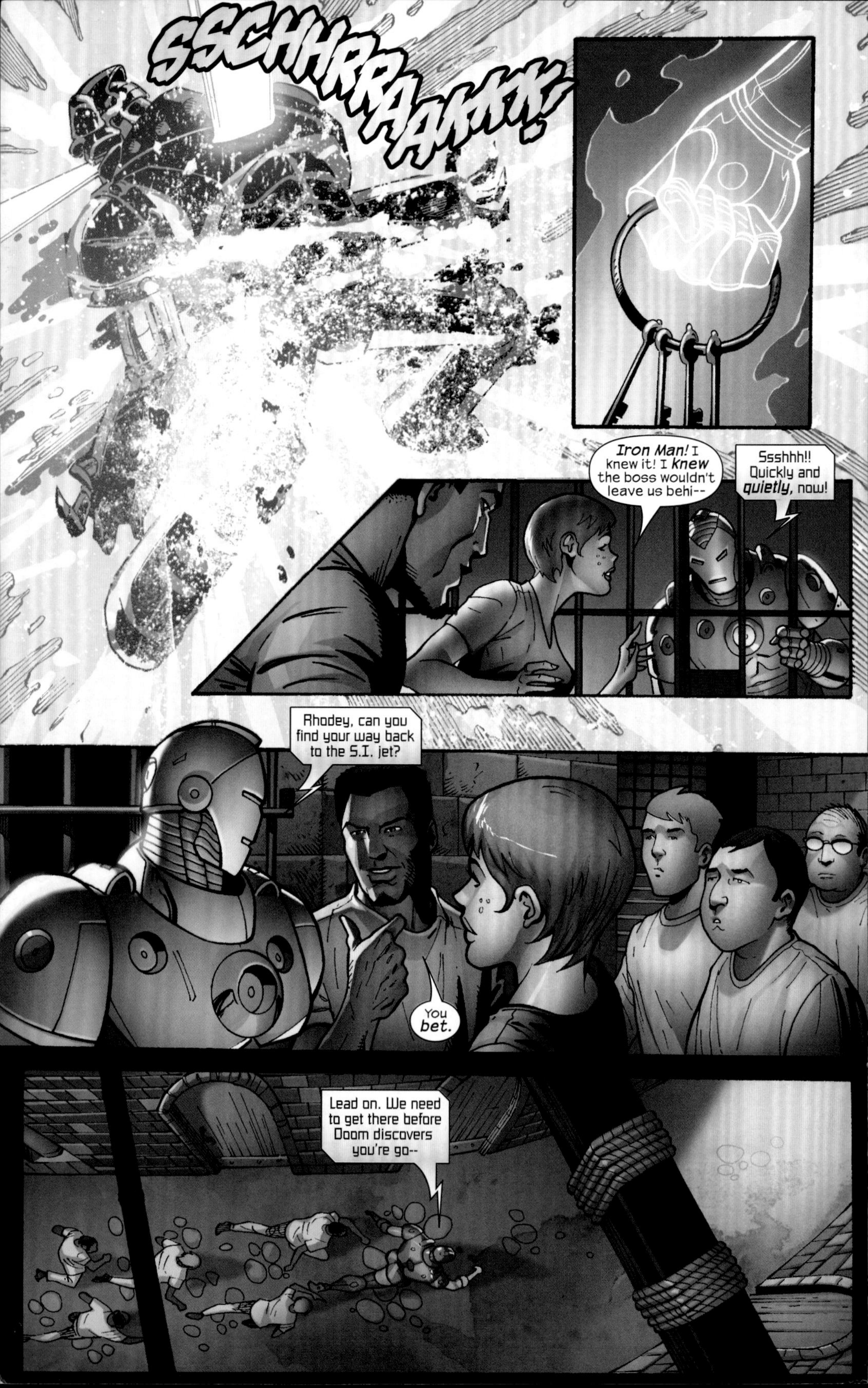
SSCHHRRAAKKK!
Iron Man! I knew it! I knew the boss wouldn't leave us behi--
Ssshhh!! Quickly and quietly, now!
Rhodey, can you find your way back to the S.I. jet?
You bet.
Lead on. We need to get there before Doom discovers you're go--

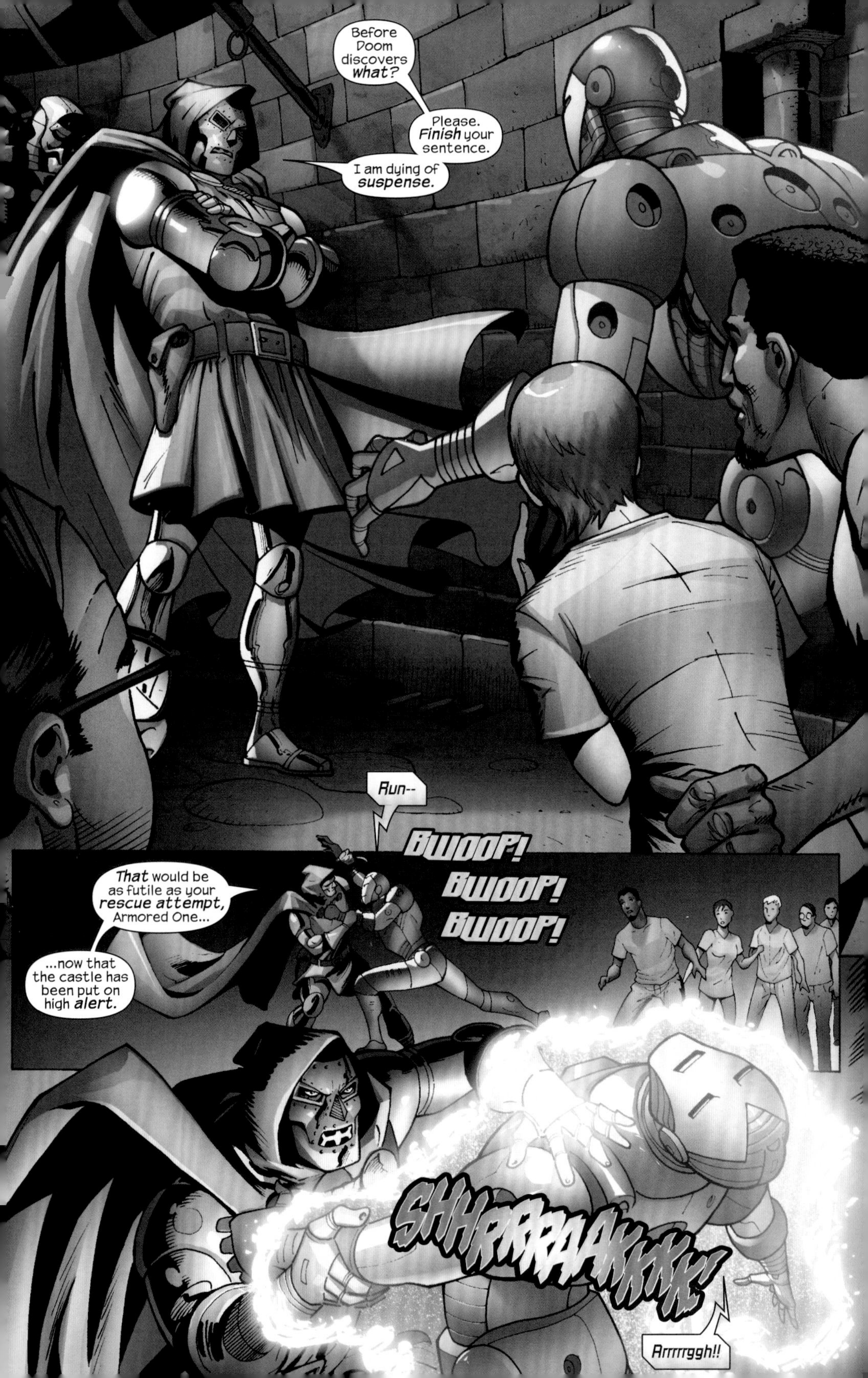
Before Doom discovers what?
Please. Finish your sentence.
I am dying of suspense.
Run--
BWOOP! BWOOP! BWOOP!
That would be as futile as your rescue attempt, Armored One...
...now that the castle has been put on high alert.
SHHRRRAAKKKK!
Arrrrrggh!!

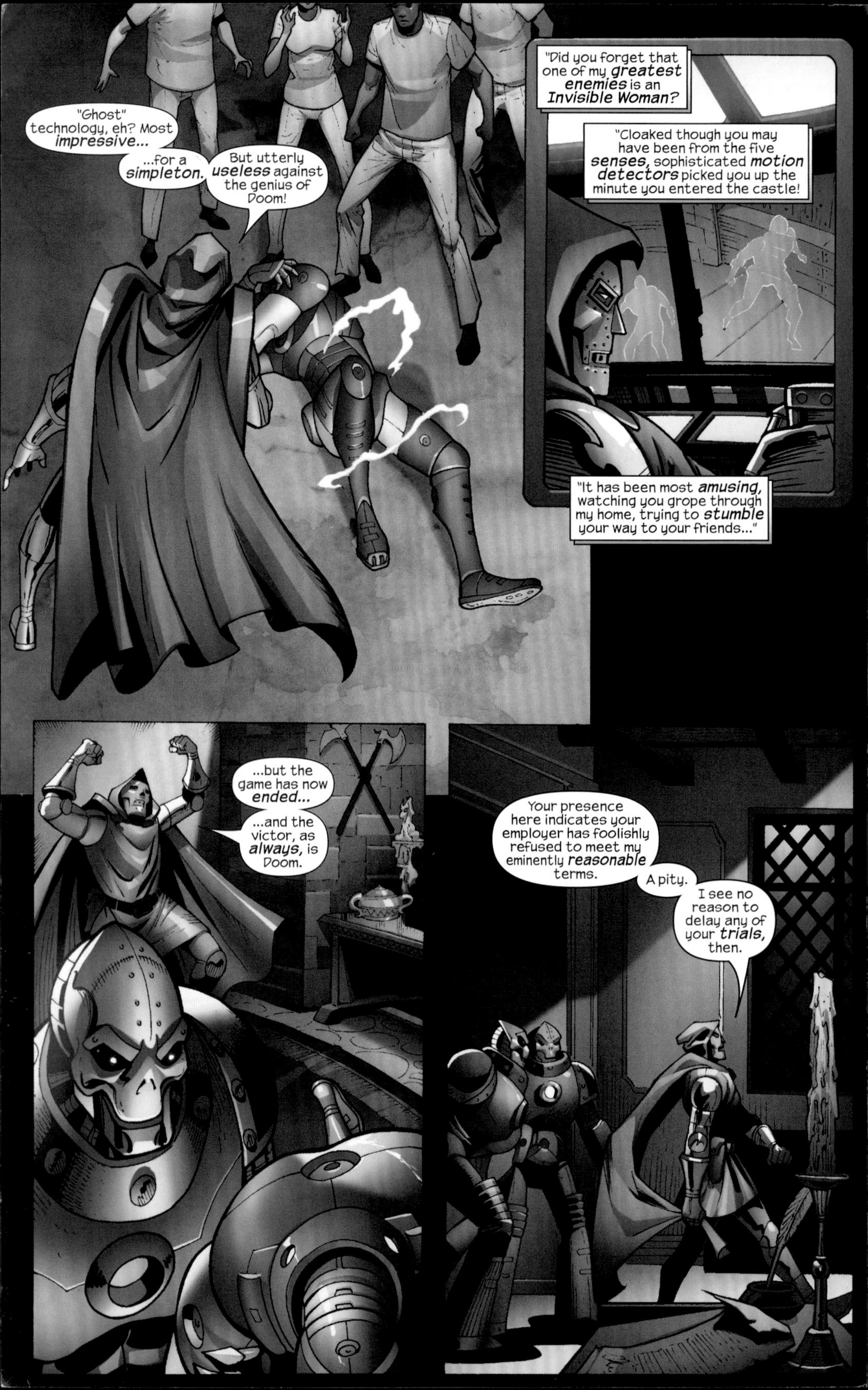
"Ghost" technology, eh? Most impressive...
...for a simpleton.
But utterly useless against the genius of Doom!
"Did you forget that one of my greatest enemies is an Invisible Woman?
"Cloaked though you may have been from the five senses, sophisticated motion detectors picked you up the minute you entered the castle!
"It has been most amusing, watching you grope through my home, trying to stumble your way to your friends..."
...but the game has now ended...
...and the victor, as always, is Doom.
Your presence here indicates your employer has foolishly refused to meet my eminently reasonable terms.
A pity.
I see no reason to delay any of your trials, then.

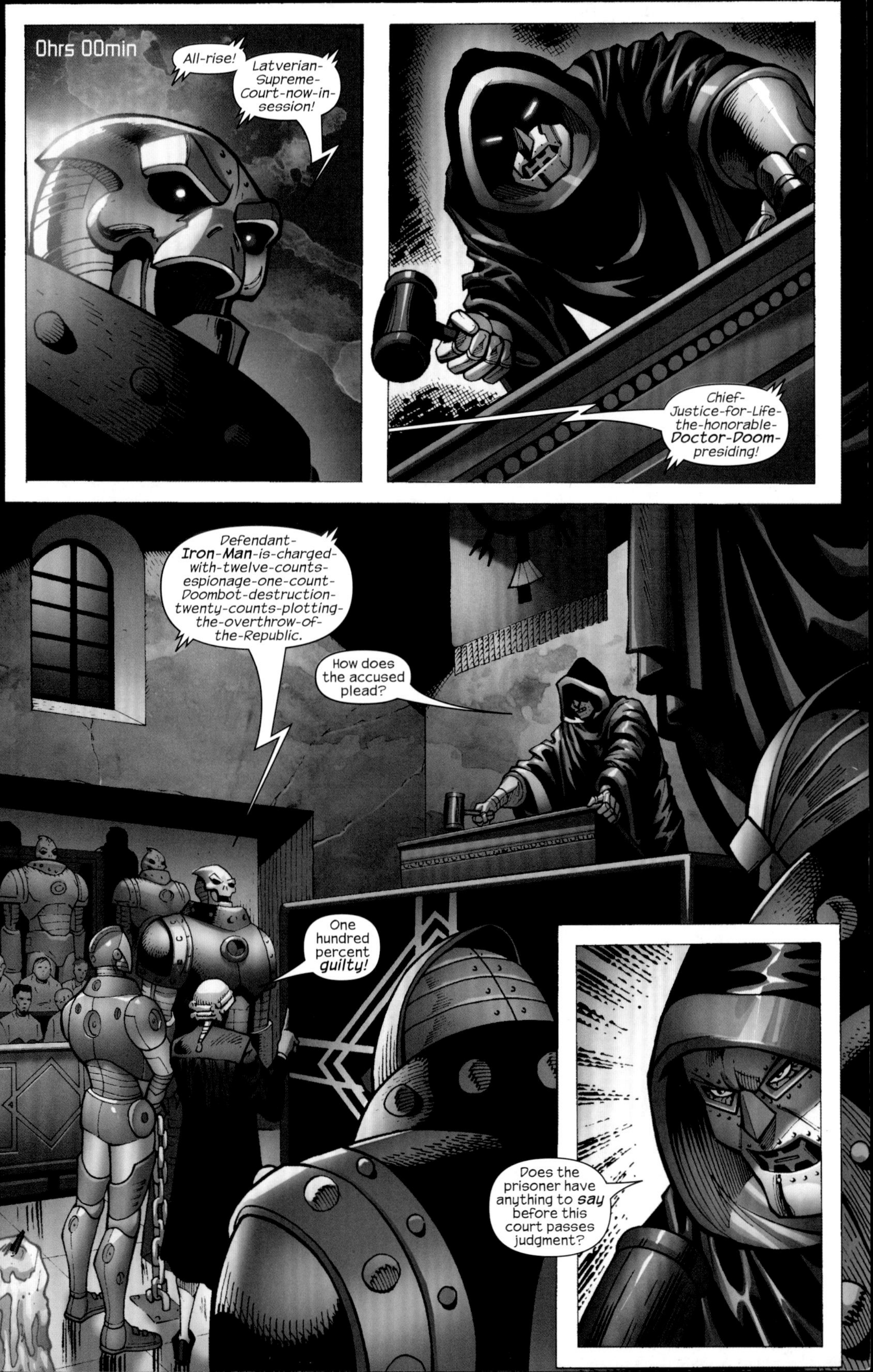
0hrs 00min
All-rise!
Latverian-Supreme-Court-now-in-session!
Chief-Justice-for-Life-the-honorable-Doctor-Doom-presiding!
Defendant-Iron-Man-is-charged-with-twelve-counts-espionage-one-count-Doombot-destruction-twenty-counts-plotting-the-overthrow-of-the-Republic.
How does the accused plead?
One hundred percent guilty!
Does the prisoner have anything to say before this court passes judgment?

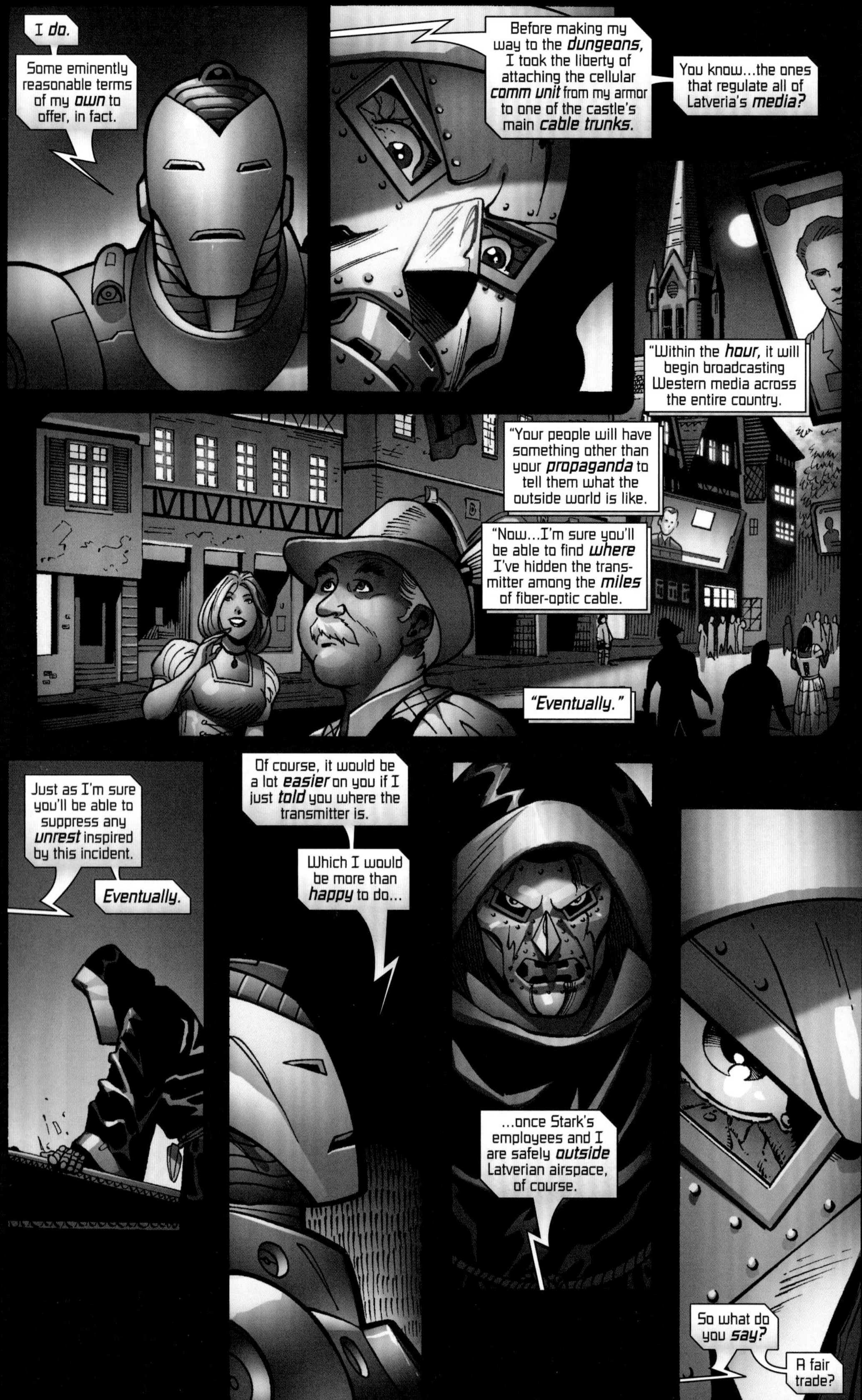
I do.
Some eminently reasonable terms of my own to offer, in fact.
Before making my way to the dungeons, I took the liberty of attaching the cellular comm unit from my armor to one of the castle's main cable trunks.
You know...the ones that regulate all of Latveria's media?
"Within the hour, it will begin broadcasting Western media across the entire country.
"Your people will have something other than your propaganda to tell them what the outside world is like.
"Now...I'm sure you'll be able to find where I've hidden the transmitter among the miles of fiber-optic cable.
"Eventually."
Just as I'm sure you'll be able to suppress any unrest inspired by this incident.
Eventually.
Of course, it would be a lot easier on you if I just told you where the transmitter is.
Which I would be more than happy to do...
...once Stark's employees and I are safely outside Latverian airspace, of course.
So what do you say?
A fair trade?

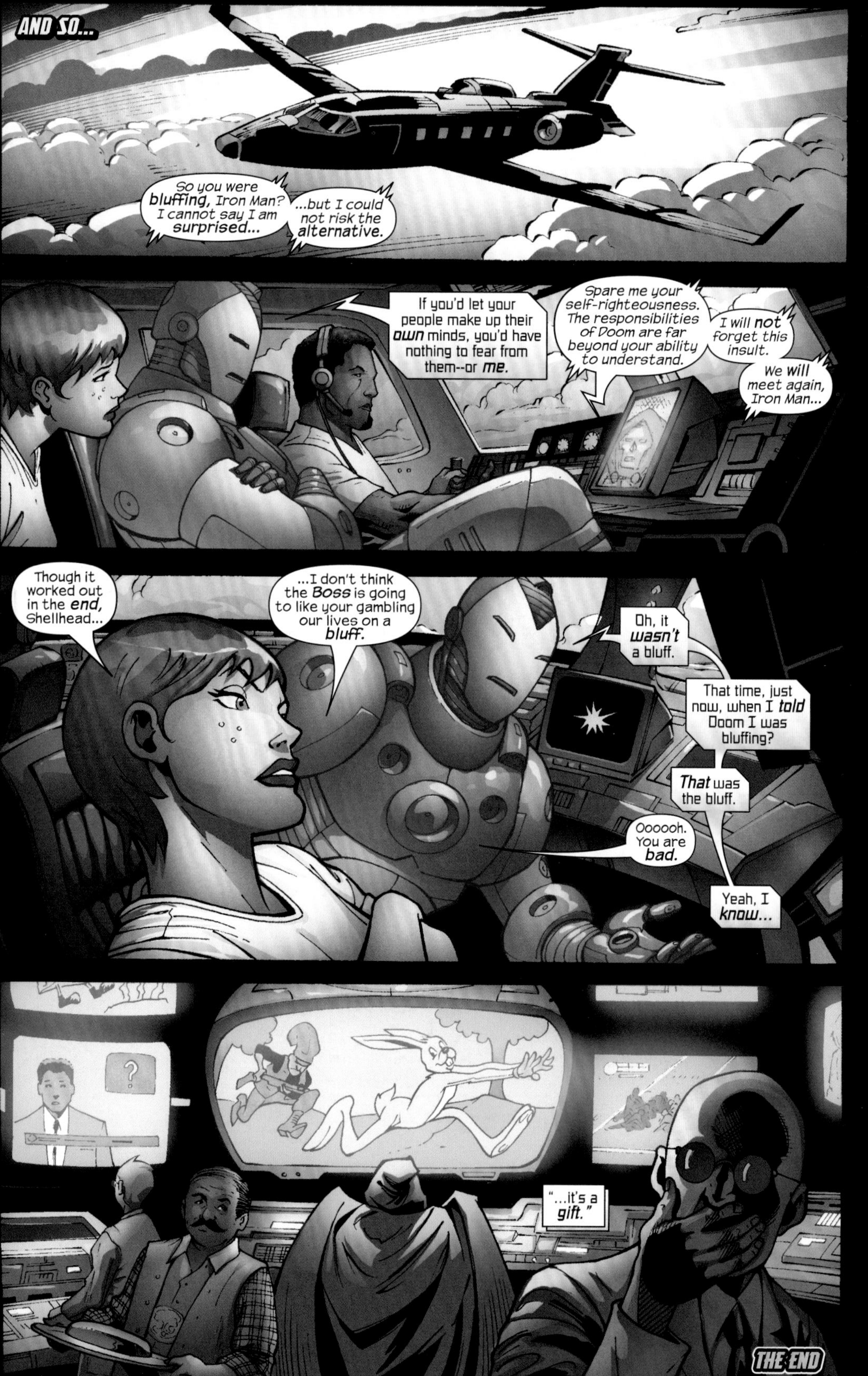
AND SO...
So you were bluffing, Iron Man? I cannot say I am surprised...
...but I could not risk the alternative.
If you'd let your people make up their own minds, you'd have nothing to fear from them--or me.
Spare me your self-righteousness. The responsibilities of Doom are far beyond your ability to understand.
I will not forget this insult.
We will meet again, Iron Man...
Though it worked out in the end, Shellhead...
...I don't think the Boss is going to like your gambling our lives on a bluff.
Oh, it wasn't a bluff.
That time, just now, when I told Doom I was bluffing?
That was the bluff.
Oooooh. You are bad.
Yeah, I know...
"...it's a gift."
THE END

MINI MARVELS

written and illustrated by **CHRIS GIARRUSSO** chrisGcomics.com

NATHAN COSBY - *editor* **JOE QUESADA** - *editor in chief* **DAN BUCKLEY** - *publisher*

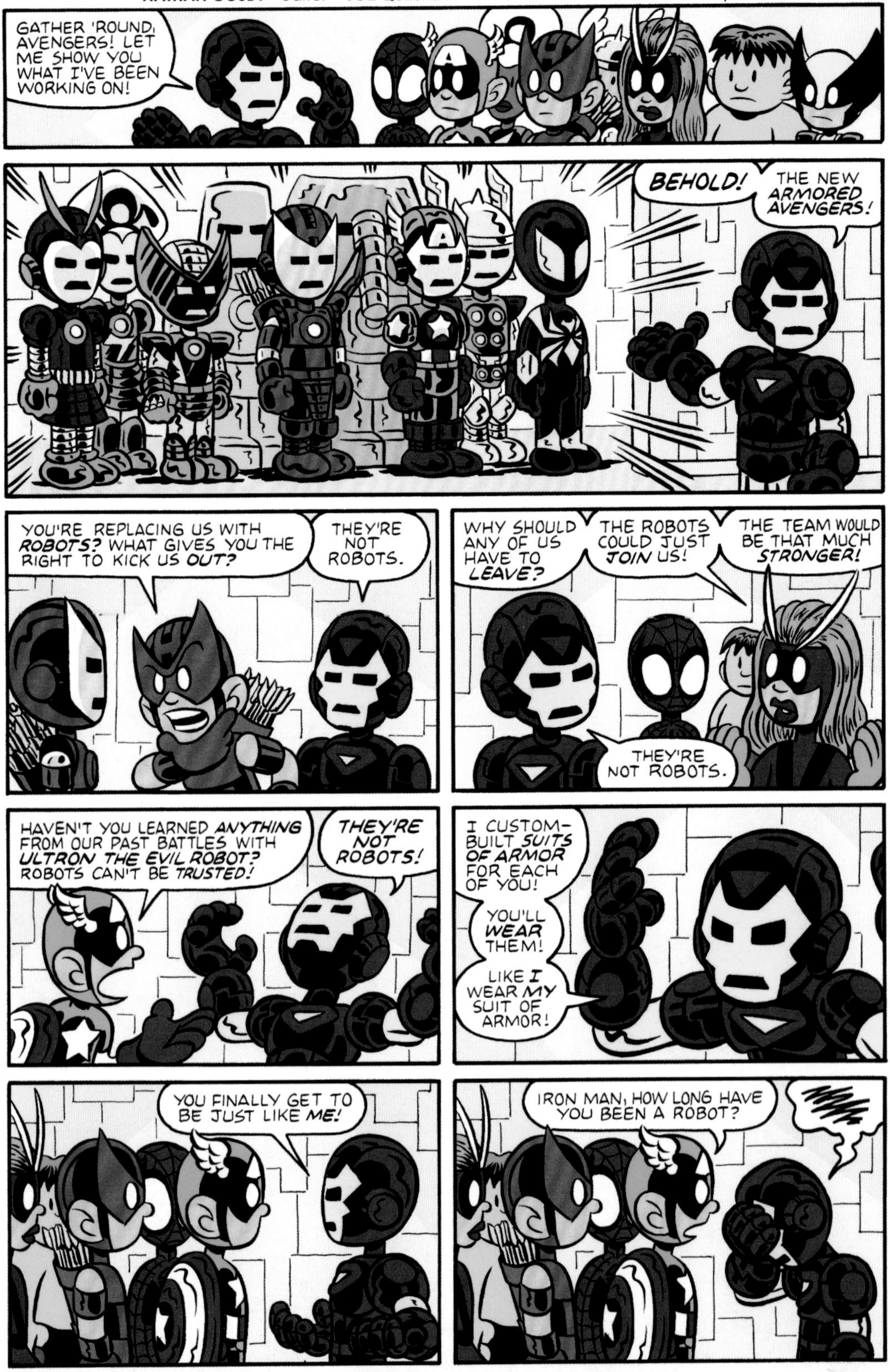

GATHER 'ROUND, AVENGERS! LET ME SHOW YOU WHAT I'VE BEEN WORKING ON!
BEHOLD!
THE NEW ARMORED AVENGERS!
YOU'RE REPLACING US WITH ROBOTS? WHAT GIVES YOU THE RIGHT TO KICK US OUT?
THEY'RE NOT ROBOTS.
WHY SHOULD ANY OF US HAVE TO LEAVE?
THE ROBOTS COULD JUST JOIN US!
THE TEAM WOULD BE THAT MUCH STRONGER!
THEY'RE NOT ROBOTS.
HAVEN'T YOU LEARNED ANYTHING FROM OUR PAST BATTLES WITH ULTRON THE EVIL ROBOT? ROBOTS CAN'T BE TRUSTED!
THEY'RE NOT ROBOTS!
I CUSTOM-BUILT SUITS OF ARMOR FOR EACH OF YOU!
YOU'LL WEAR THEM!
LIKE I WEAR MY SUIT OF ARMOR!
YOU FINALLY GET TO BE JUST LIKE ME!
IRON MAN, HOW LONG HAVE YOU BEEN A ROBOT?

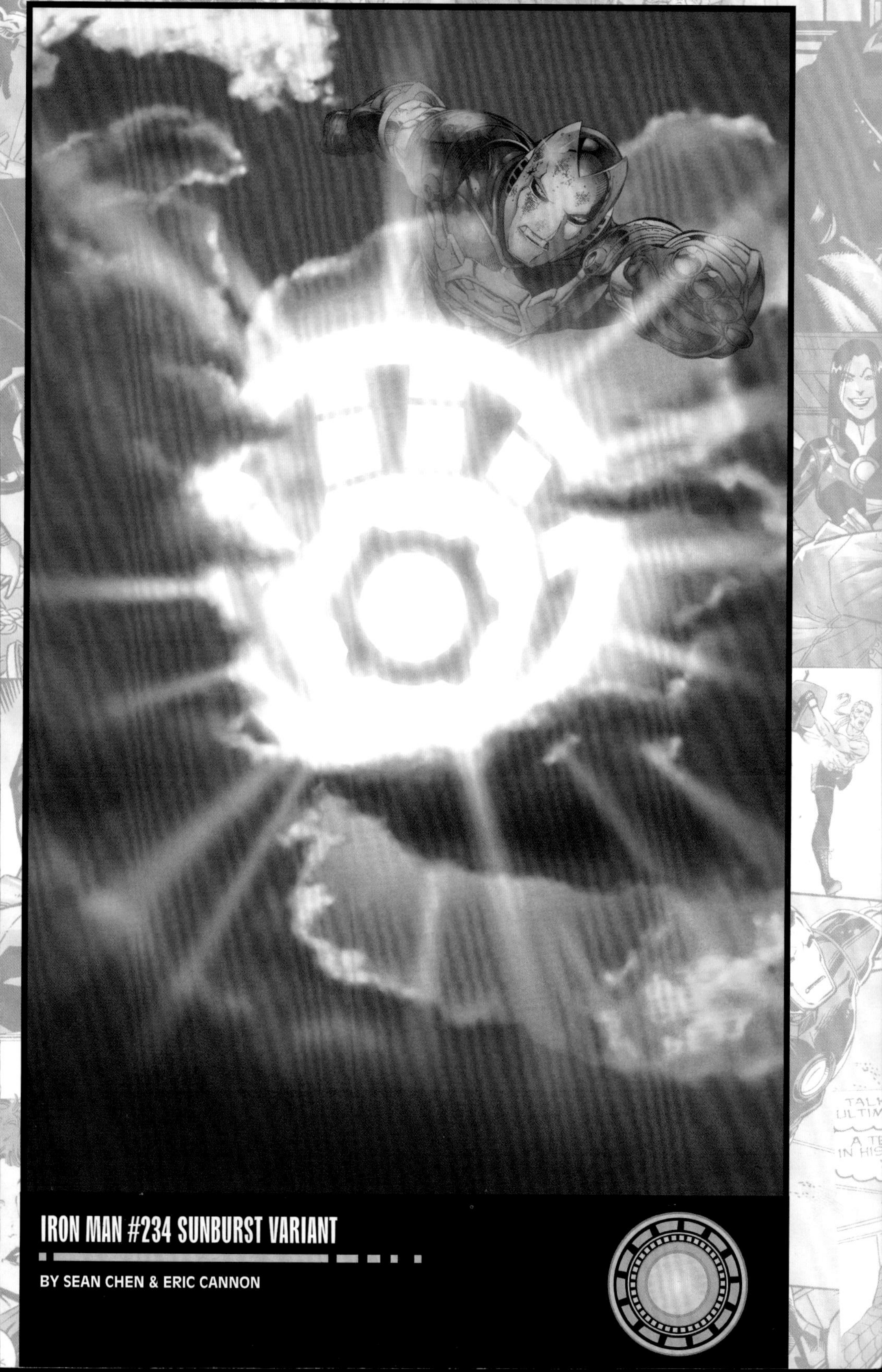

IRON MAN #234 SUNBURST VARIANT

BY SEAN CHEN & ERIC CANNON

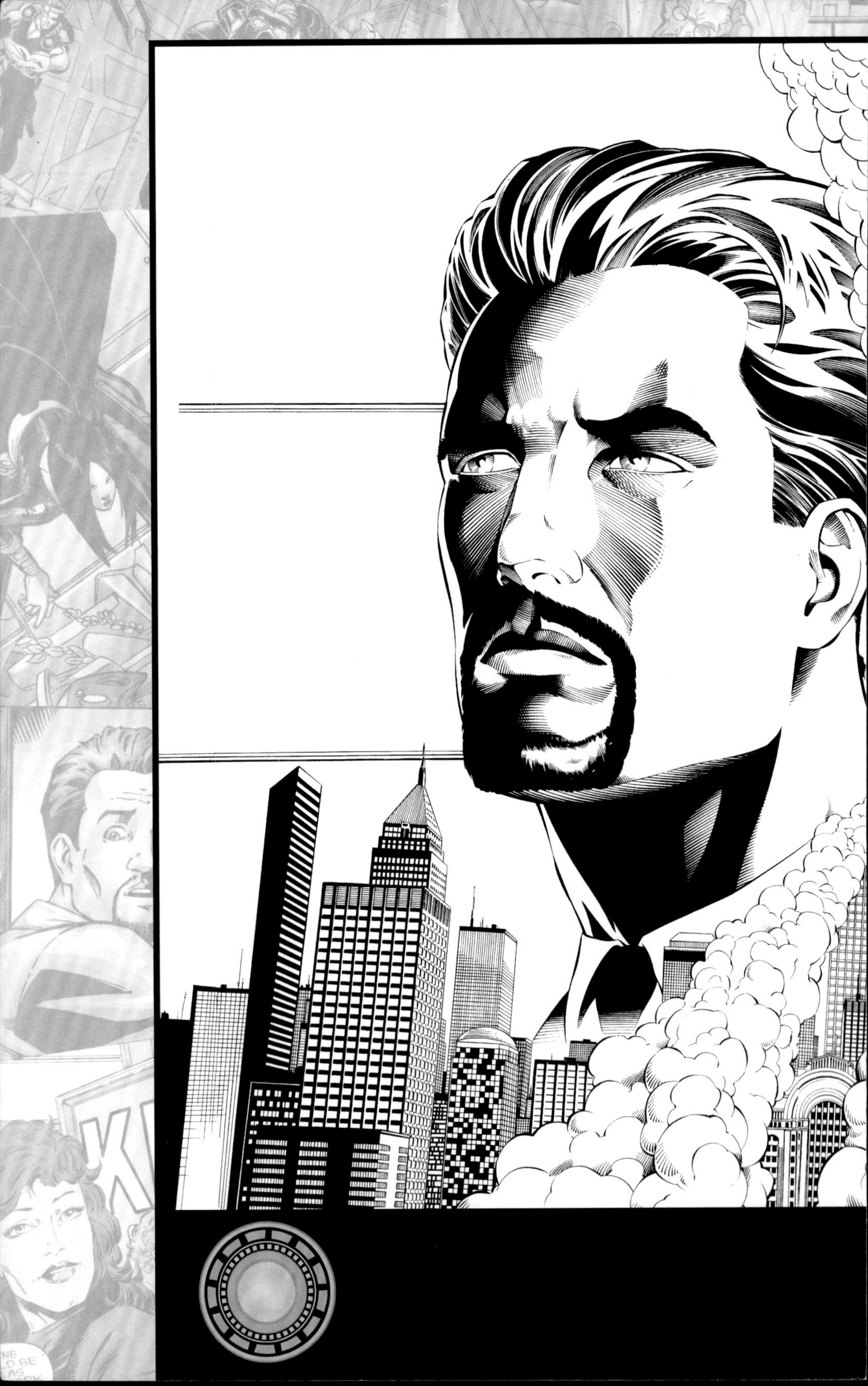

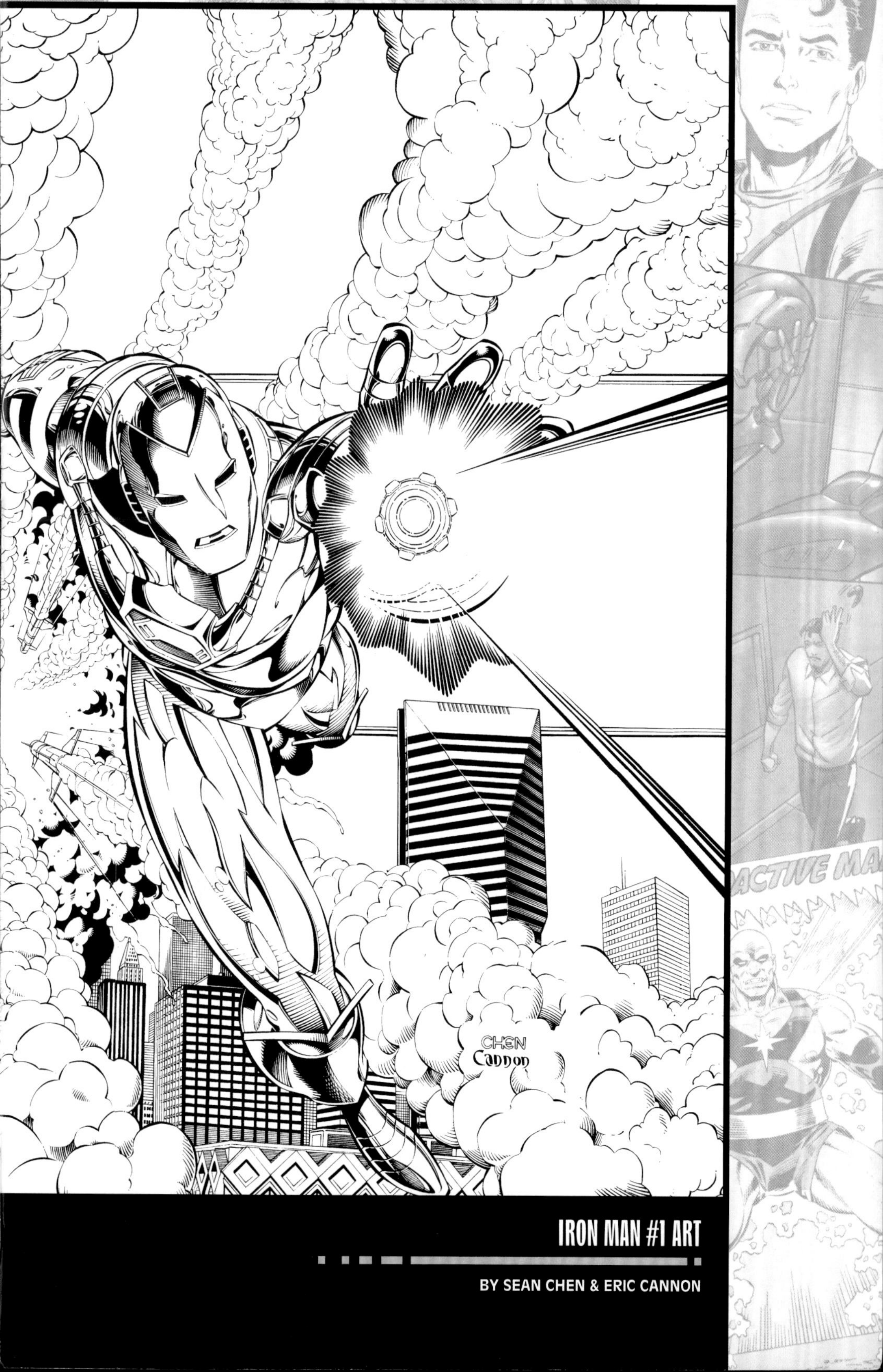
CHEN
Cannon

IRON MAN #1 ART

BY SEAN CHEN & ERIC CANNON

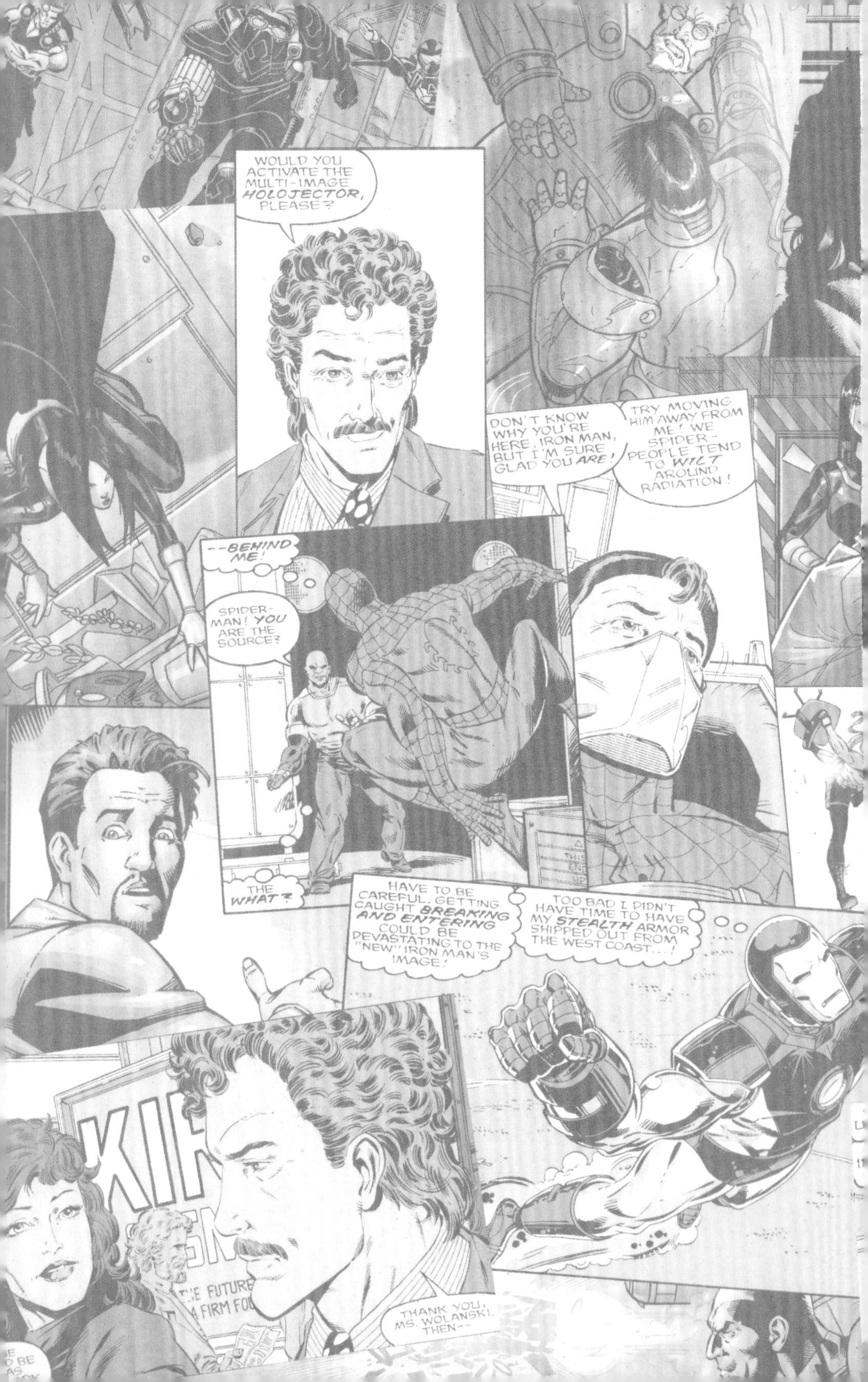
WOULD YOU ACTIVATE THE MULTI-IMAGE HOLOJECTOR, PLEASE?
DON'T KNOW WHY YOU'RE HERE, IRON MAN, BUT I'M SURE GLAD YOU ARE!
TRY MOVING HIM AWAY FROM ME! WE SPIDER-PEOPLE TEND TO WILT AROUND RADIATION!
--BEHIND ME!
SPIDER-MAN! YOU ARE THE SOURCE?
THE WHAT?
HAVE TO BE CAREFUL. GETTING CAUGHT BREAKING AND ENTERING COULD BE DEVASTATING TO THE "NEW" IRON MAN'S IMAGE!
TOO BAD I DIDN'T HAVE TIME TO HAVE MY STEALTH ARMOR SHIPPED OUT FROM THE WEST COAST...!
THANK YOU, MS. WOLANSKI. THEN--